To Selenah

At Least the Pink Elephants are Laughing at Us

By,
Chris Westlake

To my lovely friend with a wonderful heart.

Chris

C.S. Westlake

Copyright © 2017 by Chris Westlake

All rights reserved. No part of this publication may be reproduced, distributed, or transmitted in any form or by any means, including photocopying, recording, or other electronic or mechanical methods, without the prior written permission of the publisher.
First published in Great Britain in 2017
Any reference to real names and places are purely fictional and are constructs of the author. Any offence the references produce is unintentional and in no way reflects the reality of any locations or people involved.
A copy of this book is available through the British Library.
ISBN: 978-197 8215788

www.chriswestlakewriter.com
Cover Design – Demi Bernice Eslit www.graphixmotion.com
Editorial Services – Brian Tedesco www.pubsolvers.com

Prologue

August 2016

It was the same toilet his dad stood in over thirty-five years ago, just before he went up on stage that very last time.

The world had changed beyond all recognition since then. He had been just a fresh-faced teenager. Now he was a middle-aged man, with a line on his face for every year he had lived. The men's toilet at The Regency had some strange Peter Pan thing going on, though, for it had seemingly stopped in time. It *still* stunk of piss and shit and disinfectant. The tiles were still chipped. The tiny square window above the urinals was still covered in cobwebs and a heavy coating of dust.

He glanced around, feeling a bewildering sense of déjà vu. The walls were plastered with blue and red graffiti. He narrowed his eyes to read the words scrawled on the toilet door. Duncan Phillips was still waiting for someone to meet him in the cubicle at midnight. That was a bit freaky now considering Duncan had been dead for nigh on ten years.

James gripped both taps, which were slippery and smothered in white soap, and leant forward over the sink. He questioned, like he did every single day, what the hell was going through his dad's mind when he stood in this exact same spot all those years ago. James stared intently at his own reflection now. His dad must have done the same. It was unavoidable. The mirror was just there, asking to be looked at. He often wondered what or who his dad saw staring back, what he saw through his own bleary, beaten eyes. James noticed that there was a flush to his own cheeks. His nose was shiny. There was a thin, subtle smile on his lips, though.

Things were different this time. James hadn't embarked on this barmy adventure on his own. There were three of them, all in it together. That Herbert must have a screw loose. The guy had plucked James, Connor and Mandy from the darkest depths

At Least the Pink Elephants are Laughing at Us

of a place called nowhere. James still couldn't comprehend why Herbert had chosen them. The plan was surely destined to failure.

But here they were. It was Saturday night, the evening of their final gig before they headed for the prestigious Edinburgh Festival Fringe in the morning.

James had already been on stage. The adrenaline, the incredible buzz, pumped through his body. His shaking hands rattled the metal taps. The show had gone well. James felt like celebrating, felt like drinking the place dry, going wild, just like his dad, Bobby, would have done.

But he wasn't going to. James was going to find his mum and his wife. What he really wanted more than anything else was to see that they were smiling, too.

Surely, James mused, closing the toilet door slowly behind him, nothing could go wrong from here, could it...?

Chris Westlake

Part One

George
1 – Punch Lines

1950

The Esplanade curved to the left, the harbour to the right. The boy and his dad continued walking at a determined pace, passing men with their work shirts rolled up to their elbows and sunburnt women sitting on wooden bench slurping ice cream. And then suddenly – gloriously – the funfair opened up in front of them.

They were smothered by the rich smell of candyfloss and burgers and the infectious sound of children deliriously screaming. Dirty coins, earned during the day through graft and fake smiles in the factories and the shops, were now eagerly passed to men perched on stools and enclosed in small wooden booths. Wiry men operating the Waltzer ride, trousers tied around the waist by a length of string, bowed their pointed hats to the passing, giggling girls. The boy darted from the helter-skelter with the doorstep mats to the creaking, jolting roller coaster.

"Dad," George said, pointing his finger to the main gates where a crowd gathered by the concrete steps that led down to the beach. "What's that?"

"Only one way to find out, son," his dad replied, putting his hands behind his back, leading the way.

George bounced on tiptoes and looked through the gaps in the bobbing heads. A tall, skinny man with a divot in his nose stood in front of a hut with his back straight and his hands clasped together. He reminded George of a gatekeeper, or a steward at the football.

He shimmied his way through the crowd. "What's going on?"

"*Punch and Judy* show," the man announced. "Buy your

ticket here, or forever miss out."

"What if I don't buy a ticket and just stand here and watch the show anyway?"

The man merely bared his teeth and growled.

Two puppets appeared from behind the red curtain. The crowd cheered. No wonder Mr Punch was snarling, George thought; he had the most unfortunate hunchback and an enormous hooked nose that so very nearly touched his chin. The boy couldn't help but laugh when Punch spoke. His voice was a high-pitched squeak that belonged anywhere but with his face. Punch cackled gleefully as he clubbed Judy with his wooden stick. The watching children, high on sugar and the thrill of being out on a Friday night, enthusiastically joined in. The reluctant policeman tried to put Punch in jail. Said that Punch had been drinking again and his behaviour was most ungentlemanly. The policeman got hit with the stick for his troubles, too. Apparently Punch knew no limits.

"Know what that's like," one of the men shouted, and the crowd laughed.

The curtains pulled together and the crowd disappeared as quickly as it had appeared. George stared at the empty space they vacated, sad it was over. He had enjoyed the show. It was absolutely ridiculous, of course, but the stupidity was what made it funny. What really interested him, though – what absolutely fascinated him - was not the show in front of the curtains – no – it was whatever or whoever hid behind the curtains, pulling the strings. He glanced around. His dad joked with another dad, said he was glad the wife wasn't here to see the show, that she'd be none too happy. Punch really did clobber her with that stick, didn't he! His dad was most uncharacteristically jovial tonight. The boy saw his opportunity and took it whilst it was still there. He quickly nipped behind the hut.

The puppeteer was putting the puppets away inside a square wooden box. A half-eaten sandwich balanced precariously in his mouth. A fuzzy cloud of grey hair coated a round, crimson face. Blue watery eyes glared accusingly at the boy. "What the bleeding hell are you doing here?" he asked. "There are no backstage tickets for this show, you know. I'm not George Burns, kid."

At Least the Pink Elephants are Laughing at Us

George recognised the accent from the films he'd watched with his friends in the television shop on the high street. The puppeteer had the same twang as Humphrey Bogart and James Stewart, although much less eloquent and practised. He was American, for sure; a yank, as his dad would say. Those guys were on the same side as us in the war. Oh wow, the boy thought. He must be famous. Why else would an American be performing in little Porthcawl? Maybe he knew Charlie Chaplin? Went to dance lessons with Fred Astaire?

"I thought the show was great," George said.

"Really?" the American asked, quizzically. He sounded surprised. His eyes narrowed but his face softened. "Well I do try my best, kid. I always try to put on a show. I'd say I was the best show in town tonight although – as far I know – I was the only show in town..."

"I want to be a performer too," the George said, side-tracked. "I want people to look forward to putting on their best clothes and coming to see me on a Friday night. I want to make people laugh. I want them to go home to their normal boring lives feeling a whole lot happier because they've watched me put on a show..."

"I don't only do the puppets, you know," the man said, on a tangent. "I sing, I dance, I even tell jokes."

"So you're a Jack of all trades and a master of none...?"

"What *is* it with you?" the puppeteer asked. "You sure I was good, kid? It was a tough crowd out there tonight. One of them booed..."

"I think the man made a funny noise because he had a speech impediment," the boy suggested, although he was sure the man booed. "I mean," he continued. "I saw places it could have been better..."

The puppeteer raised a bushy silver eyebrow. "*Did* you now...?"

"Yes," George replied, laughing. "Like the beginning, the middle and the end, you know? And that's just for starters..."

"You're a proper little Mickey Rooney, aren't you?" the man scoffed.

"Sure am! I'm full of ideas, I am. I saw ways you could expand the show, too, make it even better than it already is..."

The man laughed. "Listen," he said. "If you really are all that keen on blowing your education and ruining any prospects life might throw your way, then maybe you *should* become an entertainer?"

"Sounds great," the boy replied. "That's exactly what I want to do."

The man shook his head and laughed, looked at the boy like he really was a peculiar one. He handed George a leaflet. *The West Virginia Wisecracker*, the boy mouthed.

The man proudly stabbed his thumb with his chest. "That's me," he said. "It's because I'm from West Virginia, in America, and I tell jokes."

The boy looked at him doubtfully. "That really needs some work," he stated. "I mean, it's *really* bad..."

The man took no notice. "Honestly," he said. "If you're as wacky as you sound, kid, and you aren't pulling my leg, then maybe when you've left school you should give me a call, see if I'm still on the circuit, see if I'm still *alive...* "

The boy thanked the man. "You'll get a call!" he said. "Mark my words, *The West Virginia Wisecracker*, you'll get a call."

And then George went in search of his dad, hoping he was still sharing bad jokes about his mother.

His dad wouldn't believe where he'd been, or the sheer significance of what had occurred when he was gone. For George was certain that, in the few minutes he was missing, he changed the whole path his life would take.

James
1 – The Boredom Epidemic

1973

Roy Hughes knew there was something wrong with Bobby Jones, that something drastic just had to change.

He knew this for certain the first time during his afternoon break at the factory. Roy was at a loose end because he wasn't able to browse through the newspaper as he routinely did. The newspaper had been torn to shreds during morning break. One of the boys had rolled the paper into a sword and used it to playfully batter another worker who'd had the audacity to mock his attempts to complete the daily crossword.

"No," the other boy had said. "Six down, five letters, a "prickly evergreen shrub", blatantly *isn't* a "bush." It's only got four fucking letters for starters! You're just obsessing about your missus's hairy fanny, aren't you?"

When Bobby Jones entered the kitchen during afternoon break, Roy was sat at the table with just his thoughts for company. He gave Roy a "thumbs up" and called his name. Roy gave him a military salute back. Bobby was light on his feet, moving so fluidly he reminded Roy of the new breed of pop stars. Was it Iggy Pup, with the non-existent hips and the wiry, veiny arms? Whatever. A large chunk of meaty sandwich quickly disappeared inside Bobby's mouth.

Bobby was only in his twenties, even though his lad, James, was in the same year at school as Roy's nipper, Terry. Roy sometimes took the Polaroid of the family on holiday at Barry Butlins out of his pocket when none of the other lads were looking. It reminded him why the long hours in the factory were worth it.

"Hear about the blonde woman who finished a jigsaw in six months, Royston?" Bobby asked. "She got proper excited because it said two to four years on the box!"

Bobby immediately continued, "I'm struggling today, Roy. I really don't think this job is for me, you know what I mean?"

Roy nodded his head. Bobby had been saying this for the last eight or nine years, ever since his first day, in fact, when he was just a kid really, straight from school, even skinnier than he was now, with dark greasy hair down to his shoulders. Bobby, though, was such an enthusiastic moaner that it was difficult to hold it against him. He made Roy laugh when he bitched about the dud hand life had given him. He talked at such pace, with such energy, that his ongoing struggles were something of a sketch show.

He knew that his own options were pretty limited – for reasons he wasn't open enough to share with any of the lads – but truth be told, he was pretty grateful for the work at the factory. There was more to Bobby, though. He *could* do better. Bobby only started working at the factory when his boy entered the world and he needed to get food on the table and an ample supply of nappies. James was nine now.

"You know how a vacuum sucks up all the dirt and grime from the carpet, Roy?" he asked. Roy nodded his head. He understood the mechanics of a vacuum; he'd watched his wife using one. "Well that's how I feel. This dire, depressing existence is draining all the enthusiasm I have for life right out of me, I tell you..."

That was when Roy Hughes knew there was something wrong with Bobby Jones. It wasn't just part of his show, his material to make the lads laugh. Bobby had been different recently. He was a loudmouth on the work floor, always shouting mock orders and singing the latest lyrics from Slade or The Kinks, and in the kitchen, which was the factory equivalent to the playground, he was the entertainer. The guy had presence. Roy had noticed a spark had gone missing. He managed to be in the thick of it whilst, at the same time, keeping his distance.

"What's the matter, Bobby?"

Roy could see the surprise in Bobby's eyes. Bobby could tell it was a serious question. Guys here didn't talk serious to other guys.

"It feels like I'm losing brain cells day by day," Bobby said,

At Least the Pink Elephants are Laughing at Us

tapping the side of his head, indicating where his brain was. "Just doing the same thing over and over again, you know? Have you read *One Flew Over the Cuckoo's Nest*, Roy? It's about one of those places people are sent to when the lift isn't going to the top floor. The main guy, though, McMurphy, well he isn't actually mad. But they put him in the electric chair so many times that by the end of it, his brain is completely fried. Frazzled. And he *does* end up loopy. I'm going to end up just like McMurphy, you understand?"

Roy understood.

"Really I should just shut up, hey Roy, and just get on with it and quit my moaning…?"

Roy smiled. That was the easy option. If it was any other bloke in the factory then Roy would have responded with an unequivocal, unapologetic "yes". But not Bobby. Roy remembered the conversation they'd had on overtime when they both sneaked in an extra break. The factory was virtually deserted. They were both tired and just wanted to get home to a nice warm plate of food cooked by their respective wives. Bobby was fighting through the tiredness by indulging in extra scoops of coffee. He was dipping his spoon in the coffee jar like it was a bowl of ice cream. The guy was manic. His eyes popped out of his head and he paced up and down the kitchen floor like Mick Jagger up on stage. He was making Roy nervous. Bobby chattered about the wonderful possibilities and hopes and dreams life had to offer.

"It takes a brave man," Bobby said, "A man of courage, to have the guts to reach out and grab life by the balls and really make the most of it, to risk losing it all, you know, Roy?"

The Bobby who had spoken to Roy that night had ideas and plans, hopes and aspirations. Roy just wasn't sure whether he possessed the courage he spoke about to go out and grab life by the balls, like he said. After all, *who* did?

"You remember what you told me a few months ago, Bobby? When we were both doing overtime?"

Bobby nodded his head.

"Well," Roy said, "I think you should go for it. But really go for it, like you mean it with every fibre in your body. Just like you said. You know?"

Bobby didn't say anything for a few moments. Roy hoped it meant he was taking him seriously, was genuinely considering what he was saying.

Bobby got to his feet. "You know what, Roy," he said. "I think I might just do that. I might just do that, Royston."

2 – Staple in the Belly Button

1979

Everything felt good about today, the fifteen year-old James thought, as he walked up the steps to the hall.

It was Saturday afternoon, for a start, which normally meant football on the radio at three, fish and chips wrapped in yesterday's newspaper for tea, and two sleeps till Monday. There was a refreshing breeze in the air but otherwise the usual dreary grey had been replaced by a cloudless, unblemished blue sky. Most importantly, though, James was out with his dad, Bobby, taking on the world.

Doors swung open. The Regency was a big venue, with metal railings and wooden benches outside and vast corridors and rooms (mainly empty) inside that made James think of a boarding school abandoned for the summer. James breathed in floor polish and stale beer from last night's party. The main hall had plastic chairs scattered in different directions, like people had been playing Musical Fucking Chairs. Long narrow tables were stained by circles that just wouldn't scrub clean. Fruit machines flashed and faded. In the corner of the hall, a blackboard marked the scores of Dave and Brian. It looked, by the way the writing became smaller and smaller to fit on the board, that it had been a long old game. A vacuum rumbled and groaned in an adjacent room like an old man with a bad smoking habit. Feint muffled voices, somewhere in the building, exchanged pleasantries; it was about time they had some sun, wasn't it, but then one swallow doesn't make a summer, does it? Nothing like the summer of '76, was it?

Bobby climbed onto the stage, wearing a cardigan that was tucked inside his baggy jeans. He followed a lead to a plug and picked up a microphone. "Testing, testing," Bobby said, his voice echoing around the corners of the empty room. He knocked the side of the head with the microphone. "This is the life hey, son."

It was hardly the Royal Palladium, James thought, but it was good enough. It was nice to get out of the house, to be honest. It seemed there was often tension between his mum and dad these days. It was difficult to concentrate, to relax, when they were shouting at each other. Often it would end with one of them slamming the front door and not coming back for hours. If it was his dad who slammed the door then he'd normally come home drunk and apologetic. They didn't argue all the time, just more than James remembered when his dad was still at the factory.

Bobby paced up and down the stage. "A comic needs to be like a racehorse before the Grand National," James had heard him say before. "I don't mean eating sugar cubes or taking a shit in the middle of a field, of course. No, I just mean nervous energy and adrenaline needs to be pumping through the body, building up to a fantastic crescendo when you walk onto the stage, ready to entertain the expectant audience..."

He'd give him some space and time, James thought. Bobby would be heading to the toilet shortly anyway, which was part of his normal routine, where he meditated and got in the right frame of mind.

James walked out of the hall and onto the grounds, which were pretty extensive for a little village outside Bridgend. The rugby season was over and the posts had been taken down and the grass was becoming overgrown and invaded by molehills. James spotted a familiar face in the corner of the pitch, idly kicking a football around on his own like he had absolutely nothing else in the world to do.

"Look who it is," Terry said, rolling the ball to James. "I hear your dad is the star of the show today, big man."

James was always surprised when he observed that Terry was no longer the fat kid. He'd always looked like his dad – Mr Hughes - with chunky arms, three chins and two bellies. James remembered the time Terry had unexpectedly turned up at his birthday party. James had thrown Terry's invite in the bin. Back in those days Terry had a habit of pinching other boy's nipples when he thought they'd done anything remotely out of line. James just didn't want him causing any drama, especially as his mum was fretting whether his dad was going to make it to the party. As it happened, Terry did pinch a boy's nipples. It was only after the boy had the cheek to say that the party was boring, though. James liked Terry for that. They'd since become best friends over the years.

Terry was still a big boy, but now he was just solid bulk, something which made him a pretty formidable opponent when he ran straight at you on the rugby pitch. Terry always talked about Bobby like he was a movie star.

"You could say that," James said, juggling the ball with his foot and chipping it into the air. James could tell Terry suddenly had a thought; they weren't that regular.

"I've just remembered that I haven't had the opportunity of sharing a recent, extraordinary discovery with you," Terry said, tapping the side of his substantial nose. "A discovery that, I might add, has become very sentimental to me over time."

They headed back in the direction of the hall. James had no idea where they were going, but he knew they weren't going to sign up with The Samaritans. Terry was no angel. James could just about see inside the window of the hall. His dad was up on stage, Jesus preaching to his disciples, even if most of his disciples were half-drunk. The hall was packed with the regulars, faces red and shiny, hands gripped tightly to their glasses. Bobby's lips were moving, but it was like one of those Japanese dubbed movies (usually with a dinosaur that had come back to life) for he couldn't understand what he was saying. It didn't matter, though, for the hall erupted with laughter. As he followed his friend past the hall, James could just about hear his dad saying "Paddy wasn't like other eleven year old kids he hung out with. He was fourteen for a start..."

James sat down on a concrete style at the back of the hall, just about managing to avoid the overflowing brambles and nettles. James thought about the man who had turned around and mouthed to his wife that Bobby was good. Was that good enough? He had accumulated a handful of regular venues, places he was welcomed, where he was appreciated by the punters. What else was there unless you made it on the telly, managed to hit the big time by appearing on *Opportunity Knocks,* like that black guy, Lenny Henry? His dad talked about the ball and chains being removed from his ankles when he left the mundane nine to five rat race, even though apparently he used to work eight till four anyway.

There was something though, that just didn't add up. His dad was free, but James was sure there was something missing when he looked at him these days.

His thoughts were interrupted by the sight of Terry's sizeable bare bottom. His friend was kneeling on the grass, stretching an arm underneath the overgrowing hedge, reaching out for something. James jumped off the style to investigate.

Terry turned around holding the prize find by the tips of his fingers, like he was dangling a dead rat by its tail. He brushed away clumps of hard mud, dry from the hot sun. The face of a gorgeous woman smiled seductively at James.

It was a dirty magazine. This *was* exciting. There was a whole stash of them. More than enough to go round!

"Don't be shy, Jimbo," Terry said. "We're all adults around here. Help yourself. Do me a favour, though?" he continued, big Cheshire grin on his face, "Promise me you'll keep that little worm of yours in your trousers, yeah?"

James was part of the secret now. They spoke in hushed tones about Jill from Manchester who liked nothing better than a Sunday roast and Jane from Liverpool who preferred to watch football on the box. James was amazed how many reader's wives seemed to love nothing better than sleeping with other men. Maybe getting married wasn't so bad after all, James considered.

"Quiet," Terry whispered, pointing in the direction of the back of the hall. There was urgency in his voice that made James nervous. Maybe somebody had spotted them? Maybe the vicar? Maybe the magazines were *his*? Terry pulled a finger to his lips. "Check this out."

They crouched down. James could see it now. His eyes grew bigger. This really was the perfect day. The door to the back of the hall was open. A woman clad in a mini skirt, pulled high over her long thighs, was being fondled by a stray pair of hands.

"What a lucky bastard!" James whispered. "He's got his hands all over her arse!"

"Shut the door, babe," James heard a muffled male voice say. The door shut and the bottom disappeared inside, never to be seen again.

At Least the Pink Elephants are Laughing at Us

"Come on, let's go," James said, flinging a magazine in the hedge. Terry was up on his feet, too, with no argument. James heard his friend struggling to catch up, taking rapid steps behind him, but he kept running fast and didn't look back.

He didn't want *anyone* to see him with tears in his eyes, let alone his best friend.

3 – Sorry, Not Today

1980

It was Saturday morning and, whilst other families were outdoors walking their dog in the drizzle or indoors biting into bacon sandwiches, Roy and Kim Hughes were enclosed within the tight confounds of their bedroom.

The door was closed. The pillows were puffed up. The curtains were pulled together but for a few significant inches, allowing some grey, gloomy light to enter into the room.

Kim spoke softly and gently to her husband, instructed him to take his time, to relax. She was his teacher. He was her pet.

Roy was anything but relaxed, though. His hands were clenched into tight fists. The nails clawed at the skin of his palms. His eyes were watery and red from anger and frustration. He cursed himself for being useless, for not being able to do what others found so easy. He loved his wife for being so kind, so patient, so understanding, but then he hated her for being so capable, so perfect, just like everybody else he knew.

He told Kim it was no good, that he truly was sorry; it wasn't going to happen, not today.

Kim brushed away his apologies with a gentle kiss to the temple.

"Don't worry, my darling" she said. "There is always next week. And if not next week, then there is always the week after, and the week after that. It will happen one day, I promise..."

At Least the Pink Elephants are Laughing at Us

4 – And In Between I Drink Black Coffee

The landlord of The Oak was concerned about Bobby Jones.

Now Bobby had always enjoyed a drink; everybody knew that, he was no Saint for sure, but he was not one of the faces who *lived* for the drink. Now, though, he sat in the corner of the fine establishment on his own, slumped over the little round table, thick brown hair down to his collars, dressed in a navy shirt that had the top three buttons undone.

Of course, Bobby was entitled to a good drink just like any other paying customer. That was the problem, though. Bobby wasn't a paying customer. Not tonight. Bobby was the goddamn entertainment. Frank had been over to his table a few times with a cold glass of water, but Bobby had dismissed him with a casual wave of his hand. Bobby's eyes were glazed and watery. Bobby was there – Frank could see the little shit - but nobody was home.

He'd really messed up this time, Frank thought. Bobby had been a little worse for wear a few times up on stage but Frank had let it pass because it hadn't really affected his performance and besides, the punters loved him. Frank had given him a little bit of rope and the silly idiot had hung himself. The Oak would manage without him. It was Bobby who would suffer. Everybody who was anybody knew Bobby had given up a perfectly good job at the factory to chase this mad dream of his. Even if he was the greatest comedian in the world, how was he ever going to make a living playing at the local pubs, British Legion clubs and maybe the occasional gig at the local University?

The wooden toilet doors swung open and Kim Hughes appeared from within the steaming cesspit, like a cowboy from out of town in a Western stepping foot in the local drinking den. Plenty of dazed, drunken eyes followed her magnetic, mesmerising strut. Fair play, Frank thought, she had a good pair

At Least the Pink Elephants are Laughing at Us

of legs, and she wasn't shy to show them off, either. Kim was obviously a fan of those Jane Fonda workout videos that Frank liked to watch when he ate his morning bacon roll. Kim was a lady who didn't mind going down the pub without her husband, Roy, who, by all accounts, preferred to settle down in front of the box in his slippers with their boy, Terry.

"Cup of coffee please, Frank," Kim said. "And make it strong and black."

Frank slowly raised his eyebrows. A cup of coffee? Did she think this was a hippy cafe? They didn't serve coffee in the Oak. They only served *coke* so it could be mixed with other, alcoholic, beverages. But Kim was a good customer, and she was good for custom, too. Any woman under the age of eighty was. Frank dutifully headed to the kitchen and put the kettle on. He told Kim the drink was on the house. He didn't tell Kim the Nescafe was out of date and stuck to the bottom of the jar.

"I'll come again, Frank," Kim smiled, heading towards Bobby and his private little corner.

"Wakey-wakey, Bobby!" Kim shouted, loud enough for the drinkers in The Coach down the road to hear.

Bobby jolted from his slumber like he'd been electrocuted. His eyes widened. His head straightened. He took in his surroundings. Kim came into focus. Bobby smiled like a kid who'd woken up in a sweet shop. She wasn't the worst thing in the world to open your eyes to, Frank thought. Kim dangled the cup in front of him like the coffee was a banana and Bobby was a monkey.

"What the *fuck* is that?" Bobby blurted accusingly.

"It's called coffee, Bobby. It's been around for some time now. You need to drink it. It is Friday night and I've put on my glam rags to watch your sorry arse – left Roy and Terry at home – and I'm not going to be happy unless you put on a show, you hear? There's going to be a riot unless you sort yourself out pronto."

Maybe it was the female touch? Bobby grabbed at the cup and jolted his head back. Black treacle dribbled down the side of his mouth, like the ninth pint of Guinness. Bobby was completely oblivious.

"Can't let my fans down!" Bobby shouted, thrusting his fist

in the air. Then his chin dropped to his chest. He closed his eyes. He slumped on his stool, drained of all energy, even more lifeless than before.

"This guy is beginning to piss me off!" Frank exclaimed.

Kim caught the eye of the woman sitting by herself a few tables away, quietly drinking gin and tonic. The woman wasn't local, Frank thought, but she'd been here a few times before. Had it been one of Bobby's nights? She was nice and polite enough when she ordered her drinks but she didn't exactly hang around at the bar to engage in idle chatter. The woman wasn't a knockout, but she had a pleasant, pretty face. She was also wearing a short skirt that gathered high over her thighs when she sat down. Maybe Kim didn't like the fact she didn't have all the attention tonight, Frank wondered, for she held the woman's gaze and then narrowed her painted eyes. For a moment they were two bulls, ready to lock horns and engage in battle. And then the other woman looked away, became suddenly engrossed in her glass of gin and tonic.

Kim smiled, like she had gained some sort of victory, then leaned forward and whispered in Bobby's ear. Something seemed to register, Frank thought, for Bobby glanced in the direction of the woman, nodded his head and then unsteadily got to his feet. He walked over to the stage and picked up the microphone.

"Ladies and gentleman," Bobby slurred. "I can always tell when the mother-in-law is coming to stay, you know?" He paused just long enough to know he had the attention of the drinkers. "I tell you, the mice start throwing themselves on the traps..."

There were a few surprised laughs. Bobby continued, "She doesn't like me much either. She said to me once, "Once you're gone, Bobby, I promise you, I'll dance on your grave." I told her, straight up, it was just as well then that I'm getting buried at sea! Mind you, my *own* mum didn't like me much, either. I was two weeks old when she asked if it was too late to have an abortion..."

Frank watched as his paying customers turned around to watch the entertainment, put on courtesy of The Oak.

Maybe, just maybe, Frank thought, possibly a tad

At Least the Pink Elephants are Laughing at Us optimistically, Bobby could pull this off after all…

5 - Stirring the Tea, Brewing the Gossip

James brushed the cue against his bum fluff (he'd recently turned seventeen and said that growing a beard was another step towards manhood), demonstrating control and composure that Ray Reardon or Terry Griffiths would have been proud of. And then...and then James slashed at the ball like a wild man, like his sole objective was to hit the ball as hard as he possibly could. James potted the black.

"Fucking cues," James muttered.
"A bad workman blames his tools," Terry offered.
"Too right he does when his tools are shit," James replied.

It was two in the afternoon and it was Saturday. The pub had been open for three hours and would be closing again in an hour. Terry looked out of the window.

"Your dad's just come in," Terry commented.
"Typical," James grinned.
"I was chatting with Frank earlier," Terry said. "He said your dad put on a good show last night. Eventually. He was a bit worse for wear, apparently. The locals can't get enough of the great Bobby Jones, can they? He has the big one down The Regency tomorrow, doesn't he?"

James nodded his head and half-smiled, like the Mona Lisa, and slotted coins into the side of the pool table. Terry had stayed home with his dad, watching the box. His mum had been at the gig, though. Terry had told his dad he should go with her, had really pushed the idea, but his dad just wasn't having it. Terry didn't like the idea of his mum down the pub on her own, watching Bobby.

James set up the balls and smashed the white ball into the pack. The black ball rolled into a waiting, welcoming pocket.

"Fucking cues," James muttered (again).

Terry thought James needed to improve on his vocabulary, stated that he couldn't put up with any more of this abysmal dross, and so they left the pub and headed in the direction of

At Least the Pink Elephants are Laughing at Us

James's house. It was all uphill and Terry felt the strain on his thighs. Terry had seen that boxer, Johnny Owen, on the news running up the bleak unforgiving hills in Merthyr in his red tracksuit, steam blowing out of his mouth, relentlessly training for his world title fight tonight. The whole of Wales was right behind him. Johnny didn't look like much, with his matchstick arms and legs and pale shallow cheeks, but the little guy had fought his way to the top of the world and he was only twenty-four. That was quite something, wasn't it?

Terry wondered whether Mrs Jones was going to be in. He liked Mrs Jones. She deserved better than Bobby, better than the life he had given her. Mrs Jones was what Terry imagined women to be like in the 1950's, before the wild excess of the 60's and then the inevitable repercussions and hangover of the 70's; she was a prim and proper housewife devoted to her family, able to cook and bake and clean, all whilst maintaining a happy disposition. Only *hot*. Terry wished Mrs Jones was more like the bored housewives he'd read about in the magazines at the back of The Regency. It seemed quite a few of the housewives were unable to resist the charms of their son's best friend. Terry remembered the first time he'd turned up at James's front door for his birthday party, when James, the little shit, had thrown his invitation in the bin. His jaw dropped and his mouth gaped open when he saw Mrs Jones stood in the doorway looking ravishing.

They entered through the front door. Women chatted in the living room. The duo snuck into the kitchen. James dipped his hands in the biscuit tin and then sat down with his feet stretched out on another chair. James was always dipping his hands in the biscuit tin, just like Terry's dad.

"Why do women always meet up for coffee?" James asked. "I hear them all the time in the shop and the post office. "I haven't seen you for ages, dear. You must pop around for a coffee." Nescafe must love women."

"The coffee is just an excuse. Women meet up to talk."

"What on earth is there to talk about?" James asked, perplexed.

James put his finger to his lips and nodded in the direction of the living room. They both went silent.

"So how is Bobby?" one of the women asked.

"Good, actually," Mrs Jones replied. Terry thought she answered a little too quickly, a tad too urgently.

"That's good, dear."

"Is he earning much money, Miriam?"

That was a bit personal, wasn't it? Terry's dad always said you should never ask about a man's earnings. It was private and confidential. Terry did suspect it was partly because he didn't earn much money down the factory. Terry thought of Mrs Jones, the perfect host, welcoming these women into her home, most likely offering them the most delicious coffee in the village, with goddamn biscuits too, no doubt, delivered on her finest china, and here they were, repaying her by asking personal questions about her finances. Well, he thought, it *took* the biscuit!

There was a pause. "Not as much as we'd like, for sure. But that is what married life is all about isn't it? We all have our struggles with money. But it is worth it to see him happy."

A longer pause. "And are *you* happy, dear?"

"Of course I am."

Terry imagined Mrs Jones squirming, cheeks flushed, avoiding their eyes, their penetrating stares.

"Well I must say, Miriam. We do all admire you for allowing Bobby to give up his job just like that. Particularly as now he really only works at night, doesn't he? We were all saying that none of us would have been quite so – now what is the word I'm looking for - *generous*."

There was hearty agreement all round. What was this? The House of Commons? *Hear, hear.* Terry bristled. He pictured the women guiltily nibbling on biscuits, worrying about their waistlines, but nibbling on biscuits, all the same. He hoped the biscuits went straight to their hips. *A moment on the lips is a lifetime on the hips,* he recited bitchily. He hated these women, although he didn't even know who they were.

"But what about James? How is *he* coping without a regular wage coming into the house? It's all about the children really isn't it, dear?"

That was enough. They were talking about his best mate now. He didn't really care about Bobby, but he did care about Mrs Jones and he absolutely cared about James. Terry started

At Least the Pink Elephants are Laughing at Us

talking, any old crap, just to make noise, about the football, the rugby, *Are you Being Served?*, just to drown out the poisonous gossip in the next room. His friend put his finger up to silence him.

"He likes his dad doing what makes him happy..."

"But Miriam, does he *really*...?"

Terry wasn't going to let James stop him now. He was bigger and bulkier than him. He jumped off his chair and headed to the living room. He brushed away James's weak arm, his feeble protests. Pushed open the door. No knock. This wasn't a time for *niceties*.

Mrs Jones was perched nervously on the edge of her chair, clasping her hands together, just as Terry had imagined her. Her eyes widened when she saw him. She smiled. Why? Embarrassment? Relief? Who knows, but she *definitely* smiled. There were three other women in the room, all older. Witches stirring a cauldron. All they needed were some wooden spoons.

"I just came in to say hello, Mrs Jones. Me and James are both in the kitchen. Ladies, would you like another coffee?"

They all said "no dear," "thank you dear," "nice of you to ask dear."

"Tidy. Oh and James says he really loves his dad being a comedian. And thank you for asking!"

The women all nodded their heads and stared down at their saucers, rattled their cups, tapped their toes, fiddled with their earrings.

"I think he wants to be a comedian himself one day, just like his dad," he added. "He has been practising in the pub. I think he has real talent. Even better than his old man."

"That's nice, dear."

Terry glanced at Mrs Jones. She smiled, briefly, gave him a subtle but definite nod of the head, as if to say thank you, and then looked away.

When Terry left the room he could hear the women saying he was a charming young man, a good example for the youth today, not like those awful punks and drug addicts, oh and don't even mention those terrible skinheads! They kept rattling on, not pausing for breath, but Terry knew it was partly because they *had* been rattled. Terry allowed himself a smug, self-satisfied smile.

Terry returned to the kitchen. James wasn't there. He opened the front door, looked up and down. The grey clouds that had threatened earlier had now opened up and the rain was firing down like bullets, rebounding from the rooftops. This was ridiculous, Terry thought. Young lads weren't supposed to talk about this sort of stuff. They weren't supposed to talk about *anything*. Yet they couldn't keep up this pretence forever. They both knew the truth.

They both saw things that Saturday afternoon out the back of The Regency.

He spotted his friend. Thank God. Walking back down the hill they'd just walked up, heading back in the direction of the pub, splashing through puddles. Only, Terry noted, now his friend was walking much more briskly, and with much more purpose.

6 – Warming Up, Falling Down

This place smells of wet dog, Bobby thought.
The weather just added to the emptiness, to the black hole. His head felt fuzzy, like he was living in slow motion, in a fog that just wouldn't clear, that was following him everywhere he went, even when he tried to lose it. He'd drunk too much last night, and the night before that, and the hangover had both numbed and heightened his senses. It wasn't just the drink, though. The news had filtered through from the radio and the television and onto the streets of Wales that Johnny Owen was in a coma. He'd put on a gallant effort in Las Angeles in the early hours of the morning, when half of Wales was listening in their dressing gowns on the radio and the other half were drunk or fast asleep, and he had been winning for most of the fight, by all accounts. But then he got hurt. The boy just wouldn't give up though, he had the heart of a lion, and he kept coming forward, until he took a hit that left him lying unconscious on the canvas. The whole of Wales was united in their prayers for the boy now. Nobody really knew what would happen. His dad, Dick, was his trainer, and had been there at ringside, had seen his son in such pain.

Bobby looked over at James, his own son. James was much more confident these days. He was changing and developing. James was no longer the shy boy who wouldn't say boo to a goose. He had an almost cocky swagger about him now, just like his dad. He'd grown handsome, too. He was a good boy. He hadn't tainted him too much. His mum had brought him up well. Bobby squinted, closed his eyes; tried to clear his thoughts, but they were just scrambled, like a TV that hadn't been tuned. It really didn't bear thinking what Johnny Owen's parents were going through right now, did it?

"This should be quite some show, hey Dad," James said.
"Sure will be."
"You heading to the toilets, Dad?"

Bobby allowed himself a rueful smile. The boy had been to so many of his shows; knew his routine far too well. They used to make fun in the pub, said that James followed his dad around like a puppy dog. Does he follow you to the toilets when you take a shit, Bobby? He never told them that up till the age of about four James actually did, that he used to park his potty up and imitate his old man; facial expressions and all.

"I guess so," Bobby said, embarrassed by his own predictability. He felt a bit pushed, though. He wasn't really ready to head to the toilets, not yet, not today. He was even thinking that now might finally be a good time to have that talk with his son.

It was too late though, he knew that. The toilets hadn't been cleaned yet and the stink was nauseating. The window was open and Bobby's hands were numb. Bobby looked at himself in the mirror. His forehead was oily and his eyelids heavy, like they had a natural urge to snap shut. Even so, Bobby often thought that considering the hedonistic life he'd lived, he should look a whole lot worse than he did. He was like a rocker that – somehow – kept on rocking. Bobby remembered that book Miriam lent to him when he was still at school, *Dorian Gray*, when she was working through the classics. Somehow the way Bobby looked was never a true reflection of how bad he felt, like his excesses were inflicted on some other poor soul. Maybe it was the guy from the butchers, who was tee-total (apparently) but still had a face like a testicle shrivelled up from a hot bath?

Bobby remembered the show the other night and felt a wave of shame. The performance truly was remarkable considering the mess he was in before the show. He remembered Kim and how she whispered to him and gave him the heads up and then he plucked up the courage to perform. In the end he hadn't let down his fans – somehow – and that was the most important thing, wasn't it?

He wondered how his life got to this point. Don't worry. It was all going to change. Bobby pulled the hip flask from his pocket and felt instant comfort. He took a swig of drink and it burnt his throat. This will be the last day I will ever have a drink. He knew that, for once, Bobby Jones wouldn't break his promise. Bobby opened his mouth and swallowed a couple of tablets the

At Least the Pink Elephants are Laughing at Us

doctor prescribed him.

He knew it was his fault, but then knowing didn't make it any better, did it? He should have been more careful when they were kids, for a start. Miriam was sweet and innocent and naive, but he wasn't. The baby didn't really make a massive difference to his life; it just meant that he was down the factory a few years earlier than otherwise predicted. But Miriam had a future. Instead, she was changing nappies and feeding the baby at three in the morning when she could have been having an adventure somewhere else at University.

Miriam could read him like one of her beloved books. She knew exactly how he felt working at the factory. It was dull and boring work, but it was safe, and he was somebody to all the other workers, just like in school. In a perverse way he was happy being unhappy, begrudging the unfairness of life. He was a big fish in a small pond. Okay, it wasn't even a pond, it was a goldfish bowl on top of the television, but he swam around in that bowl like he was a blue whale. He left because he felt he had no choice.

Bobby remembered when he came back from the factory that night. He excitedly told Miriam that he'd been speaking to Roy down the factory and he said that he should just go for it. "And you know what," Bobby told her, "I think I should!"

He had expected Miriam to bring him back to earth, to give him a reality check, tell him that he had a young boy to feed, that they had bills to pay. But she sweetly cupped his cheeks with her hands, kissed him and told him to go for it.

"What do you mean?" Bobby asked, panicked.

"Do it, Bobby. I know you're not happy. You've always been bigger and better than that place. Bobby Jones is somebody. He always has been. Just make us proud, you hear?"

"But what about the bills?" he protested.

"We'll manage," she replied.

"And putting food on the table?"

"We'll pull through, Bobby."

And he tried to talk her out of it, sure to God he did. Miriam insisted, though, he should no longer be trapped, that he should follow the dreams he talked about. Bobby couldn't possibly break her heart by telling her it was just talk, that really he was just like everybody else. She thought he was special, and he wasn't.

But he had broken her heart, hadn't he? Just rather than quickly and painlessly, he had done so slowly and cruelly. Miriam had a completely different perception of what Bobby would be doing when he gave up work at the factory. Bobby still couldn't understand why she had so much blind faith, why she was so undoubtedly naive. Miriam got carried away with Bobby turning up unannounced as a clown at James's birthday party, when he was still knee-high to a grasshopper. Miriam, bless her, assumed Bobby would be an all-round performer, that he'd be blessing lucky people with his particular brand of entertainment both day and night. She thought her wonderful husband would be a clown here, a juggler there and then transform into a stand-up comedian when the lights went down. And then, on the rare occasions he wasn't performing, he would be scribbling away in his office, creating incredibly creative new material. The reality was anything but. Bobby had an evening gig here and an evening gig there. During the day Bobby was usually sat in front of the TV or sat at the bar. He could still have put in a full shift at the factory and gigged in his spare time. There was no need for him to have quit his job! They both knew that, though they never said it.

Bobby jerked his hand away from his mouth, panicked. The toilet door pushed open. Bobby fretted.

"You know I like a little drink before performances son, just to calm the old nerves," he protested.

"I was getting worried about you, Dad. You been here some time, you know. I thought you might be jerking off or something," James said. "It's already getting busy," James hurriedly continued. "Everybody wants to see the great Bobby Jones performing up on stage. You know. Where he belongs."

They've seen it all before, Bobby thought, as he left the security of the toilet and entered the gauntlet of the hall. If he ever forgot his words then most of the punters would be able to deliver the punch line for him. He was outdated, yesterday's news and today's chip paper. Bobby realised it was no longer good enough to just make jokes about your mother-in-law and Paddy and the English. James, on the other hand, understood this new breed of 'alternative' comedy that was developing in London, talked about in hushed tones like it was a dirty phrase. Bobby rued that 'alternative' comedy was just alternative to funny. But he'd watched James from the hallway as he practised and improved his act in the bedroom mirror. The boy had talent.

Bobby was welcomed up on stage with familiar warm applause. His elaborate bow got a laugh.

"I met a new bird last week," he began. "Don't tell the wife, though." Laughter. "She told me she had a few skeletons in the closet. Turned out she really loved all that Halloween shit! She was proper impressed, so she was. She said it was nothing like the last time she had sex. She said that had reminded her of the one hundred metres race at the Olympics. "Over in ten seconds?" I asked her, feeling smug. "No," she replied, "there were eight black men and a gun."

The crowd was laughing. Bobby started his second joke, but the thoughts in his head became jumbled. He repeated the line until it made sense. They laughed, only it was quieter, less enthusiastic. More embarrassed.

He looked out at the crowd. He didn't tend to properly look at them. They were just shapes (mainly round or square). He didn't want to be distracted by somebody picking their nose or opening a packet of crisps. And now it was like he was opening his eyes for the first time. He could see the lines in their foreheads, the indents in their cheeks, the whites of their eyes. His hands were wet. The microphone felt like a slippery fish. James was there with his friend, Terry. And Kim was there, too, staring up at him, concern etched on her pretty face.

And then Bobby saw the woman, down the front, panic in her eyes; there with the little boy. He desperately didn't want to let her down. He so wanted to pull a performance from somewhere, out of the pit of his stomach if need be.

Bobby couldn't really hear himself speak anymore but he was sure the words weren't coming out in the right order. He blinked but the sweat stung his eyes and so he blinked some more. It dawned on him that he wasn't saying anything at all. He was just standing on the stage in front of the whole town, blinking and muttering random words. There was something on his arm, tugging at his sleeve. It was a hand. It was his son. His darling, faithful James. He was telling him that everything was alright. He would take over and sort it out. Don't worry, Dad. Take a seat...

And Bobby did take a seat, next to the woman and the little boy. There were movements around him but he was oblivious to what they were. His head hurt. He looked up and James was on stage, so confident and comfortable, like it was his natural environment. He could hear laughter around him, much louder than when he was up on stage, almost deafening. His boy moved up and down on the stage for some time, and the noises around him became louder and louder, almost drowning his unbearable, excruciating pain.

His heart *really* hurt. The light blinded his eyes. He closed them and when they re-opened, she was standing over him, her eyes manic, there with the little boy. He was lying on his back, on the sticky floor. James was above him now, too, like an angel, telling him it would all be alright, that it would be alright, Dad, it would be alright.

"Look after your mum," Bobby ordered, and then the painful, blinding light faded until there was only darkness and peace.

Connor

1 – John 1:9 If we Say we have not sinned, we make him a liar, and his word is not in us

1985

This lot were a motley crew, Alun considered. He glanced around at the rest of the congregation in their casual dress. Then he looked down at his handsome eight year-old son, Connor, and across to his beautiful wife, Nanya, and smiled proudly.

Alun may have been an intruder, a charlatan, but at least he had the decency, he thought, as he fiddled irritably with his tie, to dress appropriately when he entered a House of God.

All day long, when Alun was fulfilling his role as headmaster of his school, he looked little people (dear Nanya told him he must stop calling them that; they were just children and would grow taller, with a bit of luck) straight in the eye and told them that they must never, ever tell lies, that their noses would grow long if they did (okay, he only said that occasionally), and yet here he was, stood in church, surrounded by devout believers (including his only wife and only son), reciting the Lord's Prayer, and – he whispered these words quietly, even though he said them only in his mind - he didn't even believe in God.

Didn't believe in God. He repeated the words. Quietly. Even saying the words in his head made him feel guilty. Not even Nanya, who passionately embraced God and loved Him for all the wonderful things He had delivered and relied on Him to help her in times of needs, not even his darling Nanya had any inclination that her supposedly kind, reliable and faithful husband had been deceiving her all these years. But what was the alternative...? This was the lesser evil. Alun was the headmaster of a Church of Wales school. It was down on paper that his school taught the teachings of the Bible.

And although Alun didn't believe in God, and although he felt like a charlatan every time he set foot inside the sacred grounds, ironically church really *did* hold a special place in his heart. Unfortunately it just didn't have anything to do with God.

Alun met his wife in church.

It had been this very church, in fact. Ten years ago. At a wedding.

Alun dutifully stood and sang hymns and knelt and prayed on the soft cushion that provided padding for the knees, and the congregation dutifully and conscientiously worked their way through the song numbers chalked on the blackboard.

It was after the service, when Alun followed the slow trail of people down the aisle leading to the bright world outside, that it happened.

Alun fell in love with a bottom.

He had to admit, looking back, that it didn't sound the most romantic love-at-first-sight story. When he told the story down the pub, some smart Alec normally retorted that it "sounds like you got a bum deal!" or "you're such an arse!" But Alun could honestly say when he looked back that, from his perspective, it truly was a love story.

The walk down the aisle had been long and slow and if it had been a traffic jam he would have beeped his horn to hurry them up. He stared at the floor to make sure he didn't clip shoes with whoever was in front. Alun looked up and there it was. It was one of the most beautiful things he had ever seen. It was the eighth wonder of the world. The sixth Beatle. The bottom, curved like a question mark and hidden gloriously underneath an elegant silk blue dress, was so deliciously and perfectly round and large that Alun just wanted to sink his teeth into it. But Alun knew that wasn't the honourable thing to do. Not in church. And so he diverted his eyes and when he looked back in the glorious, unexpected sunshine outside, the bottom had vanished amid the crowd. Alun became just another bemused smiling face saying "cheese" to the cameraman.

At the reception it was evident Alun had been placed on the

At Least the Pink Elephants are Laughing at Us

singles table, or the table where nobody knew anybody else at the wedding. Each table had been named after a castle in Wales. Their table was Ogmore. Alun enviously eyed the Caerphilly table; they all seemed to be having a loud and outrageously fantastic time. He smiled politely at the other singletons. They killed time by folding and unfolding their napkins and staring intently at their bread rolls.

Alun swivelled in his seat to adjust his jacket that was folded over the back of his chair (it was an ideal and perfectly justifiable excuse to pass some time) when his eyes found themselves just inches from the heavenly bottom he'd last seen at the church. Oh my, Alun thought. She must be a fellow guest without a date. They already had something in common! Nerves fluttered in his throat.

"Good afternoon, everybody," the lady said. Her accent was strong and African and incredibly, relentlessly sexy. "I guess we are on the table where nobody could get a date, yes?"

Her laugh was a deep and infectious rasp. The rest of the table stopped folding their napkins and buttering their bread and laughed, too, although much more self-consciously, much more controlled.

It's nice to finally put a face to the behind, Alun thought.

And what an attractive face it was, too. Her cheeks were high and full, her eyes large and dark. Shiny black hair, with a tinge of red, was cut straight at the fringe and curled at the shoulder. The lips were plump and ruby red and oh so utterly kissable. When she smiled it revealed a cute little gap between her front two teeth. Alun thought that her skin looked so deliciously dark and smooth that she positively glowed.

Very nice to gain your acquaintance, Alun thought.

Alun glanced at her name scrupulously scrolled in black ink on white card. Nanyamka Frimpong-Boateng. Jesus, he thought, I hope they didn't pay by the letter. That was a mouthful.

"My name is Nanya," Nanya said, shaking Alun's hand. She announced her name with unabashed pride.

"Alun," Alun said. "Pleased to meet you, like."

"Darling, what a masculine name. I'm absolutely sure the pleasure is all mine."

Alun instantly transformed from the guy on his own in the

corner getting quietly drunk to the fairy on top of the Christmas tree.

"How do you know the bride or the groom, then?" Alun asked. It was one of the questions he had already recycled with other guests, but this time Alun really was interested in the answer.

"Oh, now that *is* a story," Nanya replied.

Alun had never really met a black lady before. Like most guys in the village, the closest he got was drooling over Uhura on *Star Trek*, the ebony goddess who was not completely closed to the idea of romance with a white guy. And Moira Stewart on the news was an elegant looking woman, too, of course. And so whilst Nanya was something of a peculiarity, she was a good one, for sure. Alun loved the way she spoke, demonstrating such unrestrained, uninhibited passion, the way she transformed ordinary, run-of-the-mill words into things of utter beauty, expressing herself with both those delicious lips and her free-flowing hands. Nanya was a poet, Alun thought; a freaking *poet,* like Dylan Thomas or Jim Morrison or Freddy Mercury.

Nanya said she arrived in London with her husband three years ago. Alun's heart sank faster than the Titanic.

"But he was a brute!" she exclaimed with such emotion that Alun pictured her husband to be Bigfoot on steroids. Alun hoped his pleased expression was not too evident. He was glad the husband was a brute. It gave him a better chance, if he had any chance at all.

"He had women in Clapham and women in Brixton. I phoned the family in Ghana and you know what they said? He is a man. What do you expect, Nanya? Are you with child yet? That's all they were worried about. I said no! Not with that man. Not ever with that man!"

Nanya filed for divorce and packed her suitcases. She took the tube to Paddington and stood in departures and considered where to take the train to. She hadn't heard of most of the places. They were just random letters forming random words, she said. All you hear about in Ghana is London this and London that, she added. It was a lottery, she exclaimed.

"I didn't know anything about Swansea, but I knew it was in Wales. I didn't know anything about Wales, either, but I adored

At Least the Pink Elephants are Laughing at Us

the name. Don't you think whales are the most beautiful, fascinating creatures in the whole world, Alun? I thought "Swansea is in Wales, isn't it?" I wasn't even sure. Wales will do for me."

"So you went to Swansea?"

"No. I got off at Cardiff. I needed the toilet and I didn't fancy using the one on the train." She laughed. "Crazy? Yes?"

Alun nodded his head. And then quickly shook it. Maybe he wasn't supposed to agree with her? It *was* crazy, though. And yet. And yet it was utterly fantastic. Alun felt self-conscious walking into a pub on his own, and here was this lady from a foreign country starting a new life basically on the flip of a coin. It was everything he didn't believe in. Fail to plan, plan to fail, that was one of his sayings. There had been no planning, no rationality at all. And yet it was the bravest, most courageous thing he had ever heard.

"I knew nothing about Swansea. But that was what made it so exciting. Imagine watching a film when you know the ending? Not having a clue what is going to happen is much more fun!"

"So you never actually answered my original question, Nanya," Alun smiled. "How do you know the bride or groom?"

It was the bride, Amanda, she knew. They went to the same cafe in town. Just how much coffee did she drink to get invited to the wedding? Mind you, didn't coffee come from Ghana? It was apparently where they both went for escape. Their little private place away from the rest of the world. Nanya wrote poetry and got lost in her thoughts while Amanda embroidered. Nanya made the two of them sound like Buddhist monks. They struck up a conversation, decided they liked each other and agreed to make it a regular meet.

And it was the same cafe Alun and Nanya went to on their first date.

Alun looked at his adorable wife now, in the same church, all these years later. He sometimes wondered how he got from there to here. Nanya turned and smiled. Alun still thought Nanya was the most beautiful woman in the world, just like he did the first time she smiled at him at the wedding. He felt a tinge of guilt as he looked up. He was sure Father was staring at him, singling him out from the rest of the congregation. The guilt passed. Nanya was worth lying for.

And besides, Alun reasoned, apart from that one lie, he told Nanya absolutely everything. There were no skeletons unturned in their relationship.

Well, Alun thought, as he squeezed both Connor's and Nanya's hands; there was of course *one* other thing that neither of them dared speak about.

2 – Panto at Christmas

He felt like a sea lion at the zoo. The two eyes, big and wide, stared up at him expectantly. Good old Shakin' Stevens was on the radio, doing Cardiff proud, wishing everyone a merry Christmas. The turkey and the brussel sprouts repeatedly repeated on him. The face that looked back at him in his glass was flushed and swollen and had an oily tint. Harry swished the last remains of the fizzy, gassy lager, held back his head and then downed it.

"Mum! Uncle Harry has finished his drink! He'll need another one!"

Harry felt like a king on his throne. King Harry. Sounded alright, didn't it? He was a King with his very own servant ready and waiting to respond to his every need, even if he was just an eight-year-old-boy with ants in his pants. Harry started counting again and, as predicted, he didn't get to "five." Nanya appeared in front of him, bright and breezy and full of life.

"Another lager, Harry?"

"I'm fine thank you, Nanya," Harry replied meekly. "Honestly, now," he pleaded.

"Nonsense, Harry. I can't have our special guest going without a drink now, can we?"

Harry glanced over at his younger brother by just a year. Alun arched an eyebrow and smiled. Harry was fit to burst, and Alun was loving it.

"Could you bring in the nuts please, darling?" Alun shouted. "Harry is just too shy to ask for any, aren't you Harry?"

Harry had his role to play in proceedings. He'd overheard Nanya on the phone to Ghana earlier. It was always a big event when she was on the phone to the family. Harry was sure the phone on the other end was passed to half the population of the country. "Oh yes, of course Harry is here. Of yes, of course he is still single. Oh yes, Harry is fine. Would you like to speak to him? Oh, Harry!"

Harry wasn't sure how it had happened, but he had become the Uncle who enjoyed his own company, who was happy to go to the theatre on his own. "It's just the way he is," he'd heard Nanya say. "Some people prefer to be on their own." Harry had become the Uncle who was maybe a bit different; but it didn't matter, they wholeheartedly reassured him, because he was lovely all the same.

In truth though, Harry wanted a beautiful, loving and wonderful woman just like his younger brother had. They'd had their problems, of course. Of course Alun kept things close to his chest. He was a man, after all. He had confided to Harry once. It was shortly before Connor was born, he thought. Alun said they were having some difficulties. He didn't go into details, but whatever the problem was, they came through it. Now they were happier than they'd ever been.

Sometimes Harry wondered whether his little brother knew just how lucky he was.

"You look like you've lost too much weight, Harry," Nanya observed. There was famine in third world countries, Harry thought, and Nanya was worried about a sixteen stone man. "All this diet, diet, diet all the time is no good for you. I blame Carl Lewis and those tiny red shorts of his, running and jumping all over the place, making normal men feel all inferior..."

Nanya appeared to lose her train of thoughts. She stood in the middle of the room, gazing absent-mindedly into space. Harry glanced at Alun and noticed a look of concern on his face. It was as though Nanya had completely switched off. Then, seemingly regaining her chain of thoughts, Nanya turned back to Harry and said "I do hope you are eating properly, Harry. We really can't have you wasting away."

That was odd, Harry thought. Maybe Nanya had been sipping on the whiskey in the kitchen? Oh well, it was Christmas. If you couldn't have an "odd" moment at Christmas then when could you? Harry didn't have the heart to tell Nanya he'd put on six pounds since last Christmas, since he'd last been sat on the sofa eating nuts and drinking lager and feeling so heavy and bloated he could barely move.

"Harry, we have a special treat for you today," Nanya

At Least the Pink Elephants are Laughing at Us

proudly announced. "We have arranged some entertainment. What is a party without entertainment?"

Harry waited expectantly. Nothing happened. He glanced at Nanya, who stared at Alun with noticeable venom in her eyes. Alun was sat on the edge of his chair, waiting too.

"What?" Alun asked, baffled.

"You have one thing to do and you don't do it! Your son has been practising all morning!" Nanya shouted. This wasn't strictly true, Harry thought. Connor had his head in one of his books for most of the morning. Harry could see moisture on Nanya's teeth. Her normally flawless complexion was shiny and flushed. "You are supposed to do the drum rolls, Alun."

"Oh. Sorry."

That was unlike Nanya, Harry thought. She was often loud, but normally because she was jovial and excitable and, as English was not her first language, she occasionally struggled to get her point across. Harry hadn't heard her shout at his little brother like that since the early days, since before Connor was born, since the last time her sister, the delightful Jojo, had come to stay.

He didn't think about it for long, though, because Alun conscientiously performed an elaborate drum roll and then the door swung open and Connor barged into the room, his arms swinging confidently by his side, like a soldier in the Falklands. He was wearing, unexpectedly, a purple wig. The wig was bushy and flamboyant and had loose curls. Harry momentarily wondered where he got the wig from; it wouldn't suit Nanya, and he hoped it didn't belong to his little brother.

"Where's my little Willy?" Connor asked, looking around. Nanya erupted with laughter, her deep throaty rasp filling the room. She leant forward at the waist and slapped her thighs. Harry resisted the very real temptation to glance down her top. Instead he sniggered and snorted through his nose.

"I hope that's a dog you're looking for?" Alun piped up. Harry glanced at him. His little brother looked proper chuffed with his joke. Harry always told him he was too obvious. Alun's eyes were watery and red.

The boy's face contorted into a sinister frown. Horizontal lines appeared on his forehead. His eyebrows met at the middle.

Two became one. His eyes stared accusingly. Connor held the look for a moment. "Hello, Maa," he said.

"Well you know me. I'm not one to gossip. I will stay for a little tipple – just the one – if you want me to tell you all about it...."

He was his mummy's boy, that was for sure, Harry thought. He had creativity like his mum, as well as a studious side, like his dad. The kid was good, too. Connor switched effortlessly from character to character and managed to capture their personality traits to a tee. Harry wondered just how much *Eastenders* the boy watched. Wasn't it on after his bed time? Alun should really encourage his talent, Harry thought, instead of trying to get him interested in rugby and football all the time. But he couldn't blame him; not really. Connor was the only boy Alun had, and all he wanted him to do was to *act* like a boy.

Harry took a handful of peanuts and filled his mouth. He slapped his own thigh now. He glanced at Nanya, who was laughing so hard tears were slowly trickling down the side of her face.

3 – Backwards Rule of the Forward Pass

1986

Mr Thomas bounded over to nine year-old Connor in his black tracksuit bottoms and socks rolled up over the knees. Connor knew that his dad knew that he knew rugby wasn't his sort of thing. They were both fully in the know. Connor thought his dad looked more disappointed than anybody when he'd read out his name to play Brackla Primary. Mr Thomas felt compelled to add that "Robert Davies and Matthew Proctor still have upset tummy's – *apparently* – and won't be able to play." Connor felt there was no need for his dad to shake his head at this point.

Dad put his arm around Connor's shoulder now. "Just run up and down the side of the pitch as fast as you can and catch the ball if it comes to you, okay?"

Mr Thomas blew the whistle and the captain kicked the ball high in the air. Minutes passed with no drama, and Connor thought that maybe this rugby lark wasn't as bad as he'd feared. He hid his hands inside the sleeves of his shirt and the ball didn't come anywhere near him. Connor hadn't taken his eyes off the ball. It was like a wasp with a vicious sting; it was only natural to stay away from it. But then the ball was passed down the line. *Drop it*, Connor pleaded. It was passed to another boy. *Fall over*, he begged. The ball was passed to Connor...

He caught it. Connor wanted to dispose of the ball as quickly as possible, like it was a hand grenade that was about to go off. Explode over *there,* not *here*. Connor threw it to anybody wearing green. Yes! The boy caught the ball. This was easy!

The whistle blew longer and louder than Connor had ever heard before. It had a musical shrill to it.

"Connor!" Mr Thomas shouted. "You're not allowed to pass the ball forward, you idiot!"

The game restarted and Connor knew now he wasn't going to get away with not getting the ball again sooner or later. He decided that when he got the ball next time he wouldn't even try to pass. There were too many things that could go wrong, too many unpredictable possibilities. The ball was getting closer. Connor felt familiar dread. He caught the ball. And he just ran, like his dad said. As fast as he could. Red shirts appeared in front of him and then disappeared behind him.

"Connor, put the ball down!" his dad shouted, after he'd run around the white posts and wondered what he was supposed to do next.

Connor put the ball down and the loud shrill of the whistle sounded more positive this time, almost welcoming.

He was swamped by his school friends. This really *was* easy, Connor thought, as he lay underneath a pile of muddy boys celebrating his try.

By the time Mr Thomas blew his whistle theatrically to signal the end of the game, Connor had put the ball down underneath the white posts four times.

Mr Thomas put his arm around his son again, but it felt different this time. It was no longer consoling and sympathetic.

"My son the rugby player," he said. "I really cannot believe it."

Connor saw that his dad wore the biggest smile he'd ever seen.

4 – Sick Note from Your Mother

His mother was always late waking him up. The brightness radiating into his bedroom suggested that today she had forgotten to wake him at all. Connor reluctantly took the initiative and tentatively lowered his bare foot out of his bed and onto the carpet below.

He found her stirring the contents of a giant metallic pot at the stove in the kitchen. Connor could tell from the strong, delicious scents that she was cooking cassava and plantain. It was a traditional Ghanaian dish, she said. His mum was always keen to teach him about Ghana, for him to learn where he came from. Connor already knew Ghanaian's loved spices, the hotter the better. She must be concentrating hard, Connor thought. She had no idea he was stood there on the cold floor waiting for her to pay him some kind of paternal attention.

"Morning, Mum."

Mum jumped. Both feet left the floor. Her smile widened. "Morning, Connor," she said. She parted his tight curls and planted a kiss on his forehead. "And what a beautiful morning it is. You need a haircut young man."

Connor felt self-conscious in his pyjamas. His recent growth spurt had left him "tall and gangly" according to one of the mothers, and "unusually lanky" to another. His pyjamas struggled to cover his arms and legs, let alone his skinny belly. "Mum, aren't I going to be late?"

Mrs Thomas leant forward at the waist so that she was eye-level – she didn't have far to stretch these days - and pinched his cheek. She smiled. "Dear boy, I think you could miss school today, no? You look a tad bad? Yellow like a lemon? You need to rest."

Connor shuffled on his feet. He didn't have time for this. His dad complained about him being late yesterday, and he complained about him being late the day before yesterday.

"Mum, I am not bad? What do you mean?"

Mrs Thomas edged closer. She tugged on the back of his head. Her eyes stared at him closely, like she was looking inside his brain. "You really are a funny colour. Tssk. I demand you stay at home."

Connor pictured his dad's disapproving look. It was worse now that he was the star of the rugby team. Just another reason to be teacher's pet. "Mum, what's going on?"

Mrs Thomas sucked her teeth in. She looked at him as though to say, "this boy is too smart for his own good."

She held her hands up in defeat. Connor thought of that boxing match his dad had been watching where they'd thrown the white towel into the ring. "I want you to stay at home to help me. Your Auntie Jojo is coming over from Ghana. She will be our guest. We need to prepare. I want her to see how we live, but then I don't want her to think we live like savages. It will be fun. Me and you. Mother and son. Nanya and Connor. No?"

Of course, Connor thought. She'd been talking about it night and day for weeks. He could barely remember his mum talking about anything else. Dad didn't seem so excited. He'd come home from work one day and Mum pounced on him before he'd even loosened his tie (that was his way of winding down, Connor observed) and he'd muttered something about "that flaming Auntie Jojo. You'd think she was the Queen Mother, or Madonna, or Maradona. All the fuss she's been making."

Connor was pleased she was talking about "mother and son" time, though. He was painfully aware he'd been spending more time talking to his dad about rugby recently and less time talking to his mum. It had always been the other way around. And his mum had made no effort to get involved. She hadn't even feigned interest in Connor's unexpected – no, miraculous - success on the rugby pitch. Connor was suddenly the star player, favoured even to the captain. It was like she'd been in a quiet sulk. Only it had been going on for so long that it had just become the norm. Connor suspected his mum was jealous of the sudden bond he had with his dad.

But now it seemed they were best friends again. All had been forgotten. And Connor was intrigued by the visit of his Auntie Jojo. Every woman in Ghana, it seemed, was Connor's "Auntie". His mum was forever passing the phone to him and

At Least the Pink Elephants are Laughing at Us

demanding he "say hello to Auntie", and he hardly ever had any idea who he was speaking to, let alone understand a word they were saying. But Auntie Jojo was actually family, a blood relative. She was Mum's older sister. And Jojo actually *lived* in Ghana. She was proper Ghanaian and so, Connor reasoned, she no doubt lived in a small wooden hut that was surrounded by chickens. Connor pictured Jojo walking for miles every day to the well with no shoes on just to drink some water, like all Africans did on the television. Apparently his mum was the shy and retiring member of the family. Connor struggled to imagine what Jojo must be like. He might need to purchase some earplugs out of his fifty pence a week pocket money.

Auntie Jojo had apparently been to Wales once before. "You met her, darling," his mum told him. "Only you wouldn't remember."

"Of course he wouldn't remember," his dad said. "He wasn't even born! He was still in your tummy doing handstands!"

"You will love Auntie Jojo," Mrs Thomas assured Connor. "I tell you, mothers need to lock up their sons and fathers. Wives had better keep their husbands indoors. Our Jojo is so jealous of her little sister, you know? She is on the hunt for her very own white man! She will be looking to take him back to Ghana in one of her big suitcases!"

His mum made it sound like she was going fishing down Ogmore River and wouldn't be happy until she had caught something. Mr Thomas always laughed when she said this. "I'll warn my friends to keep away," he said.

Mrs Thomas cackled. "I'm sure the men in the village won't mind some attention from my older sister. She is the pretty member of the family. All the Aunties say so. She makes me look like a member of that – oh what they called – yes, the Addams family. Oh, those large, beautiful dark eyes! And not forgetting the biggest...."

"Oh yes, I remember *those...*" Mr Thomas interrupted.

Mrs Thomas playfully slapped the side of his head, although Connor always thought that her playful slaps still had some power.

Well, Connor reasoned, if his own mum said he could have the day off school then who was he to argue? He had no idea what help he could give her, but he wasn't going to let the opportunity pass. A whole day with his mum was too good to miss. It was a bit odd, though. She didn't normally make the effort. She always treated guests like royalty, filling them with copious amounts of food and drink, but when it came to preparing their actual home, she was fond of saying she wouldn't lay down the red carpet for anybody, not even that handsome Robert De Nero. People can take us how we really are, or they cannot take us at all. She must be really excited by Auntie Jojo visiting, he considered.

Connor dressed, brushed his teeth, washed behind his ears and when he came downstairs his mum had cleared the dining table of clutter and mess and replaced it with a rectangular sheet of white cardboard, which was so large it curled at the edges like sandwiches that had gone stale.

"A blank canvas, Connor," Mrs Thomas declared. "There is nothing more exciting than a blank canvas. Think of God before he created the world and all the options he had. A blank canvas is open to endless – *infinite* - possibilities."

Connor's jaw dropped. He had never looked at a white piece of card with such fascination before. It had always been a white piece of card.

"We are going to create a collage for Jojo. We live a very different world here from what she is used to. We are going to use photographs and drawings to show her what our life is like. They say that a picture is worth a thousand words, don't you know?"

Connor could imagine that Ghana was very different from Wales. It was *Africa*. Didn't the runners from Africa always win the long races because they had to run from lions and elephants on a daily basis? Jojo wouldn't know what to make of a house made of bricks. Who knows what she'd think the television was?

"Go run upstairs and bring down the two shoe boxes that are in the bottom of the wardrobe in your mum and dad's bedroom, there's a good boy."

Connor carried the boxes downstairs, pressing the lids down with his chin. He couldn't look at the floor and he was worried that he'd trip and fall down the stairs. It would be unfortunate if he had to spend the day at the Princess of Wales, especially as he

At Least the Pink Elephants are Laughing at Us

already had the day off school anyway.
He gasped when he opened the first box. There were hundreds of miniature snaps. Men, women and children had the most fantastic garments wrapped around their bodies like elaborate dressing gowns. They were usually sat on a wooden bench (he was sure they were pews and the people were in church) or stood up holding hands and dancing at a party. Whether sitting or standing, they were always smiling. The ladies were normally dressed in gowns down to the ankles and wore elaborate jewellery on their wrists and necks. Although there were a multitude of colours, such as blue and yellow and white, Connor concluded that they loved green. Connor thought that both the men and the women carried themselves beautifully. Mrs Thomas flipped through the photos and pointed and gasped and announced, "that is Auntie. That is Nana. That is Uncle. That is Auntie. That is Nana..."
She held out one photograph proudly, like it was the prize find. "Aha," she said. "This is my darling older sister. Jojo."
Connor looked closely. Jojo looked like his mother. Her smile was wide and emanated sheer goodness. Big brown eyes looked up from the photograph and Connor felt they were staring directly at him. Connor glanced down. He could see now what his dad was talking about. They were huge and perfectly round, like melons or beach balls.
"I do so miss her," Mum sighed.
They didn't say much as they progressed with the collage. Connor quickly rummaged through the second box and picked out photos of himself, Mum and Dad. There were pictures of their house, of school, even recent ones of Connor playing rugby. The tips of his fingers stuck together and Connor had to prise them apart as he glued the photos to the cardboard. His mother drew a picture of the village church, bringing to life the green lawn, the heavy wooden door and the sloping roof. She was a fantastic artist, always adding details Connor hadn't even noticed existed. She managed to make everything look more beautiful and wonderful than it was in real life. Connor sometimes wondered how wonderful it would be to live in the mind of his mother just for a day. The church was the focal point of the collage. The photographs were just a natural progression

from it.

Connor did briefly wonder whether the collage would give a rounded, realistic view of where they lived. He loved the valleys, just like his mum did, but even Connor could tell there was another side when you scratched underneath the natural beauty. Shops on the high street were often boarded up, with a mountain of letters lying unopened inside the front door. The walls of the sports centre were forever covered in red graffiti and the grass of the playing fields was overgrown and used as a toilet by dogs. But then, Connor mused, just as his dad said there was a time and a place to stop and consider the beauty of the world, was this really the time or place to provide a realistic perspective?

The phone rang.

Connor thought that it must be Dad, asking where on earth he was. He could imagine him on the other end, undoing the top button of his shirt and fanning a text book to cool his rising temper. Connor absent-mindedly ran upstairs, not really knowing where he was going or why. He often walked into a room and wondered what he was doing there. He returned to his parents' room and pulled open the door to the wardrobe. He knelt down and looked for more shoe boxes with photos in, but all he found were reams and reams of letters on faded paper. They were difficult to read, because the writing was large and theatrical, but he could tell they were from Jojo, saying how much she missed his mum and how she wished she would return home to Ghana. Connor put the letters away and pressed the lid down tightly on the box, feeling guilty (again) for trespassing on personal items.

When he returned downstairs his mother was off the phone. Connor hoped his dad hadn't demanded that he return to school. It was just too much fun at home with Mum. He went back to the dining room, but his mum wasn't there. He glanced at the canvas. He held his hand to his mouth.

The beautiful collage they had been working on together all morning was flooded in red paint. The photographs were ruined. The church was barely visible. Somebody had picked up a tub of paint and poured it all over their work, absolutely obliterating everything they had done, killing so many memories. Connor felt anger well up until his chest was pumping. He wanted to pick up the table and throw it on the floor. How could somebody *do* this?

At Least the Pink Elephants are Laughing at Us

Connor ran into the kitchen. She wasn't there. The study was empty. He opened and closed doors. He ran around the house. He started feeling dizzy; lightheaded. Eventually he found her in the living room.

His mother sat on one of the wooden chairs, legs pressed up high against her chest, rocking back and forth, back and forth. She stared at the wall. She didn't seem to notice that Connor was stood in the room. Finally she glanced in his direction.

"Your Auntie Jojo isn't coming after all," she said.

5 – Where to Stick the Chariots?

1987

The train doors parted painfully slowly and supporters spilled out like sardines released from a tin; and then it was fast, fast, fast. Connor inhaled the familiar scent of hops from the Brains factory, but only briefly, for there was no time for contemplation and analysis, for it was like a race. His feet skipped a step, did a Lionel Blair impersonation, just to keep up with his dad.

"Best burgers you can buy in Cardiff," a round lady shouted. Wind blew dust and litter from the pavements over her stall. "Buy your programme here. The cheapest in Cardiff." Connor walked ten yards. "Buy your programmes here. The cheapest in Cardiff," another man shouted. Connor could only see the top of heads, mainly bald. "The team is nothing like the old days," a man complained. "Not like when we had Gareth Edwards and JPR and Barry John terrifying the English. Not like this lot. They couldn't scare my gran, I tell you."

Connor pushed the metal turnstiles, heard the click-click-click; worried he'd get stuck, that he'd block the entrance, that supporters would complain they couldn't get into the stadium, that he was in the way. Men stood in line at the urinals, following the rules, splashing everywhere and not caring one jot. The longest line, though, where men stood on tip-toes and nervously looked around, was at the bar. Other men, the lucky ones, stood in the wide, expansive corridors protecting their glasses and sipping on their cold beer. People looked thirsty. Connor glanced through a crack in the wall and the ground opened up in front of him. It was a glorious sight. Supporters were already beginning to take their seats or standing to attention. The ground was a sea of red and white. It was one of the most amazing things Connor had ever seen.

The players came out on to the pitch; first the white of

At Least the Pink Elephants are Laughing at Us

England, greeted with thunderous, viscous boos. Ieuan Evans led the Welsh team out, holding the white leather ball in his hands like a precious jewel. Connor was excited to see Glenn Webbe; his dad had told him numerous times that he was the first black player to ever play for Wales.

The English kicked off and a player in red dropped the ball.

"Catch the ball, you fucking idiot!" somebody from the crowd – he hoped it wasn't his dad – shouted. Other people laughed.

Smoke wafted around the ground. It had a strong smell Connor wasn't familiar with. It wasn't altogether unpleasant, though. Connor shuffled on the hard seat. It felt like his bottom was pure bone. He struggled to get as gripped by the game as the other sixty thousand or so fans in the ground. Connor had a confession to make to his dad. He was worried it would break his heart. He enjoyed the closeness they had built recently, although he hated the fact it seemed to have built a bridge between him and his mum. Connor didn't have the balls to tell his dad he didn't really like rugby. Sure, he enjoyed playing it, but that was because it seemed easy and he liked the adulation it brought. But watching it and – even worse – talking about it? It was a great big snooze.

In truth, Connor was still more interested in creative endeavours like writing and drawing, just like his mum. His dad liked books so long as they were textbooks. Recently Connor had taken an interest in the way films and sitcoms were made; the art of building suspense, adding twists and side-footing the viewers. He'd even become interested in the stories comedians told on the television shows such as *Opportunity Knocks* and the five-minute slots on *Bullseye*. Connor had watched an interview with Richard Burton where he said he would give up all his performances – including Shakespeare – to play for Wales at Cardiff Arms Park. Well, Connor was the exact opposite. He'd much prefer to perform on stage than on a rugby pitch.

"*Every* time!" a fan protested when the referee blew his whistle for an indiscretion. Connor was pretty sure it was the first time it had happened.

The referee blew his whistle for half time and people dispersed to the toilets, to the burger bar, but mainly to the bar.

Connor turned to his dad but he was content to sit and rub his hands together. Maybe this was the perfect opportunity to speak to him? The rugby was just a smoke screen. Connor needed to speak to his dad about much more important things than damn rugby.

Connor had never felt more frightened, though. It felt like he was being disloyal, a Judas. He just knew that he had to.

"Dad, I don't think mum is well..."

He knew it was against the rules to open his heart. You didn't share your emotions with Dad. Only 'sissies' shared their feelings, and no boy of Alun Thomas's was a 'sissy'. His dad stared intently at the double-glazing adverts in the programme, his eyes burning into the paper. There was a lot of noise in the ground, with people leaving and returning to their seats. Connor wondered whether his dad heard him. Maybe he needed to say it again? He hoped not.

"Don't worry, son," Dad said, looking away from the programme but not quite at Connor. "I know she's been a bit quiet but I think she is just finding it difficult. Just think. You've always been her special boy and now we've been spending more time together, what with the rugby and everything. You know?"

Dad looked relieved to see the players returning from the tunnel. He stood up and started clapping his hands, leading by example.

The second half was just as brutal and just as ugly as the first, but Wales clinched a victory and that was all that mattered. We were suddenly world beaters again. The train was just as packed as before, but now it was loud and boisterous as cans were torn open and the passengers, faces as red as their shirts, sung "You can stick your fucking chariots up your arse..."

The train stopped at Pencoed. Connor had made a decision. He was prepared to upset his dad, was ready for it, so long as he got him to listen. It was just too important not to. This was his mum.

"Dad, I don't think it is just jealousy, you know. She lost it when Auntie Jojo didn't come. She poured paint all over the collage we had been working on all morning, destroying old photographs that I'm sure were important to her..."

Dad looked at him now, like he was finally listening, that the

At Least the Pink Elephants are Laughing at Us

line had been crossed, that this had suddenly become deadly serious.

"Really?" he asked. His face looked pained. "Your Auntie Jojo not coming pushed her over the edge? Like it brought up memories or something...?"

Connor thought his father looked panicked by this, like the words somehow had a greater significance.

He felt undeniable relief. The rucksack with the bulky heavy textbooks had been removed from his back. Dad finally understood. Mum was finally going to get the help she needed. She'd be referred to one of those psychiatrists he saw in films with their reading glasses and notepads and countless letters after their names, and they'd talk to Mum in soft, hushed tones about her emotions and worries and unravel the layers and get right to the root of the problem, give her an action-plan to get better, to bring back his old mum.

"I have the answer," his dad said as they waited for the train to stop so he could stretch through the window and pull the handle on the other side. "I'm taking you all on holiday. We all need a break away from it all."

Connor felt like banging his head against the train door with frustration and despair. He was not sure his dad had actually listened to a single word he'd said.

6 – When the Sun Goes Down and the Light Goes Out

This was without doubt one of the best days of Nanya's life. Ever. She was utterly blessed. The world was unimaginably beautiful. It was unforgivable not to live and enjoy it to the fullest.

They drove down in the morning, pretty much in a straight line with a few twists and turns here and there, happily waving goodbye to the bleak, pollution-infested and intimidating steel works of Port Talbot to their left. Alun had his window down, elbow positioned outside the door, his thumb rhythmically tapping the steering wheel. He was probably drumming the beat to Madonna. Her husband liked Madonna. Alun fondly reminisced about his annual coach trips to Tenby as a child, when half the valleys squeezed onboard carrying crates of Brains Bitter, leaving at the crack of dawn and returning in the evening; sunburnt, tipsy and with an abundance of stories to tell. His sometimes stern, poker face was smiling today. Alun looked so much more relaxed now he was out of that suffocating tie and was giving those fine, muscular legs of his some sunlight. Her darling eleven year-old boy listened intently to the stories in the back, pausing only to stuff his mouth with hard boiled sweets from a white bag. Nanya optimistically started a chorus of "We're all going on our Summer Holidays," and, to her giddy surprise, the two men in her life enthusiastically joined in.

They parked the car at the train station, then gladly stretched and unfolded their bodies before rolling their suitcases along the hot, sticky pavement up the gentle hill to the hotel. This was no time to be stuck indoors, though, not on a glorious day like this, and so they quickly offloaded their suitcases. Nanya had never known Alun so upbeat and enthusiastic, not even in the early days of their love affair, when he was the most romantic man God had the privilege of creating. "You know Roald Dahl came

At Least the Pink Elephants are Laughing at Us

on holiday here every year as a kid back in the twenties and thirties," Alun informed them. "Did you know he was born in Llandaff in Cardiff, Nanya?" he asked. "He absolutely could not get enough of Tenby!"

Nanya didn't know they were walking in any particular direction or with any real purpose; she just felt blessed to be here with her two men, was happy to be led anywhere. They walked through the busy town, stopping at little shops selling magnets and buckets and spades, gazing at the church with the tower that they were able to see from absolutely everywhere, continued beyond a large department store Alun said had been run by the same family since 1903, stopped for yet more boiled sweets at Woolworths. They casually walked a little further before Alun dug his hands deep inside his pockets and treated his family to ice cream. Her little boy's teeth were going to fall out from all of this sugar, Nanya considered, without even a trace of worry.

"We'll go on a different beach every day," Alun said as they walked down a rocky slope leading to glorious sand that stretched for miles in front of them. Alun knew Nanya thought variety was one of the many spices of life. Children rode on donkeys that ambled along slowly and sleepily. Mothers unrolled the straps of their swim suits, revealing pink, sun-kissed shoulders. Dads pushed wooden cricket stumps into the sand. Children bounced on the spot and waited for both Mum and Dad to hurry up. Nanya spotted the opening to a cave. A long row of white terraced hotels stood proudly on the edge of a steep, green cliff.

"This is paradise," Nanya commented. She turned to Alun and kissed him on the lips. He tasted hot and salty. Nanya noticed the subtle twist of vanilla ice cream joining the mix. "Thank you, darling," she said, hugging her husband.

Alun carefully laid down an orange towel right in the middle of the beach and then, before Nanya had time to blink or blow her nose, he was lying on his back with his knees up in just his tiny blue trunks. What did they call then again? Budgie snugglers? The trunks certainly left nothing to the imagination, and her husband certainly had plenty to hide. "Do you see that big rock there?" Alun asked. "Well, back in my day the fort was a zoo. A zoo! With real animals! Can you believe it?"

There was no time to just sit there and let the day escape. Nanya slipped off her sandals. She looked at Connor, who was tall, angular and gangly without his tee-shirt. I must do more cooking, Nanya thought. The boy needed to eat more fine African food! Nanya held out her hand to her son. "Are you coming to explore?" she asked. Connor enthusiastically took her hand, and then they were off, their arms swinging in wild abandon.

The sand was hot, burning her soles, but then there were soggy patches where her feet sunk and disappeared beneath the surface. It reminded Nanya of the glorious beach back in Ghana, by the castle, where she used to run away from tiny white crabs that threatened to bite her. Those were happy, wonderful days, with her family and her dear, beloved Jojo. Nanya wasn't scared of crabs now. They were an example of God's creations. She wasn't scared of anything. Not now. Not today. They paddled in the rock pools, the water cold and refreshing, the seaweed straggly and slippery. Some of the rocks were sharp and pointed and dug into her feet. Nanya looked down and casually noticed that the water just in front of her feet had turned red, that it was just like the paint that had ruined their collage when Jojo should have visited; that she must be bleeding. She really didn't care.

"Look!" Connor shouted, pointing to a spot where he had just lifted a rock. "I've found a crab!"

Nanya excitedly stabbed her hand in the water and grabbed the crab. It was big, with sharp, threatening claws. It was nothing like the tiny white crabs she ran away from as a child in Ghana. Nanya proudly held the crab in the palm of her hand, showed Connor how big it was. "Watch it doesn't bite you!" Connor shrieked. Too late. Nanya closed her eyes, clenched her teeth and grimaced as the claws dug into her soft, delicate skin; bit her tongue to prevent herself from screaming, from taking the Lord's name in vain. "Don't worry," she reassured Connor, throwing the crab back in the water. "They're much more scared of us than we are of them."

The two of them continued exploring inside the little cracks and crevices of the dark caves. This was just like it used to be with the two of them. They reluctantly returned to their towels and threw ball. Father and son were good at catching the ball as

At Least the Pink Elephants are Laughing at Us

they both played rugby. Nanya couldn't catch a cold. They giggled hysterically every time she dropped the ball. It seemed a waste though, to be stood in the same spot for too long when there was the rest of the beach, the rest of the world, to explore.

Alun – the *spoilsport* – said he needed a rest. Connor agreed. Connor was always agreeing with his dad recently. They both lay down on their towels and closed their eyes. They weren't seeing sense. They weren't looking at the big picture! Days like these only came along every so often, were there to compensate for the grey, bleak days trapped indoors with nothing to do and nobody to do it with, not with Alun in work, Connor in school, and Jojo back in Ghana; and so they needed to make the most of the glorious opportunity whilst it was still there!

Nanya playfully tugged at Connor's hand, but he just giggled and said no, that he was tired. Nanya pulled more forcibly now. She could hear his elbow click. Alun would be worrying in case he got injured and wouldn't be able to play his beloved rugby. Connor moaned. "Mum," he protested. "That really hurts."

Nanya shook her head. Why was he such a wimp?

"Come on Nanya," Alun pleaded, finally interested enough to sit up, to move away from that blasted beach towel. "Come and sit down with us for a bit, sweetheart. It's been a long day. For all of us. We have plenty of days to enjoy."

Who did *he* think he was? He was back to being the stuffy headmaster again, treating her like a child! Nanya looked around. Eyes glared at her disapprovingly from every direction, stared at her from underneath dark sunglasses, behind the shelter of umbrellas. What were they looking at? They hadn't seen a black person before?

"What you gawping at?" she shouted to anybody who cared enough to listen.

Alun begged her to sit down now. There was urgency in his voice she hadn't heard for years, since before Connor was born. He hurriedly tried to shelter her with the towel, hide both him and her from unbearable, excruciating embarrassment. Nanya pushed him away and said okay, okay. It was just to keep him quiet. She sat down on the deckchair, her back straight, let the moment simmer. Nanya didn't move for quite a while, just sat there, in the fading sun, completely rigid. The yellow sun had turned orange and was falling lower and lower into the ocean. A ray of light rippled and shimmied in the water. Nanya looked at her two boys, her two men. She loved them with every inch of her being, even though – like now – they could frustrate the life out of her.

The sudden excitement had faded and her two boys – two men - were lazy and content now. Nanya was still simmering. The sea was too glorious to resist, too beautiful not to enjoy. She was going back to the great big rock, the rock that was surrounded by water now the tide had come in.

Nanya ran on the balls of her feet, the gentle wind blowing through her hair, as she quickly moved closer and closer to the sea. It didn't matter that she couldn't swim. She wasn't scared of anything. She was protected. Nothing was impossible. She would float on the surface of the water.

She entered the sea. It was cold but felt utterly glorious on her skin. Her legs kicked as the water splashed and bubbled and frothed around her. Nanya continued walking as the water circled her waist. Nanya kept walking as the water covered her eyes, covered the top of her head. It was time to swim, to float. But she couldn't swim, she couldn't float. Nanya punched with her hands and kicked with her legs, but it was all in slow-motion, all against an impossibly strong force that was fighting against her rather than with her. The salty, suffocating water filled her mouth and she couldn't spit it out...

And then Nanya lay on her back on the sand, looking up at the fading orange sun that had all but disappeared. Her husband was there, too, had finally woken up. He was very active now. He frantically pushed both hands down on her chest. She wondered what for. And then she gazed at the faded outline of her darling little boy; tall, angular and gangly without his tee-shirt.

This really wouldn't do, Nanya thought. She really needed to do more cooking, her boy really needed to eat more fine African food...

At Least the Pink Elephants are Laughing at Us

Mandy
1- Daddy's Little Princess

1999

It was Sunday afternoon, and seven year-old Mandy and her dad were headed for the beach.

It was too cold to go to the beach, her mum said. Where do you think we live? Costa del flippin' Bridgend? It will be too late by the time you get there, she protested. Daddy just laced up his shoes, kissed Mum on the lips, said we won't be late, darling; and then they were in the car, the windows down, cheeks flushed, crossing white lines in the middle of the road, stopping occasionally for sheep.

There was occasionally somebody huddled at the bottom of the gigantic, twisting hill, a part-time ticket attendant, usually in an oversized raincoat, bouncing on the spot to keep warm, but today they were free to park the car wherever they wanted, for not only was there no attendant, but there were no other cars either. The tide was out and the beach seemed to stretch for miles. The grey and black clouds looked angry and threatened mayhem, and the wind rattled the parked car like it was made of tin.

"This is absolutely perfect," Daddy said, holding out his hand, his steps large and bouncy, heading towards the sea.

The sea was never the perfect, unblemished blue Mandy saw in the movies or in the glossy brochures at the travel agents on Caroline Street. It wasn't blue, for a start; it was a dirty polluted dark green and tainted with large patches that were almost black. Mandy was both fascinated and terrified by the mysterious patches of dark water. What were they? She half-expected them to transform, to morph into something that was alive, like a whale or a sea monster.

The wind was in their faces, as it always seemed to be, whatever direction Mandy walked and wherever she walked. Mandy wiped a tear from her cheek. Held her dad's hand tighter. She was her Daddy's Little Princess, and she liked to hold his hand. Mandy looked down at her white daps, matted now with grey. She dodged blue, tangled fishing line and then kicked at seaweed. Her feet sunk into the sand. She'd be able to rinse the salt water from her socks like a wet flannel when she got home. Her mum would have put her wellies on, of course, because she was sensible, but Dad was in such a rush to get out of the house she didn't get the chance to fuss. It *really* was cold. At least she wasn't in one of those silly little skirts chasing after a stupid netball like they tried to make her do in school. She'd snuggle her hand in her pocket, nice and warm, if she had a chance, but she didn't want to let go of her daddy.

"Shoes off," Daddy ordered. "Make sure you put your socks in the shoes, like in PE. And don't sit down or you'll get a wet bum. And *nobody* likes a wet bum."

Mandy thought the sea was going to be flipping freezing. The surfers had the right idea with the rubber swimsuits that clung to their bodies and looked impossible to pull off. Even the seagulls, sitting on top of the water, were fluffed into balls and looking at them like they were mad. Her dad had already pushed his socks into his shoes and rolled his trousers up over his knees. Mandy balanced on one foot like a pelican as she tried to tear off her second sock. She looked up. Dad was in the water. He turned around. "Its proper fresh!" he shouted. Her dad was an eternal optimist. If he said it was "fresh" then Mandy knew it would be flippin' freezing.

"Come on in!" her dad encouraged.

Mandy closed her eyes and sprinted towards the water, fearing the very worst. She built up an impressive speed, like she did when approaching the sandpit on Sports Day, and entered the water with a big splash.

Mandy screamed at the top of her voice and ran out of the water much faster than she'd run in.

Her dad laughed. "It's much warmer when you get used to it," he said, his teeth chattering. That was what people *always* said when it was freezing cold, Mandy thought. Plus, Mandy

At Least the Pink Elephants are Laughing at Us

reasoned, it was often warmer because they'd had a wee in the water. It was only disgusting if somebody caught you. Dad held out his hand. "Come on, Princess," he said. "Do it for Daddy."

Mandy gritted her teeth and reached out for his hand. The soles of her feet stepped on pebbles on the bottom of the water; she hoped they were pebbles and not crabs. The waves looked harmless enough as they slapped gently against her shins. Mandy looked down and saw a horizontal line across her leg. Below the line her skin was pink and above the line it returned to a familiar milky white. This wasn't so bad, she thought, squeezing tighter on her dad's hand. Steam rose from the water. Mandy tried to look out across the channel, to Somerset, but there was a fog and she could only see out to the terrifying black patches in the middle of the ocean. She looked back and watched the green salty water turn to foam as it gently unrolled onto the shore.

Dad suddenly gripped Mandy's waist and lifted her high above his shoulders. Mandy's delirious screams travelled down the coast, all the way past Porthcawl and onwards to the Gower and beyond.

Mum was right, Mandy reluctantly considered. They walked back to the car, their socks drenched and their skin salty and uncomfortable. The light *was* already fading. It mattered not one jot though. She was with her daddy.

They climbed the concrete, bumpy path. Mandy noticed there was another car in the car park. That was strange, she thought. Even *she* knew it was time to settle down in front of the TV with a cup of tea. That's what sensible people did at this time on a Sunday. Maybe this person wasn't sensible? Maybe they were crazed? Maybe they were murderers?

A car door opened. A woman appeared. Mandy sighed with relief. It couldn't be a murderer then. Only men were murderers.

"I'm really sorry but I'm having some problems with my car," the woman said. "Could you help?"

Mandy felt a tinge of jealousy. No we can't, she thought. Call the AA or the RAC or a man with a big tow truck. Just leave my daddy alone. He is my daddy, not yours. Mandy wanted her dad to say no, to tell this stupid, infuriating woman that they needed to get back for tea, that Mummy would be worrying. She knew he wouldn't. That only ever happened in the movies and, of course, movies were not real life, were they? Her daddy was a nice daddy and he was far too kind to say that. This woman was a damsel in distress after all, Mandy guessed, and so they couldn't just leave her. Dad unlocked their car and told her to stay there in the warm, that he wouldn't be long.

But he *was* long. The light vanished and the sky turned pitch dark. It *wasn't* warm in the car at all. Mandy hated this woman more than she hated anybody, and she hadn't even met her; not really. She was ruining everything. Mandy opened the glove compartment and sucked on a mint. She turned on the radio and fiddled with the button but they were just talking about politics or religion or playing classical music. She fidgeted in the seat. She was bored. Mum would be panicking about them too, she thought, suddenly concerned what her mum thought.

Mandy never disobeyed her dad's orders, but she did now. She opened the door and walked over to the car. Mandy expected her dad to be out in the cold, under the bonnet, pulling at leads and adding oil; doing whatever men did to fix cars. He wasn't there. He was inside the car, in the warmth. Mandy couldn't see inside. The windows were steamed, like at swimming. Must be the sea air, she reasoned.

Mandy pulled open the door. There was a lot of frantic activity inside. Her dad started talking quickly, like he was in a hurry, telling the woman that her car should be fixed now and she shouldn't have any more problems. The woman looked more concerned with making her hair look pretty than with her car.

"Come on, Princess," Daddy awkwardly smiled. "Let's get you home."

Dad turned the heating in the car on and Mandy felt her fingers and toes defrost. The car chugged up the hill and they left the winding roads behind them and moved closer to the familiarity of town and home. Mandy wondered if Mum would have tea waiting for them when they got home.

At least they had a good excuse for being late, she thought, secretly hoping the woman broke down on the way home.

2 – Saying Goodnight to the Cleaners

2000

The side of her temple rattled rhythmically in tune with the movements of the bus. The floodlit town centre was replaced by darkness and nothingness as the bus began its descent along the sparse, winding roads to the vicinities. She jerked suddenly awake as the bus moved over a bump in the road. The outline of the side of her head left a feint stain, like a thumb print, on the window.

Sylvia Williams stifled a yawn. It had been a long day. It had been dark when she stood at the bus shelter in the morning, her hands sunk deep into the coat pockets, shoes carefully avoiding the glass that lay shattered on the floor, and it had been dark when she waved goodbye to the cleaners and left the office for the day. Sylvia joked to the cleaners that "now my work really begins," but it wasn't much of a joke, not really. Everybody knew she had two boys and a girl, all still in school uniforms, waiting for Mum to come home so she could cook their tea and help with the homework.

It hadn't always been like this. It hadn't been anything like this, not until that night, until *the* night.

It was just like any other work night out with her husband, Jeremy. Sylvia was perfectly willing and able to dutifully play her role. She applied her makeup, put on a pretty dress, smiled (generously) and laughed (outrageously) at his boss's sexist jokes. In truth, though the conversations were often rehearsed and recycled, Sylvia quite looked forward to these evenings. They gave her a rare opportunity to leave "Mummy" at home, put on her glad rags and feel like a woman again.

Of course, there was no need for her to look at any other man because, as usual, Jeremy was by far the most attractive man in the room. Jeremy was usually the most attractive man in *any* room, regardless how big the room was. Sylvia wasn't just saying this because he was her husband. She was saying it *despite* him being her husband. She often wished he wasn't so handsome, longed for his perfect skin to become blemished or for his thick head of dark hair to recede, but it was always in vain. It was like trying to argue that round was square or white was black. The other men wore identical tuxedos, but some had white shirts hanging out of trousers, others looked like penguins. Jeremy, though, what with his broad shoulders and narrow waist, square jaw and green eyes, looked like he was *designed* to wear a tuxedo. Sylvia hated him.

Of course, as usual, Jeremy was also by far the most charming man in the room.

"Sure I know your wife," Jeremy said, dismissing the introductions with a kiss on the wife's cheek and a delicate hand flirtatiously slivering around the waist. "We've been having a secret affair for absolutely *ages* now, haven't we Kathleen?"

Cue generous smiles and outrageous laughter. Jeremy may have been the most charming man in the room, but even he wasn't beyond recycling his lines.

He was a confident man who was used to getting his own way. Jeremy thought it was hilarious to give their eldest boy the same name as his surname. "William Williams," he enthused. "How fantastic is that?" Sylvia assured him it was neither fantastic nor original, especially in Wales, but she knew his mind was made up, and so there was no point arguing further.

Sylvia was enjoying the night more than usual, possibly because she'd drunk more dry white wine than she normally did. William had been fighting in school again, looking after his little sister he said, and so it had been a draining day. Sylvia chatted to a guy from the finance department who had square glasses and a bald head domed like an egg. He kept glancing down Sylvia's top, but he was so obvious and so cheeky with it she really didn't mind. She quite liked the man. He was funny.

At some point in the proceedings Sylvia noticed, probably with casual indifference, that her husband had gone missing. She only went looking for him because she felt good and, with the kids hopefully asleep in bed, fancied sneaking back home for some rare Mummy and Daddy time. She knew he was most likely out the back having a cheeky cigarette or cigar. Jeremy

At Least the Pink Elephants are Laughing at Us

went outside to smoke because a cigarette or cigar was always cheeky in Sylvia's mind. Sylvia pulled down the metal bar and pushed open the wooden door. Her cheeks flushed from the biting chill outside. She heard giggling and absent-mindedly went to investigate.

It was then that Sylvia caught her husband with his dirty hands snaking all over that skanky little whore, or Kathleen, as she liked to call herself.

They had been having a secret affair after all.

The end came quickly. There was no drum roll or pointless, long-winded discussions, doomed to failure. Sylvia couldn't even bare to look at the man, let alone lie in bed next to his cheating body. With the help of her two boys, one of them suddenly a man, Sylvia shredded a wardrobe full of expensive designer clothes and then dumped his suitcases onto the wet, slippery, depressing pavement outside their house, their home. A taxi with bright penetrating headlights arrived minutes later and took her husband away.

Mandy was seemingly the only one traumatised by events that night. Dad was the apple in Mandy's eye. The memory of her little girl, on her hands and knees, punching the floor, screaming for her dad to come back, still sent shivers down Sylvia's spine, probably always would.

Sylvia pressed the square red button for the bus to stop. She couldn't help but glance at her reflection in the round mirror just behind the driver's glass cubicle. She knew she looked tired, that she was the epitome of drained, but she didn't have any energy left to care. It had been a long week, a long month, a *very* long year. Sylvia now worked full-time and still brought up her three children, all on her own, with no help from anybody. Of course she looked tired.

The young guy on the seat in front was getting off too. Sylvia hadn't seen him before. He wore a long black leather jacket down to his knees and he had metal in both ears. Sylvia stepped down from the bus, gripping the railing, said goodbye to the driver, said she would see him again tomorrow. She could sense the young man walking close behind her, was painfully aware of his movements. Chunky boots stomped hard on the floor. Sylvia noticed some of the street lights weren't working, that it really was dark, that the streets were deserted and deathly quiet. Her heartbeat quickened, started beating hard and fast in her chest. The man quickened his pace too, closing in on Sylvia, and then...

He sidestepped past her, disappeared down the dark pathway without even a moment's hesitation or a backward glance, seemingly barely even aware of her existence.

Sylvia felt incredible relief, immediately replaced by acute guilt for being so horribly judgmental.

And then Sylvia felt intense, agonising pain in her arm. She collapsed on the floor, her head hitting the hard pavement. She stared up at the flickering fluorescent light and wondered why the side of her head felt so wet, like it was leaking.

3 – Desperate Den

2001

The two school friends hung out all afternoon. This was normal for a Saturday.

Dennis felt nervous around girls. They scared the living daylights out of him. They had secrets Dennis wasn't privy to. There was a circle of trust, and Dennis most definitely lived on the outside of that circle.

He'd plucked up the courage to speak to his dad about girls. Dennis was hoping his dad would reassure him there was absolutely nothing to worry about, give him a kick up the backside, warn him to pull himself together, to stop being so silly.

"You're absolutely right, son," his dad said. "They *are* absolutely terrifying. Why do you think I do everything your mum tells me to? I'm proud of you son. I think you understand women a lot better than you realise, Dennis. It has taken me forty years to reach the same conclusion. All you need to understand, son, is that women can never, *ever* be understood."

But Mandy, dear Mandy, was different from the other girls. That was why, for so long, he hadn't even thought of her as a girl. Dennis felt he *did* understand Mandy. Dennis didn't feel nervous in the slightest around Mandy. When he let rip (whether accidentally, or accidentally on purpose) Mandy didn't give him a disgusted look and call him "Smelly Denny"; no, Mandy laughed and gave him a high five. When he used some of the words his dad used when his mum wasn't around, Mandy didn't say "I'm telling Miss on you." Instead she asked if it was okay if she used the words, too. Mandy wasn't perfect like the other girls. He knew she had problems. His dad told Dennis that Mandy's old man had "done a runner" and "they won't be seeing him in a hurry." And then, of course, there was everything with her mum that people only ever whispered about.

Dennis snuck home when Mandy was in a world of her own in the den. He was good at vanishing without anybody noticing and besides, his house was just down the road. He planned to surprise Mandy. He'd ordered the present from the shop in town weeks ago, paid for it with his pocket money, emptying all the coins from his money box.

He returned quickly and was about to call Mandy's name when his path was blocked.

"What's that?"

It was Mandy's eldest brother, William. He was big even for boys in his year, and he was way older than Mandy. None of the boys dared call Mandy names. Mandy had two older brothers, but William was the one all the boys talked about. And now William was stood at the entrance to the den – *their* den – his head stooped because he was so tall, his hands on his hips.

"Nothing," Dennis replied, looking down at the broken twigs on the floor.

William snatched the pen knife. It was in his hand before Dennis could react. William eyed it disinterestedly. Flicked open the blade. Dennis hoped he didn't look too intently, prayed that he didn't examine it. Dennis held his breathe and rolled his fist into a ball. William's eyes widened. He was suddenly *very* interested in the knife. William read the engraving, the words that Dennis had asked the elderly man in the shop to write on the knife weeks ago.

Mandy.

"Did you buy this for my sister?"

Dennis wanted to lie. He longed to lie. But the letters were there, on the knife. How could he lie when the truth was engraved on a penknife?

"Yes."

"Why?"

"I thought she'd like it."

"I thought she'd *like* it," William mimicked.

Dennis felt completely exposed, had nowhere to hide. William looked him up and down, examined him, just like he had the knife. What would he find? Dennis didn't dare look up. He was sure though that William looked at him with utter contempt and disgust, just like all the girls – except for Mandy –

At Least the Pink Elephants are Laughing at Us

did in school.

"I've seen you following her around everywhere," William accused. "Like a dog. Do you fancy my sister or something?"

"No!" Dennis blurted. His hands trembled. He longed them to stop. William would be able to see what a baby he was. He dug his nails into his palms. He was sure he'd draw blood. William put the knife away, put it in his own pocket.

"Just leave her alone, alright? My little sister doesn't need a weirdo like you following her around. You know what happened to our mum, yeah? She doesn't need you freaking her out, you hear?"

Dennis bowed his head and said "yes."

William barged past him, making sure he clipped Dennis with his shoulder as he did so, nearly knocking him to the floor.

Dennis remained standing at the entrance to the den. William, thank God, disappeared down the road. Twigs snapped. Feet moved closer. Dennis acted fast. He ran across the road as quickly as his skinny legs would carry him, back to the safety of his home. He disappeared without his best friend noticing that he had even reappeared. He was good at that.

Disappearing.

Chris Westlake

4 – Fluffy Pink Dress

William looked at his sister, and then he looked at her again. William had never seen Mandy wearing a dress before and, as her older brother, he'd known her all her life. She wasn't the Barbie type. More GI Jane. Mandy joked that she was allergic to dresses. Forget peanuts. Dresses. The material brought her out in a frightful, unsightly rash, she said. It would be child cruelty to let that happen to a young girl, she reasoned. Social Services would take her away, and nobody wanted that now, did they? It was the same reasoning Mandy used when Mum tried to put her in a dress at their auntie's wedding.

"But dresses are all made of different materials," Mum argued.

"That's what they *want* you to believe, Mum," Mandy replied.

"But how do you know you are allergic when you have never worn one before?"

"I wore one in a past life and it really didn't end well. That is why it is a *past* life, Mum."

She could be quite cheeky, their little sister, and borderline witty when she got the chance, especially as she was only ten. She had grown in stature since her two brothers used her as a second goal-post when they were short of a jumper. She wasn't really a smarty-pants; William and Tom wouldn't allow that. They did let her have some lee-way, though. Occasionally. It was only fair. Mandy never did wear a dress at her auntie's wedding. She wore one now, though. Nestling on the edge of the high stool, Mandy leaned forward, her elbows pressed against the kitchen table, hands tangled tightly together. Her middle brother combed her hair. "Owww!" Mandy screamed. "That hurts!"

"Don't blame me," her brother replied. "Blame the knots in your hair. Have you ever even *heard* of conditioner?"

William knew Mandy didn't really mind if Tom tugged at

her hair, caused her some pain. Everything was water off a duck's back today.

Today Dad was coming to see them. He was taking them to Dan-Yr-Ogof caves, playing Happy Families, pretending to be a real dad. What a joke. He'd take them to the Big Pit next, or that waterfall in Neath. It would be the first time they'd even *seen* him since *that* night. But Mandy had conveniently forgotten that, hadn't she? Mandy had conveniently forgotten a lot of things about their dad. In her mind, she was still Daddy's Little Princess. William had to give her some leeway though, just like with her cheekiness. She'd only been a little girl when he left them. She still *was* a little girl. She'd always be a little girl.

Mandy had been going on and on about the visit all week. Dad this, Dad that. Of course, it was adoringly sweet, if you were that way inclined. Of course, William wanted his little sister to be reunited with her dad, for it to be a happy-ever-after story. It was the least she deserved. But he could not deny that her unflinching loyalty for the man really *grated* on him.

He glanced at their mum, slumped in her chair, staring absently at the television screen. Surely she wasn't really that engrossed in a documentary about female bodybuilders? Her two arms looked like they didn't belong to the same body, like they'd become detached and then sewn back on the wrong person. One arm twitched like a deer that had just been hit by a car, while the other was limp and lifeless and just *hung*. Her eyes were watery and unblinking, like she was oblivious to everything that was going on apart from what was right in front of her. There was an orange, crispy coating on her top lip; probably from the baked beans they'd eaten for lunch. Her nose was running. William knew it wasn't affecting her in any way, that she probably hadn't even noticed, but it irritated him; it just felt so damn undignified to see his mum that way. His brother and sister were fussing over their no-good dad when it was their mum who deserved every ounce of their attention.

William went to get a tissue, to wipe away the sauce and the snot, but his younger brother was one step ahead. Whilst William pondered and thought and just *sat* there, like the big clumsy oaf he was, Tom put down his comb and returned from the kitchen with a box of tissues. He delicately squeezed the tip

At Least the Pink Elephants are Laughing at Us

of his mother's nose and dabbed at her upper lip. He was a good boy, even William could see that. Their mother's eyes rose to look at him but her face stayed in the same position. "Thank you," she said. "You're such a good boy," she added.

There was absolutely nothing wrong with her mind at all. It was sharper than ever; compensating, it seemed, for the lack of physical activity she was able to undertake. She knew everything that was going on with all of her children, from their timetables at school to the names of their friends. She worked out the sums on the TV faster than Carol Vorderman. But emotionally she was drained. The life had been sucked out of her.

She was painfully skinny these days, William thought. Their mum had always been so attractive. When she dressed up for one of those functions with their dad she looked a million dollars. It was sheer lunacy that their dad had even looked at another woman. William didn't like seeing his mum in that drab, faded, *depressing* dressing gown. She sometimes forgot or just didn't bother – why should she – to cover up, and she exposed legs that were pale and bumpy and speckled with red, unhealthy spots. Her legs looked like they could snap like twigs from the slightest movement. It was because she'd always been on her feet – run *off* her feet - looking after us lot, William thought, and now she was hardly on her feet at all.

It was their dad who'd done this to her, who'd made her a sad shadow of her former self. The bastard. Their mum was lucky to still be alive because of him. The doctors said had it not been for the young guy who had got off the bus at her stop and heard her collapsing, who had called the ambulance and stayed with her by her side, comforting her, then she may not have made it.

All this tragedy – enough to last a family a whole lifetime - and yet Mandy still wouldn't put on a dress for her mum, would she? She'd only put one on for her dad, when he finally decided to make an appearance and take them all for a fun day out, leaving Mum on her own in front of the television.

Of course, they'd checked with Mum that it was okay to meet Dad. Mum said that it was fine, that there was no way she was going to stop her little girl from seeing her dad. She said she wouldn't take no for an answer. Then she turned away and stared absently into thin air. William noticed her lower lip quivered, that there was a tick in her cheek.

And now the so-called *real* man of the house was returning, coming home to roost, even if it was just for a day, maybe just a few hours. William was going to give him a few quiet words when he saw him, tell him a few home truths, just like he did to anybody who harassed Mandy.

And now Mandy, his adorable little sister, the one he looked out for more than any of them, was running around the place in a pink dress, excitedly awaiting his return.

The phone rang. Tom moved swiftly and fluidly to the reception room. William could hear his hesitant, confused, muffled mumblings in the other room. Tom came back into the room and William knew straight away who was on the phone and what he had said.

"I'm sorry, Mandy," Tom said, staring at the fluff on the carpet. "Dad isn't coming."

Mandy was quiet. The silence in the room was crippling. "It's okay," she said, self-consciously lowering herself off her stool. "He must have a good reason."

She patted down her fluffy dress with slow, awkward movements. William thought she looked so exposed and sad, just stood there. He felt anger welling inside of him. He remembered how pitiful she looked the night he left, screaming and banging her fists on the floor. The anger had been simmering all day, all week, ever since that selfish little bastard had left them to stew in this mess.

William tried to push himself up from the sofa, but he slumped down again and his arms and legs kicked and flailed pathetically. Fuck those stupid springs.

"It isn't okay, Mandy!" he shouted. "Just look at you. It isn't okay at all!"

William flung himself out of the seat and grabbed for the nearest item that he was able to lash out with. He picked up the china fruit bowl and threw it off the wall like it was a plastic Frisbee. It smashed into tiny pieces on the floor.

"Stop it!"

He turned.

Dad became a distant, insignificant memory. Dad became

At Least the Pink Elephants are Laughing at Us

nothing. Again. Everything that was important was in that room with them.

William, Tom and Mandy all clung tightly to their mother's frail body, for she was sobbing loudly.

5 – HaaHaa White Sheep

2002

The spotlights were bright and strong and intense. A couple of moths fluttered around them with bad intentions. Mandy thought that they had better watch their step. She had accidentally touched one of the spotlights and it had left her hand pink like a baboon's arse. She mused that one of those moths was going to end up frazzled if they didn't watch it. And nobody was going to miss a moth now, were they?

Somebody hadn't thought this through properly. She wasn't yet eleven but even she could see that the costume she was expected to wear for this production just wasn't practical. It wasn't that she was a Diva or anything, but she did have standards.

Mandy's knees dug into the wooden floor, probably full of splinters. She leant forward ninety degrees at the waist. She stuck her bum up in the air. After all, that was what sheep did, wasn't it?

Mandy didn't feel like a particularly convincing sheep. She wore her auntie's massive white woolly jumper and her brother's cricket pants, which were also far too big and kept falling down. Tom had painted her nose with a black marker pen. The stink from the pen filled her twitching nostrils. Her idiot brother must have been confused, or he must have been having a laugh, because he gave her whiskers too. She looked more like a cat than a sheep. Mandy had only noticed when she passed a mirror on the way to the stage. She couldn't help but smile. It wasn't like anybody would actually be looking at her now, was it?

She looked down at the crowd and she pinpointed her family. Only Mum looked interested. She sat upright in the uncomfortable plastic chair, her one arm rigid, staring open-eyed at the makeshift stage. It wasn't easy for her to attend these sort of events. She was looking nice tonight, Mandy thought. She had been to the hairdressers. Mandy couldn't blame her brothers for looking bored, though. She'd been exactly the same when she was dragged along to watch their performances. Her brother had played the rear end of the donkey one year, and that was just plain embarrassing.

The boy playing the lead role of Jesus waited for the cue from Mrs Llewellyn on the piano. Unfortunately dear old Mrs Llewellyn could barely see through the thick lenses of her glasses, let alone play the piano. She played a few correct notes before playing a few incorrect ones. Mrs Llewellyn cursed under her breath, then apologised to the audience for cursing under her breath. She started the song again. She stopped after a few notes and again apologised to the audience. The shit was really hitting the fan, Mandy thought. She wished she could share the moment with Dennis, but he didn't seem keen to hang out with her anymore.

Jesus turned to her with his hands on his hips. "I can't work under these circumstances! You're all amateurs!" he bellowed, and then stomped off the stage, only stopping momentarily to adjust the strap on his Next sandals.

The parents and siblings shuffled in their seats. There were a few involuntarily laughs, followed by an embarrassed silence, which was only broken by William shouting that "this is the worst Nativity play I've ever seen!"

"Hush!" one of the mums retorted. "They are only children."

"It wasn't like this in my day!" William countered. "I got a standing ovation when I played a strongman in the circus production of 96!"

Mandy could tell by the despondent shakes of the head that her brother's intervention was not welcomed. She quickly assessed the situation and concluded that it was going to rapidly descend into chaos. Somebody had to stand up and be counted. Mandy looked around and the teachers were bickering. This was make or break, Mandy thought. She pushed herself up off her hands and knees and trotted to the centre of the stage, to the spot where Jesus, who could now be heard sobbing behind the curtains, had stood. Mandy was aware what she must look like to the audience. She was half cat, half sheep, and dressed for a game of cricket.

The round heads in the audience were no longer faceless.

They all had big round eyes now. They all stared expectantly at her. Mandy could make out their features; the lines under their eyes, the dimples in their chins, the freckles on their cheeks. She could not have felt more exposed had she walked out on stage with no clothes on.

"Where do sheep get a haircut?" Mandy asked. She counted to two in her head and then said "the 'baa-baa' shop."

The mean, callous faces broke into friendly, encouraging smiles. The sound of hearty laughter shimmied around the wooden hall. Mandy felt an incredible sense of relief. She no longer had a ball and chain strapped to her ankles. Now she had string attached to the top of her head, and she was sure she had the power to effortlessly float around the hall, high above the crowd, like Peter Pan or Super Ted. Her two brothers hadn't laughed when she pulled that joke out of the cracker at Christmas. Now she caught William slapping his thigh and turning excitedly to his brother. This was fun, she thought. This was freakin' incredible.

"What do you call a sheep with no legs?" she asked. "A cloud."

The audience guffawed and giggled and clapped their hands. She could barely get a word in at home; or only when her brother's let her. Up on stage there was nobody to interrupt her, nobody to speak over her. She could just show off. Mandy continued telling jokes, one after the other, until Jesus came back on stage, fully clothed, and tried to push her out of the way. He didn't need to bother. Mandy's moment in the spotlight had come and gone. She bowed elaborately as the audience clapped and cheered.

Just before she left the stage, Mandy glanced over at her mum. She was smiling. Not the usual painted imitation Mandy had become accustomed to, but the beautiful smile that used to be ever-present and all too familiar before that fateful night when her dad had ruined it all.

And then, just as she was about to join her giggling, excited friends back of stage, just as Jesus broke into song, Mandy heard the doors to the hall swinging, and she was sure she recognised the thick dark hair that left the hall...

Part Two

James
1 - Slow Worms and Holy Water

2014

The grounds of the church were as familiar to him as his own living room.

He often came here as a kid on Saturdays, when he was bored of the endless cartoons on the television or the tedium of football on the radio; sometimes when he just wanted to get out of the house or be on his own. The cemetery was a sanctuary of peace and solitude that blended with danger and terror. Nobody knew he was there, not even his mum and dad. It was his little secret. Surely, he considered, there was something morbidly wrong about hiding away in the overgrown church grounds on his own, surrounded only by dead bodies buried underneath the very ground he walked on? When he thought about it rationally, it made his ageing skin crawl.

He'd climb the crumbling wall littered with moss and then lower himself on the other side, even though it was much simpler to just walk through the creaking wooden gate, which was usually unlocked. He scurried on the ground, lifting heavy concrete slabs, searching for slow worms that occasionally slivered underneath. Passers-by walking on the quiet, country road the other side of the wall were oblivious to his presence just feet away. Occasionally he'd wash away the dry mud and debris using the metal tap attached to the church wall, if only because he was intrigued by the concept of holy water. It was just like the water from the taps at home and those at school, but then it somehow felt utterly and indescribably different, too.

Other times he would just browse the engravings on the tombstones. He was fascinated by the older corpses, the people who lived and died in the 19th century and, occasionally, even earlier. He was aware the world was completely different then, a parallel universe, a world he could barely even contemplate. And

At Least the Pink Elephants are Laughing at Us

yet their lives were strangely entwined, for the graves were inhabited by local villagers; men and women who walked the same roads he did, probably washed their hands from the same metal tap. What happened to their souls? Did they just vanish? Did they rise to heaven or fall to hell? Or did they never really leave? Were they ever-present, watching and judging as he lightly tiptoed over their skeletons, buried deep underneath the ground? He always, always left before the sun went down, for the thought of being in the cemetery on his own, in the dark, absolutely terrified him.

It was Saturday morning now. James visited his dad, Bobby, every Saturday, without fail. James liked to think that his dad expected him, that he would be disappointed if he didn't visit. He invariably had the grounds to himself, just like he did as a kid. Sometimes he lifted a few concrete slabs, and occasionally he washed his hands at the tap. James brought flowers from Bridgend Market. He always stopped and chatted with his dad, updated him on whatever was or was not happening in his life, the news and gossip from the week. He told Bobby absolutely everything, things he wouldn't ever dare tell any living person, not even his mum. Every week James told Bobby a new joke. He always pictured him laughing. All James knew was that he felt a great deal closer to his dad when he was at his grave.

James turned towards the wooden gate, ready to return to the outside world, when he spotted another figure, stood motionless, head bowed, paying respects at another gravestone. James immediately recognised who it was. Roy Hughes was visiting Kim, his beloved wife of many years. James paused and watched for a moment, let his mind drift back to a time long gone, to when his dad and Terry's mum were both still alive. It was as though Roy sensed his presence, or maybe his gaze, for his focus slowly moved away from the grave and turned to James, looked him straight in the eye. Roy nodded in acknowledgement, then began walking along the faded green lawn towards him.

The two men shook hands. Roy's eyes watered. James knew Roy was a man of few words. James could tell he wanted to say something, something important. He could see it in his bloodshot, tearful eyes.

"What is it, Roy...?" he asked.

Roy paused for a moment, like he was uncertain whether saying anything was a good idea, like doubts still remained. "You know when we spoke, James? It was a long time ago, when we both worked in the factory. Well, I've been thinking. I think I *could* do with your help after all, you know..."

At Least the Pink Elephants are Laughing at Us

Part Three

1 - Unique Selling Point (USP)

2016

He opened the car door, pushed out his leg and then sunk a shoe deep into a dark, pungent puddle.

"Oh for..." he began, before refraining and remembering his manners. There were old people around here. Sick people, too. It was a combination that just demanded to be respected. They shouldn't have to put up with his vulgarities, whatever the circumstances. Fuck. Fuck. And fuck. It didn't count if he swore in his head. No harm done. His sock felt soggy and heavy, clinging to his foot. His new shoes must already have a hole in them, he considered, or perhaps the sole was coming away. It was his own damn fault, as per usual. His mother was forever telling him that, when it came to shoes, you got what you paid for. He could imagine her smug face now. "I told you so. Can't go wrong with strong, reliable shoes from *Clarks*." He was always tempted by the enticing cheapness of shoes from the supermarket, though. They always looked exactly the same as the most expensive brands, and yet oh-so-much cheaper, so what could possibly go wrong?

The signs pointed left, right, up, down. He ignored the lift and took the stairs to the canteen. It was best to make the most of every opportunity for exercise what with his manic lifestyle that didn't leave room for luxuries such as the gym. He didn't strive for one of those six or eight or ten packs or whatever they were these days, but he didn't fancy dropping dead just yet, either. He wasn't fifty yet and he'd barely achieved anything he'd set out to in life. A little exercise here and there all added up and hopefully kept the doctor away. He checked the step counter in his pocket. 5,018. Pretty good considering there was still plenty of the day left. He was on schedule for his 10,000 target. He looked around the canteen. Felt the usual familiar surge of nerves when he met somebody for the first time even though, strictly speaking, it was part of his job. Maybe she wouldn't be here? Maybe she'd called in sick? But no. There she was, behind the counter, serving customers. Maybe she'd forgotten he was coming? This could be embarrassing. He waited for the queue to vanish before plucking up the courage to go and speak to her.

"I'll be with you now in a minute, butt," she said, not looking up.

He was slightly bemused. There was nobody else waiting and she didn't seem to be doing anything.

"Mandy," he said, holding out his hand. "Herbert Henry. It is a pleasure to finally meet you. For real, I mean."

Mandy shook his hand and then put her same hand to her mouth and giggled like he'd said something outrageously rude or funny. Neither was typical of Herbert.

"Herbert Henry? Is that *really* your name? I mean, it's not your porno name or something? Did you change your name to make it sound all fancy? Like Elton John or David Bowie or Prince or The Rock or Tyson Fury?"

Her eyes were wide and interested. This was a decent start, Herbert thought.

"I think you'll find Tyson Fury is his real name, Mandy," Herbert replied, trying his best not to sound condescending. It was a criticism often aimed in his direction. It was sometimes difficult when he often knew things other people just didn't. "And no," he added. "For my sins, Herbert Henry is actually my real name."

Mandy looked at him carefully for a moment, as if checking to see whether his face was going to break into a smile. What was the turn of phrase people used these days? She was checking whether he was *fucking* with her, wasn't she? When Herbert's face didn't break into a smile, Mandy shrugged her shoulders and then, without any warning, shouted at the top of her voice. "Elaine! My fan is here! Can you cover the till for a bit please, darling!"

A plump, harassed-looking woman appeared from the kitchen and scrutinised Herbert through steamed glasses, like he was a very strange, rare type of species. Mandy took his hand and guided Herbert to a corner table of the canteen. She held out the palms of her hands proudly, as if to indicate it was the

At Least the Pink Elephants are Laughing at Us

grandest table in the whole establishment. Mandy waited until they were both sat and settled and ready to get going before yelling again at the top of her voice "Elaine! Two bacon and sausage sandwiches please, darling!"

Jesus Christ, Herbert thought. He wished she would give him some prior warning before she shouted like that. She was going to turn him into a bag of nerves, as if he wasn't one already! Mandy leaned closer to Herbert and whispered "They really are something special, Herbert. Keep your wallet in your trousers, you hear? These are on the house. It's the very least I can do." Mandy winked at Herbert like he was privy to a sinister conspiracy. "Plus, I get them free of charge anyway."

"It really is a marvellous gesture, Mandy," Herbert said. "But I'm vegetarian. Do they have anything that doesn't contain meat?"

Now Mandy *really* looked at him intensely. Her round sky-blue eyes narrowed into slits. Herbert dared not move a single muscle in his face. He remembered that time he had played poker, when he'd tried to mingle with the lads. He didn't win.

"Change that order, Elaine!" Mandy shouted. Herbert could sense the distaste in her voice. "Just one bacon and sausage sandwich please! And bring anything that is even *remotely* vegetarian, please!"

Herbert was keen to move things on. He clicked the buttons on his black leather briefcase and it flipped open. Herbert pulled out a pad and a pen. "I'm pleased you agreed to meet me, Mandy. I know you're a busy lady," he said, looking around at her place of work which, right at that very moment, was completely empty. "I'm truly passionate about local talent and I'll do my utmost to promote it wherever I can," he continued.

"Who did you say you worked for?"

"*The Observer*," Herbert replied, digging a card out of his pocket.

"Oooh," Mandy replied dreamily. "A national paper. You *have* done well for yourself, haven't you, Herbert?"

"*The South Wales Observer*, actually," Herbert corrected.

Mandy looked visibly less impressed. "Oh. And you are the comedy correspondent, you said?"

"Well, not quite," Herbert replied. "A small enterprise like ours cannot really justify employing a specialist position such as a comedy correspondence. I am what a layman might call a Jack of all trades. Or a Herbert of all trades," he laughed. When Mandy didn't join in, he quickly continued, "I cover all local news. But I try to spread my wings as far as I can and I cover as much of the comedy circuit as is feasibly possible."

Mandy looked at him blankly, like she didn't understand a word he was saying. It was best to get to the point. "It is not in my capacity as a busy newspaper reporter that I have contacted you today, Mandy."

"Oh, right?" Mandy said, smiling. She really did have very nice white teeth, Herbert thought. He flipped opened his briefcase again and pulled out a bulkier pad. There was a slight breeze as he flicked through the pages. Each page was covered with blue ink scribbles. Words were crossed out and corrected and notes were written at an angle in the margin. "Have you ever seen *Grand Designs* on television, Mandy? Yes? Well, this here is my grand design." He smiled proudly.

"I think you got the wrong idea, Herbert," Mandy said. "Shouldn't you have built a house out of a cave or a lifeboat station in Tenby or something? That just looks like a notebook full of words to me."

"You misunderstand, Mandy," Herbert stated matter-of-factly. "This is my project. My grand design. My book. This is the cumulative effect of my creative juices flowing freely. The book is a study of the wonderful species known as the stand-up comedian." He tapped the bridge of his nose with his forefinger before continuing. "I know what you are thinking. What makes this book different? I will tell you," he said, taking a sip of his drink, biding his time, building the tension, "What makes this book different is the angle, the unique selling point, more commonly known as the USP."

"What's your angle?" Mandy asked. Herbert hoped she would ask that. He had gained her interest. She hadn't even noticed the sausage and bacon sandwich that Elaine had unceremoniously dumped on the table next to his veggie (he hoped) burger.

"The angle, Mandy," Herbert said, ready to let the rabbit out of the cage, "is that all the comedians discussed in the book are

At Least the Pink Elephants are Laughing at Us

Welsh."

Herbert sat back in the chair and folded his arms, waiting for her excited response.

"I have to say, Herbert," Mandy said. "As far as angles go, that's pretty poor, don't you think?"

Herbert wasn't expecting this, but not to worry. She obviously hadn't understood. "Mandy, I'm not sure you are seeing the big picture. There is no other nationality of comedian in the book. No Scottish, American, not even English..."

"Yes, I know what it means to be Welsh, Herbert...

"I'm interviewing all the great and established Welsh comedians. You know, like Rhod Gilbert and Rob Brydon. I'll be honest, Rob is my favourite. Didn't you think he absolutely stole the show as Bryn in *Gavin and Stacey*? Oh the intense mystery surrounding the background to that character was a wonder to behold. Anyway. Not only them. The up-and-coming talent that have yet to hit the big time too, like you..."

"You've interviewed Rhod Glbert and Rob Brydon?"

"Not exactly. No. But I will..."

"Right," Mandy said, wiping a blob of brown sauce from her top lip with the back of her hand. "It's just, if I'm honest with you butt, your angle is pretty poor."

Herbert released a loud, pained sigh. She didn't get it at all. It was best to move on. They had plenty to cover. They continued with the interview. Herbert asked about Mandy's first gig, her favourite gig, her inspirations, her ideas and everything else he and everybody else normally asked. Mandy's responses were enthusiastic and original and they'd add value to his book.

He couldn't help but feel deflated, though. There was a shadow cast over his normally breezy demeanour. Something ate away at him; a nagging, persistent voice. Maybe, just maybe, Mandy had a point. Maybe, just maybe, his angle was, as she put it, "pretty poor."

"That's fantastic," Herbert said at the end, shutting his briefcase."Like I said, when I saw you on stage at *Junglears* I thought you had a real talent."

"Thank you, Herbert," Mandy said, getting to her feet and shaking his hand. Elaine had been poking her head around the corner for some time, asking how long they'd be. "So, I'll appear in your book then? Get some publicity?"

"Absolutely."

Mandy returned to the till, to her day job, to the mundane graft that, presumably, paid her bills. Herbert got another decaffeinated coffee and even a biscuit. He wasn't normally this fancy-free, but he needed a treat to pull him through the lull. His thoughts spiralled in different directions, bouncing off each other like a pinball machine. He would have to get back to the office soon, to do his real job that paid the bills and put food on the table.

Two old dears sat down at the table next to him. They were eighty if they were a day.

"You've had a shock, dear," one of them said. "But now you've been given the all clear and you can really get on with doing the things you always wanted to. Make the absolute most of life. Don't keep dwelling on the old memories, dear. Create some new memories, yes?"

By God, that was it, Herbert thought.

Herbert pulled his phone out of his pocket, urgently pressing speed dial. He glanced up in the direction of Mandy.

A female voice answered.

"I have an idea for the book," Herbert stated. "And the best thing is, it gives me a genuine reason to meet up with *him*, too..."

*****

"You're doing *what?*" she asked when Herbert phoned her again later. "What on earth for?"

"I just want to give them just a little, that's all. Have an element of mystery. If they are remotely interested then they will turn up. If they don't then it proves they aren't the right people for the job. I guess I'm testing them, in a way. Plus, I think it will be a curious twist for my book."

"It makes you sound like a fruitcake," she said, simply and without obvious malice. "Absolutely barmy, I tell you. It will only end in tears. And what if *he* decides not to turn up? What will you do then?"

Herbert paused for a moment. It was a good point. If that happened then it would rather defeat the object of his project. He

At Least the Pink Elephants are Laughing at Us

rubbed his chin, hoping to stimulate some inspiration.

"I'll cross that bridge if and when it happens," he replied.

2 – Arousing Mr Right

Herbert did as his friendly and professional female roadside companion instructed him to do. After all, his satellite navigation had never let him down before, so why would it now? People changed. Robots didn't. Herbert prided himself on being a man of logic though, and logic told him this just *couldn't* be right. Herbert was torn between following his beloved logic and being at a total loss for a more suitable alternative. And so Herbert flicked the indicator switch down, closed his eyes and hoped for the best. The car bumped up and down as it drove over the mole hills and rabbit holes, and then there it was, appearing in front of him, in the exact spot his satellite navigation told him it would be. Why had he ever doubted her? How *dare* he doubt her! Hallelujah.

He pulled at the door handle and....Jesus Christ! Don't swear, Herbert. But where the fuck did that wind appear from? It wasn't blowing a gale just four miles or so up the road in *sunny* Bridgend! Ogmore-by-Sea suddenly felt like a different world; a much colder and windier world. The car door almost flung off its hinges. Herbert shut the door and then navigated past the sheep droppings and the cow dung, his briefcase in one hand. He'd just bought another pair of new shoes from the local supermarket, straight after his recent hospital visit in fact, and he was particularly keen to keep them clean. He waved away the dreary drizzle with his hand, like a bad fart. A couple of hens idled over and clucked and pecked at his feet. A black and white dog lay lazily on his back and made a show of scratching his balls. Who actually lived here, Herbert wondered. Dr Doolittle?

"I'm not a man who likes to use obscenities," Herbert said to the hens. "But piss off. *Please.*"

Herbert pushed the shop door open. It chimed loudly. He heard movements out the back. There was life. The place was still open, then. It hadn't been abandoned during the Second World War. A tall, slender light-skinned man appeared. That was

At Least the Pink Elephants are Laughing at Us

him, of course. He was exactly as she had described him. He was very distinctive, especially around these parts. For starters, the man was undoubtedly good looking, and also, he was not white. He wore red shorts down to his knees, like he was on *Baywatch*, with white socks and sandals. Herbert was no style guru. He struggled to keep up with the latest trends. He was aware that sometimes his clothes were a mismatch. But even *he* had the nuance to look at this man and ask the question: just *what* was he thinking?

"Welcome to my humble establishment," the man said, without a flicker of enthusiasm. "We stock a range of products that cater for a variety of interests," he said, mechanically. "How may I help you today?"

Herbert looked around the shop. It sure was a strange little place, he thought. A kind man would say that it was quirky. An unkind man would say that it was chaotic, even crazy. It reminded Herbert of a programme about hoarders that were all the rage these days. Slanted wooden shelves were packed full of seemingly unrelated items, from buckets and spades to key rings and mugs. The walls were plastered with paintings and photos. A freezer in the corner that stocked lollies and choc ices quietly hummed. Next to it stood a coffee machine.

Herbert turned to the man, sheepishly grinning from the corner of his mouth. "I think the question should be," he began, "how can *I* help *you* today?"

The guy wasn't as enthusiastic as Herbert had hoped. The man sighed deeply and unravelled his long body so that it slumped over the counter. Herbert wasn't convinced by his commitment to customer service. "I am sorry but I had one of your people here last month," he explained. "I've been through all of this before. I respect your beliefs, okay? My views on the matter are personal. I am just not interested in buying into your big plan, whether you can offer me eternal salvation or not."

"What? Oh. Sorry. No, that's not what I'm here for."

"And you're not selling those dodgy videos? The German ones?"

"No."

Herbert snapped open his pristine leather suitcase and pulled out a red envelope. He shut the briefcase and handed the envelope to the gentleman.

"My sole objective at this point, Connor," he said, "is to stir your curiosity. Please read the letter inside the envelope and if the said curiosity is appropriately stirred then I look forward to seeing you soon. If not, then I thank you for your time and I bid you good day."

Herbert spun around on his new supermarket shoes and walked out of the shop, the door chiming happily behind him.

Outside, battling the dreary rain and the ferocious blizzard, he again told the hens to piss off. Pulling open his car door, Herbert allowed himself a slightly smug, self-satisfied smile.

*****

The solid, sturdy door brushed against the mat. The darkness inside was quite a contrast to the light outside. The thick concrete blocked walls and the low arching ceilings gave the place the feel of a tent or an igloo. The uneven tiled floor was slippery. An orange and red fire cackled invitingly in the corner. A photo of the local rugby team, all big bellies and long moustaches, hung from the wall. There were a few dusty medals and cups in an otherwise sparse glass cabinet.

"Not seen you around here before," the barman said, friendly enough. He was a stocky chap in a polo shirt that was speckled with grass clippings. He had a large hoop in his ear that Herbert thought probably looked good back in the nineties, or maybe the eighties. "I make it my job to remember every face, although I'd prefer to forget a few, if you know what I mean," the barman said, laughing.

Herbert wasn't overly competent or comfortable with idle chatter. He smiled as energetically as he could.

"What can I get you?" the barman asked.

"I'm looking for a gentleman called James Jones. I understand from reliable sources that he frequents this fine establishment."

The barman wiped his hairy forearm on his nose. The arm was plastered with blue ink. "That's him over there."

James hadn't aged very well, Herbert considered sadly. Life had obviously thrown him a tough hand. A large jelly belly hung

At Least the Pink Elephants are Laughing at Us

uncomfortably over his faded, grubby jeans. What little hair that remained was lazily plastered down unevenly with a handful of gel. He looked ten years older than he actually was. Best get this over and done with, Herbert considered.

"My sole objective at this point, James," he said, flipping his briefcase open and holding out the red envelope, "is to stir your curiosity. Please read the letter inside the envelope and if the said curiosity is appropriately stirred then I look forward to seeing you soon. If not, then I thank you for your time and I bid you good day."

Confused, blank eyes stared up at him. The envelope remained dangling mid-air.

"Not *him!*" the barman bellowed. "*Him* over there," he said, pointing his big hairy arm.

Herbert apologised to the stranger, who sat motionless, frozen with fear.

Of course, Herbert thought. James was sat at a round table with an attractive woman and a young boy, a toddler. He didn't look too bad for his age, just slightly grizzled and worn, like he had been left out in the rain for too long with no coat; better than he expected, all things considered. Herbert was nervous. He had rehearsed in the mirror at home, of course. But he hadn't expected to get the wrong man. That was a schoolboy error. He was feeling light headed. Maybe his sugar levels were down or he had eaten something that didn't agree with his lactose intolerance.

"Hello James," he said. "My name is Herbert Henry."

Herbert followed this up by cursing loudly, and he followed the loud curse up with an apology for his foul and inappropriate language. There were children around. He hadn't intended to give his name. That merely detracted from the mystery.

James and the woman looked at each other and smiled.

"Is that a made up name?" James asked. "You know, like Lady Gaga and Tyson Fury..."

"No. And anyway...actually, it doesn't matter."

Herbert went to hand James the envelope but it flew from his hand and landed on the next table, where two men were sat drinking.

"I'm sorry," he said, returning to James. Herbert could feel his cheeks burning.

"My only aim at the moment is to arouse your curiosity. If you are not aroused then you are not the right man for me," he blurted.

James looked at the woman and the woman looked at James, and they both laughed. The little boy started laughing, too, although it was clear he didn't know what he was laughing about.

"Just read what's inside the envelope please and if you're interested then I hope to see you soon," Herbert quickly added.

Herbert pulled his shoulders back and pushed his chest forward and headed purposefully to the door. He struggled to get it open.

"You need to pull, not push," the barman said from behind his newspaper.

Herbert was glad to see the beautiful light outside, which contrasted very nicely indeed to the grim darkness from inside the pub.

At Least the Pink Elephants are Laughing at Us

3 – Feeling Flat

She lived on the top floor of a block of flats with a lift that hadn't worked for as long as he could remember.
It was a struggle climbing the unforgiving concrete stairs, even for a male of average age (middle age was so difficult to determine these days) and of reasonable health (he was still breathing and he was still managing 10,000 steps per day) and he never quite got used to it, even though he was a regular visitor. Herbert shuddered to think what it was like for say, a woman of advancing (old) years carrying her shopping in those 5p plastic bags that tore painfully into the palms. He counted the steps to each floor. Sixteen. It wasn't really the physical struggle that troubled him. It was the emotional turmoil. The stairs stunk of urine, the walls were plastered with graffiti of all different designs and colours, and the lights on the ceiling flickered, like the bulb was ready to explode. The end effect was that by the time Herbert made it to the top floor and knocked on the door, he was already abysmally depressed.
"Hello, Mum."
Herbert sat down on the sofa in the living room. The heating was on full pelt and his mother's sizeable underwear stood proudly in the middle of the room on a clothes dryer, obscuring the view of the television that flickered on the stand in the corner. Herbert wished that his mother's underwear was *not* stood proudly in the middle of the room. A red jumper had been abandoned on the seat next to him with knitting needles still intact. It looked like his mum had got half way through the Sun crossword and then given up. Herbert noticed there was a new addition to the row of books on the windowsill, which included a Danielle Steele and a Catherine Cookson. The bulky hardback had pushed the fruit bowl containing, as normal, one black, bruised banana and one blue, moulding tangerine, into the corner, partly obscured by the curtain. His mum must have borrowed *Skagboys*, by Irvine Welsh, out of the library. Herbert

knew that this was a prequel to *Trainspotting,* but he did not know how his mother could possibly have considered this a suitable addition to her collection of books.

His mother returned from the kitchen with a tray holding two cups of tea and a marzipan cake. She sat down and didn't say anything for a while. Herbert had bet himself he would not be able to count to ten without her asking. Seven. Eight. Nine...

"So...?" she said.

His mum liked to leave questions hanging. She liked him to take the bait.

"So....?"

His mum took a sip of her tea, a bite of her cake and then wiped her lips with a tissue before continuing. "So, did you go ahead with that ridiculous idea of yours?"

"I certainly did," Herbert replied proudly.

Mrs Henry sighed heavily and shook her head. She cut up another piece of cake into a perfect, tiny square, ate it and wiped her mouth again with the tissue. "So when are you meeting, then?" she asked.

"Wednesday."

She sighed heavily and shook her head again. She was making the most of this, Herbert thought. He could understand her being dismissive of the whole plan, that he had actually gone ahead and executed it, but she was going a bit far chiding the fact the meeting was on a *Wednesday.* She would have given exactly the same reaction if he said they were meeting on Tuesday or a Thursday or, God forbid, a Friday.

"This will all end in tears," she said. His mother thought most things would end in tears, but she was adamant this time. "You mark my words! And it could even end in blood, too! And, most likely, it will be yours!"

"Sometimes you just need to take risks, Mum."

It was Herbert's turn now to take his time, to enjoy the moment. "And besides, it will give me the perfect opportunity to introduce you to him again, after *all* these years. And maybe – possibly more importantly – an opportunity to meet her, too..."

Herbert was sure his mother's face turned a paler shade of grey. Her hand visibly shook and the saucer holding the cup of tea vibrated. He had rattled her cage. Herbert felt regret at

At Least the Pink Elephants are Laughing at Us

pushing things too far. It was his mum, after all. He didn't want to upset her. She didn't deserve that.

"Another cup of tea, darling?" she said, pulling herself out of her chair and heading to the kitchen without waiting for him to answer.

Chris Westlake

4 – Comedy Club Versus Fat Club

They had all sorts of groups in this hall, Babs considered, as she sprayed the kitchen window and then wiped away the polish with her duster, but this lot really *were* a strange assortment. The hall had never looked so interesting on a Wednesday evening.

Eavesdropping was the best part of her job. There weren't all that many perks clearing up other people's mess, if truth be told. It was a necessary evil of being a caretaker, she supposed. Babs had mastered the art of *pretending* to clean. She did a lot less cleaning than people actually thought. She was highly proficient at looking busy when, in layman terms, really she was just 'fannying around' with a feather duster. Just how much work did they expect a seventy year-old lady to do? Her dear old ma, God bless her soul, had always said she had an alert and curious ear, and it came to use here. They charged up to a fiver each for some of these meetings (including Fat Club on a Tuesday night where members stood up and got a clap even when they put weight *on*) and Babs got a birds-eye view for free, so she couldn't complain. It was like being a steward at the football; only, she accepted, with no football and no stewarding.

It was just a run-down communal hall with a flat roof, a low ceiling and holes in the walls. The thin brown carpet was littered with gruesome stains and precarious rips. You had to climb a narrow, bumpy twisting path just to reach the car park at the top, and cars were adept at beeping their horns as they went round the corners. The hall was sheltered by impressive oak trees, which the Cub Scouts climbed on Monday evenings. The smell of wet dog, from people coming in from the rain, was always there, no matter how much Babs sprayed the hall with air freshener. She used a red traffic cone to keep the fire escape door open to let in a welcome, refreshing breeze on the rare warm summer nights.

The guy running the meeting was already waiting at the front door with a white flip chart and an impressive array of felt-tip pens when Babs arrived with the key to open up. He wore grey flannel trousers and a white shirt which was unbuttoned at the top and tucked in at the bottom. The man was unusually tall, unusually slim. He looked like he did plenty of walking, was the sort of person who went everywhere with a step counter in his pocket.

"Herbert Henry. Pleasure to meet you," he said, shaking her hand.

Babs wondered whether this was his real name, or some sort of stage name, like Tyson Fury, but decided she didn't have the time or energy to wait for his explanation.

Once inside, the man scurried around the hall, all arms and legs, manically getting things ready. Babs could see him taking slow, deliberate breaths in and out, like he was familiar with yoga, presumably to calm his nerves. Herbert boiled the kettle, buttered bread and put biscuits on plates. Babs almost felt guilty when she caught him practising his lines in the bathroom mirror, for he put his hand to his ear and pretended to be talking into an imaginary phone.

"Don't mind me, darling," Babs smiled, waving the toilet brush around like it was a light sabre. "Mark my words," she reassured him, "I've seen men doing much more embarrassing things on their own in that toilet."

When the rest of the troops arrived, Babs understood why he had been psyching himself up.

They looked like they would benefit from that motivational talk they delivered at Fat Club. The girl arrived first, still in her uniform, presumably straight from work. A pretty thing, Babs considered, if only she'd washed her strawberry blonde hair and perhaps applied some make-up. There was *no* doubting she carried some heavy goods underneath her tired old uniform too, for the buttons visibly strained to keep them under wraps. The girl gave Herbert a hug and then said "hello sweetheart" to Babs. She wasn't shy with the biscuits either, sticking two in her mouth and two in her pocket, justifying her appetite with comments like, "I'm wasting away over here," and "people say I've got hollow legs, you know. I don't know where it all goes."

A tall, handsome black guy with great bone structure, a sprinkling of freckles on his cheeks, a wide jaw, a deep dimple in the chin and sultry brown eyes arrived, wearing jeans so tight it was as though they'd been spray-painted on. Babs wondered

At Least the Pink Elephants are Laughing at Us

how his bits were able to breathe in there. *She'd* give them the kiss of life, she thought. If only she was twenty years younger, she mused. Maybe that was a bit optimistic. If only she was thirty years younger. Babs liked dark chocolate, and that included her men. His hooped blue and white tee-shirt wouldn't have looked out of place in Popeye's wardrobe; it was as if he was trying to distract attention away from his good looks by wearing some pretty questionable clobber. The man looked like he spent the evenings playing *Dungeons and Dragons* and his weekends at *Star Trek* conventions.

Herbert bound over and vigorously shook his hand. "So glad you came, Connor," he said. "I've prepared some food and drink for you to enjoy. Nothing special, mind you."

"You can say that again," an older guy agreed. Where had he appeared from? He'd sneaked in through the fire escape, the cheeky bugger. This one sure knew how to make an entrance. The guy held out his hand for Herbert, who enthusiastically accepted it. "Only kidding, Herbie," he said. "You've put on a marvellous spread here. Absolutely grand. A feast fit for a king, no less."

Babs noticed that Connor eyed the plastic bowls filled with crisps, the sandwiches (which visibly curled at the sides) and the squash in tiny plastic cups that would have left a child asking "Please sir, can I have some more?" with a neutral, placid face.

"Connor," Herbert said, "I'd love you to meet James. I would say that James is the comedian of the group, but then that wouldn't be quite right now, would it?" He laughed. Nobody else did. "I don't want to give too much away too soon. Let the cat out of the bag, as they say. I've got this hall for an hour, and Babs over there said there are strictly no refunds if we finish early."

Babs waved her broom in his direction to good-humouredly acknowledge his (she assumed) joke. The two men shook hands and guardedly nodded their heads. Neither looked massively impressed with the other. These two were hardly a perfect match. James was much older, probably in his fifties, and was clad youthfully from top to toe in denim. Despite his advancing years, he still had an impressive head of silver hair, which he tied back in a ponytail with an elastic band. His stubble gave him a grizzled look, as did his bloodshot eyes. Did the studs in both ears make him a rebel? Babs wasn't sure whether the bloke was a nice bit of rough or if he needed a good scrub down. If it was the latter then she had just the tools for the job, she considered, eyeing him up and down.

"And not forgetting the rose amongst the thorns of the group, of course," Herbert enthused, opening up his hands. "This is Mandy."

The girl smiled and pointed to her mouth to indicate that she was eating. She held up her thumb as a sign she was friendly, though.

Babs got the dustpan and brush from the cupboard and swept the skirting boards. She had a perfect view of events from this angle. The trio swivelled the plastic chairs so that they faced Herbert, who stood next to the clipboard with a felt tip pen in his hand. Babs could tell he meant business.

"You're probably wondering, who is this strange man? Why me? What am I doing here?"

Three blank faces glared at him.

"Free food and drink," James eventually piped up, rubbing his hands together.

"I thought you may be looking to formulate a mad cult with the sole objective of brainwashing us into doing whatever you ask," Connor added, without even a glimmer of a smile. "I have one thing to say to that; count me in, buddy."

"Yes, very good," Herbert said through a pained smile. "Now call me a traditionalist, but I always think a good place to start is at the beginning. Mandy, would you care to tell these two gentlemen about our meeting last week?"

"I was going to keep that between you and me, Herbert," Mandy said, winking. "Seriously though, gents. Herbert interviewed me for the book he is writing about stand-up comedians. He said I am an up-and-coming local talent, which was nice of him. And he said that I was a real hottie, too. I've no idea what you guys are doing here though," she said, laughing.

"And what did you think about the angle I told you about, Mandy? Don't be shy. Don't hold back. We're all adults here. I've got a pretty thick skin."

"Herbert here thought the fact his book only included Welsh

At Least the Pink Elephants are Laughing at Us

comedians was a real winner. I said "I'll be honest with you, butt, I think it's a pretty poor angle, you know?" You really need an idea that will grab the reader by the balls and give them a big squeeze, don't you think?"

"Abso-fucking-lutely," James replied, holding up a hand up for Mandy to slap.

Babs could see Herbert was a bit miffed that Mandy had opened up quite so much, that maybe his skin wasn't quite as thick as he'd cited. "You're absolutely right," Herbert said, unconvincingly. "And Mandy, I thank you. You made me think. And that brings me on to why you're here."

The three of them glanced at each other, apparently nonplussed.

"Let's begin with a question, shall we? We all studied history at school. It was compulsory on the curriculum. Now what do you think the problem with history was?"

"It was really boring," James offered, looking sincere, leaning back in his chair. That chair was going to topple over any minute, Babs thought; then there would be some drama. She would have to charge him for breaking property, even though, strictly speaking, the left leg was already loose. They were trying to raise whatever money they could to fix the roof, and had been for the last twenty or so years. "Everyone was dead and they were forever talking about foreign policies and sinking ships. It never seemed to relate to gritty valleys life in the late twentieth or twenty-first century, did it?"

"In a roundabout way, I think you have hit the nail on the head, James," Herbert replied.

Connor looked at Mandy and Mandy looked at Connor. They both wore the same expression: there was absolutely no way in this world that James had hit the nail on the head.

"The problem with history is that the story has already been told," Herbert explained.

"Exactly what I said," James agreed, folding his arms smugly.

"Would you prefer to be a commentator talking about a football game, or a footballer creating the action? I've given you a taster. I've pencilled an outline. Now let's colour it in. Why do you *specifically* think I have brought you here this evening?"

"I have absolutely no idea why you brought us here," Connor said.

"I have even less of an idea than he does," Mandy added.

"I'm really worried why you've brought us here," James stated.

"Okay. I'll give you some background. I am, in a roundabout way, the comedy correspondent for *The South Wales Observer...*"

"In a 'roundabout way'?" Connor questioned.

"You said you weren't," Mandy added.

"Okay, I am *not* the comedy correspondent for *The South Wales Observer*. But I *am* passionate about comedy and I do whatever I can to cover the local gigs for the paper. I've even seen you guys perform. Connor, remember your gig in *The Prince* a couple of years back...?"

Connor nodded his head hesitantly. "That was my last gig. The audience didn't understand my material."

"*I* didn't understand your material," Herbert said. "But you know what I did understand? What you were trying to do. Sort of. And I saw potential. I think."

"Thanks," Connor said. Babs wasn't sure he looked too grateful.

Herbert turned to James. "I've seen you more than once..."

"How many times?"

"Twice. And you got a mixed reaction on both occasions. But *I* liked you. Or at the very least, I liked some of your act."

James shimmied his chair forward. Babs worried that it might tear another hole in the carpet. "So you don't think either of us are very good? Fair enough. I haven't even performed a gig for donkey's years. So what are we doing here?"

Herbert flipped open his briefcase. He loved flipping that flipping thing, Babs thought. It looked lethal. This time he pulled out a thick bundle of paper. He leafed through the pages with a smile on his face. "This is the book I have been working on," he announced. "And now I'm going to show you what I'm doing with the book. I hope it demonstrates just how serious I am about my proposal, about my commitment to the cause..."

Babs watched as Herbert gripped both sides of the paper. Unfortunately it was apparently more difficult to tear the paper than he'd imagined. Herbert adjusted his position and bent his knees and grimaced. Still nothing. His face went red from the physical exertion. The four of them watched Herbert trying in vain to tear up his manuscript. You could hear a pin drop. This was getting embarrassing now, Babs considered. Eventually Herbert decided his best option was to tear just a small section of his book, which he successfully managed to do. He wiped his forehead with his arm. "I'll do the rest when I get home," he said.

"Wow, you've thrown away all that work, Herbert," Mandy commented. "I am impressed."

Herbert dismissed her with a casual wave of the hand. "I've got a back up on my memory stick, don't worry," he said.

Babs wondered what the *fuck* was going on with this meeting.

Herbert was in his stride now. He pulled over the first sheet of paper on the flip chart, stabbed at the canvas with his felt pen and smiled broadly, exposing big, polished teeth. He pointed at the bold words written in red.

"Edinburgh Festival Fringe," Herbert announced. He paused. Waited for a reaction. When none was forthcoming, he continued, "I want us to *get* good. Think of yourselves as David, and the Edinburgh Festival Fringe as Goliath. Or you are Rocky and the Festival is Mr T. You are going to, in simple terms, "kick Goliath's butt." I want the four of us to work together to put on a run of shows at the Festival. I'll arrange the venues and you provide the entertainment. Right now we are not even close. Not even near. They say the sky is the limit. Well *I* say, how come there are footprints on the moon? I want us to make a mark in the greatest comedy festival in the world. You create the history. I record it in my book. It is a win/win all round. It is February now and the Festival is in August, so we have six months to get ready. What do you say?"

Babs didn't even bother to pretend to clean any more. She stood with one hand on her slim hip, the other holding the dustpan. There was silence. The trio just looked at each other. James pulled at his chair, finally tearing a hole in the carpet.

"I'm not even sure where Edinburgh is," James said. "Where is Edinburgh?"

Herbert glared at him. "Is that even a serious question?"

James got up onto his feet. Babs was worried there might be a commotion. She would have to stay late if there was any extra mess, and she didn't get paid overtime. Plus, she had another date later with a younger guy she had met on the internet.

"I don't know much about Edinburgh, but even I've heard of the Festival" James said, waving his hands in the air and heading to the fire exit. "You have to be proper good for The Festival. From what I've heard tonight, we're no-fucking-bodies. I can sure see what is in it for him, but I'm struggling to see what is in it for us. This guy is just using us for his own benefit, to create a plot for his disaster novel. Well, I'm not going to be one of the main characters. I'm out I tell you! Out!"

James left through the fire escape and slammed the door behind him. The hall went quiet.

Babs resumed pretending to clean. She hoped Herbert pulled the group together, got them over this little mishap, managed to work something out. After all, she thought, this was the most entertaining gathering since the sex addiction group!

*****

Herbert kicked off his shoes and allowed his tired feet to breathe. It was good to be home, especially after this exhausting day. He pressed the button on his phone, which was flashing red. The voice on the line sounded like it came from a pub.

"Herbie, me old mucker. Its James. I'm sorry for my little diva outburst earlier, like. Just to tell you – count me in, butt!"

5 – News on Sunday

Connor stopped and turned to face a shop window. Most of the shops had their metal shutters down, keeping the burglars at bay, but this was an estate agent's, and Connor imagined there wasn't much to steal apart from the odd phone or swivel chair or photograph of a house. Even if the house was a splendid detached dwelling with a garage for two cars and a garden front and back, a house that made Phil and Kirsty foam at the mouth, it was *still* only a photograph of a house. There were streaks in the window where presumably it had been washed the day before. Connor hooked his fingers inside his belt, pulled up his slacks, adjusted the crotch with a firm grip of the hand, brushed down the creases in his shirt, and finally fiddled with his favourite Bart Simpson tie to try and ensure it was at least remotely straight.

It was the same every Sunday morning. Same street. Same shop window. Same trousers. Same crotch. Same shirt. Same Bart Simpson tie. Connor was a man of routine.

The only difference this week was that Connor jutted his neck forward and actually looked inside the shop before fiddling with his tie. He had learnt his lesson. Last week he had stood in the shop doorway, pulling faces and adjusting his crotch, when he noticed a guy was actually *in* the shop, pen in hand, paper on the desk. Probably finalising that big sale from the day before or maybe just paper pushing, rinsing the overtime budget for all it was worth. Either way, Connor hadn't expected to see him there. He thought that he had the luxury of pulling as many faces in the window as he so desired without any negative comeback. No such luck. Connor recognised the look the guy gave him: just what on Earth are you *doing,* bozo?

The streets were normally deserted at this time on a Sunday morning. Mind you, Connor considered, the town centre wasn't exactly thriving anymore even on a Saturday afternoon, either. Respectable chain stores had been replaced by charity shops and empty windows. Connor blamed the cost of car parking, the out-of-town retail centres and the one-way streets. The only people he encountered on Sunday mornings were occasional strays with sore heads that looked like they were trying to remember what happened the night before. Some still stumbled around, their mouths dry and thoughts scrambled, the effects of the drink not yet worn off.

Connor continued walking until he reached his destination. He took a deep breath and pushed the glass door open. Sausage and bacon sizzled on a grill. An egg cracked against the side of a frying pan. The greasy, early-morning food tangled and wrestled with the fresh powerful smell of disinfectant. Connor looked down. The floor was wet. The lines suggested the mop had taken the long route around the floor. Connor noticed there was no yellow sign warning you not to fall on your butt. He was glad *he* didn't have a hangover. The smells would be too much, and with a dazed and disorientated mind, he might end up on that wet floor. He looked around at the tables. The cafe was long and narrow, like a shoe box. He dismissed the comparison from his mind on the grounds that it wasn't made of cardboard, it didn't have a lid and there were no shoes. Rectangular plastic tables were spread evenly on each side, leaving just enough room down the middle for somebody carrying a large English breakfast in both hands to navigate comfortably. It could be any cafe anywhere in the country.

But it *wasn't* just any cafe.

The owner, a lady of advanced years with black hair blended with streaks of silver cut in a straight line at the shoulder, appeared from the kitchen, her face pink and shiny. Her expression lit up when she saw Connor standing at her counter. He was a familiar, welcome face. She didn't say anything. She just nodded over Connor's shoulder, to the far corner of the room.

Usual seat then, Connor thought.

A couple of workers with dirty hands and yellow jackets bit into bacon sandwiches. One of them nodded at Connor. A young mother smiled pleasantly and pulled at a pushchair to give Connor more room. He walked steadily and carefully to make sure he didn't slip on the wet floor.

At Least the Pink Elephants are Laughing at Us

Connor hovered over the table in the corner of the cafe. "Hello, Mum," he said.

*****

Mandy picked up the papers from the newsagent and crossed the familiar streets, keeping half an eye open for anybody she recognised, maybe a friend or foe from school, possibly somebody to say hello to or run away from. The only people up and out of their pyjamas this morning though, held a lead in one hand and a plastic bag in the other, ready to scoop up any messy brown deposits their dog left behind. Mandy sometimes wondered why she still needed to dodge so much poo on the pavements when the plastic bag brigade seemed bigger and stronger than ever. Did rebel dog walkers only come out in the middle of the night when the rest of the world was in bed and counting sheep, oblivious to their gross misdemeanours?

She knocked on the door and a fuzzy, blurred figure grew larger and clearer through the stained glass. Her eldest brother, William, appeared from behind the door. She'd recognise that outline anywhere. Mandy saw him every Sunday, without fail, and often during the week too. Her brother had always been a lump as a child, but with the passing of the years he had toned his soft edges and now he looked like he belonged on the cover of a glossy magazine. The handsome, moisturised looks that had made Mandy's school friends giddy with excitement were still intact and stronger than ever. Bastard.

"Morning, sis," William said, bending at the knees and planting a kiss on her lips. "We thought you'd got lost," he smiled, glancing theatrically at an invisible watch on his wrist.

"I'm only ten minutes late, Pretty Boy," Mandy protested.

Mandy walked through the narrow hall, past the hexagon mirror (that was likely an antique) on the bumpy wall, glanced at their embarrassingly toothy school photos in the glass cabinet, and continued on to the lounge. Her mum sat in *her* chair, just feet from the television, staring at the screen, oblivious to the new addition to the room. The blue jumper on the windowsill, that had one arm last Sunday, had two arms now. No, hold on; did Mum realise the jumper had three arms? It must be a jumpsuit, Mandy reasoned, or maybe a 'balls-up.' Mandy leant over and kissed her mum on the temple. She smelt of soap and water and all things clean. Mum turned around slowly, almost mechanically, seemingly not at all startled. Her face broke into a smile.

"Mandy," she said, gripping her hand. Mum's hand felt surprisingly strong. "How lovely to see you, dear." Mum glanced down at Mandy's spare hand, like she did every week. "I see you've brought the papers. I don't care what anybody says about you, dear. *I* know you're a good girl."

"How are you, Mum?" Mandy asked. "What's new...?"

*****

Connor stood up and held out his hand. His mother slowly rose to her feet, pushing herself up using the edges of the table.

They waved goodbye to Amanda, the owner of the cafe. "Give our love to that husband of yours," Nanya said.

Amanda was an old friend of Nanya's. They met in the cafe years ago, before she even met Dad, or so the story went. In fact, if Connor remembered correctly, his mum and dad actually met at Amanda's wedding. She was part of their history. Amanda fell in love with the cafe and bought it some years back, initially for nostalgia and then, when reality struck, to pay the bills.

"I told you, didn't I Connor? What have I always told you, huh?"

Connor wasn't sure what his mum had told him. She told him a lot of things. Connor shrugged his shoulders, tried to make sure he angled them in such a way to indicate that he was perplexed rather than dismissive.

"I told you that you had a creative side that just had to be released. Didn't I? Yes I did!" she said.

Oh yes, Connor thought, she was always saying that. He'd never given Mum any real indication that he possessed a creative side. He'd merely demonstrated enthusiasm and willingness, especially as a child, before rugby came along and changed (ruined) everything. But then, he wondered, did it really matter if he wasn't any good at something? Could you be an artist and yet be terrible at art? His mum was talking sense though; at the moment at least. She'd always unconditionally and

At Least the Pink Elephants are Laughing at Us

enthusiastically believed in his creative endeavours, to an almost deluded degree, with no solid foundation whatsoever.

"I wouldn't say they have been released," Connor mumbled. He didn't really want to dampen her spirits, just maybe give her a subtle and gentle reality check. "I've just joined forces with a couple of other comedians with the same objective, that's all, Mum. We have plans, admittedly, but then we haven't actually done anything with those plans. We're like runners who want to complete the London Marathon, but so far have just bought the trainers and shorts and haven't done any running yet."

Nanya stopped walking and turned to face her son. She talked slowly and passionately, like she was pleading with him. "Nonsense!" she said. "Make it happen! If you don't believe in yourself then who will? I have a good feeling about this." She looked up to the clouds in the sky. "God tells me it will work out real good. Do you hear?"

She held out her hand and they continued walking as if no words had passed. Connor could hear the church bells chiming, becoming louder the further they walked. He always found the church bells comforting, reassuring.

"There he is!" Nanya enthused. She held out her arms and hugged the man wearing a smart, perfectly cut suit and a subtly curled, wary line for a smile. Nanya kissed him on both cheeks like a long-lost brother.

"Nothing like a good old-fashioned French kiss for one of my favourite men in the whole world," Nanya stated.

Connor nodded at the man, and the man nodded back. Connor noticed that his mum had left a perfect red lipstick kiss on his ruddy cheek.

No need to tell him about his developments with the comedy, Connor thought. He'd let him find out in his own time.

"Dad," he said.

"Connor," Dad replied.

*****

Mandy wasn't sure why she asked what was news, but she always did. There was only so much that could be new when your mobility was restricted and you rarely left the house.

Her mum smiled, though. She didn't seem to mind the pointlessness of the question. She seemed more content these days, had accepted the hand life had delivered her. The bleary-eyed woman that stared at the television screen for hours on end had progressed and moved on. "I'm good, thank you, honey. I cannot complain. I've been well looked after, as usual," she said, glancing at William. "News? It's been very rock n roll here, dear." She rubbed the tip of her fingers on the walking stick that balanced at an angle against her knee. "You know that Paul Hollywood? The one with the lovely tan and silver hair off the tele? He's been calling me night and day, so he has. Wants me to come over for tea and cake. Don't tell Mary Berry. She gets ever so jealous. Oh," she continued, "and your brother over there has bought me a computer. So I've been having a play with that."

Mandy smiled. It would have been nicer if *she* had bought her mum a computer, but there again, it was nicer that her brother had spent money and not her. He had a good job, in an office where he had to wear a suit, and he earned more than she did. She couldn't imagine what her mum would do with a computer. Her mum wasn't exactly the type to download tunes or collect followers on social network sites. What else was there to do on a computer? Oh yes. Of course. "So you've been busy watching porn have you, Mum?" Mandy cackled. "I can recommend a few sites if you fancy..."

Her mum excitedly rocked back and forth. William shook his head in mock disapproval. William was a free spirit in his spare time, when he wasn't working or looking after his dear mother, and he had a lifestyle that verged on the hedonistic. It was one of the things Mandy envied about him. If only she could get a hedonistic lifestyle of her own! Despite all this, he was still apparently mortified by the open relationship she had with their mum.

Mandy ventured to the kitchen. It was good to get some brownie points, especially as she was lagging so far behind William, and especially if any were on offer that wouldn't affect her purse. The kitchen was immaculately clean. There wasn't a single china plate or cup left on the draining board. Damn it. She needed to invite her brother round to her own gaff a bit more often, she thought; it could do with a tidy and some spit and

At Least the Pink Elephants are Laughing at Us

polish. Why was her brother so annoyingly perfect? David Beckham had nothing on William, Mandy thought. William was the original Golden Balls. He was making her look bad, and she didn't need any extra help in that respect. "Cup of tea, Mum...?" Mandy asked.

"I'm alright thanks, dear. William just made me one."

Mandy mouthed the words, "William made me one." It was different when they weren't with Mum. William returned to being her cool, handsome older brother, the boy with the easy, mischievous smile, the tough guy who looked out for his little sister. William was far from a being a goody two shoes when he was out and about or getting into trouble in his "bachelor" pad. He was such a mummy's boy though, and he didn't even realise it, Mandy mused.

Mandy searched desperately for something else she could do. "Do you want me to mow the lawn, Mum? You can never count on the weather can you? I could mow it now it's dry, like."

"It's okay, sweetheart. William mowed the lawn yesterday. Just come here and tell your mum everything that has been going on. How's work, dear?"

Mandy sighed and lowered herself onto the settee. She told her mum that work was just great, although to the best of her hazy recollection, it was exactly the same as it was last week. Oh, there had been an unexpected and unexplained surge in the sale of sausage rolls. Did that count as news?

"And what about your comedy?" Mum asked, not waiting for a reply. "Have you done any more gigs? I keep looking out for you on *Live at the Apollo* with that lovely Michael McIntyre. And whoever said the Chinese aren't funny?"

"Mum!" William protested, laughing. "Michael McIntyre isn't Chinese."

"Give over," Mum replied. "You can't pull the wool over my eyes. My body may not be perfect but my mind is in perfect order, thank you very much."

Mandy wanted to spill the beans about Herbert and his insane idea, tell her that their endeavours were going to be chronicled in a book, because that really *was* news. Mandy knew her mum would be excited. She would tell Ethel from next door when she popped around with the morning papers, and Ethel would tell Phyllis at next-door-but-one, and then the news would spread all down the street. But right now she didn't have much to go on. So far they'd just had a single, highly unsuccessful meeting. James had thrown his toys out of the pram and walked out. It seemed like such a pie in the sky, such a sketchy farfetched plan of action. Mandy wasn't sure she had much, or any, faith in the other two so-called comedians, either. It was best to keep quiet about this one for now, Mandy considered.

"No gigs since last week, Mum," she said. "I've been working on some material though. I've got this idea about a secret society of dog walkers who only go out in the dark and never, ever pick up their poop."

"Oooh, sounds amazing," her mum said, without even a hint of sarcasm. "I've always said that you had funny bones, Mandy." She turned to William. "Can you remember when she started making jokes during that nativity play, William? She had the crowd in her hands, so she did. Mandy was an absolute natural, a born performer. She was like Victoria Wood, I tell you."

"She wasn't as good as my strongman from 1996," William mumbled.

"You and that goddamn strongman performance! You had no choice but to be funny, did you darling? You had to do something just so you could get heard with your two older brothers making so much noise all the time. I remember how they used to use you as a second goalpost! You had to make yourself known somehow, didn't you, love?"

Mandy scanned her mind for anything else that could pass for "news." Her mum was always fascinated by her lack of love life. She just couldn't fathom how her gorgeous, utterly hilarious little girl wasn't beating the guys off with a broomstick, or just beating them off full stop. Mandy had told her that men said they were interested in women with a good sense of humour (GSOH) but this was just a cover. Really men just wanted a woman who was skinny. Mandy was proud that she was not a skinny woman, especially as it gave her more freedom to eat. So what could she say about her 'love life?' There was that guy at the bus stop who had started talking to her. But there again, Mandy hadn't eliminated the possibility yet that he was a serial killer. What about that night she got lucky at Sax nightclub? But there again,

At Least the Pink Elephants are Laughing at Us

it turned out, after she had drunkenly opened her heart to him, that he was only looking for a one-night stand. No. She didn't want her mother thinking she was a floozy. Mum was already suspicious she'd be a floozy if only she got the opportunity. There was no reason to confirm her suspicions. It was all just *too* embarrassing.

"I'm just nipping to spend a penny," Mandy said.

Mandy weighed herself in the bathroom, as she did every week. She hated those cold-hearted scales. They were always such doom and gloom and had no consideration whatsoever for her fragile feelings. She had been working so hard on her weight, too. She had really cut down on those delicious bacon sandwiches at work. She was down to two a day. Even when they met at the hall she had gone easy on the food. Damn you. She had put on another two pounds. Mandy stepped off the scales and stood back on them again, just in case they weren't working properly. Two and a half pounds now! Mandy got down and did some press-ups and, after reaching five, she got back up again, hot and flustered and with dribble trickling down her chin. That wasn't such a good plan of action, she considered.

Mandy always found it difficult to pass the stair lift. She wanted one for her house, just so that she could go up and down and kill some quiet moments, but she didn't think she could justify one on the NHS and she *definitely* couldn't justify paying for one when she struggled to cover the rent. She strapped herself in and rode down the stairs and then back up again. It was just like the log flume at Barry Island, she thought. "Pleasure at the fairground on the way," she sang, mimicking Mick Hucknall. Mandy shut her eyes and swung her head from side to side, bopping like she was back in The Peny-y-Bont on a Saturday night. When she opened her eyes again, William stood at the bottom of the stairs, hands on his hips.

"Your mum is in there waiting for you," he scowled. "And you're here playing with the bloody stair lift!"

Mandy unstrapped the belt. She was the naughty little school girl all over again.

That was it, she thought. She was *definitely* going to go ahead with that plan of hers, and the sooner the better.

*****

Connor sat down opposite his dad and listened to his mum in the kitchen, pulling out drawers and banging pots and pans together. Father had delivered a wonderful and inspirational service, apparently, and so Nanya was in exuberant spirits. Connor thought Father must be about one hundred and seventeen by now, and he was cynical that he only shouted his sermon so loudly and passionately because he could barely hear himself speak. Father had an excuse, but Connor couldn't fathom how his mum managed to produce so much noise when she was only supposed to be making a cup of tea. There again, he thought, Mum followed different rules when she did absolutely *anything*, so why was he surprised?

It was apparent Connor wasn't the only one who longed for Mum to return to the room. Well, *he* could suffer. Dad sat with each hand dug firmly into the arm rests. His knuckles were white. His nails clawed at the fabric. His back was ramrod straight. His hefty size eleven's were planted onto the floor. He looked out of the window. The light was fading outside. Connor wondered whether he was going to start talking about the weather.

"Doesn't look like Cardiff will get promoted this year, son," he offered.

Connor tried to look vaguely interested, but not *too* interested. He raised his eyebrows. Slightly. "Hmmm," he replied.

"It's that red kit, isn't it?" his dad persisted. "How can you be called the Blue Birds and wear a red kit and still expect to win football games?" He shook his head sadly. "I don't know what the world is coming to, honest to God I don't."

This was one of the things with his dad that really irritated him. It was one thing filling a void with small talk, but why choose a subject Connor had no interest in whatsoever? Rugby was slightly different. Connor had played rugby to a decent level, and it could have been so much higher if only he had taken the time to learn the actual rules. Dad had been so grateful all those years ago when it turned out Connor had a talent for the game. It gave them a common ground and brought them closer

At Least the Pink Elephants are Laughing at Us

together. But *football?* He was talking about that damn red kit four seasons ago, before they did actually get promoted, before they got relegated again. That was what his dad did all the time. He painted over the cracks by getting engrossed with tiny immaterial matters in the vain hope the big issues would be smothered. Connor wanted to talk about his shop, about the sudden, outrageous and totally unexpected developments with his comedy, but most of all Connor wanted to talk about his mother. But he knew his dad would flick randomly from one subject to the other – it would probably be Brexit next, or the Zika virus that was threatening the Olympics – but he would never talk about the stuff that really mattered to Connor.

He'd had enough of this nonsense. Sometimes his resentment bubbled over unexpectedly, often out of nothing. "Well, Dad," Connor said, holding eye contact for the first time since they'd been sat in the room together. "I still don't know why you didn't tell me the truth until it was nearly too late, you know? Until it nearly killed your wife, my mum..."

His dad turned away sharply. Connor had seen that look too many times. It was a question Connor had asked many times over many years, when he had the urge, the compulsion, to hurt his dad.

Nanya returned to the room and there was an audible sigh of relief. "Cup of tea for my two favourite men," she announced.

The two favoured men reverted to normal as though no crossed words had been spoken.

*****

Mandy had been thinking about this for some time. *Years.* Recently the thoughts had gathered momentum until they now dominated her mind. The pendulum had swung both ways, back and forth, so one moment she was decided and the next she changed her mind. Now, though, she was definitely decided. There was no stopping her. The straw had broken the camel's back.

She headed to the smallest room in her house, which was really saying something because most of the rooms in her house were small. Upstairs. In the far corner. Away from the passing traffic and kids kicking coke cans on the pavement. The kind of room visitors stumbled across when searching for the toilet or a secret porn stash.

Mandy sat on the computer chair and wiped the monitor with her fingers, leaving the tips grey and unhealthy. She only did these kind of things when nobody was there to tell her off. Her reflection in the monitor was just a dark, unidentifiable shape; a blob. Mandy pouted her lips and looked up at an imaginary camera, her eyes wide and suggestive. She spoke with exaggerated mock modesty. "Thank you for all your 'likes'! It wasn't my intention at all when I posed like this for you to tell me how beautiful I look, honestly it wasn't!"

The computer revved up. It was old and cranky and gathered such enthusiastic momentum it sounded like it would take off. Now it was time to be serious, Mandy considered. Just for a little while. Mandy knew her actions would have monumental consequences, and not just for her but to those closest and dearest to her. She knew that she was probably being selfish, just thinking of herself and neglecting others. She had made her decision though, and she was sticking by it.

The keyboard was making it difficult to articulate. The plastic 'p' button had fallen out, and Mandy struggled to find suitable words that didn't have a 'p' in them. Mandy was not the most articulate even when she could use 'p' in her sentences. She asked herself once again whether this was the right person to send the email to. She reassured herself that she'd spent hours on the internet researching and that – yes – he ticked all the boxes.

Mandy re-read the message. Her eyes scanned left to right and right to left, making sure each word had its rightful place. She knew she was pathetic for caring about him so much, but she couldn't help it. It was in her genes, it was the way she was.

I would be most grateful if you could take suitable actions to locate my dad.

Her finger hovered over the keyboard. She closed her eyes. She pressed Return.

Mandy switched off the computer and waited for events to unfold.

At Least the Pink Elephants are Laughing at Us

6 – Just Look Who's Been in Court

Herbert's briefcase was snapped open and he busily scribbled on a pad with one hand and slurped tea from a chipped mug with the other. He drained the contents of the mug and then pinched the top of his nose and closed his eyes, trying to order his thoughts. They say fact is stranger than fiction, Herbert thought. Well, it was going to take a lot for the reader to believe any of this! Herbert sat in this position for a few moments and when he opened his eyes again and returned to the world that was outside the realms of his imagination, his cup had been refilled with piping hot tea.

"Thank you, Amanda," he said. Herbert came to the cafe regularly to put his thoughts into order, mainly when he should have been working. It was like most other cafes, but then it had a homely, welcoming feel. Herbert liked that Amanda filled the walls behind the counter with her own embroidery and poetry written by her best friend. Amanda was the happy, friendly aunt Herbert never had. His aunts were neither happy nor friendly. In fact, none of them were even alive.

"How is work with your newspaper?" Amanda asked, hovering next to his table holding a metallic jug. Herbert wondered how heavy the jug was. It was balancing quite precariously. Amanda was of advanced age. "You know Tony?" she continued, not waiting for his response. "The one who comes in here regularly and always sits in the same spot by the window? I saw he made an appearance in the Just Look Who's Been in Court section of the paper last week. It's the only part of the paper where I know anybody, if truth be told. Oh and not forgetting the obituaries, of course. Tony got caught urinating on the pavement in the town centre on a Saturday night, apparently. I imagine quite a few folk do that on a Saturday night. The trick is not to get caught, isn't it? He never mentioned it when he came in here, funnily enough. He did look a bit sheepish though."

Herbert smiled. He wasn't too busy with the newspaper at

the moment. Herbert hadn't been running around anywhere near as much as he used to, and he was even struggling with his daily step count. His boss, the editor of the paper, sent him to the local Comprehensive to interview a boy who was taking his GCSE French examination three years early. Oh, the excitement! When Herbert was introduced to Pierre it was apparent he was taking his French exam early because he *was* French. It summed it up really. Herbert didn't feel the newspaper was utilising his full potential or maximising his many strengths. It was just as well though, because Herbert had other priorities in his life right now. It gave him an opportunity to push forward with the book.

"We are experiencing an unexpected lull at the moment, Amanda," Herbert explained. "We are only as busy as the news of the day in the town we report on. In fact, I am currently taking a rare break from my schedule and I'm working on my book."

"Ohh," Amanda said, suddenly very interested. She put the jug behind the counter and both hands on her hips. "Have you interviewed any more comedians yet? Has that lovely Rob Brydon returned your call yet?"

"Not yet," Herbert quickly replied. "But last time I turned on the TV he was busy on a cruise ship, so I guess that provides an explanation for the lack of contact."

"Must be a very long cruise," Amanda stated.

Herbert put his pen to his mouth and then took it out again. His mother was forever telling him to stop chewing things, that you never knew where things had been. He noticed some ink had leaked onto the tips of his fingers. That was always happening. That and leaking in his trouser pockets. He hoped he didn't have blue lips. "To be honest, I've scrapped that idea for now, Amanda. I've started a new venture. I'm chronicling the escapades of three relatively unknown Welsh comedians as they take on the might of The Edinburgh Festival Fringe this summer."

Amanda thought about this for a moment. "Does the Festival clash with Gareth Bale and the rest of our boys playing football in France?" she asked.

Herbert shook his head and informed her that the football was in June and the Festival was in August.

"How very exciting, Herbert," Amanda said. "That's proper

At Least the Pink Elephants are Laughing at Us

tidy, that is. I'll be honest, I did think your last book sounded a dud. It was best to scrap it..."

"You did? Well, I haven't scrapped it as such. Just put it on the back burner for now. I may still go back to it, actually..."

"But this new idea," Amanda interrupted, apparently not listening, "I imagine the story hasn't actually been told yet, has it?"

"Yes! That is exactly right, Amanda. I'm glad you get it. I'm not sure many others do. I'll be introducing the characters first. They all have an interesting if slightly tragic story to tell."

"Oh, most of them do, don't they? It's like that poor Forest Gump who discovered he was fast when running away from the bullies, isn't it? I imagine there are a lot of comedians out there who told jokes in the playground to stop the bullies taking their dinner money. Don't you think?"

Herbert assured her he certainly did, but really he suspected Amanda was guilty of generalisation. It might be worth asking the gang – mainly Connor – whether they told jokes to keep the bullies at bay though, for it would certainly be good narrative for the book, add some additional conflict.

"Maybe you could describe how you used to come here to write, dear? It could be like the coffee houses JK Rowling wrote *Harry Potter* in. I'm certain that woman had a caffeine addiction if she was in those coffee shops as much as they say she was. It could be a constant. Maybe you could write a small but important role for me in your book, Herbert? It is just a suggestion, of course..."

"Hmm," Herbert replied.

"And of course," Amanda continued, "it could all go disastrously wrong, couldn't it? But then I imagine that would make for quite an exciting story, wouldn't it? And I guess," she continued, moving closer, speaking her words quietly, "you could have some influence on how events unfold, couldn't you Herbert? You're like a puppeteer really aren't you dear? Like a *Punch and Judy* show."

Herbert couldn't help but smile. "I must be coming here too often. You know how my mind works, Amanda. Maybe I could write a small part for you after all, who knows....?

7 – Flushing the Terrible Twos Down the Toilet

James kept a watchful eye as his three-year-old boy proudly rolled the green basket purposefully along the aisle. Rory loved shopping. It was best to get him involved, give him some responsibility, some independence. "Can you put a toothbrush in the basket, please Rory?" he asked.

"Yes, Daddy" Rory replied. He dutifully picked up a toothbrush and placed it in the basket.

"Thank you, Rory. Good boy, Rory. Can you please put toothpaste in the basket now?"

Rory did precisely as he was told.

"Thank you, Rory. Aren't you a good boy?"

"Yes, Daddy. Rory is a good boy, Daddy."

Rory got carried away, though. He was having far too much fun. He grabbed at other items with his overactive little hands and threw them in the basket.

"No, Rory, put that tampon back, please," James urgently asked.

"No."

"What do you mean 'no'?"

"No, Daddy," Rory stated. "I will *not* put the tampon back."

James removed the box from the basket, but Rory lunged himself at it and then threw himself on the floor. His little angel turned into a monster just like that, with a metaphorical click of the finger. James had to take urgent action, before things got out of hand. He knelt down and tried to gently wrestle the cream from his son's hands. Rory rolled on the hard floor, kicking his legs like he was riding an imaginary bike.

A woman passed and smiled knowingly. "Terrible twos?"

James returned a flustered smile. The woman was passably good looking. He managed to retrieve the box and safely return it to the shelf. "I don't think so," James replied. "The little git is three, for starters."

At Least the Pink Elephants are Laughing at Us

The woman didn't look too happy with that comment. Rory got back to his feet and wiped away big raindrop tears with his sleeve. The trauma was over and Rory's world was back on an even keel. Rory pushed the basket up and down the aisles, only adding discount items as and when he was asked to do so. He waited patiently in the queue and only walked to the till when he was called.

"Oh my," the cashier gushed. "He is an absolute cutey, isn't he?"

She was a proper sort this one, James thought, what with her peroxide blonde hair and whitened teeth. "He sure is," James replied. "God only knows who his real father is..."

The woman's smile turned upside down and cracks appeared in her foundation. You just couldn't get the banter going with people these days, James thought. Everybody was far too serious.

They moved to the large home improvement retailer, with more room to run around on the spacious concrete floor. They'd already killed some time by staring at the rabbits in the pet shop and riding around on the scooters in the toy store, and James was rapidly ticking the usual options from his list.

"Car!" Rory excitedly shouted as he ran to the amusement ride by the entrance. Noddy and his damn car, James thought. Noddy had cost him a lot of money over the years. Noddy and Lightning McQueen. Rory climbed inside and spun the steering wheel. I'll let him have a play in there for a minute or two, James thought. It was only a matter of time before Rory remembered the car moved when you stuck a pound coin in the slot.

James pressed his hand to his forehead as he remembered Shirley had asked him to buy nappies. She wouldn't be happy if he forgot. "I asked you to buy one thing," she'd say. Nappies were considered to be a necessity in their household. Rory should have been out of nappies last year. Potty training hadn't been going too well. Rory kept pissing on the floor or, worse, on the Sky box. They had progressed to pull-ups which, as the kid still didn't use the toilet, were the same as nappies only much more expensive. Rory had only managed to go to the toilet on a few occasions. There had been a big celebration in the house each time. James had never imagined he'd ever celebrate a kid taking a dump, but times had changed.

James stopped the next assistant. "Sorry mate, could you tell me if you sell nappies?"

"For you?" the boy asked, looking James up and down with ill-disguised disdain.

"You what...?" James replied. Who *was* this dumb kid? "Are you 'twp' in the head or something? No, not for *me*. For my little boy."

The assistant smiled sympathetically. "I'm sorry sir, but this is a DIY shop," he said. "We sell DIY things. You had best try a supermarket."

James thanked him for nothing and continued with his shopping. Rory stayed right by his side, contentedly holding his hand. It was best to make the most of his angelic behaviour whilst it lasted. James had a good browse. The thought of being stuck indoors when they got home, watching the same cartoons again and again until it was finally time for Rory to go to bed, frightened him.

He only let go of Rory's hand when they reached the baths. They weren't like the basic tub his mum bathed him in when he was just a kid on Sunday evenings at five on the dot before tea at half past five, James thought. The retailers could charge whatever they wanted to if the bath arched at a certain, pompous angle. It wasn't going to get you any cleaner though, was it?

"Poo-poo, Daddy."

"Okay, Rory," James replied. He had pretty much accepted the inevitable. They'd been out for hours and it was only a matter of time. At least these places had changing facilities for kids. "I'll take you to the bathroom now," James said.

He absent-mindedly turned to Rory and then did a double-take. "Hold on. What the *fuck...?*"

Rory had a celebratory smile on his face. It was a big moment for him. He had his trousers and pants down by his ankles, and he was sat on a toilet. "No toilet paper, Daddy."

"That's not a real toilet, Rory!" James protested, frantically tugging at the boy's pants and quickly glancing at the gigantic turd that his son had plonked at the bottom of the exhibit toilet.

James just knew he shouldn't have let go of that hand...

At Least the Pink Elephants are Laughing at Us

8 – Bus Trip to the Coast

Connor liked being his own boss. It meant he didn't need to follow orders from anybody else and he didn't need to look busy. Even when he was doing admin for that solicitor's firm on Caroline Street when he left University, he was never particularly busy, but trying to *look* busy was absolutely exhausting. *I'm not a machine*, he was fond of saying. He wasn't a Terminator. He was a human being with limited energy supply that regularly needed refuelling. The British took pride in grafting, like it was a badge of honour, Connor considered, but he never really understood why. He conveniently thought himself to be European, and much preferred the French's relaxed approach to life and doing, or not doing, much of anything really. It was just as well that the frightful Brexit campaign had no chance whatsoever of success, he considered. Connor genuinely thought he'd have moved to a country like France long before now if it was not for his mum.

Owning the shop had advantages. His mum always told him not to be a sheep, to be a shepherd. He remembered she sat him down in Peacocks one time as a child when he was seriously deflated as he had no idea what to buy because he didn't know what was in fashion. His mum told him not to care one bit what was in fashion; just wear what feels good and let fashion follow you! Connor had been living by her advice ever since. And he genuinely despised following the orders of somebody else, of doing things just because they wanted him to. The thought of working hard (or at least pretending to work hard) to make somebody else rich made him sick. Connor much preferred instead to work to make himself poor. He was very aware he could have done a whole lot more with his life, but then he couldn't pretend that he was particularly bothered. This shop was his way of being free and at least trying to be, in some way, creative. He could do whatever he liked with the place. It was, as his mum said, just as she had with that collage when Aunt Jojo was supposed to come and visit, a blank canvass. The fact that he did very little with the shop and the canvas mainly remained blank was his choice.

The shop was his own very small pond, his very own kingdom. Connor owned the hens and fed and housed them. Frankie, the dog that could usually be found rolling around and licking his balls on the grass outside, was not strictly Connor's, but he visited the shop every day and was part of the furniture. Frankie *wanted* to be there every day, and that said something. Connor didn't possess much, but he was proud of what he did possess.

Connor enjoyed being part of the community. The postman knew his name and he was always greeted warmly in The Cups and The Pelican and as far afield as The Fox. Connor liked to help the locals where he could, which was why he was always willing to display folk's art or scribbles, however horrendous they were. The walls were covered with adverts for handymen, window cleaners and Weight Watchers. The poster of the teenager who had mysteriously gone missing was on his wall for years.

The boy was called Sam. He never met him, but he felt he knew him, that he was inexplicably part of his life. Sam had plenty of friends looking for him, including the black guy, Den, who always complimented Connor on what he referred to as his high quality of "banter." Connor remembered the day the boy's mother came into the shop in floods of tears and said they'd found Sam. The boy had been in London all the time. His mum had made the effort to come and tell Connor. That meant so much to him.

This job gave him ample opportunity to pursue other interests. This whole comedy thing was an odd one. Excitement didn't come easily to Connor, but he had to admit his interest had most definitely been stirred and maybe even shaken. They'd only had one meeting, but the next was imminent and Herbert was already talking about their first gig. The whole set-up was so unexpected, so random. Connor had never really thought he was particularly funny and, as far as he was aware, nobody else thought he was particularly funny, either. He wasn't a natural as a kid. He laughed at jokes in all the wrong places because he

At Least the Pink Elephants are Laughing at Us

wasn't able to identify the punch line. Connor only tried comedy as an adult through a process of elimination; all his other creative endeavours had been unsuccessful. It was to please his mum more than anything. Predictably, it was a failure, and Connor quickly moved on to the next venture.

Herbert, though, had seen something in him, hadn't he? Herbert was nobody's fool. He must have recognised something that was beyond the perception of the average man. Connor was determined to give this comedy lark his best shot. He wanted to develop his own style, to create an act that was unique to him. They didn't have long. The clock was ticking. It was February and the Fringe was in August. Time was of the essence. For the time being he'd merely copied routines from established and celebrated performers by watching countless clips on *You Tube*.

Something was distracting Connor though, something he just couldn't work out, something that he just didn't seem to be able to piece together.

Herbert openly said he'd plucked James and Connor from obscurity. Connor hadn't performed for years. Mandy and James didn't realise that he'd only been on stage twice in his entire life, and both times had been to small audiences.

And he was sure Herbert wasn't in either audience.

Connor was slumped over the counter, bent almost ninety degrees at the waist, showing less energy than a hibernating hedgehog, when the bell chimed and the shop door opened.

"Mum?"

He was suddenly alert, like he had downed a can of Red Bull or stuck a rocket up his arse.

Her cheeks were fleshy and shiny, like a polished snooker ball, and it was difficult to tell whether it was moisture from the drizzle outside, that had been so constant and dogmatic, or sweat from exertion or anxiety. Mum wasn't smiling. She didn't reply to his enthusiastic greeting. She wiped her feet on the mat and then glanced around the shop curiously like it was Aladdin's Cave. She raised her eyebrows and then pottered around his humble establishment. Nanya fiddled with a plastic wind-up penis, a novelty toy primarily catered for the hen market. The neutral expression on her face suggested this was not the first time she had fiddled with a plastic wind-up penis.

Connor glanced at the door and waited for his dad to appear, irritated from the attention of the dog. Nanya closed the door carefully behind her, mindful not to let in any cold, even though she had already been fiddling with a toy penis with the door wide open. Connor rushed to the other side of the counter, holding out his hands to assist his mother, like she was a decrepit old lady with a walking stick.

"Mum?" Connor asked. "How did you get here?"

His mum waved her hands dismissively. "Tssk. I caught the bus," she said.

"On your own...?"

Mum narrowed one eye and widened the other. It was not a good look. "Yes," she replied. "On my own."

She had the hump, Connor thought. That was unusual. His mother could be as high as a kite, floating on the clouds, or she could be on the floor, low and paralysed, but she didn't normally have the *hump*. And his mum didn't normally catch the bus anywhere, either. Connor felt a sliver of anxiety. Maybe something was wrong? He wanted to ask a string of other questions: Have you and Dad had an argument? Have you taken your medication? Did you *really* catch a bus? But he knew it was best to give her some space. He wouldn't get anywhere with her like this. And so Connor returned to relative comfort and safety behind the counter.

Nanya continued to browse the items in the shop, like she was on holiday searching for a fridge magnet. She picked up a plastic bucket and scrutinised the inside and then the outside. What was she expecting to find? It was a *bucket*. A bucket is a bucket is a bucket. Unless it was a spade, of course. She cast an analytical eye over the local art work. His mum was normally enthusiastic about anybody who showed any sort of creative endeavours. Now she just sniffed and shook her head dismissively. Did she really come here to buy something? Don't be ridiculous, Connor thought. Nobody *ever* came here to buy anything. Most of the punters saw the shop merely as a tourist attraction, as something to do before they crossed the stepping stones to the sand dunes or, more likely, headed to The Pelican. That was why he hardly had any money.

"I want to tell you something, Connor," Mum announced.

At Least the Pink Elephants are Laughing at Us

"Yes?" It crossed Connor's mind that maybe she had found the magazines he'd hidden in his sock drawer in his old bedroom, the ones he bought over twenty years ago and never found the need to replace, just in case he ever stayed over. The women may have aged in real life, Connor pondered, but they still looked damn good in the magazines.

"I don't ever want to hear you speaking to your father like that again. Enough is enough. You're not a child any more. You're a grown man, nearly forty. Do you hear?"

Connor paused, shocked by the abruptness, by the tone of her voice. His mother was not asking him. She was *telling* him. He briefly wondered what occasion she was referring to, for he was often not polite to his dad; frequently it was deliberate, and sometimes it was just because he couldn't help it. Connor quickly dismissed this question. He knew all too well she was referring to the Sunday when he was alone with dad in the lounge after church.

He nodded his head up and down, and he was still nodding after his mother had turned and walked out of the shop, closing the door behind her, minding that she didn't let any cold in.

9 – Make Me Hard

Herbert returned from the bar with a glass of apple juice (for himself), a medium dry white wine (for Connor), a pint of lager (for Mandy) and a packet of cheese and onion crisps and a packet of dry roasted peanuts (for general consumption).

"Bon appétit," he said, clinking glasses. "Light food and liquid refreshments. Just what the doctor ordered, I'd say."

Connor looked at the nuts and crisps and crinkled his nose like they wouldn't be prescribed by any doctor.

"Not drinking, Herbert?" Mandy asked, eyeing his drink with suspicion before slurping loudly on her own alcoholic beverage.

"I'm not much of a drinker to be honest, Mandy," Herbert replied.

"You don't *say*," Mandy said.

Herbert felt he needed to justify his general abstinence further. "It tends to make me very sleepy."

"Why don't you just get wasted and then go to sleep straight after?" Mandy suggested. "Washing the drink down with a kebab before bedtime always works a treat, I find."

"I'm not saying I don't let my hair down and go mad from time to time, Mandy," Herbert said, laughing. "But it does tend to go straight from my mouth to my head. I can be a touch outrageous when I've had a tipple. And so I tend to stick to lager shandy with a dash of lemon. Very refreshing. I'm more of a coffee shop kind of guy though, if I'm completely truthful."

"We'd prefer the truth, Herbert," Connor dryly stated.

Jesus, Herbert thought. He knew this misadventure was going to be tough, but he didn't expect it to be *this* traumatic. Herbert was aware he had significant work to do to counter Mandy's suspicions, but he was worried about Connor this evening. The guy normally had a calm exterior that bordered on the disinterested. He was hardly a little ball of energy. Tonight, though, he was on edge. His bright red and yellow flowery short-sleeved Hawaiian shirt was in direct contrast with his low mood.

At Least the Pink Elephants are Laughing at Us

What was *with* this guy and his clothes? Connor had already torn a beer mat into tiny pieces and left it to soak on the sticky, beer-drenched table. Connor was an intelligent guy, that was clear. Surely, therefore, he realised that tearing beer mats into tiny shreds was anything but intelligent? It was going to be difficult to cut through his persistent cynicism to make this project a success. Connor must have some interest though, Herbert thought. He wouldn't be here if he didn't, and he wouldn't be so nervous if he didn't care, would he?

James wasn't helping matters, either.

"Herbert, you told him half past seven, right?" Mandy asked, pausing to offload a handful of nuts into her mouth. Mandy swallowed the nuts before continuing. "And it's now twenty past eight. I think it's groovy to allow a bit of time for a man of his age – you know - for unexpected back twinges and all that, but fifty minutes is beginning to take the Mickey Mouse, don't you think?"

Mandy wasn't one to mince her words. She was no shrinking violet, as they called it. If there was something on her mind then she'd apparently let you know, plain and simple. Herbert could work with that. He had enough experience with his mother. It was passive aggressiveness Herbert struggled with; people who told you everything was fine and then suddenly erupted like a volcano. Herbert was fully aware though, that he still had a challenge ahead to persuade and influence her that this was a worthwhile plan. Oh yes. *How to Win Friends and Influence People:* what an utterly marvellous book that was, Herbert considered. The other two didn't have much to lose. Mandy was only performing on a small scale and at local venues, but she was good and she had a small following. It was only a matter of time before somebody important and influential noticed her, somebody much more important and influential than Herbert. It was perfectly reasonable for her to think she didn't need help from this trio of male mavericks.

"I'm sure James has a perfectly good explanation," Herbert said, offering Mandy some more peanuts as a distraction technique. "He called me up after our meeting and was very enthusiastic about the proposed project."

"You mean he was pissed?" Connor asked. "And this was

after the meeting he had walked out of?" he continued.

"I did detect some level of intoxication," Herbert meekly accepted. "But then some of the best artists enjoyed a drink or two, didn't they? I'm thinking of Dylan Thomas, for starters. And Tommy Cooper was hardly tea-total, was he?"

"Dylan Thomas drank himself to death after drinking eighteen straight whiskies," Connor countered.

He was like a bleeding *Encyclopedia*, Herbert thought. Or was it *Wikipedia* these days? If ever he got another team together for the quiz at the Three Horseshoes then Connor was getting a call. "I'm sure we've all woken up a bit worse for wear after a night out," Herbert said. "Besides, James being a little tardy with the time gives us a great opportunity to discuss some ideas I have. I think we should all be thinking about our comedy styles, about the persona we are intending to portray. I'm looking at you two, at your chemistry, at your very different outlooks and mannerisms, and you know what I'm thinking...?"

"Not to bother?" Connor asked. "To quit whilst we're ahead?"

"Cheeky!" Mandy said, playfully punching Connor on the arm. Connor grimaced.

Herbert shook his head, like these were serious suggestions. He smiled. "I'm thinking 'Double Act.'"

Connor and Mandy turned and faced each other. It was like they were looking at each other properly for the first time. Connor crinkled his nose. Mandy shrugged her shoulders. "But we'd clash, Herbert," she said. "I have my angry woman act whilst Connor has his whole grumpy geek thing going on, doesn't he?"

"I do?" Connor asked, perplexed. "That certainly wasn't my intention..."

"The contrast is what will make it so interesting, so explosive," Herbert interjected. "You do realise that Alexander Armstrong and Ben Miller performed at The Fringe and were nominated for a comedy award? And look at them now!" Herbert followed their eyes. Connor and Mandy weren't listening properly anymore. Three had become four.

"Evening, people," James said, holding up his hand and giving them a group wave. He must have already been to the bar,

At Least the Pink Elephants are Laughing at Us

for he plonked a half drunken pint on the table. He looked down on them from a great height, for his stool was so much higher than their chairs, with long wooden legs that could have belonged on a giraffe.

Herbert noticed that his eyes were bloodshot and his forehead was waxy. There was a feint whiff of booze to him. He hoped that the other two didn't notice, but he suspected Connor, for one, probably wasn't lacking in observational skills.

"I am most sincerely sorry that I am late. You know what it's like with children. I've been tearing my hair out all day, so I have. It is most unacceptable," James said, bowing his head to Mandy as though she was the Queen.

"Too right it is," Mandy replied, but she was smiling.

Herbert blew her a playful kiss across the table and Mandy pretended to catch it in her hand.

"I've just been moaning about you being late!" Mandy said.

"I *bet* you have," James replied.

Herbert interjected. "I was just putting forward to our new colleagues here, or should I say our new teammates, that they would make a great double act. Quite a unique selling point, don't you think James?"

James paused for a moment. Herbert wondered, with trepidation, what on Earth was going on in that fuzzy mind of his. Then James smiled and wagged his middle finger at him. "This is why this gentleman is our manager. It certainly is a unique concept," he agreed. "A black man and a lesbian. Together. I bet my right testicle it's never been done before. Genius, Herbert! Absolute genius, squire."

Mandy found this hilarious. She snorted and then put her hand to her mouth. "What do you mean a 'lesbian'?" she asked, high-pitched.

James held his hands up in protest. "I am sorry, Mandy," he said, suddenly Mr Innocent, Mr Squeaky Clean. "I've been told off about this before. I struggle to keep up with political correctness these days. What is acceptable one day becomes blasphemy the next. Do you guys go by "homosexual" or is it "gay" these days?"

Mandy was pink in the cheeks. She couldn't stop giggling. She wiped something from her eye. "It's not what you call it that I find funny. You think that just because I drink pints and don't wear frilly dresses and don't gossip about Kim Kardashian then I must be gay?"

"Nothing wrong with being gay," James accused.

"Nothing wrong with it," Mandy agreed. "Apart from the fact I'm not fucking gay!"

"Of course you're not," James said, unconvincingly. Mandy responded with another playful punch to the arm. James yelped.

Silence around the table.

"Well this is going well, isn't it," Connor said, rubbing his hands together.

Mandy's initial excitement appeared to have run out of gas. She busied herself on her phone. She had been distracted by the phone a fair bit tonight. Was it possibly another example of her lack of enthusiasm for the plan?

Herbert was surprised when Connor engaged in idle chatter. He did not seem the idle chatter kind of guy. And he just presumed him and James would be a total mismatch. "So how did you get into the comedy scene, James?" he asked.

"My dad was a comedian," James replied, proudly pumping his chest out. "He was a natural talent, my old man. Typical old school, you know? It was a different game back in the seventies, of course, when you didn't need to worry about upsetting people so much. We were built of stronger stuff back then. Just think of Bernard Manning, only good-looking. If there was a mother-in-law, blonde or Irish joke out there that my dad didn't tell, then I'd sure love to hear it..."

Herbert could tell the others were warming to James's enthusiasm. "So what happened to your dad?" Connor asked.

"He died on stage," James replied.

"We've all been there, hey butt!" Mandy said.

"No, no, you don't understand, Mandy..." Herbert urgently interrupted, but James dismissed his protests. "Don't worry, Herbert, its fine. Dad was up on stage, doing what he loved, when he got ill. He couldn't finish his act and he died shortly afterwards."

Silence. "I'm very sorry, James, honest to God I am," Mandy said. She made the effort to be more positive. "I can think of worse ways to go," she chirped, and then she clinked

At Least the Pink Elephants are Laughing at Us

James's glass, and the others urgently joined in.
"So do you work, James?" Connor asked.
James laughed. Herbert wasn't sure why. "No," James replied. "I've been claiming job seekers for years now."
"I'm sorry to hear that," Connor replied. "I do seem to be asking all the wrong questions, don't I? I imagine it is incredibly difficult to find a job in this current market, although things have picked up in recent years in the aftermath of the recession."
James appeared perplexed. His brow furrowed. He rubbed his nose with his sleeve. "Oh, I get you," he said, slapping his hand down on his thigh. "Sorry. There has been a misunderstanding. I said I've been *claiming* job seekers. I never actually said I've been seeking an actual job."
Connor started tearing into another beer mat. He seemed more frustrated than ever. "I've been thinking," Connor said. "This plan of yours, Herbert? I understand why you want to chronicle us going to Edinburgh for The Fringe. And I understand the concept of the underdog. We're Welsh. It is what we thrive on. But are we even underdogs? Wouldn't "no-hopers" be a more adept description?"
"Speak for yourself, butt," Mandy laughed, but her tone indicated a subtle warning.
"No, Mandy is right," Connor accepted. "I can understand why you've chosen Mandy. But I haven't done a gig for ages and James has already said that he hasn't done one for donkey's years." Connor turned to James now. Herbert could tell that he was on a roll, that he was gaining confidence, that he had started something and so he may as well finish it. "And, to be fair, James, you're not exactly a new kid on the block, are you? And you walked out of our first meeting and now you've turned up late tonight. I really have no idea why Herbert has plucked me out of nowhere, but I have even less of an idea why he has chosen *you.*"
"Don't mince your words, darling!" Mandy loudly protested, seemingly trying to ease the tension. It was needed. Colour filled James's face. He eyed Connor with wide, manic eyes. Herbert feared there would be a confrontation, possibly a physical one. Herbert wasn't adept when it came to fisticuffs. Then James looked around at the whole table and spoke surprisingly calmly,

unexpectedly softly. "Listen, if you don't want me in the team then its best I leave now, don't you think?"

Mandy reached over and rubbed James's thigh. "I'm willing to let you show me what you can do," she said. Herbert wondered whether she meant to sound so suggestive.

James turned his head sharply to Herbert. He was looking for his contribution. He was supposed to be the leader, the motivator. Herbert wasn't ready to spill his ulterior motives just yet, though. He struggled for a genuine reason why James should be part of the team. Herbert decided to put the onus back onto James. "Well, James? What do *you* think? Why should you be part of the team?" Herbert asked.

James went to speak. His top lip quivered, like a baby who'd been crying uncontrollably. Herbert could tell he didn't know what to say, that words failed him. Herbert looked at Connor. He leaned back on his stool with his arms tightly held against his chest. It would be impossible for James to find the words or the order or the vocabulary to convince Connor that he was the right man for the job. Evidently James thought so too. He stood up and kicked his stool back a few inches, took a long gulp of his drink and then slammed the glass down on the table.

That was it, then. It had ended before it had even begun. James was going to walk out. Quit. Edinburgh was not going to happen. The book would not materialise. She would never meet any of them. But instead James turned away and just stood there, chest pumped out.

And then he spoke, loudly and clearly for the whole pub to hear.

"Ladies and gentlemen, I am sorry to disturb you," James said. "Actually – no - reverse that. Ladies and gentlemen, I am ecstatic to disturb you. I am going to give you some free entertainment that would be at home in the *Comedy Store* in London..."

The punters stared glumly into their drinks, wishing they could be swallowed up inside the glass. One guy, probably a pint or two worse for wear, groaned loudly. Another sunk his head in his hands. This was a ruthless crowd, Herbert considered. He felt a familiar sense of dread.

"I've been working on getting really hard," James shouted to

At Least the Pink Elephants are Laughing at Us

the pub. Groans turned to boisterous cheers. James held his hands up, all innocent, like they had him all wrong. "No, not like that." He turned his attention to an old dear with, presumably, her husband, and said, "Although I'm sure I can work something out in that respect, sweetheart."

The woman smiled, and so did her feller. James returned to the punters. "I mean "hard" as in Jean Claude Van Damme "hard." Tough. Or "tidy" if you prefer around these parts. So I got a book out by one of these so-called "hard bastards." You know the type: they always talk like they have a mouthful of nuts in their mouth. No, not those nuts...So what this guy was telling me was to always be alert. He said you could be down the chip shop when somebody calls your missus a slag. He kept using the same example. You're down the chip shop and somebody calls your missus a slag. I thought, either his chippy is rough as hell, he lives in Newport, or his missus is a proper goer..."

Herbert glanced at Mandy and Connor. Both watched intently. There was a vague, barely noticeable smile on Connor's lips. Mandy was beaming. James had their attention, Herbert thought, contentedly. Maybe, just maybe, this was a start...

*****

Mandy waited in line in the chip shop, tapping her shoe on the floor, glancing – out of habit and boredom – at her reflection in the glass. She wasn't really the type to keep looking at herself. She always looked the same anyway. They always took ages in this place. How long did it take to batter a fish, for God's sake? And didn't they suspect that in a chip shop punters would regularly order chips? It was all about avoiding wastage. Every time she came in here – every *single* time – the first thing they ever said was "it will just be a few minutes on the chips, love." She felt like saying "Of course it fucking will," but she just wasn't that type of girl. Her mother had brought Mandy and her brothers up to at least be polite. Scoundrels maybe, but *polite* scoundrels. Mandy glanced at the flashing fruit machine, sticky with grease from fingers that had been handling chips. She looked at the posters and adverts stuck to the wall with sellotape. There was yoga in the hall on Thursday nights. She had an excuse not to be there, Mandy thought - she worked Thursdays. Thank God for that.

She thought about James and his act. Fair play, the bloke seemed like a ticking time bomb ready to explode, but it took guts to get up in the middle of the pub. It was different at a comedy club because the punters expected you to stand up and tell jokes. They just got upset when you told *shit* jokes. Mandy had just assumed James was all talk and no trousers. Just as James had assumed Mandy was a lesbian. Cheeky bastard! He had walked the walk though, just like Eddie Jones, the new England rugby manager. *Bastard.* He was good, too. The guy was genuinely funny. She wondered whether they could possibly make a go of this project. Mandy had been keeping a very open mind so far, half-expecting it to fall flat at any moment. She'd been going along for the ride regardless because it took her mind off things and kept her busy. Besides, it wasn't as if she was taking the South Wales comedy circuit by storm on her own, was it? Plus, she quite enjoyed hanging around with three blokes. She was *far* from a lesbian, if truth be told.

Connor was an interesting one. She wouldn't mind unravelling some of his layers, and not just those crazy clothes of his. She smiled. There was a whole lot going on in that pretty head of his. She did think he could have gone easier on James tonight though. It was like he had an ulterior motive. Mandy had yet to identify any characteristics that suggested Connor had the balls or personality to get up on stage and make an audience laugh. He had a dry sense of humour, for sure, but it was one thing to make a small group of acquaintances laugh, and a whole other thing to make a large group of hostile beer-drinkers laugh. Mandy had dismissed the double-act idea, too. Angry man and grumpy woman was too much misery for any audience to take. It just wouldn't work.

Mandy glanced at her phone again. Nothing. Zilch. She pushed the blasted thing back into her pocket. Stop checking it, Mandy. Stop being so frickin' desperate.

"You want salt and vinegar with your chips, love?"

Hang on. Was that a vibration in her pocket? Maybe her mind was playing tricks again? "Yes please," she said. "And can you please give me a few more chips than that? Don't be shy."

At Least the Pink Elephants are Laughing at Us

Then she pulled the phone out of her pocket. She was her own worst enemy, a glutton for punishment, basically a sadomasochist. All she needed now was a leather bodice and a whip.

She opened up the message and read the words on the screen. She smiled. Mandy could see her teeth reflecting back at her in the glass. She did look different now.

This was finally becoming real, Mandy thought.

10 – The Park (in the Middle of the Day, in the Middle of the Week)

It was dry, which James thought was good, but overcast, cold and drab, which James thought was not so good. This was the dreariest, bleakest time to go to the park: the middle of the day, the middle of the week. The park was usually deserted, because normal, decent folk were expected to work, weren't they? When they were joined by an occasional other, they always looked like the walking lost, that they were there because they literally had nothing else to do. But it had to be done, James reasoned. It wasn't every day you could treat your kid to *Folly Farm* or *Peppa Pig World*, especially on the stupid money he received claiming job seekers.

James blew steam on his fingers, pulled the zip on his leather jacket to the top and then nestled his chin inside. He poked his head out like a tortoise. Rory's chunky little legs dangled from the swing. He looked grateful that his ears were covered by his *Thomas the Tank Engine* bobble hat. James eyed his darling wife. Shirley didn't appear to be affected by the cold. There was no pink flush to her cheeks or steam emitting from her mouth. Shirley was clad in a tee shirt and blue jeans that had rips in the knees and thighs. James sometimes joked that Shirley was really from Newcastle, and not Ponty, where she claimed she was born and bred.

James stood facing Rory and, bending at the knees, gave the swing a big push.

"Higher!" Rory pleaded. His eyes were big and his face was frozen into a smile.

James pushed harder.

"Higher!"

James pushed harder.

"Too high!" Rory protested. "Stop Daddy! Stop!"

Shirley put a question to James. "So you stood up in front of

At Least the Pink Elephants are Laughing at Us

the whole pub, like?"

"Sure did."

"And there were actually people in the pub? I know pubs are closing all over the place nowadays..."

"It was busy, full of hardened drinkers who weren't pleased to be interrupted."

"So how did you feel at that precise moment in time?"

"Well, you know when you're in a changing room full of men and you're worried your tackle is smaller than everybody else's...?"

"I'm a woman, James, so not really..."

"Fair enough," James replied. "Well, maybe your boobs...? Your lady...? Something...? No. Okay. My point is that at first I was absolutely bricking it. It felt like I was naked, Shirley, and all these people were staring at me. Studying and evaluating me. And boy, they did not look impressed. It's been a time, you know. I was terrified that I wasn't funny anymore..."

"You're the funniest man I know, James, the funniest man in the whole of Bridgend..."

"Yes, well thank you" James smiled. "You know that and I know that. But right at that very moment it felt like it would be the end of the world, a potential Armageddon that even Bruce Willis and his bald head and big kick-arse drill could do nothing about. If nobody laughed then what would that mean? Where would it leave me? It would confirm that I wasn't really funny, that's what. It would confirm that this dream I had been relentlessly chasing all these years was really just that: just a dream. You know?"

Shirley smiled. "But you haven't really been *chasing*, have you, James? And definitely not *relentlessly* chasing. You haven't done anything about your dream for years."

James ignored her. There was no reason to get hung up on technicalities. Or facts. "I longed to sit down and hide away, to disappear amongst all the other drinkers, back within my warm and cosy comfort zone. That was the easy thing to do, right enough."

"But you didn't, did you? My husband was a big brave boy, wasn't he?" Shirley teased.

Oh yes, James thought. Your husband was a very big, brave

boy.

"Mikey!" Rory excitedly exclaimed, pointing his middle finger at a dog pissing against a tree. Rory called every dog Mikey, as that was the name of the dog that lived down the road.

"So I told my first joke, and people laughed. They really laughed! Not out of politeness. This was a rough group, I can tell you. They actually thought I was funny. Me." James put his finger to his chest. "James Jones. It was the most fantastic feeling in the whole world, Shirley. And then I just couldn't get enough. Like that song. I craved their laughter, like it was a drug."

Shirley stepped off her swing. God, James thought, as he eyed her smooth pale flesh under the rip in her jeans; skin coated with cute goose bumps. It had been six long years since they'd exchanged vows down the rugby club, and James honestly thought she was still the sexiest woman he'd ever seen. She was fifteen years younger than James, and looked even younger. Shirley stood behind James now and put her hands on his hips, gently nestled her lips on his neck. She smelt good. James considered telling her he had a boner, but then reconsidered. He was a romantic, after all. Maybe he should let her find out instead? If he arched his back just a little that way and let those hands go...

"Higher!" Rory shouted.

Exactly what I was thinking.

Rory started whining, building up to a tantrum. He wanted his swing to be pushed higher and he wouldn't stop until it was. The moment had gone. "Little shit!" James involuntarily bleated, under his breath.

"Language!" Shirley protested, playfully slapping James's arm. "That is no way to speak about your darling son. And you know how he picks up words these days. This is the time that their minds are most absorbent. He is a like a sponge."

Rory looked at his dad and smiled, like butter wouldn't melt in his mouth. "Little shit!" Rory mimicked. His words were clear and they were loud.

"See!" Shirley said.

James looked at his son ruefully. The kid was on a continual mission to get his dad into trouble. If he didn't wash his hands after a leak then Mummy found out. James put his finger to his lips. Rory chuckled.

"So the other three rate you now?" Shirley asked. "They want you on board?"

James thought about this for a moment. He nodded his head. He wasn't sure about Connor, but there was potential there he could work with. He thought Mandy was close to being on his side. He didn't appear to have put Herbert off yet.

Shirley put her hands back on his hips, and then they slivered inside his leather jacket and under his tee shirt. Naturally, James pulled in his tummy, tried his best to turn the wobbly jelly into a rock-hard six-pack, and he tightened his doughy chest. He hoped she didn't tickle his nipples with her fingers. It would be far too much to handle and, after all, they were in the park, with their little boy.

"Seriously though James, I am really proud of you. We've had our tough times and I know life hasn't been a barrel of laughs, but things are looking up, don't you think? I've always had faith in you. Blind, stupid faith. But you're going to prove me right this time, aren't you? You're really going to make things work with this comedy thing, aren't you...?"

James nodded his head. He thought about what Shirley was saying. She was right. They weren't exactly in a good place – not yet – but at least now there was a platform. He did have an opportunity to do something really good. For once, he might not let her down, let himself down, let everybody down.

And then suddenly the clouds looked black and threatening and his cold fingers felt numb, like he couldn't sense the tips. His thoughts scattered. He felt dizzy, like he was floating above the park.

James pushed little Rory higher, and higher...

11 - The Accidental Astronomer

The ground was bumpy and hard and smothered unevenly with moisture, but that was how he liked it. This was his chosen spot, a sloping stretch of green evenly placed between river and the road. Connor could hear the gentle, natural flow of water from the river. Occasionally his thoughts were interrupted by the bright lights and revving motor of a passing car. He lay somewhere between obscurity, which he loved, and the real world, where he was not quite sure he fitted. This was genuine peace. Connor rested the back of his head in his upturned hands and gawped open-mouthed at the night sky above.

Connor wasn't really into astronomy. For example, he didn't own a telescope. He was not sure he had the courage to own one, for he had this irrational fear that somebody, somewhere, would misinterpret him to be a Peeping Tom, and Connor could not think of *anything* worse. But he was aware that a telescope was a basic component for a budding astronomer, like a chess board was to a chess player. However, when Connor stared up at the glorious and infinite possibilities of the galaxy, he could not possibly fathom that that there was no other life out there. It was just impossible to envisage. The Earth was such a tiny piece of the jigsaw that was the universe that it just seemed unbelievably egotistical to think we had sole rights to it. And so, when Connor lay on his back and stared at the sparkling stars above him, he wondered whether there was somebody else, millions of miles away, staring at Earth, wondering exactly the same thing.

Don't cha wish your girlfriend was hot like me? Don't cha wish your girlfriend was a freak like me? Don't cha?

Damn that ringtone, Connor cursed.

He tugged at his phone and put it in his pocket. Put it to his ear. "Hello?"

"Connor," the faintly familiar voice on the other end said. "I've got you a gig."

12 – Flashing Lights and Bingo Calls

The hall was on the top floor of the corner pub. The pub was mainly visited by regulars with beaten faces who drank slowly but determinedly and loudly cursed the day the smoking ban was introduced. The drinking hole catered for what could most kindly be called a "mature" clientele, and less kindly be called "old people." Most of the drinkers were young – once – usually a long time ago, and had been coming here with their parents since they were children and were now coming with their own children and sometimes with their children's children. They didn't know any different, didn't know what else to do. Bowling? The cinema? *Nandos?* The steep, awkward stairs that led to the hall were at the rear of the pub, behind a flimsy wooden door that clung to the hinges for dear life. The door was difficult to spot and easy to confuse with the toilets. You were instantly hit by the waft of sweat and soggy leather: the hall was used for boxing classes in the week. Punters were pleasantly surprised when they reached the top of the stairs and the hall opened up in front of them. It was spacious and airy. The floor was polished. Their expectations had, for good reason, been low, and they were usually surpassed.

The four of them sat at a small, round wooden table, close to the stage. They huddled closely together like footballers having a pep talk before a big game. They'd arrived early. The hall had been empty of people then. Forty-five minutes and a few drinks later and the venue was slowly beginning to fill. Just about right, Herbert thought. It would be overwhelming to perform to a full house at this stage in their development. There again, there was nothing worse than standing up to one man and his dog, especially if the dog, or the man, were asleep.

"When you said you had got us a gig, Herbert," Connor said, flipping a beer mat and catching it, "I thought you meant a proper one. Isn't the point of an "open mike" night that any Tom, Dick and Dirty Harry off the street can come along and do their thing?"

What was *with* this guy and beer mats? Connor was a bag of nerves again tonight, Herbert thought, but then, who could blame him? Performing was frequently traumatic for even the most established of comics. Disguising fear and anxiety was often part of the act. Tommy Cooper was apparently as sick as a dog before every show. Connor hadn't performed for a long, long time and by all accounts the last time he did was hardly a roaring success. The report Herbert got back was far from positive. The guy had good reason to be panicking.

Connor was talking faster than Herbert remembered, but only his lips seemed to be moving. His face appeared completely numb. He reminded Herbert of a ventriloquist dummy, or maybe a *Thunderbird*. A glossy layer of sweat covered his forehead, giving it an impressive shine.

"These events are very popular nowadays, Connor," Herbert explained. "They are a suitable starting point for budding comics. There are waiting lists, and those lists can be very long. But I've used my contacts and pulled a few strings and you have jumped the queue. This is a perfect venue to try out new material, to hone your act. Even the most established performers practice their material at small venues before they hit the big stage. The crowd don't expect much, Connor, and I'm sure you won't let them down."

Herbert wasn't sure whether his choice of words helped or hindered his cause. He turned to Mandy and James for support, but they both seemed in their own little world. He hoped they were in the zone, psyching themselves up, ready to take centre stage, but that seemed overly optimistic. Mandy was busy checking her phone again. James was quieter, more subdued than usual. Maybe he was exhausted? It wasn't easy bringing up a young child. Or maybe he was nervous too? Either way, James didn't seem interested in playing the jester or the motor mouth tonight. Both James and Mandy dutifully nodded their heads, but Herbert wasn't even certain they heard his question.

Herbert swiftly moved things into a higher gear. His role was to be a leader, to motivate and inspire the troops. "Just think of this as a training session guys. All we're looking to do is try out new things, see what works and what doesn't. Nothing more,

At Least the Pink Elephants are Laughing at Us

nothing less. Rome wasn't built in a day, and neither is a quality, well-polished five-minute comedy routine."

The MC was a round man with a puffy face and a terrifically lopsided fringe. His hairdresser must have been having an off-day, or maybe he had a vendetta, Herbert considered. His role was crucial. The guy was supposed to get the crowd in the mood whilst calming the rising nerves of the acts. Sometimes they were the main attraction. However, this guy looked uncertain and agitated. "We are very fortunate tonight, ladies and gentlemen, because we have a star performer in our presence. She is a regular on the comedy circuit and is building quite a following. Later in the proceedings we'll be welcoming on to the stage our very own girl from Bridgend, Mandy Williams."

His over-the-top enthusiasm was met with lazy, muted applause. It was apparent nobody had heard of Mandy Williams.

Herbert hoped Connor would be encouraged by the standard of the other acts. Most were amateurs, there to either cross an item off a bucket list or to build confidence for a best man speech. Some read from scraps of paper and others forgot their lines. It was a relief just to get to the punch line. "Don't worry, Connor," Herbert said. "However bad you are you are, you're still going to be a whole lot better than this lot. I hope." He gave him an encouraging wink. Connor didn't respond well. He downed his shot. One leg was shaking, banging and vibrating against the underside of the table.

The low standard of the acts seemed to have an adverse effect on Connor. The crowd was getting more confident and increasingly boisterous. A couple of loudmouths at the front seemed to relish shouting abuse at the performers. James and then Mandy managed to get through their acts relatively unscathed, but both were fairly lacklustre, subdued performances. Mandy did make Herbert laugh when she said, "Some guy asked if he'd seen me working as a stripper in a strip club in Swansea. I told him he was a cheeky little git. I'd never work in Swansea!"

"Calm down, Connor," Mandy said when she returned to her seat. She put her arm around his shoulder, finally showing an interest. "You'll be just fine, butt." James joined in. "Yes mate," he said. "Just give them what for."

Connor was pumped up now, Herbert observed. The adrenaline, or maybe the shots, appeared to be racing through his body. Connor looked like he'd start thumping his chest with his fists like it were a drum at any moment. "I'll fucking show them!" he yelled. "The grumpy bastards!"

He took to the stage, which was a small wooden box, and Herbert feared the worst.

But, when Herbert updated his book later, maybe just a tad gleefully, he reflected that it was much, much worse than that.

"When I said I was going to be a comedian, they all laughed," Connor said, looking bitterly depressed. "Well," he continued, "they're not laughing now, are they?"

There was a loud groan from the front row. "Jesus," a heckler shouted. "Bob Monkhouse said that back in the seventies!"

Connor bowed his head and talked so fast people could barely understand what he was saying. He walked around, but on the spot and in a circle. When nobody laughed at his third joke, he stopped and spoke directly to them. "You don't find that funny? What's the matter with you?"

The audience heard *that* clear enough.

This was rapidly turning into a fiasco. Herbert could see what Connor was doing. He'd seen it all too often before. Connor was viewing the audience as the enemy. They were working against him rather than with him. He wished they weren't there, that he was up on stage on his own and performing to any empty hall. Also, all of the jokes were very familiar.

Connor kept glancing distractedly at a guy on the fruit machine, slotting coins and pressing buttons, holding plums and making things flash. What was that thing even doing on this floor? A woman appeared from the darkness of the stairs and started working the tables, apparently oblivious or indifferent to the poor guy covered in sweat standing on a box holding a microphone, desperately trying to entertain the crowd. "Fancy buying a raffle ticket, love?" she asked. "There's a bottle of bubbly up for grabs tonight."

"Oh for *fucks* sake!" Connor protested, not even trying to hide his frustration.

At Least the Pink Elephants are Laughing at Us

The woman turned around. Her face looked crushed.

"Don't have a go at her, mun," somebody piped up, one of the guys who had been shouting abuse and who had suddenly become a good samaritan, a flippin' martyr. "She's only doing her job."

There was a chorus of approval from the other punters. Connor had made himself the pantomime villain. Only he wasn't big and lovable like *Wolf* from *Gladiators*, in their eyes he was just a nasty bastard, picking on the poor raffle woman who was only trying to do her job, bless her. Herbert went to put his head in his hands but resisted. That wouldn't set a positive example. He looked at James and Mandy and was partly glad to see that they both looked worried. So they *did* care, at least.

Connor was undeterred. He pointed his finger at the guy who had shouted his support for the poor woman. "You can shut up too! Do you know how difficult it is to get up and perform in front of a load of village idiots like you? Well? Do you, Popeye...?"

Popeye got to his feet and headed towards Connor at a thunderous pace. He was a big lump and Herbert realised this could turn bad. Very bad. Herbert got to his feet and was followed by James.

They needn't have bothered. Connor responded to the angry man like a Poodle chased by a Rottweiler. He bit first. Or more accurately, Connor swung at the guy and landed with a punch square on the nose. The guy stopped charging and dropped to the floor with a thud.

"Come on," Herbert said, picking up his coat. "Let's get out of here. This isn't a receptive audience."

Herbert fled towards the narrow stairs down to the pub below, and the other three were right behind him.

13 – Let Me Entertain You

James had only come out for a quick pint, but then quick pints were often deadly, weren't they? Quick pints were almost mythical. James had been out for a quick pint more than once and then woken up on the sofa with his trousers around his ankles, *Babe Station* playing in the background, wondering what the dear Lord Almighty happened last night.

Tonight though, the first pint was a bit of an uphill struggle. The amber nectar wasn't mingling well with his taste buds which, frankly my dear, was a tad unusual. James wasn't going to waste a good pint though, not when there were people out there starving, and so he closed his eyes and forced the drink down his throat like a trooper. Might as well stay for another now I'm here and I really didn't enjoy that one, he considered. He'd informed Ron when he arrived he was only staying for one, and yet the cheeky bastard didn't even bother to feign surprise when he returned to the bar with a crinkly five-pound note (one of the new ones, no less) in his hand asking for another. That bloke was a cynic just like his dad, Frank, James thought.

James did most of his thinking when he was drinking. It didn't say much for his thinking that James didn't drink all that much nowadays, just the odd pint or two here and there and the occasional unexpected session there and here. James rarely drank in the house. He had duties at home. He needed to think tonight though, and therefore he needed to drink. *I think and drink, therefore I am.* James did occasionally dip into all those books on his mum's bookshelf. He was like a bodybuilder, James optimistically considered, who needed protein shakes to provide fuel to his developing muscles; James needed alcohol to fuel his developing mind. It didn't *really* make sense, did it? He didn't imagine the greatest thinkers of the world needed a tipple before their brain cells worked. Stephen Hawking didn't hit the vodka shots hard before developing a theory on the history of the Universe, did he? James conceded he wasn't comparing like with

At Least the Pink Elephants are Laughing at Us

like, something he tended to do on a fairly regular basis. He'd watch Arsenal v United on the tele, for example, and then compare the goals to the ones he'd scored down the Bridgend Rec on a Thursday night, back in the day. This whole drinking and thinking theory was probably just an elaborate excuse to get drunk, he accepted, as he took a long, pleasurable slurp from his lager.

To be fair, most of his thinking when he was drinking *was* creative rather than destructive. James didn't tend to dwell on negatives and the old days, like some doom and gloom folk he knew. He preferred to blank some of it out. What was the point? You couldn't do anything about what had already happened and besides, he knew he was luckier than most: you only had to turn on the television to know the horrors that were going on in the world. People were at war! People were starving! James liked to think he was a glass half-full kind of guy; unless he was on a bender, of course, and then his glass was always in need of refilling! He was the joker, after all, the *comedian*. James didn't pretend to be the sharpest knife in the box, or was it tool in the box, but he felt he was smart enough to know that if you looked after today – gave it your undivided attention and devotion - then yesterday and tomorrow would look after themselves very nicely all by themselves. There was probably a name for that theory, James considered.

Recently, though, James had to admit that his thoughts had been troubled. There was trouble in Paradise. There was bleakness to his thinking that not only made him feel uncomfortable, but scared.

Things were going pretty damn well. Anybody could see that. For once in his life he had the opportunity to really make things work. But that was the problem. He was used to letting people down. That was what people expected. He had done it in his past life, with his ex-wife, when he was still working at the factory, before he met Shirley, and now he was going to do it all over again, wasn't he? That's what he did.

"This isn't you doing well," the devil on his shoulder said. "Just who the hell do you think you are?"

After his third, utterly delicious pint, James decided that tonight the only way to turn off his thoughts was to drown them in a steady and continual flow of alcohol. The drink could fuel his thoughts, but hopefully they could destroy them, too. Tonight he was content to be the irritable bloke in the corner of the pub getting sloshed.

It was a quiet in The Oak. As Tom Jones would say: it's not unusual. James exchanged the usual chitchat with some of the regulars (*How's your job? You lost it? How's your dog? Dead? Sorry to hear that, butt, honestly I am*) but they'd gone home for tea and had been replaced by others who had already had their tea. James was just – tentatively - beginning the process of at least *thinking* about calling it a night, when she walked through the door.

The few heads that were left in the pub turned, even Joe's, who'd been off work with a stiff neck for the last six months. It was a woman, which wasn't all that common, and she was a woman who wasn't a regular, which really *was* unusual. The woman looked to be in her mid-forties, but she had a well-preserved, pampered style which suggested she was probably older and just looked good for her age. Her fingers were donned with sparkling jewellery; gems that didn't look like they were picked from an Argos catalogue. Her nails were perfectly manicured and polished. A black skirt clung comfortably to long, gym-toned thighs which probably appeared longer and more gym-toned because they were attached to black high heels. The woman glanced quickly around the joint, swivelling 360 degrees, a little flustered, cheeks slightly flushed. James knew she was asking herself the same question everybody else was asking: why in earth did she end up in a place like this on a damp Tuesday night?

He could almost visibly see her body relax; her shoulders drop, her grip on her handbag loosen. She obviously made the decision that she was here now and so she may as well stay for a drink; probably easier than walking straight out of a pub when all eyes were on her. And so she strolled purposefully to the bar, all smiles and good intentions, like she couldn't be happier to be there. Made eye contact with Ron behind the bar. Ordered a vodka and coke. And then she slowly, hesitantly made her way to a spare table, any table would do so long as it was away from the boozy, bloodshot eyes that were fixed on her. James noticed

At Least the Pink Elephants are Laughing at Us

she had a mesmerising sway of her hips, that her butt shimmied every time she took a step in her high heels. It was like a pendulum swinging from left to right, hypnotising him.

"Of all the gin joints in all the world, you come into this one..."

James knew he'd mastered the devilish smile. He'd had quite a few years to do so, he was so old. Even with a few gallons of beer inside a belly that was ready to pop, James was still wise enough to know exactly what he looked like: a dishevelled, middle-aged man with an optimistically youthful ponytail, drinking on his own in a dingy little drinking den. James also knew that, however dishevelled and pathetic he looked, he still, mysteriously, offered a certain amount of charm to a certain type of woman. There was still a chance, albeit with diminishing odds with each passing year, that this was that certain type of woman.

Her reaction was lukewarm, like a piping hot cup of coffee that had been left standing for a tad too long. That was much more positive than James had anticipated. The woman took James in, became a terminator, quickly assessing whether this unidentified specimen was friend or foe. She smiled and then emitted an over-the-top laugh. She pulled her head back and James noticed her neck was not quite as smooth and creaseless as her face, like her face had been plonked on a different body. The woman didn't look disturbed by his uninvited attention, but neither did she give the impression she was going to stop to chat. James kicked at a stool and missed, hurting his shin, then kicked at the stool again, more successfully this time.

"Why not let me entertain you for a little while?" he asked, grinning. He raised one eyebrow like Roger Moore. He'd practised that in the mirror, too. "It's a quiet night in The Oak tonight and I have nobody to share my most excellent stories with."

The woman put her hand to her mouth and giggled. "Just who do you think you are? Robbie Williams?"

James could tell this lady *thought* she had a good sense of humour. This was a good sign. James was old school. He tried his best not to be chauvinistic but he often failed miserably. James was sceptical of the number of women who were actually funny. Victoria Wood (God bless her soul)? Dawn French?

Jennifer Saunders? Amy Schumer? Caroline Aherne (God bless her soul again)? It seemed unlikely this woman would be added to the list. James wasn't in the mood for somebody who was uptight though, somebody who took life too seriously. It would only end in tears. For him. James just wanted somebody to pass a few hours with, to share a laugh and possibly a mild flirtation. The fact this woman thought she had a good sense of humour was at least encouraging.

"James," James said.

The woman reluctantly held out her hand, and James kissed it.

The woman giggled. She looked at the stool. And then she sat on it.

*****

Shirley needed an escape, a release.

There was only so many times her wonderful, precious little boy could climb the metal steps to the top of the slide, stop to give a dazzling smile, whoosh to the bottom, pull himself up and then start the whole process again – repeat, repeat, repeat – before the initial, genuine excitement faded. Only so many times he could say "Mummy" before she pleaded for him to fall asleep and please, *please,* darling, stop making so much damn noise. And only so many times he could roll down his pull-ups and wee on the Sky box before she desperately wanted to shout at the top of her voice, "Will you please, please stop pissing on the frickin' Sky box!"

She planned the surprise tonight though, not just for her but for her husband, too.

James had things on his mind. He was tense. She knew it was the comedy. There were expectations on his shoulders now that he hadn't experienced for a long time. Now he had no excuses. Shirley wanted him to do it because she knew he was the funniest man put on the earth. And she knew that, deep down, beneath his anxiety and fears, James really wanted to do it too. But it was worrying him. *Really* worrying him.

Shirley knew James had ruined everything before, with the people he loved, people who loved him back. Now he was scared

At Least the Pink Elephants are Laughing at Us

of doing it all over again. James was *terrified* of letting her and Rory down.

James was blissfully unaware Shirley had arranged for Nan and Gramps to come over and 'babysit' tonight whilst Rory was tucked up under his *Thomas* duvet. James had no idea Shirley had dabbed herself with his favourite perfume and put on her special black silk underwear, that she was surprising him with a night of romance and passion in a hotel just out of town.

Shirley knew James was busy drowning his worries at the bottom of a dirty glass. She didn't mind that. She would get to him before it was too late, revitalise him with some coffee and sweet promises. Shirley was on her way to the pub right now, walking the pavements, a subtle smile on her red painted lips. She was going to cheer him up tonight, goddamn it.

Her man was worth it.

*****

"Well, I'm very happy that I stopped for a drink with you, James," the woman said. She circled the rim of her glass with her finger. "You certainly have entertained me. Robbie Williams had better watch out."

James looked at her through glazed eyes. Her shape morphed. One moment she was wider, more rounded, the next she was longer, like a pencil with a face and arms. Maybe not a pencil then, he reconsidered. Occasionally, when he looked at her for long enough, one became two. This wasn't necessarily a bad thing. The allure just doubled; intensified. Her voice was becoming louder, the words she spoke making less sense. His thoughts were slowing down, like they were stuck in mud.

This woman had become increasingly attractive. When she perched on the edge of the stool and James examined her closely, he noticed a shadow of light hair on her top lip and faint, barely visible blue thread veins that zigzagged down the side of her scalp like a bolt of lightning. But a few drinks later and these imperfections (*were* they even imperfections, or perhaps just idiosyncrasies) were long forgotten and now his sunken eyes followed every subtle movement of her beautiful, red voluptuous lips. James wasn't even sure he was listening to anything she actually said any more, he was just watching and wondering.

James clawed two fingers into his thigh, pinching like a crab, hoping this would jerk him awake. "I do try," he said, slurring only a little. "Is it such a bad thing to want to make people laugh?" he asked, like he was on a selfless crusade to save the dolphins. "Is there a more positive emotion in the whole world than a good old laugh?" He'd heard that expression before, and then remembered who used to say it.

She straightened her back, looked deadly serious. "Absolutely not!" she said defiantly. "You're a good man, James," she said, looking him straight in the eye. James wanted to say that no, he wasn't; but he was too tired, too flattered, too everything to refute her compliments. "And I'm a good woman. I know I am. I don't care what my husband says."

She wiped her lips with her forearm. James wasn't quite sure why, for the effect was merely to leave a streak of lipstick on her chin. The woman nervously twisted and played with her wedding ring, spinning it around her finger. She held out her hand. James thought she felt surprisingly cold. "I deserve to be happy," she said. James thought she looked incredibly sad. "To have some fun. Don't you think?" She squeezed his hand.

*****

Shirley pushed open the door to the pub.

The heat inside, in contrast to the typical South Wales cold outside, blasted her cheeks like a hair dryer. It was deadly quiet. She wasn't exactly expecting it to be Saturday Night at the Palladium, but it was like a morgue. She wasn't much of a regular anymore. She hadn't been here since Herbert had surprised James with his elaborate, secretive plans. Now it was her turn to surprise James. Shirley felt unusually nervous all of a sudden. Maybe a quick drink would help.

"Where is that husband of mine?" She smiled. "Is he hiding in the toilets again?"

Ron looked around nervously, liked she'd caught him behind the bar in just his underpants, or maybe in stockings and high heels. "You've just missed him I'm afraid, Shirley," he said.

Shirley couldn't quite put her finger on it, but it was like Ron

At Least the Pink Elephants are Laughing at Us

wanted to tell her something, but either didn't have the courage or the tact to do so. His dad was just the same, always covering for punters, especially James's old man, by all accounts. Shirley felt deflated. She had made these plans, and now where was that blasted husband of hers? Maybe he had stumbled back home in a drunken stupor or was walking the streets, completely lost. Either way, he was probably no good to man nor beast, let alone a woman with passion and romance flowing through her veins. She felt foolish. Even Ron could tell that she had dressed up, had tried to surprise him, by that bleeding pitying look he gave her. She felt like she had been stood up for a blind date.

"Stay for a drink?" Ron asked. And then he reluctantly added, "on the house, like."

Shirley smiled weakly. It really was sweet of the man. Everybody knew Ron didn't dish out free drinks lightly. Again, just like his old man, apparently. "Thank you," she said. "But I better be off. See if I can find that blasted husband of mine." She gave him a wry look and added "Give him a clip round the ear hole for being such a pain, if you see him."

She let the heavy wooden door shut behind her and headed into the cold, in search of her wayward husband.

*****

James gripped both hands on the rusty metal chains and casually swung back and forth on the black plastic seat. He had been on these swings so many times, just him and Rory, and sometimes with Shirley. The woman, this relative stranger, did exactly the same on the swing next to him.

"It's funny how things work out, don't you think," she said.

"It certainly is," James muttered, but really he was thinking, when did this woman become a flipping philosopher?

"These swings are obviously intended for young children, but I bet my bottom dollar, or at least my husband's bottom dollar, that the most vivid memories of the park are when you are a teenager hanging out with your mates, drinking cider and you know..."

"Yeah," James added quickly, although he was still thinking about Rory on the swings asking him to pusher harder, to push higher.

James felt that he was sinking lower and lower though. He didn't want to be here with this woman anymore. It was suddenly bitterly cold. The effect of the drink was beginning to wear off. His thoughts were racing and the park around him was spinning. Maybe he had reached the high and was now on the way down, head first and without a parachute. There was part of him that was on the floor, heavy and low and lifeless. He guiltily wondered what Shirley was up to, whether she'd be worrying he wasn't home yet, if Rory was sleeping through soundly. It was time he headed home. Part of him felt fantastic, on top of the world, and another part of him wished that he had never started speaking to this woman; this woman who now saddled him, who had both legs round his waist, on this flimsy plastic seat that was designed for a child.

She kissed him.

James panicked. He couldn't think straight. He wasn't sure how he could push her away without toppling her over, banging her head on the hard floor below. James wasn't sure whether he wanted to push her away. He didn't want to hurt her head or her feelings. And she wanted *him.* No. He needed to do the right thing. Tell her to get off him. Go home to his wife and child.

James pulled away, struggled to explain that this was all a mistake, but when he opened his eyes, nestled his chin on the woman's shoulders, he stared straight into the eyes of the most beautiful woman in the whole of Bridgend, who was stood there, watching him.

"Shirley!" he shouted, at the top of his voice, but he knew all too well that it was far too late, that it was impossible to do anything about something that had already happened.

14 – Every Cloud has a Silver Lining. Doesn't it?

The park was as flat as the Sahara Desert and stretched for miles. The grass was well maintained, cut short, and it was primarily a healthy luminous green, with lighter, worn patches where cricket was played and muddy, barer sections where goalmouth action took place.

This was Wednesday morning, though, and the park was void of activity. Mandy sat in the middle of the wooden bench, her knees pressed together. She wished she had something to occupy her hands – nothing weird or sordid; she was in the middle of a park, after all – just a book or (slightly more "out there") a Rubik's cube. There just wasn't much to do but check her watch every ten – oh, twenty now – seconds.

There was a tiny dot on the grass on the other side of the park, on the lawn. It looked like an ant, Mandy thought, but then didn't everything that was far away? A second dot moved towards the first dot, and then a third, much slower dot followed in pursuit. What was it all about? What was going on? Mandy concluded, with as much rationality as she could muster, that the first dot was a person who had been lying on the grass in the middle of the park until they had been woken by a dog and its owner. Wow, she thought, I bet that first person has a story to tell! But that rationale seemed a bit out there, even for Bridgend. Mandy concluded it was early and she needed more caffeine.

A jogger caught her attention. The jogger didn't have much competition on the attention stakes, not anymore. The jogger was another tiny dot that grew bigger with every painfully slow, steady step. Really, Mandy thought, was this guy even moving *forwards*? Was he jogging on the spot? She felt guilty when he eventually moved close enough to identify that he was a gentleman of advanced years or, less politically correct: an old dude. She thought of James then, not because he was old, although of course he was getting on a bit, but because he was always belittling this politically correct world they lived in. Mandy was careful to respect anybody over the age of fifty: after all, they probably fought for us in the war, didn't they? Good on you, she thought. Did that sound condescending. Was Herbert rubbing off on her? The jogger, though, had the steely perseverance and determination of a rambler climbing Snowdon. Apart from a red patch circling his nose and mouth, the rest of his face was deathly grey and sprinkled with liver spots. He had dark prominent sweat patches under each arm. Mandy gave him an encouraging smile, but – cheeky shit – the jogger glared and grizzled at her like *she* was the crazy one. That was *it*, Mandy thought. She wasn't going to do any more deeds for these coffin dodgers like *ever* again.

"Has he stood you up?" the man gasped.
"What?" Mandy asked, perplexed.
"Your blind date."

Mandy was about to explain that she wasn't waiting for a date, that she was far too popular and attractive to ever be stood up, but she could see that the man wasn't listening, for he was focussed on the long, unforgiving path ahead. It troubled her that he would probably go to the grave thinking the poor girl sat on a park bench that Wednesday morning was stood up.

This was seriously not a good idea. Her life was better than this. She shouldn't be sat on a bench in the middle of a deserted park on a Wednesday morning, anxiously checking her watch, receiving sympathy from an old man in a tracksuit, not when it was somewhere between coat and no coat weather (it was early spring, after all, and it was always a dilemma in spring) and, as she'd optimistically opted for no coat, her fingertips were now pink and she left a cloud of steam every time she flipping breathed out! Mandy checked her watch again. Quarter past.

Fifteen minutes late.

*****

James was awoken by a wet, slobbering tongue enthusiastically and hungrily licking his face.

He jumped to his feet with his hands held out, trying to give

At Least the Pink Elephants are Laughing at Us

the conflicting signal that yes he was friend but also, please, *please*stay away. Please! They say dogs can smell fear, James thought; in which case he must absolutely reek. This was one of those athletic dogs with long legs, impressive muscle tone and low body fat percentage; the personal trainer of the dog world.

"Polly, come here!"

The dog turned and dutifully sped off in the direction of its owner, who proceeded to crouch down and put a lead on the collar. That beast should be muzzled, James thought. Just look at those gigantic, sharp teeth. Dogs love balls, and this one would be able to chew off *his* balls without breaking sweat. And what was with the name? She wasn't a budgie. That dog should be called Tyson or Bruno or Fury or Vin Diesel or something; not Polly. Dear God Almighty.

"Don't worry, she wouldn't hurt a fly," the owner, a middle-aged lady with red apples for cheeks, said.

That's what they said about every dog, James thought. "It's fine," James said. "I'm a dog lover myself," he lied. James only loved dogs if they won him some money on the races. James kept his eyes on Polly, just in case she made a move for his crown jewels.

The woman wriggled her nose. Concern was etched on her face. "Are you quite alright, dear?" she asked, looking him up and down. She was the sort of woman James could imagine working down a charity shop, sorting through dirty linen and disregarded possessions, because it was the right thing to do and not just to fill the gap between *The Wright Show* and *Judge Rinder*.

James was disorientated. He felt like he did when he stayed on the roundabout at the swings for too long with Rory and when he got off he stumbled around like he'd finished off a six pack of Stella. Nothing was quite in focus. Swings. That was where it had all gone wrong. James was aware he'd been lying on the ground for goodness knows how long, his eyes to the heavens, his arms straight and to his sides, a perfect stance to be measured for a coffin. He knew the grass was wet, because he could feel it seeping through his clothes, probably leaving his skin pink and blotchy. James was under no illusions; this probably wasn't his greatest moment ever. These were not ideal sleeping conditions.

When he looked around now, he was still amazed to realise he hadn't bothered trying to hide or blend into the surroundings. No, he'd decided to sleep right in the middle of the playing fields, where he was probably most exposed to ridicule and most vulnerable to attack. He was glad the park was deserted. Was that a jogger in the distance? Was that jogger even *moving*?

He instinctively grabbed for his suitcase, then let go of it.

"Oh, yes," James said, nervously tapping his foot on the soggy grass. "You know how it is. One of those mad, mad nights! It's good to let loose once in a while, don't you think?"

James was aware that the woman's idea of a mad, mad night was probably very different from his own. She probably felt like a rebel when she bought an extra card down the bingo on a Thursday night. The woman didn't say anything though, just kept looking at James with those sympathetic, concerned eyes. James remembered people looked at him like that after his dad died.

"Seriously though," James continued, "I'll be fine. *Promise.*"

James could tell the woman was far from convinced, but convinced enough to know she wasn't going to get any more information out of this stray. The woman smiled and walked away, leaving James alone in the middle of a field, clutching his suitcase.

*****

Mandy jumped, her buttocks nearly leaving the hard, unforgiving bench.

"Jesus Christ," she said, high-pitched, like she was pre-pubescent again and her voice had yet to break. "Are you trying to give me a heart attack? You scared the life out of me."

The man was sat right next to her, looking straight ahead, his face expressionless. "It is my job, Ms William, to not be noticed."

Mandy took the man in. He was probably about thirty, but looked like he had a seriously committed moisturising routine, like Patrick Bateman from *American Psycho*. Apart from some subtle laughter lines, his skin was as smooth as a baby's bottom.

At Least the Pink Elephants are Laughing at Us

But it was his physique, or lack of, that astonished her. He was a grown man with the build of a boy. Sat upright, back ninety degrees, his legs dangled, the tips of his shoes barely touched the floor. He really was some sort of man-child, Mandy thought. He'd obviously decided this was coat weather, for he was wrapped in a navy duffel coat Paddington Bear would have been envious of. Tied elaborately around his neck was a black and white woollen scarf.

"You're late" Mandy stated. "I've been sat here on a bench in the middle of the park with nipples like bullets for twenty minutes."

The strange little man was unaffected by her outburst. He continued looking straight ahead. His voice was monotone. "I apologise for that," he said. "But I had to ascertain whether you were genuinely serious. If you were not prepared to wait then I would know you weren't. Not really. I only work with people who are serious, you see. I've been here the whole time."

Oh Jesus, Mandy thought. Was this guy actually *trying* to piss her off? And possibly more importantly, was he some kind of weirdo? Where had he been? When she looked at him though, when she took the full extent of him in, she just couldn't imagine he could possibly be any threat. She'd just sit on him if he tried any silly business.

"So, Ms Williams. Do you have as we agreed?"

Mandy unzipped her handbag, pulled out the sealed brown envelope; handed it to the man. He slipped it inside his coat in a single fluid motion. He didn't utter a word. Not even "thank you." It felt like a drug deal. Or, at least, what Mandy considered a drug deal would feel like. Or maybe a porn DVD exchange. Mandy didn't need to imagine that one.

"Don't you want to count it?" she asked.

"I now know you are serious, Ms Williams, so I see no need to count the money. I know you are as committed as I am to finding your father."

They both sat there, not talking, not doing *anything*. Mandy wondered what was supposed to happen next. "Is what we are doing illegal or something?" she asked.

The man smiled now. He chuckled. "No. Why would you ask that?"

"I don't know. It all feels so very secretive."

"I'm a private detective, Ms Williams," the man stated. "Things are supposed to be secretive."

The detective stood up, held out his hand and Mandy shook it.

"I will be in touch," he said, bowing his head, before disappearing as soundlessly as he had appeared.

Mandy was left sitting on the bench on her own again.

I'd better get up and go, she thought, before some old jogger starts giving me abuse again or I get attacked by a dog.

*****

James didn't know what he was expected to do now or where he was expected to go, but he did know he couldn't stay standing in the middle of the playing fields. And so he walked. Anywhere. James dragged the suitcase up the slippery steps. Slippery when wet, he thought. No shit. Bang. Bang. Bang. His body felt itchy. He scratched at his arm and became aware that he had been bitten. The sweat on his forehead felt cold, but it felt much worse when it trickled into his eyes. He wanted to get somewhere – quickly – where he wasn't exposed, where he wasn't the guy everybody stopped and pointed at, somewhere he could try and put his thoughts into some kind of order. He wanted to hide, to escape, anywhere that was away from where he was now. That was his initial aim. He couldn't think beyond that.

Maybe more out of habit, James pulled his wallet out of his pocket. His expectations were suitably low. There were too many coins of the wrong colour and not enough notes of the right colour. James wondered, half heartedly, whether there was enough for a cheeky Chinese. He needed something to pull him through this lull. It could be his last hurrah. He dismissed the idea as fantasy. There was a bank card in one of the slots in his wallet, teasing and mocking him. The last time James had used the card he'd closed his eyes and hoped for the best, and was relieved when the machine spat out some money. Shirley was the one who looked after the money. Shirley was the one who looked after absolutely everything. She joked that there were two

At Least the Pink Elephants are Laughing at Us

children in the house. James knew she wasn't really joking. Shirley did the shopping, bought all the necessities for the family. "No, James; fags and booze are not a necessity." She distributed anything that was left over from the budget to James as and when, like a schoolboy given his pocket money.

Shirley.

James held down the button on the side of his phone in hope. It was dead in the early hours of the morning when he was walking the cold hard streets, and so it should be dead now, too. There was no reason to believe his phone had miraculously been brought back to life. He just wanted the phone to have enough energy for him to make a single call, like he was under arrest. He stared at the screen, waited for it to illuminate. It stayed dark. Dead.

James continued walking, pulling the suitcase along the bumpy pavement.

He hoped that, if he kept busy, for long enough, then he would be able to blank out the thoughts that were relentlessly trying to invade his mind, the thoughts that were trying to tell him he had absolutely – totally – fucked everything up.

*****

The phone rang. Although he wanted it to be answered, hoped he could get the conversation completed at the earliest possible opportunity, there was a real part of him that dreaded the thought of it being answered, wanted to delay the conversation for as long as was feasibly possibly.

"Hello."

"Hello Dad."

"How are you, Connor?"

"I'm good thank you. Listen, Dad, I'm sorry for what I said the other day, okay? Sometimes I just say things I shouldn't, you know?

"I know. And thank you. But listen, we need to have a proper chat soon. There are things I want to say to you, Connor."

"Okay, Dad. We will..."

*****

This cul-de-sac is pure suburbia, James thought. Suburban hell.

And it had been one hell of a day. James quickly realised it wasn't easy appearing invisible in your home town when you were a fairly familiar face and you were carting your life's possessions around in a suitcase. There weren't as many quiet, derelict streets in Bridgend as he'd imagined, and the streets that *were* remotely quiet and derelict were unnecessarily long and straight, which meant people spotted you, as their sole target, from miles away. There were also many more schools in Bridgend than James had ever bothered to notice, and each school seemed to educate an overflowing abundance of cheeky bastard Chubby Brown clones with an endless supply of jokes about homeless people. James was tempted to say it wasn't like that in his day, but he wasn't a hypocrite and of course it was fucking like that in his day. In the end James gave up and he spent the majority of the day from hell in the leisure centre. He parked his suitcase in the darkest, remotest corner, squeezed between two vending machines, and then tried to blend in, roaming between the drinks machines, the sports halls, the swimming pool, the gym and the library. He thought about trying to sneak into the showers during the afternoon quiet but thought better of it. James was everywhere, but nowhere for too long. The tedium and monotony and sheer loneliness of it all was unbearable. When he'd had as much as he could possibly take, James returned to the darkest, remotest corner he could find and was relieved to find his suitcase still squeezed between the two vending machines.

And now James was in suburbia, a setting straight from a glossy brochure, where the residents were young and beautiful and *smiled,* the dogs were bouncy and free of fleas, the lawns were cut in straight lines and the identical houses were adorned with colourful, blossoming hanging baskets. On Sundays the dad's washed their cars in short-sleeves, the mum's donned their apron's and cooked the roast whilst the children happily practised their French or attended their piano lessons. Perfect lives in an imperfect world, James thought. He couldn't stand it. He much preferred his messy life, with his rascal of a kid and his

At Least the Pink Elephants are Laughing at Us

sexy wife plucked from the depths of Ponty. Or, he grudgingly admitted, allowing memories to enter his throbbing head just momentarily so he could at least take a reality check, hand burning from pulling the suitcase for too long, he much preferred the life he did have yesterday. *Yesterday, all my troubles seemed so far away.* James stuck a middle finger up in the air. Fuck you, Beatles, he thought.

James was aware he was a blot on the landscape, like an old unoccupied building with boarded windows and graffiti on the walls in a modern, clinically revamped shopping centre. James stood with one hand on a wall. His forehead felt like a woodpecker was viciously and cruelly tapping away at it. James glanced at the impressive black metal gate with an almost impulsive regularity.

All of this was familiar to him, of course. He had hardly wandered onto unchartered territory. James had been here many times before. He breathed deeply and wiped his salty forehead with the grubby sleeve of his shirt. He needed to just go for it. There was nothing to lose, and it was now or never. One. Two. Three. Four. On "five" James pushed open the metal gate, entered the wide and expansive block drive and then shut the gate gently behind him. A forecourt light illuminated the driveway. James stood in the porch and then tapped at the door.

There was movement inside the house and then the door opened.

The familiar face that greeted him looked alarmed.

"James," he said, courteously, almost a question.

"Terry," James replied. "It's good to see you, buddy."

*****

It was like most things in life, he thought, as he pushed a fistful of popcorn into his ready and waiting mouth: you build things up and then you're always let down.

He told himself he was having a great time. His *Facebook* page would most likely confirm that later, too. But, as he shuffled uncomfortably on his seat, transferring weight from one buttock to the other and then back again, he knew that – really – he was damn bored.

Everybody asked if he'd seen the movie. Oh, you must see it! If you see one movie this year then it must be this one! All the usual clichés, of course. But – again – he allowed himself to get wrapped up in the hype. Sure, he was in no doubt it was a good movie. There was plenty going on, it was a complex and clever storyline no doubt, and the special effects were truly exceptional. He could imagine the critics gleefully scribbling away an array of superlatives. But the biggest problem, the one he just couldn't get away from, was he didn't have a clue what was going on. Not the foggiest. Not since the opening minute. Maybe even since the opening credits. Everybody was trying to kill everybody else, he knew that. He did feel (perhaps a little cynically?) that once you'd seen one person shot in the head at close range then you'd seen a hundred and one people shot at close range in the head. It was like the Red Light District in Amsterdam all over again. *Oh, a dildo! How very exciting and outrageously naughty!* Once you'd seen one dildo though, you'd seen them all, however much variation they offered with shape and size and bumps and curves.

He leaned over to the woman sat next to him.

"Do you know what the flying *fuck* is going on?" he whispered.

Luckily, she was not just a random woman trying to watch the film. She was there – intentionally – to watch the film with him. She still looked at him like he was an invalid. "This is like the most basic plot ever," she stated. "How can you *possibly* not know what is going on?"

He shrugged his shoulders, like there was no rational explanation for his stupidity, that he was possibly just born this dumb.

His pocket vibrated. There *is* a God, he thought. This gave him a bona fide, genuine reason to get up out of that damn tiny chair and leave the cinema. Get some light! Even if it was still dark in the foyer! He'd already been up for a piss twice and people were beginning to give him dirty looks, like he had a bladder problem or was taking drugs in the cubicle. If he held his phone up high by his chest then they would know the score. This guy had friends who were actually calling him! On the phone! It was nothing to do with a weak bladder, okay!

At Least the Pink Elephants are Laughing at Us

"I better get this," he whispered. "It could be important."

The doors swung behind him. He clicked the button and put the phone to his ear.

"William."

"Mandy."

"I thought you said you were in the cinema?"

Why did she phone him if she knew he wasn't supposed to pick the phone up?

"I am and I'm having a great time, thank you very much. If you watch one film this year, you must watch this one! But I answered the phone because it was my dear little sister, didn't I?"

There was a heavy, knowing chortle on the other end of the line. "You *hate* the cinema, William. I know you. You can't sit still for more than two minutes without fannying around and getting ants in your pants. I bet you couldn't wait to get out of there, could you?"

"How can I help you, sis?" William asked, feigning impatience. "I really need to get back to this film. I've been following the plot very closely."

"*Whatever*," Mandy said. "I'll cut to the chase. We're both *very* busy people. I just wanted to tell you that I have received an email."

"Your first one? Well done, Mandy. I hate to tell you, but people have been exchanging emails for quite some time now. Even Mum is on the World Wide Web now you know. I bought her a computer. Before you did."

"An email from him. The detective. I met him this morning in the park and then he emailed me this evening and said he already has a lead."

Silence.

"William?"

"Yes. Sorry. That's great. Does he know where Dad is then?" William asked.

"Yes."

"Where?"

"Apparently he is in Cornwall."

"*Cornwall...?*"

"Yeah, you know, where they make pasties and talk funny.

What's wrong with Cornwall?"

William was struggling for words. He started using his hands to express himself, but that didn't work well on the phone. "Oh – err- nothing," he said. "It's just difficult to picture him there, isn't it?" he offered, before continuing. "Just be careful, okay, sis? I don't want you to get hurt. I do love you, you know? Better get back to the film, okay...?"

"Oh, okay. I love you too, bro."

"Oh," William continued, remembering something, something important. "Does Mum know? Have you told Mum?"

Pause. "I'm working on that," Mandy whispered. "Bye then, bro."

The phone went dead. The doors swung open. His girlfriend appeared, hot and flushed and panicked.

"Will? Is everything alright? You look like you've seen a ghost or something."

William faked a smile and bounced on the tips of his toes back towards the cinema. "Sorry! Everything's just fine! Now let's get back to this movie! I can't believe I'm missing it!"

*****

Terry had been working all day, just like every day.

He put his daughter, Cat, to bed and read her a book, one of those that combined entertainment with education, which were all the rage nowadays.

"Night night, Daddy."

Terry needed to work all day because his eldest daughter was twenty and in her second year of University. It was fortunate Terry owned his own building firm that had survived the recession and come out stronger for it, because he needed every penny he could get. Sally had been meticulously planned after visits to the fertility clinic and plenty of worry and anguish. Cat, on the other hand, twelve years and countless grey hairs later, had been a beautiful surprise; a miracle.

With Daddy duties completed for the day, Terry headed downstairs and tidied up in the way he normally did; he put some stray magazines in the recycling bin and wiped the odd surface. Michelle called it "Daddy Cleaning"; he was "Half a Job

Hughes" when he was at home. Michelle kissed his forehead, stroked his chin and said she would see him upstairs. Terry was old enough (far too old) and wise enough (plenty of room to get wiser) to know this didn't necessarily mean Daddy and Mummy time. It was normal for Michelle to sneak under the covers an hour before Terry with one of her beloved Catherine Cookson's. Terry didn't mind, but they did need to make sure they didn't let things drift. He'd known others in the same place who were suddenly sipping coffee on the marriage counselling settee (apparently you always got a complimentary cup of coffee, which was possibly a silver lining) or in the divorce courts (where you had to pay an extortionate price at the machine that gave no change). He loved Michelle too much for that. Tonight though, as with last night, Terry was content to settle down with his feet up and browse the multitude of pointless channels on the television.

And then there was a knock on the front door, a meek and tentative tap, like a child in a goblin costume (or any other costume, really) at Halloween.

"Oh for *God's* sake," Terry said. Cat was in bed, but that didn't necessarily mean she was asleep. It was odd getting a visitor at this time, he considered. His initial, gloomy thought was that maybe it was a door-to-door salesman, trying to plug him yet another charity or a new drive or triple or quadruple glazing, whatever the latest craze was, but he glanced at his watch and thought it was too late for that. Terry opened the door thinking this could not possibly be good news.

And boy, was he was right.

Terry's best friend in the whole world stood at his door, but Terry still did a double-take. James looked like he'd been sleeping down Merthyr Mawr sand dunes or washed up ashore at Ogmore. Dirt was ingrained into his face. His eyes looked sullen and heavy. He stooped forward with his shoulders hunched. The long hair was still tied back in a ponytail but was greasy and oily and just a little pathetic.

"James," Terry said. He was aware his tone was probably pretty neutral, but it was the best he could fathom.

"Terry. It's good to see you, buddy."

James held out his hand and Terry shook it. James squeezed

hard, like he was trying to compensate for something, maybe to show he was still a strong alpha-male. His hand felt rough and flaky. James talked fast, words firing out of his mouth at a rapid rate. "Hello mate," he said. "Listen, I know it's late and I'm dead sorry like, but is there any chance of coming in? I wouldn't normally ask. You know me. I won't stay long. Promise."

Terry glanced at the suitcase and smiled at the irony of the promise. "Of course, mate," he said. "Come in."

James looked around the place with big, awe-inspired eyes, like it was the first time he'd been there. James ran his middle finger in a line down the wallpaper and glanced at the impressively high ceiling; an estate agent evaluating the house.

"Tea?" Terry asked, already heading to the kitchen.

"That would really hit the mark, big man."

"Make yourself at home. Take your coat off. Take a seat."

Terry was aware he wouldn't normally be so hospitable. He felt untypically on edge. He didn't need to ask James to make himself at home. James was more than capable, and very willing, to dump himself on the settee and pull open a cold one. "We have the house to ourselves, mate. Michelle and Cat are both in bed. My dad is down the pub. Good timing, really."

It *was* great to see him. It was *always* great to see James, and he saw him often. They'd been close as thieves since childhood. Michelle joked that she didn't worry Terry would run off with another woman, she worried he would run off with James. She was forever asking "so how's your *boyfriend*, Tel?" It was all in jest. Terry knew she thought their friendship was sweet; cute even. She was glad Terry had a friend he could rely on, even if the guy was a million miles from being perfect.

Terry didn't walk around with a bag over his head though. He was no longer the big, dumb kid at school. He was now the big, responsible kid who worked. Terry knew even James didn't normally turn up late and unannounced at his front door with a suitcase. James normally turned up unannounced earlier in the evening for beers.

He sat down opposite James, who stared at the Big 50 mug held between both hands like a precious stone. There were a few chips in the china now; the mug was a good few years old. He puckered his lips and blew at the steam, causing a slight ripple.

At Least the Pink Elephants are Laughing at Us

"This is just the ticket, mate," James said.

"Keeping well? How's Shirley and the little man?" Terry asked. Jesus, he thought. He couldn't keep up this pretence for too long. He dreaded the answer his mate was going to give.

James placed his tea down on the coffee table. Terry pondered why it was called a coffee table when it welcomed all sorts of beverages, hot and cold, alcoholic and non-alcohol, fizzy and still; but then he told himself: *focus*. His friend was obviously gearing up to tell him something important and he was getting embroiled in a trivial, albeit interesting, personal discussion.

"Well, it's a bit of a mixed bag to be honest with you, mate. Despite a recent couple of set backs, I'm still confident about the comedy lark I told you about. If we sort out our differences then I still think the three of us and Herbert could make it to the Fringe, and that would be quite something."

"That's great, then..."

"But on the downside, Shirley has thrown me out. She caught me in, how should I call it, a compromising position? I'm basically homeless, mate. My life is pretty much over, you know?"

Oh right, Terry thought. Bit of a shit sandwich really, wasn't it? And the "shit" really, really stank.

Terry felt saddened, and confused, and disappointed. Hadn't his best friend learnt from the last time? Was he going to blow it all yet again...?

He needed to say something, and snappy. "Sorry to hear that, mate," he said. "But as you said, at least the comedy is going well. Every cloud has a silver lining and all that, you know?"

Damn. Damn. Damn. Terry wasn't happy with his reply, but then he had no idea what else he was supposed to say. He wasn't trained for this. He wasn't a counsellor. And he wasn't a woman. They were blokes. They weren't built to talk about these difficult things. They were best mates and the two of them still had secrets they still hadn't talked about since they were kids. What was he supposed to say? Tell him that it was awful, that he had probably ruined his life? How would *that* help?

"So the Edinburgh Fringe?" he asked. "Isn't that the big comedy festival in, er, Edinburgh, like?"

"That's the one," James replied, smiling, seemingly happy that his mate recognised it. "Fuck knows where Edinburgh is, but it's going to be magic. But tough. Performers from all over go there. The best in the business. And so the crowd won't accept any old rubbish, you know?"

"You'll be fine. You're made for comedy. I've always said my mate is the funniest guy in South Wales," Terry said, truthfully. He remembered that time in classroom when he had told that funny story about what love meant to him. Or at least, Terry assumed it was meant to be a funny story.

James beamed. It seemed for a moment that James had forgotten he'd been thrown out of his house, that he was effectively homeless (well, there was really no need for "effectively" was there?) and his life was in absolute tatters, for just in that brief moment Terry's best friend had a glint in his eye, pondering the possibilities of the Edinburgh Festival Fringe.

"More tea, mate?" Terry asked.

"Aye," James replied. "That will be golden, like."

15 – Mr Demotivator

Babs was glad the comedians were back for their second meeting. They made her laugh. Admittedly, not necessarily for the right reasons, but it was a step in the right direction, she guessed.

The hall was getting in the way of her busy social life, and so she was glad tonight was a group she actually liked. Her online dating had been firing on all cylinders lately. It seemed there were plenty of young, sterile men in Bridgend interested in older women, and Babs was more than happy to oblige to their affections. At times it had been wild. She had relived her youth. Things had taken an unexpected turn recently, though. Babs had met a gentleman in the same age bracket, a gentleman who was looking for a lady to spend the rest of his life with. Babs so had so enjoyed their nights at the theatre and meals out in fancy restaurants. He was so kind and considerate and funny. The thought of becoming the woman the man spent the rest of his life with was becoming more and more appealing.

Babs kept her mind clear by analysing the mood of the group. It was another of her fruitful distraction techniques. This group was such an unusual assortment that they were more difficult to understand than most. At the first meeting there had undoubtedly been confusion amongst the group. Maybe "bewilderment" was a more apt choice of word? Only Herbert appeared to have any real idea what they were there for, and even that was debatable. And there was suspicion. Did Herbert, who seemed to be an intelligent guy, *really* think this assembly of misfits had a chance of succeeding at this big Edinburgh event? Excitement. Maybe he knew something they didn't? Perhaps one of them had what it took to become the next Joe Pasquale or Jim Davidson? And hunger. That Mandy definitely had an appetite, demonstrated by the way she quickly devoured the sandwiches.

It had been a few weeks since that first meeting and the

mood at this meeting was undoubtedly even worse. Suspicion had turned to cynicism. Hope had turned to despair. It was not so difficult to analyse the mood this time. The group were all, plainly speaking, properly "down in the shitter."

Herbert arrived early, again, and again he was the poster boy for positive energy and charisma. The man oozed self-help book with every step and every breath he took. Herbert had his flipchart and array of felt-tips with him and, of course, his black briefcase. They exchanged pleasantries when Babs unlocked the door and she could tell, by the pleading look in his eyes, that if she asked any questions then he would open up, tell her all his woes. Babs didn't ask any questions. She didn't think it would do any good and, besides, she was paid (peanuts, she might add) to clean and look after the hall, not to counsel. Who did he think she was? *Dear Deidre?*

When the others started trickling through the door in single numbers, like lemmings ready to walk off the cliff, Babs could tell why Herbert was struggling.

The older guy, James, was keen to make sure everybody was aware of his presence at the first meeting, but now he limply shook Herbert's hand and muttered a few harmless pleasantries. Who pulled *his* chain? The black guy, Connor, apparently thought it was a fancy dress event. He wore baggy shorts below his knees and a multi-coloured Hawaiian shirt that would have made Magnum PI's moustache bristle with jealousy. Connor shook hands and nodded his head, but then tapped his feet and paced around in a circle at a distance, making it clear he was not up for conversation. The girl, Mandy, was the last to arrive, all smiles and bouncing bosom. Unsurprisingly, after getting through the required pleasantries, Mandy was straight into the sandwiches. It was if the girl thought food was still rationed. Babs considered that Mandy was definitely the shining light of the group this evening.

"Let's get this show moving!" Herbert exclaimed, hurrying over to his beloved flipchart, felt tip already in hand. His enthusiasm was met with groans.

Herbert flipped the cover to reveal a blank page and then, meticulously, he drew a straight line down the middle from top to bottom. Babs could tell he was the type who liked order, who probably made a shopping list before he ventured to Asda. On one side of the page he wrote "positives" and on the other he wrote "negatives." He turned to his audience exposing a nervous grin.

"It was a bit of a rollercoaster ride that last show," Herbert began. "Full of "ups" and "downs" and not so many "straights." But sometimes life is a rollercoaster and you just have to ride it..."

"Fuck you, Ronan Keating," James plainly retorted.

Herbert continued without pausing for breath. "Can one of you start me off with what you thought went well, and maybe what didn't go well?"

The trio looked at each other, waiting for somebody else to pipe up. When nobody did, James shrugged his shoulders and offered, "It was shit, Herbie, that's what it was."

Herbert seemed happy enough with this response. He pointed his pen at James, said thank you for getting the ball rolling, turned to his flip chart and wrote the response word for word on the sheet of paper. "Any others?"

"My act was an absolute embarrassment," Connor stated. Babs noticed James nodded his head in agreement. Mandy glanced at her phone, like she was checking a message.

Herbert took exception to this response. He was the leader, after all, Babs considered, and he was responsible for keeping the pack positive and their eyes on the ball, to inspire them, like Winston Churchill. "Oh I wouldn't say that, Connor," Herbert said, shaking his head. "It had its moments."

Connor stared at him with wide, disbelieving eyes. "Some guy tried to *hit* me," he said. "They *hated* me."

"Ah, yes," Herbert countered, "but they were passionate with their hate, weren't they! There is nothing worse than having an audience who is indifferent to you. You provoked a strong reaction, you stirred their emotions, and that can only be a good thing, Connor. Mind you, one thing I will say is that it was as though you got your jokes from watching comedians on *YouTube*..."

Babs stifled a laugh with a loud cough. All the eyes in the group turned to her. Babs quickly busied herself with her duster.

"I have no idea why you would think that," Connor replied.

His eyes flickered to the floor. "It was a nightmare. The hecklers were getting personal. I don't know why the security didn't do anything about it."

Herbert didn't even pause before replying, with a deep sigh, that "It was the security *doing* the heckling, Connor."

James put his feet up on the chair next to him and folded his arms. "Let's be open and honest about this, Herbie," he said. "Tell us what you really thought about our acts."

Herbert didn't appear too keen to do this. The poor man was going to need plenty of prodding. He wiped his forehead with his sleeve, leaving a dark patch. "I don't think it is a good idea to put question marks in your mind at this early stage," he said. "We are still developing and honing our act. Nobody expects it to be perfect."

"Go on," Mandy encouraged. "We need to know. Better coming from you than a boisterous, critical Edinburgh crowd crying out for blood, don't you think?"

The others guffawed and snorted their approval.

"Okay, if you are *sure* this is a good idea," Herbert said. "Remember that this is early days and, apart from Mandy, you guys have not performed for a long time. It is natural to experience some initial difficulties. I therefore set my expectations very low. And, admittedly, you performed at a much *lower* level than I expected. A comedian should be looking for six genuine, heartfelt laughs per minute of their act. I counted zero of these. None of your acts were what I would call "tight." They were all over the place, like you were making it up as you go along. If you perform like that at Edinburgh, we will be run out of town. But the good thing is that I am confident we can improve and, rest assured, we *will* improve."

The three of them didn't speak for a few moments. James, who had taken his feet off the chair and unfolded his arms, put his feet back on the chair and folded his arms. Connor put his hand through his tight locks.

"Listen to Billy Big Bollocks," James said.

Mandy cut in quick, "It's easy for you to stand up there and criticise us like that, Herbert, with your big pen, your big flipboard and your even bigger ego," she said, her cheeks puffed out, her bosom jiggling, "but I'd like to see you up on stage!"

The others shouted their agreement. Babs decided to join in. She waved her duster in the air like it was a flag.

"But you said you wanted me to give it to you straight," Herbert protested, trying to hide his pen in his pocket and seemingly missing the hole so he stabbed his leg. "You were the ones who said to tell you how it is. I was the one who said it wasn't a good idea."

"You're supposed to be encouraging us," James said. "Building our confidence. Not putting us down and then sticking the boot in!"

"I was thinking of quitting before tonight," Connor added, "and I was hoping you would talk me out of it. But now after your little talk, I am *definitely* quitting!"

Herbert clawed his hands into his scalp and literally looked like he was going to pull his hair out. The ship was going under water, and it wasn't a submarine; it was sinking, and fast. James was already on his feet, heading to the door, but he was walking painfully slowly. Babs could tell he didn't really want to leave, that he was just putting on a show. The poor guy was crying out for somebody to call him back. Moments passed and James was almost walking on the spot. It was getting embarrassing, Babs thought, with a wry smile.

"James, not so quick!" Herbert finally bleated, putting him out of his misery.

James sighed. He stopped walking and waited for Herbert to reel him in like a fish that had taken the bait. This was last chance saloon for Herbert, Babs thought. Make or break. She clung to her duster for dear life. The excitement of it all was beginning to get to her. She absent-mindedly brushed the fabric against the skirting board; she could virtually see her face in it by now whilst she waited for Herbert to make his next move.

"Take a seat, James," Herbert said. Babs was surprised and – possibly - impressed by the forcefulness of his instruction. She thought he looked awfully handsome when he was strong and commanding. Like a young Gregory Peck. Babs willed him to deliver the goods, to get going when the going got tough. Herbert pulled his shoulders back and pushed his chest forward. "I think my intentions were good but my delivery was poor. I just don't want to put you under any false illusions of the work that needs to be done. I'm not going to lie to you. We have a mountain to climb – bigger than Snowdon – if we are to perform at Edinburgh..."

"This isn't getting any better, Herbert," Mandy muttered.

"But the fact is," Herbert continued, gaining pace and volume as his words flowed. "I just know I have the right team to take the place by storm. We just need to work out our strategy and put together a plan. Let's write tonight off as a bad day at the office. We have our gig on Friday night. I want us to go ahead with that, put everything into it, and then meet again next week as usual. If at our next meeting we agree that the idea is unworkable then we will call it a day. But at least we can say we gave it a good go. Are you in?"

They glanced at each other. They were each daring one another to make the first move.

"I'm in," Mandy said, jutting out her considerable chest.

"Count me in Herbie. Count me in," James said.

Now all eyes, including Babs's, zoned in on Connor. Babs squirted some polish on the kitchen window. Connor rolled his eyes. "I'll give it one more shot," he said. "But if it doesn't get any better, then next week, I'm out!"

Herbert clapped his hands together, and James gave Connor a high five. Babs felt like going over and giving him a big hug. She was sure that slim chocolate body of his would feel mighty fine.

They all idled out of the hall in no great rush. Connor was the last to leave. He stopped, as if he had thought of something, and then turned to Babs. Maybe he had taken a shine to her, after all? These young men certainly did love a cougar, didn't they? And she *had* put on an extra layer of Coca Cola red lipstick especially for the meeting, which her new friend had said brought out the very best in her skin tone. He really was full of wonderful compliments. Babs would have no choice but to tell Connor she had met somebody now, that the poor sod was just a few weeks too late.

"I just wanted to say that I am very impressed with your ability to look genuinely busy," he said. "It is something I strive for. I salute you, Ma'am."

And he did indeed salute Babs, before leaving the hall and

At Least the Pink Elephants are Laughing at Us

joining the others outside in the car park.

16 - And From a Little Acorn Grew a Big Oak

Connor knew that this was last chance saloon. If this was a repeat of the open mike night fiasco then it was game over. His dream of actually achieving something in life and making it to the Edinburgh Festival Fringe would remain but a figment of his imagination, a missed venture he would bitterly recall whilst playing cards with his mates in the nursing home.

He arrived at the pub as early as possible. It was a deliberate and reasoned ploy to make sure he was the first one there, to give him time to physically, psychologically and emotionally prepare for the torture that lay ahead. Connor had not managed to eat any of his two shredded wheat that morning. His hand was too jittery to shave.

Of course, Herbert was already there when he arrived at the pub, nervously snapping and unsnapping his briefcase in the far corner. His broad smile brought light to the dim dreariness that surrounded him. He reminded Connor of a spotlight on a lonely stage. His stomach churned.

What *was* it with this guy? What time did he actually turn up to these events?

Mandy arrived shortly afterwards and quickly retreated to the bar, returning with a smile, a warm hello and a pint of lager, a white wine spritzer for Connor, a black coffee for Herbert and another pint of lager for an old guy who'd made himself welcome at their table.

"I used to own this place," the old man, Frank, proudly announced. "And now my son has taken the reigns. But not half as well as I did, I might add. We'd only ever serve coffee in my day if it was an absolute emergency," he stated, eyeing Herbert.

The Oak was already full by the time James arrived. This was his local, and the locals greeted him with wolf whistles, cheers and open arms.

"Your dad performed here all the time, James," Frank said, pulling up a chair. "I remember the last time. It was only a few – right, forget that – anyway, there was this time when your old man was completely out of it. He could hardly stand up. He was beginning to piss me *right* off. But I offered him a free black coffee because it was an absolute *emergency,* and he got up on stage and blew them away. Didn't let his fans down. Just couldn't do it."

"No pressure then, Frank," James muttered.

Mandy took to the stage first. Connor thought she'd been distracted beforehand, not really paying attention to the conversation around her, but once she got on the stage she put on a solid performance. She was much more practised and clinical. He suspected she lacked some passion, though. It was like she was just going through the motions and was holding something special back. She still had more to give.

"You try growing up as the youngest child with two older brothers," Mandy said. "It is just assumed that you will spend your days brushing Barbie's hair and dreaming of the day Ken asked you on a date. To be fair, my brothers were keen for me to be involved in their games of football. My brother said to just stand there please, little sister. To the left a little. Back a little to the right. It was only when the ball hit me full in the face that I realised they were using me as a second goalpost!"

The drinkers in The Oak liked Mandy. Connor could see that plenty of the old men had taken a shine to her. Mandy played on their attention. Connor noticed an almost sexy swagger to the way she walked up and down the stage. "Of course, you may have noticed how deliciously curvy I am," she said, putting her hands on her hips and thrusting out her pelvis. This brought a loud roar from the punters. "I attract a certain type of man. There is the one type that stares at my tits the whole time. And then there is the other type that desperately wants to stare at my tits but are absolutely determined not to do so. And so instead they just stare resolutely and madly into my eyes, without blinking, until they are red in the face and look like they are ready to explode. I feel sorry for these guys and so sometimes I feel like saying "Listen, just have a look if it makes you feel better!" But I'm just not that type of girl..."

James was next up. Connor thought the roof would come off when he took to the stage. Drunken men everywhere raised their pint glasses to the local hero of the hour.

Connor could see James was nervous. This made Connor feel less nervous. Sweat coated his forehead. Round patches had formed under his armpits. James tentatively approached the microphone in the same way a child approaches a large dog.

"Most of you old bastards will remember by dad, Bobby, performing here," James began. There was a loud cheer around the pub. "My old man wasn't so bad really. I remember when I was seven I sat down on his knee and asked whether I should write a letter to Santa asking for a BMX for Christmas. He folded the South Wales Echo in half. Right then I knew I had his attention. They put a man on the moon and Bobby didn't look up from the paper. The poor bloke was panicking. Those bikes were fucking expensive back then! He tried to find a way out. Dad said that now I was seven it was time we had a little father and son chat. My mum pleaded with him not to! "Everybody has been lying to you all these years," he said. "There *is* no Santa, and so no, you can't have a BMX for Christmas." I ran out of the room crying. My whole childhood dreams had been ruined with one father and son chat. My mum made Dad buy me a BMX just for traumatising me. My dad never realised that this was my plan all along! I knew there was no Santa when I caught him sneaking into the bedroom and eating all the mince pies and drinking the malt wine the Christmas before!"

Connor could see his shoulders loosen now. James was much more relaxed. And he had an audience listening to his every word and so he was going to make the most of it. "People have got me all wrong," James said.

"No we haven't," Frank piped up. "We really do think you're a twat!"

The Oak erupted. James grinned and gave Frank a wave. "I want to tell you all something," James said. "For real. I need to get it out of my system before I explode..."

"Keep it in your trousers!" somebody in the audience shouted. Connor was surprised to realise the words came from his own mouth.

"I remember when I was in school," James continued. "The

At Least the Pink Elephants are Laughing at Us

teacher asked us what our idea of love was. Now even the girls were saying that it was sex. The more the merrier. One back and one front, please. But I was the one," James said, digging his thumb into his chest, "who said my idea of love was of a happy couple walking hand in hand together through a field on a sunny Sunday afternoon. I said they didn't need to be going anywhere or saying anything; they just needed to be together. There was probably a young child playing and a dog running after a stick..."

James shook his head now, like he was trying to rid his mind of horrible thoughts. His hands took on a life of their own, moving theatrically like a puppeteer as he struggled for suitable words. James wiped his brow with his sleeve. "I had all that," he blubbered. "And you know what I did? I threw it all away! What sort of a man does that...?"

There was silence around the pub. James stood on the stage, head in his hands, not saying anything. He looked so exposed, so sad, so pathetic. Connor looked around and everybody stared at the glasses, at the floor, at anything but at the lonely man up on the stage.

Connor jumped to his feet and moved quickly. His decisive actions felt alien to him, like he was acting from his heart and not his mind. He put his arm around James's shoulder. "Come on, mate," he said. "Take a seat. Just relax and watch the rest of the show, yeah. I'll take over from here..."

James walked slowly and awkwardly back to the table. The silence was replaced by a few punters clapping. They were joined by a few more, until eventually the whole pub was clapping.

"It's not often enough us real men show their true emotions, butty," Frank said, raising his half empty pint glass. "But that was some proper brave shit right there. That was a proper tidy show, James! Your dad would have been proud."

Connor was up on stage. He didn't feel nervous now. He didn't feel like anybody really cared whether he was funny or not. He cleared his throat. Connor had an idea. He decided he would just run with it. He was going to throw away the material that he had meticulously crafted all week and just go with what was on his mind, right now.

"Now that James has set the theme, I thought I'd continue

running with it and talk about my own dad," he announced.

"For the Son of God, please don't start crying on us!" somebody pleaded.

Connor continued with his idle chatter. "We don't exactly get on anymore, but James has made me think. It hasn't always been like that. I remember when I was just a kid. I sat on his knee, too. I asked Dad how the Tooth Fairy knows when to leave money under a pillow. My dad said that the Tooth Fairy has super powers, like Superman and your mother. The Tooth Fairy can see through houses. I asked how she knew when she needed to look. I said I'd left a tooth under the pillow last night but when I woke this morning there was no money. My dad said that the Tooth Fairy had been on a short mid-week break to Aberystwyth but was due back today and to leave the tooth under the pillow tonight. I asked whether the Tooth Fairy would make an extra payment for being late. My dad said that the Tooth Fairy had a strict pricing policy and if he made any exceptions then the result would be absolute bedlam! Thinking back, it was mission impossible to get an extra 50p out of my dad even in those days!"

Connor heard some laughter. He looked up and noticed that some faces were actually smiling. They weren't exactly ecstatic and standing on tables and dancing, but they looked moderately happy enough for him to be stood there talking to them. Connor felt ten feet tall.

"My mum, on the other hand, is one step away from being a hippy. I used to walk to school with her every day just so we could absorb the beauty of the world. All my friends would wave at me from the back of the bus as it passed. I couldn't catch the bus because it polluted the beautiful world God had gifted us. I said, "But Mum, the bus will go to school whether I'm on it or not!" She did not give a flying shit about logic, though! We were always late. My dad was the headmaster of the school. He was like, "Listen, I appreciate your need to absorb the beauty of the world but can you please do it outside school hours!" But my mum is Ghanaian, and those people are late for absolutely everything..."

Connor finished his act to polite applause. He returned to the table and Mandy gave him a hug. James looked awkwardly at

At Least the Pink Elephants are Laughing at Us

him. "I had to do what you did one time," James said. "And I know how difficult it is. I just wanted to say thank you, yeah?"

Connor smiled and said no problem.

Herbert was on to him like a rash.

"So," he said, rubbing his hands (which were plastered in black felt tip pen) together, "are you going to give it another shot?"

Connor bided his time. He took a sip of his drink. "I'm in," he said.

The whole table, including Frank, cheered.

17 – Playing God

"So should I even bother to ask whether you're busy with work, Herbert, or should I just ask how you're getting on with that book of yours?"

Herbert ran his fingers through his hair and smiled. He had been spending less time in the office and more time in the cafe recently, drinking tea and plotting his book. Luckily they had a new work experience recruit who was keen to do as much as he could, and it cut the slack for Herbert. Amanda was wise to his game. Herbert didn't even pretend anymore.

"I can only write as quickly as the plot unfolds," Herbert said. "But I'm managing to stay on top of things. There has been plenty of burning the midnight oil recently, Amanda. I'm surprised my energy levels have been able to sustain this level of output for so long, and that my immune system has managed to remain robust..."

Amanda looked at him with a pained expression. "So how are the comedy trio getting on?" she asked.

It was a good question, and one he had frequently posed himself recently.

"Well, they say the road to success is always under construction, don't they, Amanda?"

"Huh...?"

"And it is worthwhile taking your time to get the fundamentals right, because there is no point clipping the leaves if the roots are damaged and rotting, is there?"

"You what...?"

"Where the tailor rests, the needle rusts."

"What the...?"

Herbert really enjoyed his conversations with Amanda. She was one of the few people he felt really understood him.

"It's been a good few months since we first got together," Herbert continued, "and the good news is that we are still together, and we're all still alive. I do not exaggerate, but the

At Least the Pink Elephants are Laughing at Us

gang were one gig away from calling it a day after that first, challenging show. They were like a bottle of pop ready to explode. But the next show went just about well enough to keep the hopes up. And practice makes perfect, doesn't it? We're doing a couple of gigs every week now, and not just in Bridgend but in the valleys, Swansea, Cardiff and even Newport. The crowd has been reasonably receptive; I'd say lukewarm at worst. The trio are trying new material and styles and are being a sliver more daring. It is all practice until they enter the big arena. Put it this way, nobody has been punched since that gig at the open mike night a couple of months ago, so that can only be a good thing..."

Amanda put her hand to her mouth and gasped. She poured Herbert another tea. It was the mid-morning quiet between the breakfast and lunch rush. Herbert was her only customer. "Oh my," she said, "so somebody actually got punched? Mind you, that must have been great for your book, Herbert. It wouldn't surprise me if you had orchestrated the whole thing, you dirty dog. So tell me, how long have you got until you're supposed to go to Edinburgh then?"

"Three months," Herbert replied.

"And do you think you'll make it, dear?" she asked.

Herbert took a sip of his tea. "Well from my side things are all in order. I have booked the venue and the accommodation. We have five shows running from Tuesday with the final show on the Saturday. Our shows will be free, with just a bucket passed around for tips. You know, like in church? But that is the straightforward part; just basic administration. Do I think our performers will be ready? You know what," he said, "It is very early days, but I think they very well might, Amanda. I think they very well might be..."

18 – It's a Cracker Joke

I'm glad that day is over, Terry thought, as he pulled up the handbrake and pressed the button on the radio to silence *Five Live*. He shut a handful of plastic sweet wrappers away in the glove compartment. Terry took a quick, final glance at his reflection in the car mirror. His eyes were outlined with a red tinge and he was sure that white eyebrow wasn't there yesterday. I must stop wishing my days away, Terry mused, as he tiredly pushed open his car door.

"Daddy!" Cat shouted, when Terry entered the house. She jumped from the sofa, her arms outstretched and lips puckered. Terry lifted his daughter off her feet and gave her a kiss.

"You're getting so *big,*" Terry said, like he did every night when he returned home from work. Then he turned to his dad, Roy, and shook his hand, which had become something of a ritual between the two men.

"Uncle James has been telling us jokes!" Cat exclaimed.

"No shit."

"Terry! Watch your mouth," Michelle warned, appearing from the kitchen with a plate of biscuits. Cat put her hand over her mouth to stop her giggles. Terry gave her a wink. He liked being the bad boy of the household. It made him feel like a cool dad.

It was no surprise James had been telling jokes. That's what James *did.* He had been telling jokes every night in their house for months now. Some people devoted their lives to discovering a cure for cancer. James told jokes. He'd been telling jokes since they were kids in school and he would be telling jokes when old and decrepit and barely functioning in the nursing home, trying to impress the old dears.

"Do you want me to tell you one of the jokes?" Cat asked.

"No, you're okay."

Cat widened her eyes, indicating that was *not* the correct

At Least the Pink Elephants are Laughing at Us

answer. "Okay, I'll tell you anyway," she said, smiling. She sure was cute. Terry thought this every single evening. He tried his best to remain objective, as he was sure that, as her father, he just had to be biased. But Terry knew an ugly kid when he saw one - he saw them all the time with their mums in Lidl - and Cat was *not* an ugly kid.

"Why do French people eat snails?" Cat asked.

"I don't know," Terry replied. "Why do French people eat snails?"

"Because they don't like fast food!"

Terry smiled. This was pretty funny for an eight-year-old. He wasn't sure it was the sort of material to take the Apollo by storm, though. Had he really been out a couple of times a week working on his act? Terry couldn't see the Queen giving an appreciative wave of her hand at the Royal Palladium. Terry glanced at his best friend. James was wearing blue denim jeans, but for some reason he had pulled white socks over them to the knee. His red and white checked shirt had a button undone at both the top and the *bottom*. Was this part of his comedy act? Black hairs sprouted from his chest, like spider legs. Terry wondered why his chest hair wasn't going grey; the hair on his head was speckled with a multitude of grey and white. James had one leg crossed over the other. His buttocks sunk into the chair. He didn't look like he had the world on his shoulders, like he was desperately trying to keep his life together. Terry raised a sceptical eyebrow at his friend.

"Hey, a good performer adapts to his audience," James said, holding up the palms of his hands. Terry walked over and shook his friend's hand.

"I think Uncle James is hilarious," Cat stated.

Of course you do, Terry thought.

"A drink each for the men of the house," Michelle announced, dishing out cold beers in long glasses. Service with a smile. Michelle kissed Terry on the cheek. Terry was aware he was prickly and rough. He didn't have time to shave this morning; Terry had been waiting for the bathroom door to open and when it did, James appeared with a magazine and a sheepish smile. Michelle stroked the back of Terry's neck with her middle finger. *That* felt good. "Tea is ready," Michelle announced.

"Wash your hands please, Cat. And use soap."

"These wives are fantastic, aren't they?" James said, winking at Terry. "Where can I get one?"

Dinner was salmon with green, orange and yellow vegetables and boiled potatoes. The knife and fork sunk effortlessly into the salmon. Butter melted from the potatoes. "This is absolutely delicious, Michelle, "James said. "This is absolutely delicious, Michelle," James said. Again. Change the record, Terry thought. He knew he was being unfair though; Terry would be livid if his friend was anything other than gracious for their hospitality. And Terry knew the meal was delicious, of course. Michelle always prepared delicious meals. All their invited dinner guests said so.

There were the usual please don't speak with your mouth full, if you don't eat your greens then you won't grow up to be big and strong like Daddy. James had parked his greens to one side of his plate and Terry had no doubt this was in preparation to hide them under his knife and fork, and he hadn't stopped talking and eating at the same time, usually waving his cutlery in the air like dangerous weapons. Cat followed his every word. It was like Mr Tumble had come for dinner. It was exciting having somebody stay with them, especially her Uncle James. Terry knew she had been telling all her friends in the playground that they had a famous comedian living at their house.

Terry expected this from his daughter. It was his old man who surprised him though. What was it with those two? It was like they had a secret code nobody else was privy to. Roy seemingly adored James. He sat opposite him at the dinner table now, listening intently, nodding his head in all the right places, even smiling and – occasionally - laughing. This was a rarity.

Of course, the two men had history. His dad worked with James's dad, Bobby, in the factory and then, later, he worked with James in the factory, too. Terry always knew his dad had a twinkle in his eye for Bobby, although even that seemed to fade a little towards the end. Terry had his own, more distorted memories of Bobby, but kept them tightly locked inside his head.

Terry had always known his dad was a good man. A gentleman. But he had always blissfully lived in the shadows of his mother. Kim passed away a long time ago now and Roy had been part of their household for many years. Cat adored him. He was her big, cuddly bear. Roy lived more and more in his mind these days but, as far as Terry could tell, it was still a mind that functioned on all cylinders. When Roy spoke, he spoke sense; he just didn't speak very often, that was all. The arrival of James, though, appeared to have lit a spark. Terry had noticed a visible change in his dad over the last few months. He was more alert. He listened to what was discussed at the dinner table. He asked questions. He was living more in the present than in the past, not the good days when Kim was still alive.

"Things are looking up," James announced to the table, to his captive audience. Terry examined his friend closely, really scrutinised every curve and contour of his face, but no; there was not the slightest inclination of a smile. "Our acts have really picked up since that initial open mike night. It was bad news all round when Connor smacked that bloke. But it was nerves. The guy had been off the circuit for a long time. He'll be alright. Him and Mandy have funny bones in their bodies, I tell you. We've been really well received recently. The audiences are really warming to us, you know?"

"But is Connor actually committed?" Terry asked. "You said he was ready to just pack it all in after one bad gig?"

Michelle gave Terry a sharp look.

"Well, that's what he initially said. It was a knee-jerk reaction..."

"I thought he said at the time to shoot him if you ever saw him on a stage again?"

"Terry!" Michelle protested. "I don't think talk of shooting people is appropriate dinner table conversation, do you?"

"Connor fell off the horse and got back on the saddle. The guy is back and stronger than ever. He's got the bug," James continued, apparently unaffected by the sudden outburst. "And let me tell you, it is like the most addictive drug in the world. Laughter to a comedian is blood to a vampire. You need it to keep living, to keep breathing. Once you have been on stage and made an audience laugh, you can't eat and you can't sleep until you are back up there..."

"But you weren't up on stage for years? And I didn't think Connor made people laugh? That's why that bloke ran up on stage..."

Terry felt a sharp twang to his shin. Michelle was on to him, giving him a warning. James didn't seem to notice. James just waved his hand dismissively. Terry noticed his friend had waved his hand dismissively on a regular basis since taking up residence. Who needed rational arguments when you could just wave your hand dismissively?

"Didn't you say you all kicked off with Herbert at one of the meetings?" Terry asked. On this one occasion he was prepared to put up with the threat of a shin splint. It had been a long, hard day at work and he was tired and he was irritable.

James nodded his head. "We did give him some grief, that bit is true. That Mandy has a big mouth, and I wouldn't fancy my chances against her in a wrestling fight, that's for sure. But it's best to get it all out in the open really though isn't it? We cleared the air and came out stronger for it. He's an odd feller that Herbert, I'll admit to that. He isn't the sort of bloke I would normally hang out with in the pub, you know? He likes his long words, that's for sure, and I'm always suspicious of people who like long words. But he has passion pumping through his veins, I tell you. Reminds me of Chris Coleman in that respect, only without the navy jacket and the slicked-back hair, you know? He isn't what you would call a conventional leader, not one of the greats. I'm thinking of Churchill and Skargill and Cowell right now. He is one of those jumpy nervous types. But he is determined we make a go of it and he won't let go until we do. But listen to me, getting carried away," James said, looking around innocently. "I'm R Kelly, floating on the ceiling. I need to get real, don't I? Be realistic about it all?"

"No, not at all!" Michelle said. "I think it's marvellous, especially with everything else you have going on in your life at the moment. You aren't just lying down and feeling sorry for yourself. This Edinburgh gig gives you something to strive towards, doesn't it? You are so brave to get up on that stage in front of all those people. I couldn't do it. I'd get all giddy and tongue-tied."

"Good work young man," Roy added, nodding his head.

James bowed his head, stared intently at his broccoli, propping up from its hiding place beneath his knife and fork. "I just wish my dad was here to see me perform."

Terry wondered how long it would be before Bobby reared his ugly head. It was just a matter of time, a ticking time bomb. Terry groaned. He didn't mean to, it just slipped out like a bad fart. He tried to stifle the groan with his hand, but he was too late. He glanced up. James hadn't noticed, thank God. His wife had, though; she gave him angry, penetrating daggers. It was the stern, disappointed look his dad gave him that really affected him, though.

Terry pushed his chair back and stood up. All eyes were on him now. For the first time since they had all sat down to dinner, he had a captive audience.

"I'll do the dishes," Terry said, quickly retreating to the kitchen.

19 – Digging a Hole

Mandy knew there was a psychology book out there, probably sat lonely and unloved on a dusty shelf in a charity shop, a book that explained the phenomenon. It was all to do with pink elephants. At least, Mandy *thought* the elephants were pink. If you tell somebody not to think of pink elephants then those bleeding pink elephants will dominate your mind, mocking you with their over-active trunks, squirting water in your face (metaphorically, not literally). And now, even though Mandy told herself in no uncertain terms to stop looking at the clock, that time would pass so much quicker if she occupied herself some other way, like gazing at the pigeons with their chests pumped out, looking like they owned the place and were up for a fight with you and all your mates if you thought you were hard enough, she just couldn't help but stare at the hand that went round and round; slowly, slowly, slowly...

The emails had bounced back and forth over the last couple of months, distracting Mandy both at work and with her comedy. The conversations had flowed with surprising ease, without any apparent tension. He was even funnier than she remembered him, even more charming. He had changed, but for the good. And then focus had turned to making arrangements, had built to this damp and dreary day...

She'd arrived ridiculously early, and now she was paying the price with restless boredom. Mandy wanted to be ready at the station when the train arrived, there to give her dad a big hug. Just like in the movies.

The guy on the speaker had until now only announced that the next train was not stopping at this station and so please stay away from the edge of the platform. He now dutifully informed all passengers that the next train *was* going to stop. It was *his* train. There could be hundreds of people on that train, but Mandy only cared about one person. Finally. This was real, then. Mandy stood up. The train was coming around the corner. Fast

At Least the Pink Elephants are Laughing at Us

and focused. Was it supposed to be going that fast? Was it going to slow down and stop? *Stop being so silly, Mandy.* There were a few other people on the platform, all of whom appeared infinitely less bothered whether the train stopped or not.

The train stopped. Mandy imagined people standing the other side of the door, tapping their feet on the sticky floor, impatiently waiting for the button to light up, to turn green, questioning whether it actually was going to change colour, whether they should be pressing the button regardless, just in case. And then the doors opened and people from all different carriages disembarked. Mind the gap between the train and the platform edge, Mandy mechanically thought. It was engrained in her mind now. There were people with suitcases, people with hats, people with children; an older lady with a suitcase, a hat *and* a child. It was a long train with plenty of passengers, not one of those local trains where first and second class were distinguishable only by a napkin on the back of the seat. Mandy tried to pick him out amongst the figures. Did she even really remember what he looked like? Had she fabricated his handsome features? Maybe the photograph hidden behind the china clock on the fireplace at her mother's house exaggerated his movie star looks? Perhaps he had changed, and not for the good. Put on blubber? Become stick thin? No. She dismissed the idea. Not her dad.

The platform was quickly clearing of people, like a football stadium after the final whistle had blown, when the fans slumped off in the drizzle to their cars, anticipating inevitable traffic. There were less and less people to choose from now who could possibly be her dad. One by one they disappeared, too, crossed the bridge to platform one, following an orderly and civilised line.

Mandy began to panic. It hadn't even crossed her mind that he wouldn't turn up. Not really. She felt a sharp pang of stupidity and anger. Why hadn't it crossed her mind? It should have been the first thing to cross her naive, dumb mind. He had let her down all his life, even though she had manically tried to convince herself otherwise. Of course Mandy knew long before her mother that her dad had was up to no good. Was she supposed to believe that damsel in distress had just randomly arrived at the beach all those years ago, when she was just a kid? She should have spoken to her mum about meeting Dad. She shouldn't have been such a coward. Her mum deserved more. Maybe this was her punishment, her karma, for her selfishness, her cowardice.

Her two older brothers were right. Oh God. She dreaded telling William. She could tell by the way he went silent on the phone that he didn't want her to meet him, but she just went ahead and did it anyway; she just didn't care.

That was it, then. There was just one tall gangly bloke with round black glasses and a long mackintosh left on the platform. Mandy turned to head back, her mind frazzled, her body heavy and tired, not looking forward to the journey up the short flight of stairs to cross the bridge.

"Mandy?"

She instinctively turned, excited. She'd missed him. But no, it was just the young guy in the mackintosh. He looked at her awkwardly, embarrassed, like he was back in school and one of his mates had sent him over to tell her he fancied her, which happened regularly because Mandy always had the biggest boobs in her class. She stopped and - cautiously - waited for this stranger to tell her how he knew her name.

"Mandy," the man continued, his face distorting into different, changing shapes. "It's me you've been emailing..."

*****

Connor's dad opened the door and smiled awkwardly. He held out his hand and Connor shook it. The strength of his handshake hadn't diminished with the passing years.

"Hello, son."

"Dad."

"You've come at a good time, you know. We have some unexpected guests. I've put the kettle on for a nice cup of tea."

Connor removed his shoes and pushed them under the wooden table in the hall. There was a fresh, appealing smell in the house. Connor noticed flourishing yellow flowers in a long vase in the hallway. He wondered who the guests were. Probably somebody his dad thought Connor knew when, actually, he

At Least the Pink Elephants are Laughing at Us

didn't. Connor walked into the living room in his socks, ready to exchange pleasantries, ready to pretend he knew who the person was. But no, Connor did know the guest. It was Uncle Harry, Dad's older brother. It was nice to see him. He liked his Uncle Harry. Connor did consider that his dad was probably exaggerating the "unexpected" guest part, though. Uncle Harry was often popping around for some free dinner and a pint of lager, and not just at Christmas.

Harry stood in the middle of the living room with his hands tucked tightly inside the pockets of his blue jeans, shoulders rounded and relaxed, legs bent slightly at the knee. He wore a blue polo shirt that was just the right fit. Connor was surprised to observe that he looked unusually trendy for an old guy. There was something different about him. Oh yes, that was it. He'd lost quite a few pounds, around the midriff and especially in the cheeks.

There was something else, too. Something significant. Something unusual. Something he hadn't noticed when he first entered the room. His uncle wasn't on his own, like he invariably was. Stood next to him was a smart, attractive brunette lady wearing cream slacks and a bright, flowery blouse. The lady was in the same age bracket. She was very familiar. Connor had met her before. Oh God, he thought, where was it? It was on the tip of his tongue...

"This is Babs," Harry said, holding out his hand and proudly gesturing to the woman. "Babs, this is Connor. The comedian of the family. Literally..."

"I know all about him being a comedian," Babs said, smiling.

Of course! She was the caretaker from the hall, the lady who was remarkably skilled at looking busy. Connor saluted her; a wild and extravagant gesture he had fretted about later. The woman had already gained his respect. It was strange seeing her in a different environment, in his parent's house of all places! She looked remarkably attractive out of her blue cleaning overalls, probably quite the catch for folk of her generation. Harry put his arm around the woman's slim shoulder. His smile, which had never disappeared, now broadened. Connor could physically feel his face unfolding as reality hit. This woman was *with* his Uncle Harry.

"We met on the internet," Harry informed him, as though to pre-empt any awkward questions.

"That's very modern and fashionable," Connor said, genuinely impressed. He turned to Babs. "It is very nice to properly meet you, in a civilised environment. I must say, it is a remarkable coincidence, don't you think? It's a small world and all that..."

Babs smiled wolfishly and shook her head. "To be honest, Connor, I've been on that dating site for quite some time and I've had so many dates that it's probably not all that surprising that one day I would date one of your friends or family, if you know what I mean, chuck?"

Connor glanced at his uncle. He didn't seem affected by this revelation. There was still an undeniable twinkle in his blue eyes. Babs seemed to pick up on Connor's concern (possibly because he wasn't very good at hiding his facial expressions), for she turned to Harry and planted a big wet kiss on his cheek. "I've never met anyone like Harry," she said. "This one is a proper keeper, you know?"

This was all quite a bombshell for Connor. He had never seen his uncle with a woman. Connor never pictured him with anybody. He was just Uncle Harry, on his own. He had always given the impression that was how he liked it. It obviously wasn't. He had found a companion, and at this late stage of his life! Connor was genuinely made up for the guy.

"Well done, Uncle Harry," he said, shaking his hand. He was aware this might sound slightly condescending, that maybe Herbert was finally rubbing off on him, so he quickly turned to Babs and said, "Or should I say, well done Babs?" The woman beamed, like she had been complimented on her prize catch. Connor thought about it for a moment; his uncle probably *was* quite a good catch once you unravelled the layers.

"Your mother is out the back garden, Connor," his dad said, interrupting the jovial niceties.

Connor wondered whether he had forgotten about the cup of tea he mentioned when he arrived.

"She's been looking forward to seeing you..."

At Least the Pink Elephants are Laughing at Us

*****

Mandy sat at the plastic table, on a plastic seat. She stared out of the window. The constant drizzle had left the pavement damp. Originally Mandy had been proper tamping. Mandy no longer felt angry. She had given up on anger. That had passed. The anger had been replaced by something less visible and prominent but much, much worse. Mandy felt heavy, numb emptiness, like she had pins and needles in her very being. She felt like she was beyond caring, like none of this really mattered, like there was no point to it all.

"So who exactly *are* you?" she asked the man who returned from the counter with two piping hot mugs of tea. He'd even treated himself to a chocolate éclair, the cheeky little git.

"Oh, I'm Dave," he said, like he couldn't possibly be called anything else. He held out his hand. His fingers were very long and slender. "It's very nice to meet you, Mandy."

Mandy couldn't believe this guy had the cheek – the gall – to stand there (or sit, now) in front of her, all smiles and politeness like any of this was even remotely normal. The bony hand dangled in front of her like a wet fish waiting to be gobbled up by a seal. Mandy remembered Chinese burns from school. Was it appropriate for an adult to give a Chinese burn in this situation? If there was any situation that was appropriate then this could be it, she considered. She couldn't be bothered. Her energy was beat. Mandy reluctantly shook the hand. She cursed herself for doing so.

"Are you 'twp' or what?" Mandy scowled. "I don't want to know what your name is," she said. "I want to know who you are!"

He had one of those boyish, cute innocent faces that looked hurt by even the remotest suggest of ill-intent. Who? *Me?* None of this added up. There must be something sinister with this situation, she thought; but this guy? He had Bambi eyes, for God's sake. She really wanted to hate the bastard. It was almost like he was *trying* to make her mad.

"Well that's a deep philosophical question, Mandy," he began, but Mandy gave him such an evil look – a look which suggested that if he pushed her further she might stab him with her fork - that he visibly flinched. "I know I owe you an immediate explanation. You deserve that and I had better hurry things along. I'm the man you've been emailing."

"You're not my dad!" Mandy spluttered.

Two old dears from the next table looked around curiously. These two looked like they split their time between the park, the library and this cafe, Mandy thought. Mandy knew what they were thinking: dads often started young in the valleys, but this was ridiculous! This guy must have been about ten when he dipped his wick and got a girl pregnant.

"Well, yes, I know I am not your dad. But I am the person who has been emailing you in the guise as your dad. I guess the correct term is that I am the one who has been masquerading as your dad."

Mandy took a sip of her tea and then plonked the cup down with a thud. She had considered throwing the contents of the cup over him. She imagined him squealing, making a horrendous scene. The familiar anger had returned, and pretty quickly. She was ready to blow. "You have ten seconds to tell me exactly what has been going on before I pour this tea all over your head," she said.

The lady who owned the café, Amanda, looked up concerned from behind the counter. Mandy knew she wasn't worried she'd make a scene. She just wanted to make sure Mandy was alright. She came to the place a fair bit. They sold nice cakes. They chatted when it was quiet. Amanda had spoken passionately about her embroidery. Mandy told her about her comedy once. They got on. Mandy held her hand up to let Amanda know everything was under control.

Mandy had expected the guy to start gibbering, to start spluttering out pathetic, desperate excuses. "You're right," he said. "I knew you'd be angry, and of course, you have every right to be. I guess I'm just nervous. Well, let's start at the beginning. Roger is my best friend from school..."

"Who the fuck is Roger?" Mandy asked.

The man snorted. "That's like that song from back in the day. You know, "Alice, Alice, who the..."

Mandy interrupted him by putting a single, threatening finger to his lips. Dave got the idea. He stopped this line of conversation and got to the point. "You know; the private detective?"

"That tiny little shit with the moisturised skin is called *Roger*?"

Dave laughed. "Yes. Roger."

This guy had better stop laughing, Mandy thought. He continued, "Well, Roger has always been a clever guy. Like Stephen Fry. You should see him when *Countdown* is on. He eats up eight letter words like there is no tomorrow. But he has never really known what his true calling in life is. So he has drifted from job to job and never really committed himself fully to any of them. Last I heard he was selling PPI. It didn't really work out. Roger has an expensive lifestyle. He is a "metrosexual" male. And now he is in debt. He told me about this idea of earning a few pounds from the private detective game..."

"Game...? So what you're basically saying, *Dave*, is that I've given my hard-earned money to some conman who has run off with it? I've been properly screwed, yeah?"

Dave pulled a face. It didn't suit him. "No! Sort of. Well, yes. You need to believe me, Mandy," but Mandy gave him another look and so Dave continued "That guy you met was an act. He wanted to be mysterious because he didn't know what he was doing. Roger really did want to find your dad. He was trying all sorts of things on the internet even before he took any money from you. Truth is that he was a bit shit at the private detective game. He asked me to help when he knew he was hitting his head against a proverbial brick wall. He created a false email address and asked me to start replying to you. The guy just knew he couldn't pull it off himself. Then he asked me to arrange a meeting so that he could keep the payments coming in. The debts really are coming out of his ear holes. He is my best friend. What could I do...?"

Mandy had a few ideas what he could do. He could have told him where to go, torn him a new...she just didn't care if the poor guy had tried. He had tried and he had failed. Fair enough. But then the prick had instigated a cover to keep the payments coming in, so he could steal from her, hadn't he? She had been scammed. She was a bigger mug than she'd ever feared. This was much, much worse than her dad not turning up, than being made to look a fool in front of her brothers.

"So why did you come? *Dave?* How could you *possibly* think that was a good idea? Why did you agree to meet me when you knew I was expecting my dad? And even once you'd agreed to meet, why didn't just leave me waiting, like a dumb-ass bride standing at the altar? Any of that would have been preferable to *this,* don't you think?"

Mandy knew that her voice was breaking, that her eyes were watering. And she hated herself. It felt pathetic. Her mum wouldn't cry. Her mum remained strong and dignified, regardless what shit life threw at her. There was just that one time she remembered her mum crying, and that was all Mandy's fault for making a huge fuss about her dad coming back to take them out for the day. It was always to do with Dad. Mandy was strong, too. Normally. Her brothers never let her cry in public, to feel sorry for herself. But no. She was blubbering, like that little girl she barely remembered waiting in her pink dress for her dad to turn up to take them to the caves.

Dave spoke quickly now, firing the words out, trying to get them in quickly before the situation rapidly deteriorated into total chaos. "You know when you dig a hole? With a bleedin' great big shovel? And you keep digging in an attempt to get out of that hole? I was torn up about what happened. I couldn't sleep. I *haven't* slept. I didn't know you when I agreed to help. I knew it was wrong but my main priority was my mate. It had all gone too far, had become a big mess. I could tell you were a good sort from your emails. I really liked you. I felt you deserved an explanation face to face."

"*I haven't slept...? I really liked you...?*" Mandy mimicked. "Well bless your little cotton socks..."

The man really needed to stop. He put his hand in his pocket. He pulled out a brown envelope. That envelope looked familiar, Mandy thought.

"Look, I know it doesn't make up for everything, and I know it really isn't the point. But it is all there. Every penny. And it isn't my money either. I've spoken to Roger. Made him see sense. You have to believe me; he is very sorry. It's your money, Mandy."

He carefully placed the envelope down on the table, like it was delicate and valuable china.

Mandy stood up. She pushed her chair back and it screeched on the floor, like long nails scraping down a blackboard. All the other customers in the cafe turned around and faced her, accusingly. "You can keep your money," Mandy said.

She walked off. Mandy half expected the other customers to start clapping their hands. But they didn't. They turned around and started talking amongst themselves. She felt a bit stupid now.

And so Mandy returned to the table, picked up the brown envelope, waved goodbye to Amanda, and *then* walked out of the cafe.

*****

Connor never knew what he'd find with his mum. It was all part of the condition. Part of him fancied hanging about and chewing the fat with Harry. He knew that was just an excuse, that he was just biding time. His dad would see straight through him. He could be very observant when it suited him. Connor was too much like his mum and, for all his faults, Dad knew everything there was to know about Mum. He worshipped the very feet she walked on.

Connor said that he wouldn't be long.

He looked through the sliding glass windows. There she was. His dear mum. At the rear of the garden, on the flat stretch of grass on the higher verge, diminutive with the tall impressive pine trees overlooking her. Connor's mother was a lady of fashion, a woman who took great pride in her appearance. Now, though, she was in her gardening clothes; her scruffs. The navy tracksuit bottoms were baggy and speckled in white paint and pulled high up over her legs, like she'd borrowed them from a child. Her tee-shirt was spotted with holes, like it had been kept in the back of a wardrobe for too long and been nibbled by a moth. She was sitting down on the damp lawn with her legs outstretched.

She turned around when Connor moved close and her smile was instant and undisputedly magnificent. Connor felt his nerves subside and his mood blossom, like pesky weeds pulled up out of the ground. Whatever was or wasn't going on in his life right now, or any time, it was worth persevering with just to see his mother smile like that.

"Connor!" she exclaimed. Nanya pressed the flat of her hands into the grass to try and push herself up. It was drizzling, ever so faintly, and the grass was wet and her cheeks were shiny.

"Don't get up," Connor replied, quickly reaching out before she could move any further. "You look very comfortable just as you are, Mum."

"The ground is the best seat in the world," Nanya proclaimed. "God's natural surface. Come and sit down and tell me all about it, Connor," she said, invitingly patting the patch of grass next to her. "How are you?"

"I'm doing alright, really," Connor replied. "Things are picking up with the comedy. We are working with and off each other. We've adapted the Welsh football team anthem. You know: Together Stronger. And it is proving pretty powerful stuff. We all have our weaknesses; of course we do. In fact, James is a completely flawed individual. But together we make up for those faults and we are better for it. And on a personal or individual basis – call it what you like - I have managed to embroil myself in a positive cycle. My act is getting better, which is making me more confident, and the more confident I am, the better my act becomes. Does that make sense or am I talking nonsense again?"

His mother smiled encouragement. Connor knew that she would never, ever say he was talking nonsense, even when undoubtedly he was. Not because she did not want to hurt his feelings or because she was prone to flowery fluffiness, but because she genuinely believed her son always talked sense. Connor could argue that the world was flat or that blue was black and she would be in his corner, backing him up.

"No, no, no!" she said loud and emphatically, pointing her finger at him. "You are not talking nonsense. I say *no*! You talk sense. It's always been a *nonsense* to me why you have never been more confident. You don't get it from your dad and you sure don't get it from your mum! Is it some sort of brain defect? Some people who are skinny think they are fat, don't they? Some of the most beautiful people in the world look in the mirror and an ugly person looks back at them. My boy is the cleverest in the whole of Wales and yet he does not think he is clever at all. Why is this?" she asked. She shook her head forcibly from side to side. "I tell you, Connor, I am right! And are you still going to Edinburgh?"

Connor thought about this. He was normally non-committal about everything. People had asked him this before and he tended to shrug his shoulders and say "who knows? How long is a piece of string?" He was aware that this response didn't even make sense. "Yes," he said. "I think we actually are."

His mother smiled. "And what about the young girl? Mandy, is it? She seems very fun. Are you going to make an honest woman of her? Are wedding bells ringing? Are you going to bring me a grandchild?"

Goddamn, Connor thought. He had only ever spoken about Mandy in factual terms. He had never indicated any interest in her in *that* way. Connor knew his mother's mischievous ways and he loved her for it. He was tempted to play along. He almost had to bite his tongue. It was wrong to put false ideas in her head, to paint a picture that was mere fantasy rather than reality. His mother was an incurable romantic. She dreamt of the day a little grandchild entered the world. It would happen. Connor was not certain of many things in this world, but he was certain of that. Just not with Mandy. He liked Mandy, and she definitely *was* fun, but he just didn't like her in that way.

"She'd good, Mum. She's a real sweet girl." And then he turned and smiled at her. "Nothing romantic is going on, though."

"That's lovely," she said, seemingly unaffected by the announcement that – no – there would not be any wedding bells or the tapping of tiny footsteps any time soon. She smiled. "We both know you admire a particular type of girl, don't you darling?"

Damn. Would she ever forget that he had a childhood crush on Velma from *Scooby Doo?* Velma possessed such undeniably fantastic attributes, such as intellect, humour and a short skirt, that Connor assumed it was perfectly natural to fancy her. Okay, so she was a cartoon character. Connor recalled the time (when he was all of ten) he told his mum and she just couldn't stop laughing. His mum was being mischievous now and – truthfully – Connor adored her for it.

He wasn't here to talk about himself, though. There were much more important things to talk about. "So," Connor said, dreading the upcoming question. "How are things with you then, Mum?"

Her smile was wide and genuine. "Oh, you know," she said. "It's a blessing I'm alive really isn't it? So I thank the Lord for every extra day I have on this world. Your dad is the kindest, most gentle man in the world and I am grateful every morning when I wake up next to him. We've been getting out of the house as much as possible, just enjoying the great outdoors, going for walks, spending time in the garden..."

This was even better than Connor had hoped. Of course, it was dreadful when Mum was low, when her body was there but her mind seemed vacant, but it was much more frightening when she was high. When his mum was on a high she was absolutely delirious and totally unpredictable. Connor still had recurring nightmares of when she ran into the sea in Tenby. He shut it out of his mind as much as he could, to calm his fear, his anger...

Right now his mother seemed to have a real, rational perspective on life. He needed to savour these moments. Connor glanced around, interested. The garden did look fantastic. He knew it had absolutely nothing to do with his father. His dad didn't have green fingers. Connor was no expert – he wasn't an expert at anything– but he could imagine how wonderfully mediating it must be to focus all your intentions into gardening. He would do some himself if it wasn't for the hard labour, the hidden brambles and the fact his house didn't have a garden.

The unofficial break was apparently over and his mother was suddenly busy, sinking her bare hands into the soil, digging a hole. She was going at a rapid pace. Her hands delved deep. She stretched at the shoulders and her arms disappeared inside the tunnel. What was she, Connor thought, some kind of gerbil?

"What are you working on now?"

His mum did not look up at him. She continued gazing into the depths of the ground, blissfully mesmerised by whatever it was she saw. Connor noticed now the intenseness on her face. She was on a mission. Her nose was shiny from exertion and a blue vein throbbed and pulsated on the side of her forehead. "I'm digging a big hole," she said.

Those eyes looked too big, too wide, too manic. The calm he felt just moments before vanished. He feared a terrible storm now.

"For my sister, Jojo," Nanya added.

The eerie silence that radiated across the garden must have alerted her, for his mum sprung up, high on energy, like an addict who had just injected a much-needed hit. Her face looked panicked. She realised something.

"I haven't told you, have I? Dear God, I haven't told you!"

Nanya swiftly and urgently took Connor in her arms, gave him a big, suffocating hug. Her body felt warm and full of moisture and her hair tickled the side of his face. "I am sorry," she said, her eyes just inches from his. "It must be the blasted medication. It's no good, I tell you! I forget things. But that's not an excuse. Connor, darling. I really should have told you."

"What is it?"

"Your Auntie Jojo is dying, Connor."

Connor took in the words. Auntie Jojo was dying? It was awful. Tragic. It wasn't his greatest concern, though. Connor just couldn't look beyond what was in front of his eyes right now; the terrifyingly deep and gaping hole his mum was digging. It suddenly took on a much more sinister demeanour. Why was she digging it? It seemed to grow bigger and deeper the more Connor stared at it. Connor nodded down at the ground. "And what is that for, Mum?"

The pain etched on his mother's face was instantly replaced by exuberant, energetic excitement. Her sister dying was a bad thing, a *terrible* thing, but it seemed that, in contrast, this hole was undoubtedly a good thing.

"Don't you see? I'm digging a hole for Jojo to be buried in. What better place could there be? Then she can finally be close again to her sister. It is what she always wanted."

Connor gently pressed his temple against his mother's forehead. Hot sticky tears, big blobs like raindrops, trickled down her face. Connor kissed his mother's cheek and told her everything would be alright, everything would be absolutely fine.

He desperately needed to get away. Right now. Connor got to his feet and strode quickly to the house.

The three of them were still in the living room, chatting and laughing. How did they have the gall to be happy, to chat and *laugh*, when his mother, his wonderful mother, was outside on her own, with only her mad thoughts for company, digging a hole to bury her sister in? Connor stormed into the lounge, shrugging past Harry and his new girlfriend, and pointed his finger accusingly at his dad. "This is all *your* doing!" he shouted.

Before his dad had time to respond, to challenge him, to ask how *dare* he speak to him like that, especially in front of their unexpected guests, Connor had already slammed the front door and escaped from the house.

20 – Reading Between the Lines

It was his day off.

Everybody was entitled to a day off, after all, Terry reasoned. He had one on a regular basis to let some fizz out of the metaphorical can of coke to prevent it from bubbling over and causing an almighty mess. Terry worked hard. Most days he put the foot down on the pedal full throttle. And, just like a high-performing race car, every so often he needed to come in for a pit stop. On these days where he slowed the pace and re-charged his batteries, Terry was like Greta Garbo: he just wanted to be left alone.

He'd booked this day in the diary months ago, in his previous life when James was not an essential and ongoing part of the domestic equation. Now James threatened to be a proverbial spanner in the works.

Terry slumped in front of the television in his boxer shorts. He had a scratch and a sniff. It was good to escape from the serious and practical and *adult* world. *Fireman Sam* had quite an involving and complicated plot today, he considered.

The back bedroom door opened, the one hidden away in the corner, and James appeared wearing his grubby navy dressing gown that had unidentifiable stains down the front. James displayed an unwanted eyeful of bumpy white leg. He rubbed both his eyes with his fingers. James noticed Terry sprawled on the sofa from behind his hands and mumbled "So have you been sacked then?"

"Day off," Terry replied. He considered using the racing car/pit stop analogy to explain why he was sat in his boxer shorts watching *Fireman Sam*, but then thought, how could he explain the crucial requirement to take an occasional break from work to somebody who hadn't worked for years?

James grunted his apparent understanding. Terry thought he sounded like Daddy Pig. James offered Terry tea and toast and said, "Don't mind me, mate. I won't be under your feet. I'll be busy on the computer keeping track of developments in the employment market. You won't even know I'm here. I'll be like The Invisible Man"

He always made searching for a job sound so fancy. He was like a stockbroker monitoring the rise and fall of shares. James had the ability to make a dreary, tedious day in front of the computer sound incredibly exciting. It was a talent really, Terry mused.

"Any luck with any jobs, mate?"

"I have a few ongoing enquiries I hope to hear from very shortly," James replied. "It's kind of ironic really; I've managed to successfully avoid employment for so many years and now that I actually want a job, I can't find one. I will say, though, that one of my applications in particular is extremely positive. To be honest, employers are not desperately seeking an unqualified man in his fifties, especially one who, due to circumstances out of his control, has been in-between jobs for a lengthy period. My CV usually disappears into a black hole and I never hear anything back. Back in my day they told you when they weren't interested. Just common courtesy, wouldn't you say?"

Terry enthusiastically told his mate to keep trying, reassured him something was sure to come up soon. He privately wondered though what these mysterious circumstances that led him to be "in-between jobs" that were so out of his control were.

Roy came through the front door wearing baggy grey tracksuit bottoms. He had been walking again. It was part of his daily routine these days. Terry could only see it as a good thing. His dad had lost some weight and his skin had more colour; he no longer looked like he was jaundiced. His dad saluted Terry and then asked James, in a hushed voice, whether they were still on for later. James smiled and replied quietly (for him) that you bet your bottom dollar they were.

This irritated Terry. James was supposed to be *his* friend. Roy was supposed to be *his* dad. When had the roles been switched? Why was he excluded from their little private arrangement? Why were they so secretive? Had his invite mysteriously been lost in the post, just like on James's seventh birthday? Terry was fully aware there'd been simmering tension between him and James since he moved in, but surely that was to be expected? Couldn't his dad see things from his perspective? Why wasn't he supporting him? James was making a mess of his life and Terry was just expected to budge over, make some space, change his equilibrium and then just watch him do it. He wasn't just going to let his mate get hurt. He didn't when they were teenagers, when he stormed in on his mother's little tea party and he wasn't going to now. But besides, did any of the tension really mean he should be left outside their precious circle of trust?

"We're just going to the pub," Roy said as a parting gesture a bit later in the day, with his shoes on and one foot already out of the door. "We've just got something to chat about. We'll only be a few hours, son..." And then he slammed the door.

We're just going to the pub, Terry mimicked, from the sofa. *We just got something to chat about.*

Of course you are, he thought. Of course you have, he added. *I sniff a rat!*

Terry made an instinctive decision. He frantically scrambled around on his hands and knees for his trainers. Terry pushed open the door that had only just been shut and rushed outside.

He hadn't done anything like this before. He was an amateur playing a professional game. Terry wasn't a spy. He wasn't a jealous husband. He wasn't a nutcase. He wasn't a stalker. What other possible reason was there to follow somebody without them knowing...?

He had no idea what a safe following distance was. How were you supposed to remain inconspicuous? His adrenaline flew straight off the grid. Terry half-expected one of the deadly duo to glance over his shoulder at any moment. Terry looked out for hedges and garden walls he could launch himself over if push came to shove.

His suspicions were further aroused when they continued walking past their usual watering holes, The Oak and The Fox, without giving either a second glance. I knew I was on to something. Terry smiled smugly. Self-satisfaction quickly turned to panic. So what were they up to? They were walking further into the depths of town and seemed to know exactly where they were headed. And then, without warning, both men disappeared inside an inconspicuous building on the high street.

Terry decided to set up camp in the cafe across the road. It was just lucky he would be able to mix business with pleasure, like James Bond slurping on a Martini (shaken but not stirred); Terry had to blend in and be incognito and so why not treat himself to a coffee and maybe some delicious cream cake in the process?

This was new too, Terry considered. He had unsurprisingly never been on a stakeout before. He had seen it in the movies, of course. Was it *Beverley Hills Cop*? Oh, and *The Stakeout*. The cafe was quiet and it didn't require a great deal of acting ability to make it look like he was just absent-mindedly gazing out of the window, lost in his flowing – possibly creative - thoughts. The clock ticked slowly and Terry bought another coffee and then another. The old dear who owned the place was very friendly and keen to quench his thirst. Terry was beginning to feel jittery from all the caffeine, and anxious from the boredom, and so he was relieved when James and his dad finally appeared from behind the glass door across the road.

Terry counted to thirty. He was used to counting from his games of hide and seek with Cat. Terry was on his feet, out of the door and quickly across the road, waving to the nice lady on his way out. He felt like Jason Bourne. Terry could tell from the outside that it was some sort of training centre. He pushed open the door and was instantly struck by the warmth inside. It was like entering a smoky pub on a cold December evening. The radiators were clearly on full blast with no consideration for the gas bill, even though they were now into summer.

He glanced around. There was a line of computers on both sides of the room and spiralling wooden stairs led to another room upstairs. A young guy sat behind the counter playing with his phone. He didn't raise his eyes when Terry entered, despite the chime when the door opened.

"I'm looking for my dad," Terry blurted. Terry was aware that his forehead was seeped with sweat. The guy raised a single eyebrow, a possible prompt for Terry to provide more specifics.

"He is doing a course here and he asked me to meet him," Terry elaborated. Terry was aware that his hands were now doing a lot of the talking. He waved them in the air like a puppeteer. "He is an old guy; looks like he hasn't got all that

At Least the Pink Elephants are Laughing at Us

many years left to live. He was probably here with a younger guy who is getting on a bit himself, to be honest, my age to be exact..."

"Oh, Roy and James," the man interrupted, the light bulb suddenly illuminated. "You've just missed them. Sorry about that, mate."

Terry idled, looking around, trying to think of something to say. He moved his feet, but only on the spot. The guy looked up again with a tired, irritated expression.

"I'm thinking of joining my dad and doing a few courses myself," Terry explained. He hoped his nose wasn't growing. This perked the kid's interest. Dollar signs always talked. The guy raised *both* his eyebrows now.

"Remind me, what course is my dad doing at the moment?" Terry asked.

The man paused for a moment but then shrugged his skinny shoulders. Terry imagined he was probably trying to recall his data protection training but then thought better of it. *Nobody really concentrated during data protection training.*

"Basic English. He is learning to read. James is just helping him. Those two seem like good mates."

Terry absorbed these words. Repeated them slowly in his head.

"Learning to read?"

The young guy appeared less comfortable now, realised that he had probably given information away that he shouldn't have. He stroked his chin with his thumb and waited for Terry to say something, to fill the awkward void.

Terry, though, turned around in a daze and left the shop without saying another word.

Chris Westlake

21 – Little People Looking Up

Connor went to the house to see his mum, but she barely let him through the front door. Sure, she gave him a warm hug and a kiss on the lips, but then she waved her middle finger under his nose and said that she wouldn't even make him a cup of tea until he spoke to his dad first and apologised for his recent, outrageous outburst. She reminded him that she had warned him about this before in no uncertain terms.

She was right, of course. He did owe his dad an apology. And she had definitely warned him. It wasn't Dad's fault. It was his mother's condition. His dad couldn't keep taking the blame for what happened now just because of his mistake years and years ago. Connor had been told time and time again the erratic, unpredictable behaviour was to be expected occasionally. Sometimes it would be much more outrageous and frightening than other times, but it would always pass. The key was to anticipate it and be completely aware it was just part of the condition. Connor just got too involved when his mum was at her best though that he unconsciously convinced himself she was absolutely normal, just like every other mum. He was his own worst enemy. He never learnt. When Mum did then say something that was totally unexpected and completely off the radar, Connor usually exploded with worry and frustration, and usually diverted his emotions directly onto his dad.

Connor clasped the rusting metal rail and climbed down the concrete steps that were smothered in mud and clumps of grass and then the large expanse of playing fields opened up in front of him. This place brought back memories. The wooden cricket pavilion was sheltered by overhanging trees. Dead fish sometimes floated on the surface of the murky river water. Connor played rugby here on Sunday mornings as a kid. The touchlines were usually filled with excitable dads and children too big or too small to make the first team. Things used to be so simpler in those days. If you had a pound and a pair of boots then you were good to play. One time Connor forgot his boots and scrambled around on the boggy pitch in his black leather school shoes. Any dad who showed any willing and was able to give a lift to away games became an integral part of the coaching staff. These days it was all about checks and certificates and fitness. Connor knew that some of the changes were needed, some of them were crucial, but sometimes it felt like the fun had been taken away from being a kid.

Connor was still thinking about his mother's irrational moment when he reached the bottom of his steps. It did have one positive outcome: it had brought back to the forefront happy memories of Auntie Jojo. He had only met her on three occasions – once when she came to stay shortly after the Tenby trip and twice when the family visited Ghana – but even so, it felt like they had an incredibly close bond, that she was a massively important part of his life. Connor absolutely adored his auntie. She was just like his mother, just even more bubbly and colourful and confident. He was so glad this sickness his mother spoke of was just a creation of her own disturbed mind.

The rugby season was over and now it was all about pre-season training. Connor walked towards the group of little players in green tops who were training on the pitch right in the middle of the park. This was the time of year that knees were grazed and blisters like bubbles blew up on the soles of feet. Connor whistled and hummed and wondered why they didn't choose the pitch closest to the car park. Connor moved closer and noted that the players were very little indeed, probably the under ten's. There was no shortage of enthusiasm from the high-pitched, excitable players. Connor tried to spot his dad. He slowed his pace until he was virtually walking in slow-motion. Connor worried that anyone interested enough to notice would think he was taking the piss.

"He's over there," a dad said, pointing his finger to the thick of the action.

"Thanks," Connor replied. His dad still had his socks rolled up to his knees outside his tracksuit bottoms. Connor was surprised to see he still looked a formidable figure, despite his obvious age. It probably helped that he was surrounded by juniors, or "little people," as his dad still liked to call them.

Then Connor had a thought. How did this dad know he was looking for his own dad? The guy held out his hand and Connor shook it. The guy's big, affable face seemed vaguely familiar, like it was from a life long-forgotten.

"Ryan Evans," he said. "Remember? We went to junior school together. You were one of the best players I've ever seen. Once you sort of learnt the rules. Once you stopped passing the ball forwards."

Of course, Connor thought, nodding his head and smiling. Ryan had been the captain of the rugby team, and that always meant something. Connor didn't feel so bad now about not recognising him. It must have been way over twenty-five years or so since he'd seen him last, and the lean kid with knobbly knees was now coated with an overflowing abundance of soft padding. Plus he had a beard.

"Your dad's still going great guns, isn't he?"

Connor looked at his dad, following the play with his whistle in his mouth, and was surprised to acknowledge that - yes - he did seem to be going great guns, didn't he? It was difficult to relate this vibrant, athletic guy with the old man he normally envisaged sat on the sofa in his slippers reading the newspaper.

"The young kids still love him you know," Ryan continued. "They still respect him just like they did back in our day," he smiled. "Although now he is older they do make fun of him a bit more. It's all good fun though, and he takes it how it is meant."

"We respected him?" Connor asked, half-joking. "I thought we were just terrified of him?"

Ryan found this funny, and slapped Connor on the back, quite forcibly. Connor was finding it easier to make people laugh these days. This was a good sign with Edinburgh looming, even if some of the laughs weren't intentional.

Alun blew his whistle with a theatrical, rhythmic shrill, just how he liked to back in the day. The children all shook hands and congratulated each other on a good game, and then they each shook Alun's hand, too. Who said the kids these days didn't have manners? They headed off in the direction of the changing rooms a little further down from the cricket pavilion.

"Dad," Connor called.

Alun turned around. He looked alarmed to see him, and

At Least the Pink Elephants are Laughing at Us

looked around cautiously. Connor hoped he didn't think he would make a scene, that he thought he would embarrass him. Surely he realised he wasn't that heartless, that whatever resentment he held it didn't stoop that low?

Connor urgently attempted to ease his concerns. He held out his hand from a distance and quickly walked towards his dad.

"You were looking good out there," Connor said. "Very fit."

"Thank you."

His dad's upper lip glistened with moisture. He struggled for breath.

"I just wanted to say I'm sorry for the other day, you know?" Connor said. "I was upset but I over-reacted. I know she has these moments from time to time."

Dad smiled cautiously. "I appreciate that, son. I know it isn't easy. I know how much you love her. We both love her."

"Yes," Connor said, feeling awkward again now. "I'll let you get changed. I know you give a few of these guys a lift home. I'll see you soon, yeah?"

Connor turned and walked toward the concrete steps. That didn't go too bad, he considered.

"Connor."

Connor turned. "We'll have a proper chat sooner rather than later. I do need to speak to you about your mum. Yes?"

"Sure, Dad," Connor replied.

22 – Promise to Keep in Touch, Yeah?

It was Sunday morning and, because life was predictable, Mandy was on her way to her mum's house.

She had already picked up the Sunday newspapers, and she was already contemplating what she'd say when her mum asked what had been going on in her life since last Sunday. Her mum deserved to know the truth. Mandy should have told her everything before she even arranged to meet her dad, just like she had reassured William she would, but she was scared, and she was a coward. Mandy was sure it would upset her, and what was the point of that? But really Mandy knew she was making excuses, that however much it hurt, the truth was still better than lies and deception. Now there didn't seem much point telling her. There really wasn't any news. Her so-called 'dad' was a fraud, a fake. Truthfully, the stone was now best left unturned.

Mandy had decided she was just going to smile (as usual) and tell her Mum everything was absolutely fine. As normal. She might even treat herself to a quick ride on the stair-lift after all the recent heartbreak she'd endured.

"Mandy? How are you? Wow, it's been years."

Mandy's thoughts were interrupted by a young guy heading towards her pushing a buggy. The man's face was kind and gentle, and it was familiar. Of course. His face was just like it had been when they were children. It really *had* been years.

The man introduced Mandy to his wife, who was pretty and young and had a warm smile, and then to his baby daughter, who was just utterly adorable. He was unquestionably happy, but then he had all the things in life that Mandy didn't. Mandy didn't feel envious or bitter; she was genuinely happy for the guy. Mandy knew that, from the memory of the man as a little boy, he deserved all the happiness life had to offer.

All Mandy could think however, after they had parted and promised to keep in touch – which, of course, they wouldn't – was that she really deserved a little bit of that happiness herself.

23 – Two Men Talking

The rest of the household, excluding James (of course) were in bed. Naturally James was on the sofa in the lounge, with his feet up, watching television. It was déjà vu from last night, Terry considered.
Terry wished they could turn back the clock just a few months, to before James moved in. He longed for the image of James turning up on his doorstep with his suitcase to become just a figment of his imagination. Terry loved it when his mate popped around unannounced for a few beers. The banter always flowed back and forth at a relentless pace, often wild and uninhibited. It was such a welcome escape from an otherwise serious and predictable world. Terry longed to brush everything under the carpet and revert back to how it had been. But that was delusional thinking. Terry knew he had no choice but to speak to James, to clear the air and get some answers.
Terry took two cold ones out of the fridge and handed one to James.
"I've gone teetotal," James casually stated, placing the unopened can down on the table.
Terry spat his own drink on the floor. It bubbled and frothed on the carpet. Terry rubbed at it with his sock. "You what...?"
James looked at him and, with no additional creases in his worn face said, "It might not be a long-term thing mate, and I know I'm always starting things and giving them up, but for now, I'm off the booze. It's no big thing."
Terry wasn't sure what to say, which had become the norm recently. His mate was having a tough time and so it was great he wasn't drinking himself to oblivion. It was probably a clear sign he was taking positive, constructive steps to sort himself out. But right now it didn't feel positive, not for Terry. Nearly everything in their friendship revolved around booze in one way or another. He looked forward to their drinks together. It felt like

their friendship had been given another blow to the stomach.

"That's good, mate," Terry offered, as convincingly as he could muster. "Good on you. I've got your back on this one."

James continued to stare intently at the television screen. He seemed very interested. A giraffe was giving birth to a baby giraffe. The two men sat and watched in silence. It was unsurprisingly messy. The newborn giraffe shuffled around on the dusty ground like Bambi on ice. This was becoming awkward. Terry knew it was a perfect opportunity for him to break the silence and open up, tell him what was on his mind. Terry was always the big, tough boy in school but now he felt like a frightened little schoolboy. Terry wasn't sure whether talking would leave their already fragile, flailing friendship in tatters. He desperately didn't want that.

James was the one who spoke first. His gaze moved from the television and he – mechanically and almost robotically – turned to Terry. "So tell me. What is your beef with me mate...?"

Terry was suddenly on the back foot, taken aback by his friend's directness. This wasn't in the script he had rehearsed in work earlier. James was loud and brash and sometimes boisterous, but he was not a serious talker, not one for confrontation.

"Beef...?" Terry asked. "How do you mean...?"

Sure, Terry wanted to talk. However, when he pictured the chat in his mind he a) got his mate drunk and then b) dipped his toes in the water, tested the temperature and then slowly moved into choppier territory. Now a) and b) had been given the cold shoulder in no uncertain terms because his sober friend had jumped straight in the deep end, creating an almighty splash. Terry was seriously vexed by the sudden and unexpected turn of events.

"Yeah," James replied. "I'd like you to be open with me, mate, so that I can fix what I'm doing wrong. I don't want to be pissing you off. Not you, my best mate in the whole world."

What was this, Terry mused. Marriage counselling? Terry was surprised by his friend's apparent display of maturity. It sounded like an open invitation to talk like adults. This was new. Terry put his beer down, ready to talk. Terry picked his beer up, took a sip and then put his beer down again, ready to talk.

At Least the Pink Elephants are Laughing at Us

"Okay, now you've mentioned it, I guess I do have a few things to get off my chest. Firstly, what is the score with you and my dad, mate...?"

James laughed. That was unexpected, Terry thought. "That is a fairly obvious question, I guess. I knew you had some concerns, otherwise you wouldn't have followed us the other day, would you?"

"You knew I followed you?"

James smiled. "Mate. You are hardly inconspicuous. You've always been a big boy, haven't you? To be honest though, I half-expected you would, the way you were hanging around giving us funny looks and eyeing up your scruffy trainers, like you were ready to jump up and run out of the front door as soon as we shut it."

Terry couldn't help but smile. He quite enjoyed playing private detective (until he started finding answers) and he imagined he was pretty good at it. It was apparently like the karaoke machine all over again though; Terry imagined he was good, thought had a voice of an angel, of Aled Jones, but then in reality he was bloody awful.

"So you've been going to reading lessons? Why? What's the point of that? My dad can read."

"Well he can read just a little now, yes. He is picking it up really well. Your dad is doing great."

Terry took another gulp of his lager. He had pretty much reached this conclusion over the last couple of days, had accepted his dad had been conning them all these years, pretended he was just like everybody else, when in reality he had been hiding something monumental from them. He could see why his dad didn't want to shout it from the rooftops. It was a shock, but he'd accepted it. That wasn't his main concern anymore.

"But why is he going to lessons with *you?*"

James cleared his throat. "I'm not fully sure myself," he began, "but I met Roy at the grave a couple of years ago and he asked for my help and I said yes. Listen, I've always liked your dad. I'll admit, I liked the fact he got on with my dad. Those two had a bond. Me and your dad got pretty close at the factory, too. We often talked about Bobby. Your dad said he had always felt guilty about what happened to him."

Terry *was* shocked now. His voice went high-pitched. "You what? That makes no sense? What did Dad have to do with it? He wasn't even there when he died. Dad was never at any of the shows. My mum always went, not Dad."

James seemed to pick up that he had touched a nerve, for he spoke quieter, with a level tone. "Apparently they had a big discussion in the factory one night. Roy apparently told Dad that if he was serious about performing then he should go for it. Dad respected Roy and so he listened to him. He gave his up job at the factory to concentrate on the comedy. But listen," James said, holding out the palms of his hands "in my mind your dad had *nothing* to do with what happened to Bobby. I want to make that clear right now. Bobby was his own man and he made his own decisions and, truth be known, deep down I know most of them were wrong."

Terry shook his head. James was undoubtedly right. There was only one person who was responsible, and that was Bobby. How was his dad to know Bobby would go off the rails, make a total mess of everything? But he felt for Dad. If he did really feel guilty for what happened then he'd been living with it all these years, eating away at him. That must have been utter torture.

"Anyway, I kind of figured Roy couldn't read by the way he browsed the newspapers during breaks in the factory. He clocked on I'd noticed. He was embarrassed, and I felt bad for the guy. He said he wanted to read and had tried for years to learn with your mum, but he had failed every time. He said one day he might try again; but not today. It was never today. Roy said when the time was right he would need to ask somebody for help. We never mentioned it again until we met at the cemetery, when I was visiting Dad and he was visiting your mum."

Terry wasn't sure what to think now. The lager was beginning to mix with his scrambled mind; it was potentially a deadly cocktail. Terry was gutted his dad didn't ask *him* for help, but at least he has asked somebody. He was grateful James had tried. It was kind of touching James thought so much of his dad.

"Well, I thank you for the help you've been giving him."

"It's an honour."

They sat in silence. Terry's mind was overactive; he just

wasn't sure how to get the words out. Speaking from the heart was difficult. It just wasn't what they did. James had opened up though, and so it was now or never.

"But what about you then, James? You've obviously done wonders to help my old man, but what is going on with your life? Shouldn't you be out there fighting to get your wife and son back? Don't you need to sort yourself out first?"

James bowed his head. He looked incredibly sad, absolutely distraught. Terry quickly continued "Listen, we both know we saw things we never talk about. Do you really want to live your life just like your dad?"

James looked intently at Terry now, with open, challenging eyes. "What does that mean?"

"You really want me to spell it out, mate?"

"Spell it out..."

"We were both there, James! Behind The Regency, when we were teenagers. We both saw it! We were both in the same boat..."

"How were we both in the same boat?" James asked. "It was *my* dad, not yours. I'm fully aware my dad was messed up, that he could be a prick, but he was still my dad, you know?"

Terry was shocked, absolutely flabbergasted. He thought his mate had seen everything. He hadn't. Terry's head felt like it was going to explode. He was determined to pursue what was important now, what could actually be changed.

"You say all that, so why are you suddenly hell bent on following in his footsteps? You've been living a blessed life. You have a wonderful wife and a cracking little boy, and yet you seem desperate to throw it all away, just like Bobby did. Why, mate? Tell me that...?"

James stood up. He hovered over Terry, face flushed, fists clenched. He looked like he was ready to pounce. Terry tensed. His friend was going to hit him. Terry desperately didn't want to hurt his mate, but he'd have to defend himself. He waited for James to make his move.

But it didn't happen. James completely relaxed and unravelled his body. Straggly, long greasy hair fell lazily over his eyes. James put his head in his hands then started pulling on his hair with frustration. His face crumbled into a pinched, pained expression. James sobbed, loudly and freely. It broke Terry's heart to hear his mate in so much pain, so hurt.

"He wasn't a bad man. I just know he wasn't. And I just loved him to bits. He just really struggled, you know...?"

Terry was on his feet now, offering his arms to James. "I know, mate. I'm sorry. I shouldn't have pushed it..."

"But I *don't* want to be like him. I promise you, I really don't. And I'm trying to sort things out. I've called and called Shirley but she just won't get back to me. I miss her and Rory with all my heart, you know? God knows I'm trying, Terry, honestly I'm trying..."

Terry felt his friend's wet cheek pressing against his shoulder, his body trembling, and he said "I know you are mate. I know you are..."

24 – Lying Down and Looking Up

He turned off the engine and parked his car in what always felt like the absolute middle of nowhere, the perfect spot to ditch a dead body. He looked down at the ground, tried to avoid the divots and the nettles, but then it was so dark he could see very little, and so instead he mainly listened to the faint but mesmerising flow of the river somewhere in the distance for guidance. There he was, lying on the hard grass, his arms by his side and his eyes fixed to the sky. Without any introduction or warning – without hardly any sound at all - he slowly unravelled his own body so he lay down on the grass next to him.

"Son."

"Dad."

Connor didn't turn to acknowledge him, and neither did he sound remotely surprised his dad was there with him on the grass in the middle of nowhere, despite the fact he had never been there with him before.

Weeks had passed since they had met at the rugby pitch. He was so glad his boy had come to see him, even though he knew he was prompted by his mum. It was only a few more weeks until the big Edinburgh trip. Alun knew the tour was a massive thing for Connor and the last thing he wanted to do was add to his worries, but he desperately wanted to speak to him; no, he *needed* to speak to him.

Instead they sat in silence, just staring at the multitude of stars that filled the perfect night sky.

"Do you ever fear that a psychopath might sneak up and kill you, Connor? You know, just lying here like this...?"

Alun wasn't sure this was a good opening gambit, or if it was a tad too random, but then it was a genuine question and besides, he was dipping his toes in the water. When Alun was a teenager he'd pitched a tent with his friends close to this spot, down by the castle, and in his mind he was certain every noise, every movement and every shadow belonged to a psychotic killer with a sharp knife and even shaper teeth, hungry for blood. It was one of the rare moments Alun wished he believed in God, for he so wanted somebody there to look over and protect him.

"I have an overactive imagination, Dad, as you know," Connor replied, "and so at some point, yes, it probably has crossed my mind. But then humans are prone to irrational or disproportionate fears, don't you think? We worry about being bitten by a spider or eaten by a shark and yet you really are more likely to get run over by a bus, or maybe struck over the head by a flying can of baked beans in Aldi…"

"It really is nice, though," Alun added. "This. I know your mum has always been the one to appreciate the beauty of the natural world and I've been more engrossed with mundane practicalities like turning up to school on time. I'm not entirely sure what she thought the school bus was there for, honest to God I don't. This place brings you closer to the way your mum thinks, doesn't it? You really are at one with nature here, aren't you? The older I've got the more I think your mum was right all along. We're all so wrapped up in our own busy lives we forget how trivial we actually are. It puts things into perspective, don't you think, when you look up and see the big picture?"

Alun waited for a response. Alun knew he was stepping into Connor's territory here, that anything he said about the wonders of the world were probably nothing to the big questions occupying his son's mind. Connor had always been a deep thinker, even as a child. Alun knew that when he was asking childish questions about the Tooth Fairy, he had a layer of deeper questions left in reserve. He really hoped Connor did not give a sarcastic, belittling reply. He was speaking from the heart. Moments like these were one of the rare occurrences he genuinely questioned whether there might – just might – be a God.

"It really does. That is exactly what I've always thought. To be honest, I thought I was mad. It's kind of reassuring to know I'm not thinking these things all on my own. If I am mad then it's reassuring that at least my dad is too."

Phew. It felt easier to open up here, Alun considered, because they shared the same mesmeric distraction. They did not need to look at each other, be conscious of eye contact or any of

At Least the Pink Elephants are Laughing at Us

the other signs that the discussion was so painfully difficult.

"You know I think about what happened with your mum in Tenby every single day, don't you son? You do know I regret it with every bone in my body?"

"I do, Dad. I've honestly never doubted that, not for a moment."

"That's good to hear," Alun replied, his voice breaking. His hands nervously snapped at the grass on the floor, rolled the clippings around in his fist. "I know I was wrong not to do anything when all the signs were there, were plain to see. And I know I was an absolute imbecile to just brush the problem under the carpet, to take you away to Tenby like the problem could be painted over..."

Connor interrupted him. Alun could feel his tension growing, his emotions rising. "You know that's what I've always struggled with. You must have known what was happening, that Mum was ill, because it had happened before. She had been ill before..."

"I know, I know. I honestly didn't think it would happen again..."

"*Honestly?*" Connor questioned. There was real doubt in his tone.

Alun paused. He thought about the question. He so wanted to be honest. It was just so difficult, so painful. Sometimes he doubted if he even knew the truth.

"So obviously you know your mum had a breakdown when she was pregnant with you. They said the underlying condition was worsened by pre-natal depression. That's why we only had one of you. We just couldn't risk going through that unbearable pain again."

It hurt Alun to even remember that period of their lives. It had been the only time they had struggled to survive as a couple. He had even confided in his brother, Harry, and as a rule, men never spoke about real things.

"And you know that is why Aunt Jojo came over from Ghana to stay?" Alun continued. "She comforted your mum in her moment of need, and boy did she need it. I don't know how we would have got through it without Jojo, to tell you the truth. I don't know how *I* would have coped, let alone your mother. And the signs were there again before Tenby, of course. I saw them loud and clear and I know you tried to warn me that time at the rugby match. But the circumstances weren't the same. Of course, your mum wasn't pregnant, was she? I just hoped and prayed it was different this time, that everything was different, you know? But...but..."

"But what...?"

"But I guess I just *wanted* to believe it, son. It was terrible the first time your mother broke down, so goddamn awful watching the beautiful woman I love with all my heart suffering so very much. And of course, she was so delicate and fragile that first time because she was carrying you inside her, this beautiful unborn baby. If I am as honest as I can be then I just don't think I was strong enough to accept it could happen again. I was too weak, son. There you have it. Alun Thomas was too damn *weak!*"

Alun knew he was crying because his eyes were smothered in tears and the beautiful night sky he had moments before admired was now blurred and out of focus. He felt Connor turn so that he lay on his side now, so he was able to look his dad in the face.

"You're not weak, Dad. You're the strongest man I know. You hear? You hear me...?"

Alun nodded his head. He managed to force words out. "I hear."

Connor continued. "We can't let it happen again though. She is losing it again. Mum thinks Aunt Jojo is dying. She is digging a hole to bury her. We can't just let this happen. We need to do something now before it is too late..."

"Son," Alun interrupted, "I am very sorry to tell you this but your mum isn't having an episode. She is telling the truth."

"What? What do you mean? What are you talking about, Dad?"

"Your auntie is dying, Connor."

"No?"

"I'm sorry, but yes. Your mum reacted bizarrely by digging the hole, you're right enough about that. But what can we expect? It is her beloved older sister. It is her way of coping. There was some muddled reasoning here. Your mum just wanted her close and in a place she would be comfortable and loved. She knows it was ridiculous now. Your mum has filled the hole back up. We did it together. Her approach has been much more pragmatic and positive recently. She has considered what Jojo's last dying wish would be. She's made arrangements for Jojo to come and stay with us, one last time, before it is too late."

"No way?" Connor exclaimed. "When is she coming?"

"She lands tomorrow, son. That's why I've come to speak to you tonight, to finally have that chat I've been putting off for far too long..."

Alun held out his hand and Connor took hold of it. He could barely remember the last time his son had shown him genuine, heartfelt affection. Alun knew he'd be strong enough to handle things this time.

This time he wouldn't need to handle things alone.

25 – Supermarket Sweep

The pushchair was attached to her that often these days it felt like an extra limb. Shirley glanced down at her little adorable boy, with his rosy cheeks and crusty dried snot coating his upper lip. He stared back at her with those fascinated, big beautiful eyes. His eyes had never lost their apparent wonderment for the world they possessed as a baby. Rory was such a darling, Shirley thought, the most important thing in her world, her absolute everything.

Rory kept those fascinated, big beautiful big eyes fixed on his mother, the woman who brought him into this world and then, with a swift brutal single motion, lobbed his Paw Patrol dog out of the side of the pushchair and onto the filthy pavement. His adorable, innocent face morphed into a mocking snigger.

He was such a flipping brat! How many times did she need to tell him? What part of "no" did he not understand?

Shirley dug her teeth into the inside of her upper lip so hard she nearly drew blood. One, two, three...she rigidly and mechanically forced her lips into the shape of a smile and then bent at the knees and picked up the toy. The dog stared back at her with that smug grin. Shirley gave the toy a quick wipe with her sleeve. Keep calm. Don't show frustration.

"Here you go, darling," Shirley said, handing the toy back to Rory for the umpteenth time that day.

"Thank you Mummy," Rory said, his smile a picture of innocence. "I'm sorry, Mummy." And then he threw the toy out of the pram again.

Keep calm, my arm! The process started again.

Shirley knew Rory had outgrown his pushchair, that when he was with James he held his hand and walked everywhere and that other mothers gave her sly, disapproving looks. But James wasn't here anymore, was he? James had messed up. Again. Rory thrived on misbehaving when he was out with Shirley. He loved to run off with an infuriatingly infectious smile, saying "chase me, Mummy, chase me." Or worse, he threw himself on the floor like one of those prima donna footballers. Only the other day Rory had decided to lie down in the middle of a puddle. Shirley just couldn't manage with the bedlam, not anymore, and not on her own. Something had to give, and she chose the pushchair. Rory hated it and so, after she'd strapped him down, with his arms flailing and his legs kicking, then he rebelled. Throwing his toy out of his pram was one way that Rory told Mummy he was not happy.

Life was unquestionably tough without James. She really didn't want anybody to feel sorry for her, she didn't even want anybody to know she was struggling, but it definitely *was* a struggle. This was the most difficult period. She hadn't adjusted yet. But at least she was no longer living in denial. Shirley looked in the mirror every morning and told herself she was a strong, independent woman who deserved to be treated with respect. They were deliberately powerful and straightforward words. She didn't believe them, of course. Definitely not after a sleepless night, waking up to another dreaded day ahead. But one day she would.

The real problem right now, apart from the bleeding obvious, was that Shirley didn't have enough purpose in her life. Shirley missed adult company. She felt painfully guilty for thinking that; like she was an ungrateful bitch, an awful mum. She couldn't deny the truth, though. She was lonely. She couldn't remember the last time she'd a good old-fashioned laugh with an actual grown-up person.

Shirley darted in and out of shops like Lewis Hamilton overtaking cars at Silverstone. She walked up and down the aisles, balancing frozen sausages and bottles of coke on the hood of the pushchair (she used to store the items in the basket at the bottom but a woman accused her of stealing). Choosing the best till was not always straightforward. It wasn't like Shirley was in a great rush to be somewhere but still, she liked to play the game. This queue was longer but the woman looked fast and on the ball while on the other till the guy looked like he needed a nap. Oh hold on: a gap had opened up. She pushed the pram to the till and smiled. Shirley was nothing if not polite and friendly.

"Hello, Shirley."

Her initial thought was *wow*. The customer service on this till was first class! The guy even knew her *name*. Her second thought was, what the...

Shirley looked at him like she had seen a ghost. She was undeniably shell-shocked. "What are you doing here?"

James smiled. He put his hand to his plastic name badge. "I work here."

Of course he was working here, Shirley thought. Why else would he be sat at the till serving customers? There was really no need for him to show his badge to seal the deal. Shirley felt her cheeks flush. What was going on? It had been so long since he had worked it seemed alien to see him now, sat at the till.

Shirley was jittery, like she had been living on a diet of cigarettes and coffee. Was she looking a mess? What would he think? She had put on any old grubby clothes to come down the shops. How could she feel flustered around James, the man she had loved for so many years, the father of her little boy, the man who had let her down more than anybody else in the whole world...?

"Daddy! Mummy, look! It's Daddy! Sat down! In the shop! Daddy...!"

Rory frantically and aggressively wrestled with the straps of his pram, struggling to get out; like a wild, caged animal. His face reddened and his mouth frothed. Saliva literally dribbled down the side of his mouth. He took hold of his Paw Patrol doll and lobbed it out of the pushchair. It flew further than Shirley had ever seen it. These were sure signs of a monumental meltdown.

"Could I give him a hug? Please?" James asked.

Shirley glanced over her shoulder. The woman behind her had given up and taken her chances in the queue with the sleepy guy. Shirley had so many powerful and conflicting feelings for this man but, ultimately, she wasn't going to deny her son a hug with his dad. It broke her heart to see how sad her little man had become without his dad. Shirley unfastened Rory and lifted his heavy bulk onto the counter. Rory threw himself into his dad's arms. James closed his eyes and held him, squeezed him tight.

"How are you?" he asked Shirley over Rory's shoulder. His voice was breaking. "You look well."

"I'm doing good," she replied. She had a compulsion to rub it in, tell him she was doing absolutely amazingly, that catching him with some trollop was the best thing that had ever happened to her, no thanks to you, you dirty little cheating shit. But she resisted. It wasn't her style and – besides – she wasn't into fantasy.

"And how are you?" she politely, and reluctantly, asked.

James had been calling her regularly and persistently recently. Shirley had just been letting the phone ring. She had nothing to say to him. He had knocked at the door, too, and she longed to open it, just to say hello, to hear his voice, remind her of the life she so missed, but she resisted and pretended they were not in. Shirley knew James desperately wanted to see Rory. Shirley knew that whatever happened between her and James moving forward, James had to see Rory. It wasn't fair on her boy not to see his daddy. He adored his daddy and his daddy adored him. None of this was Rory's fault. She just hadn't been ready to speak to James; not yet.

Another woman had joined the queue behind her now, almost a replica of the first; impatient and intimidating, and Shirley could sense her looking around, tapping her shoe, ready to bubble over. The woman wasn't in the mood for happy families. Shirley wasn't entirely comfortable conducting this conversation in the middle of a supermarket, either, but on the other hand, she did want to know how James was.

"Not too bad, really," he said. "As you can see, I've got this job. It's not what I grew up dreaming of but it pays with real money. I'm living with Terry and his family. They've been so good to me. And I've been much more active with the gigs. The Edinburgh Festival Fringe is only a few weeks away..."

Shirley was taken aback. She expected him to talk it up; to try and impress her, maybe win her back. He was playing it down. It sounded like things were getting a little better; like *he* was getting a little better. And it really was good news about the comedy. She still wanted him to make a go of that.

There was suddenly a commotion. Rory released his dad's hold and then slapped him angrily on the cheek. Shirley put her own hand to her mouth and gasped. "You left us, Daddy!" Rory shouted.

James held Rory's hand and pressed his nose against his. "I'm sorry, Rory," he said. James kissed Rory's lips and Shirley lifted the boy off the counter and put him back in the pushchair. This time Rory did not kick and scream when she strapped him up.

"Would it be okay to call you about making an arrangement to see Rory?" James asked, placing change in Shirley's hand. He had already been calling. He was asking if she could maybe *answer* some of his calls.

"Bye, bye Daddy," Rory shouted, waving from his seat.

"Give me a call," Shirley replied. "We'll see." She smiled.

It was muggy outside now. There had been a shower and it had washed the pavements clean. Shirley wiped a cold sliver of sweat from her forehead. She passed another mother, looking tired, pushing a pram. She guessed she was probably her age. Shirley smiled and the mother smiled back.

A rainbow appeared in the blue sky above the dreary shops; clear and lucid and beautiful. It suddenly came to her. Shirley remembered the last time she'd had a good old-fashioned laugh, with an actual grown-up person.

It had been the last day she was still with James.

26 – When Relatives Come to Stay

Dad opened the door and then immediately stepped aside to let Connor through.

"In the bedroom, son," he said, as Connor kicked off his shoes, pushed them under the table and then hurriedly climbed the stairs with the thunderous footsteps of an elephant.

Connor took a deep breath in the musty landing and then pushed open the door, which opened slovenly as it brushed against the thick, luxurious carpeted floor. The room was dark. The room was quiet. The curtains were pulled tightly together. It didn't feel like the bedroom that belonged to his parents, the bedroom he remembered from childhood. Connor stepped inside, no idea what he'd find.

And there she was, sitting on the bed next to Mum, her legs dangling over the side, like a child on a seat that was much too big. Auntie Jojo.

"Connor!" Jojo gasped, white smile stretching the circumference of her face. "It is wonderful to see you! It has been much, much too long. And just look at you. Haven't you grown *big*!"

Now his auntie was familiar again to him. He remembered her magnificent warmth and affection, her incredible love and passion for life; the charming woman who made him and his dad feel so welcome in her country all those years ago when they first visited Ghana, when they were both strangers – and in a minority - in a foreign land. As he held her in his arms though, physically she felt a shell of the healthy, vivacious African lady he remembered. Jojo was painfully frail. Her skin clung to her flimsy bones. Her whole frame had shrunk and shrivelled, like an apple that had been left in the fruit bowl for too long.

Connor didn't need telling that the news was true. He could see with his own eyes now. His auntie was dying.

He glanced at his mum. She was always the first person he noticed in any room. But not today. She had one leg crossed over the other. The whites of her eyes were crimson. Her nose was running. She sniffed. She'd been crying. She held out her hands too and embraced him, held him so tight it was like she was scared to let him go. Connor looked at his auntie again. His wide, sympathetic eyes must have told a story.

"Don't you go feeling sorry for me, young man," Jojo warned, playfully wagging her middle finger. She patted the space on the bed next to her. Connor felt unusually heavy and bulky sat next to her fragile frame as he sank into the mattress. "I've had the most wonderful life, Connor. Every day has been a gift. And do you know what is a blessing now?"

Connor shook his head. His thoughts were slow and muddled; the confused thoughts of a serious hangover.

"They've told me there is no way I will get any better, Connor. And do you know why that's a blessing?" Jojo squeezed Connor's hand. "I will tell you why. It is because I know exactly where I am heading, and I can plan for it. I can live my last few days knowing it will end shortly. I can enjoy them and savour them without any false hopes I might just get a little bit better."

Connor smiled. He understood. There was no enjoyment or dignity spending your final days suffering in a hospital bed, clinging dearly to some false hope. He had always thought that. Auntie Jojo had great and infallible faith, just like his mum. She knew a better life was waiting for her.

"So what do you plan to do?" Connor asked. "You know – with the time that you have left?"

Jojo laughed now. "When I said "plan," that may have been an – what is the word now – an exaggeration? I am looking to spend a week or so here with my darling sister and her beautiful family and then head back to Ghana to be with the rest of my family. But what I will do with each day has not been planned. I'll thank the Lord for each extra day that is gifted to me and then I'll just live each day as it comes. I'll just be grateful to have the people I love around me. Do you understand?"

Connor looked up and noticed his dad was in the room, quietly and patiently standing by the door. "Cup of tea for anybody?" he asked.

Connor smiled. "I do understand, Auntie," he said. "Oh, and Dad...milk, no sugar, please..."

27 – Do Not Play God. Understand...?

"So how long have you got left now until the big tour, Herbert?" Amanda asked, standing like a teapot with one hand on her hip and the other outstretched and leaning against the counter.

Herbert absent-mindedly put his pen in his ear, fiddled about and then pulled the pen out again. He wanted to quickly check whether any earwax had attached itself to the pen, but he considered that as Amanda was stood by the table waiting for him to reply, the odds of him getting caught were unrealistically high. And so, instead, he stopped fidgeting and gave her his full attention. Their conversations had become more frequent recently as Herbert had been spending less and less time doing the job he was actually paid for and more time sipping tea and working on his project.

"Two weeks now, Amanda. It is unbearably exciting. We have our final show at The Regency on the Saturday night and then we are off to Edinburgh first thing Sunday morning."

Amanda smiled. "It's almost like going off to war, don't you think? It *must* be exciting, for sure, because I'm delirious and I'm not even going, Herbert. How are the three star performers bearing up? Any more drama for your book? Have you managed to conjure up any? That book of yours must be getting mighty thick now. Any more punch-ups?"

Herbert laughed. "They're doing just fine, Amanda," he reassured her. "Their development is growing all the time. And don't worry, nobody had been punched since that first show. I'm convinced it was completely out of character. If I was a betting man - which I'm not - I'd say Connor was normally a practising pacifist..."

"Connor?"

"Yes. Don't tell me I haven't told you? Of course. I know you told me a long time ago that you're good friends with his mum. One of the performers is Connor. I must have told you that, surely?"

Amanda narrowed both eyes now. "No, Herbert," she said. "You didn't tell me that."

"Oh. Right."

Herbert was certain the conversation had taken a sudden turn for the worse. He fiddled with his pen again and considered sticking it back in his ear, but managed to resist. Just.

"You are right, Herbert. Connor's mum is a *very* good friend of mine. Can you remember what we discussed about creating some drama for your book?"

Herbert coughed and then blinked both eyes, like they were smothered in salty sweat. "Yes. I seem to remember something about that."

"Well," Amanda continued, leaning closer. "When it comes to Connor, just *don't*. Do you understand?"

Herbert shuffled about in the plastic seat. "I think I understand you loud and clear, Amanda. Loud and clear."

Amanda smiled warmly. "Good. More tea, dear...?"

At Least the Pink Elephants are Laughing at Us

28 – The Perfect Son

Shirley had left the pushchair at home this time.
Rory's moods changed with the wind. Right now he was going through an independent stage. He didn't want any help with anything whatsoever, and that included getting dressed, eating, and, of course, walking. At this rate, Shirley considered, she'd be sending him out to work by the time he was four, earning some extra pennies through a morning paper round; it would definitely help with the dreaded bills that dropped through the letterbox at an alarmingly regular rate. He happily held his mother's hand and trotted along the pavement at a steady, leisurely pace, like a horse performing the dressage.
"You alright?"
"Yes," Rory replied, nodding his head. "I am alright, Mummy."
Shirley knew all too well that he would tell her, and in no uncertain terms, if he wasn't alright. Her little three year old boy wasn't one to hide his emotions, probably because he *was* a little three-year-old boy.
She knocked the front door.
An outline grew larger through the stained glass. The door was opened with by a familiar face with lips which greeted Shirley with a kiss.
"How are you, dear?"
"Can't complain, Miriam," Shirley replied.
"Nanny!" Rory said, bouncing excitedly up and down on the spot. He was so adorable when he did that, Shirley thought.
Miriam leant forward and gave her grandson a big hug. "Look how big you've grown!" she exclaimed, smiling. "You must be costing your poor mother a fortune in shoes. You'll be playing second row for Wales one day soon, you mark by words. Come in! Don't stand on the pavement like a couple of beggars. Oh I know that's not the correct term these days, but you know what I mean, dear."
Shirley and Rory followed Miriam through the narrow

hallway. Rory was keen to get past her, but he knew much better than to do that and so he bided his time by tapping his feet on the floor, like he was running on the spot. He was like that when he was stuck behind a younger kid at the slide, Shirley thought. He was always amazingly considerate of both younger children and elderly big people. They passed the study with the pine bookcase that spanned every wall in the room. Eventually they reached their destination. Rory sprinted. "Daddy!" he shouted. "Daddy, Daddy, Daddy...!"

Rory was on top of his dad, smothering him with hugs. His dad held him at the waist, tickling his skinny belly. Rory fell about in hysterics.

"I hope this isn't too awkward," Miriam said, smiling wryly, stirring the pot with an invisible wooden spoon. "I know you two love birds aren't getting along too well at the moment. James here was just visiting his mum, aren't you son? To tell you the truth dear, I'm a bit upset James didn't choose to stay with me all this time. That Terry Hughes has been a good friend to James all these years, there is no doubt about that. He always stuck up for him even as kids. Remember when he pinched that boy's nipples at your party for saying something rude? I've always liked Terry. I think Terry had a soft spot for me, too. My point is, I'm sure he must be fed up of you staying there by now, James..."

James held his son outstretched in his arms, and was pretending to launch him in the air like a rocket. Miriam had a mischievous streak in her, Shirley considered. And it seemed to be getting more and more mischievous the older she got. Apparently she came out of her shell when Bobby passed away. And she had continued growing ever since.

It *was* a bit awkward, but Shirley was glad James was here. She hoped he might be. The odds were pretty decent. It was a slightly ridiculous predicament. James didn't need to justify visiting his mum, did he? He visited her all the time when they were together. There was no reason he would stop now. If anything the regularity of the visits had probably increased. Shirley knew James would have loved to have stayed with his mum after she threw him out, that he adored spending time with her. She knew the only reason he didn't stay with her was to avoid her fretting. James may have idolised his dad, but he truly loved and adored his mum.

He obviously hadn't told her why they weren't getting along too well though, had he? James didn't want to break her heart. He knew Shirley thought the world of Miriam, and Shirley liked to think the respect was mutual. The first time Shirley met Miriam she couldn't believe how young, elegant and attractive she was. Shirley could imagine Terry lusting after his best friend's hot mum when they were kids! Miriam looked more like a sister than a mother. James explained to Shirley that she and Bobby were childhood sweethearts and his mum gave birth at a very young age. He told her – with undoubted pride – that after Bobby had passed away Miriam had returned to college, passed her exams and become an English teacher. It was fitting, as she absolutely devoured books. James told Shirley his mum was the cleverest person he knew, and Shirley had no doubt whatsoever that he was right.

Miriam would be the first to give her boy a clip if he got caught up to no good. Admittedly she wore rose-tinted spectacles when it came to her little (middle-aged) angel, but she did manage to see clearly at some point, and when she did, she took no prisoners. Miriam had strong morals. Shirley thought about making James squirm. James feared nothing more than the wrath of his dear mother.

"She is right enough," James said. "I'm just visiting my mum." He glanced at Shirley, daring to hold eye contact for just a fleeting moment. "You know how I try and visit my mum when I can. After all, she makes a lush cup of tea, so she does."

Shirley accidentally caught her own reflection in the big oval mirror on the wall, the mirror above the wooden sideboard with the permanently moulding fruit in a round, plastic bowl. She was pleased – and surprised - to note she didn't look too bad. Not really. Her hair wasn't too tangled and there was at least some resemblance to colour in her cheeks. She was surprised – and possibly disappointed – to notice that, just like in the shop, she still cared what she looked like when it came to her husband.

"Did James tell you why we're not getting on too well, Miriam?" Shirley asked. She had taken Miriam's wooden spoon and was doing some stirring of her own. This was fun, she thought. Shirley made sure she waited until she saw the whites in

James's eyes, staring back at her with blind panic, before she winked at him.

"He said he'd been a very naughty boy. If I know my son then that means he got drunk again."

Shirley made sure she wasn't looking at James any more when she said "Something like that, Miriam. Something like that."

Let him squirm!

Rory was jumping on the sofa like it was a trampoline. Seeing those two together was a stark reminder of something she had tried to blank out. Her little boy wouldn't want any other dad in the whole world. Shirley felt much, much worse about the split for Rory than she did for herself, and that really was saying something.

"Have you heard the good news, pet?" Miriam asked.

"What good news?" Shirley absent-mindedly replied. She didn't mean to be so flippant. She knew there was some good news out there at the moment. She just couldn't think what it could possibly be.

"James getting a job!" she said, happily slapping her hands together like a sea lion. "I thought there was no chance I would see my good-for-nothing son doing an honest day's work again before he got his eager mitts on the measly state pension. It has been so long since he worked at the factory, hasn't it? But he has proved me wrong. And I couldn't be happier."

Shirley smiled. Miriam was clearly proud her ageing son had managed to get a job working on the till. It was endearing, to tell the truth. But Shirley couldn't deny she was surprised, and impressed, too, that James had got a job. James could write a book on excuses not to work. Apparently it used to be so different, though. He worked at the same factory his dad did for over twenty years. James worked hard too, by all accounts. And then he got made redundant. James hit the self-destruct button, drunk himself into oblivion and then cheated on his wife. One day he was living as a respectable married man and then next he had lost it all. Shirley knew that for years James was reluctant to add too much to his life because he was frightened of losing it again. She was so aware James had been terrified of repeating the same mistake and that it was partly because of this fear that he had.

There was something else nagging in Shirley's mind too. Was it just coincidence he'd managed to get a job so quickly after she'd thrown him out? Okay, it had been months, but then he had been out of work for *years*. Was James putting himself out there, totally out of his comfort zone, so that he could win her back?

Now that really *was* cute.

"And that's not all," Miriam continued. "The way James is going with his comedy shows, that Billy Connolly is going to have to watch his step!"

Miriam did make her laugh. She was like a never-ending, walking and talking advert for her son. Rory would never want a different dad and Miriam would never want a different son. Sometimes it was just adorable. It was something she worried about with her and James splitting; that she wouldn't have a genuine reason to stay close to Miriam, that they would drift until there was nothing left. Who wanted a daughter-in-law hanging around like a bad smell?

"James has asked me to come to his next gig," Miriam enthused. "It is the final one before they head off to Edinburgh. He warned me there could be swearing and adult themes. I said, in which case, 'count me in!'"

Shirley put her hand to her mouth and giggled. Rory did the same. He loved mimicking his mum.

"Why don't you come with me, Shirley? Next Saturday night? At The Regency."

Now this *was* awkward. Miriam's mischievous side was stronger than ever tonight, Shirley thought. Sure, things were improving between her and James. Shirley didn't want to slam James over the head with an iron every time she saw him, for starters. That was an improvement. Shirley still needed him to know she was the boss in this situation though, that he had some major making up to do before she could even *think* about taking him back. Ideally Shirley wanted James to think she was squeezing him in between the rest of her very important, unusually busy daily schedule. Going to one of his shows with his mum wasn't part of the equation. Shirley wanted to watch James perform, especially this close to the Edinburgh gig; she just didn't want James to know she did.

Shirley struggled for the right words.

"For me...?"

Shirley was sure Miriam slumped her shoulders forward, like a tired and flattened pillow that desperately needed plumping up, just to emphasise her frailty. *Would you really let an old lady like me go out by herself at night...?*

There was another thing, too. Miriam said the gig was at The Regency. That was where Bobby did his final show. It was going to be a tough night for both James and Miriam. They could probably do with her support.

"Go on then."

She couldn't help but glance at James.

Shirley was pleased to see her husband was smiling.

Chris Westlake

29 - Let the Plane Wait

Connor was really going to miss his Auntie Jojo.

He was generally pretty philosophical about these things. He successfully managed to put himself in other people's shoes, to see the big picture, to take a step back and all the rest of it. Connor was sad when his granddad died, for example, but his initial thoughts then were for his dad, even though they weren't exactly getting along at the time.

But now he felt irrationally sad. This was only the fourth occasion they'd spent time together. And she was only returning to Accra. She was still alive, for now. He told himself to look at the big picture, to consider how his mum must be thinking. But his emotional self was kicking his rational self into touch, was really giving it a pummelling. And it was way beyond his limited capability to imagine how his mum was feeling right now.

The three of them sat patiently on the chairs at Heathrow Airport, periodically glancing at the departures screen and keeping their ears alert for the flight to Accra to be announced. Connor's dad was with them, somewhere, but he had ants in his pants. Every time he sat down he looked around for something else to occupy his time. And when apparently nothing met the challenge he slapped his knees and said he was off. He had returned, on different occasions, with a newspaper, a cup of coffee and a new pair of shoes. Connor was exhausted just watching him.

"The hand dryers in the toilets are truly first class," Dad announced when he returned this time. "Very powerful. Nothing worse than an airport full of people with wet hands or hand prints on their trousers, don't you think?"

Connor nodded his head slowly and then glanced at his mum and auntie, who were doing the same. He was sure they couldn't think of anything to say either. Connor felt like saying it was probably worse to have somebody carrying a bomb at an airport, but he didn't feel this was worth raising as a discussion point.

"It's just amazing isn't it," Jojo said, big brown eyes looking

At Least the Pink Elephants are Laughing at Us

around like a baby taking in the world for the very first time. "All these people. All these flights. All these countries. All at the same time. And everything still runs like clockwork. How on Earth do they do it?"

Connor was fascinated by the way Jojo looked at the world through completely different eyes from the average man or woman. Connor knew his mum looked at the world through similar eyes. He knew his own life would probably be so much more enhanced and enriching if he followed suit. But he was just too much of a cynic, a realistic, a grumpy old man to do so.

As if on cue, a tired voice announced that the flight to Amsterdam was delayed. Jojo didn't seem to notice, or if she did notice, didn't seem to care, for she continued beaming.

Connor had realised over the last few weeks that Jojo truly was amazing. He'd initially been deflated when he reunited with her. Back in Ghana she had been a magnificent lion, the king of the jungle, possessing a thunderous roar that all the animals feared and respected. Now she had been reduced to a fragile bag of bones that could barely raise a meow due to this terrible illness. Connor was sad when he saw her. But when she spoke he instantly realised that she was just as magnificent as she always had been. Just because her body was sick didn't mean her mind was any less beautiful and unblemished as it had always been.

"The world has always been the same size, Connor," Auntie Jojo said, as if announcing something new. "But years ago – and I *mean* years ago – it felt so much bigger. If you were born in Ghana you lived in Ghana. All your life. The rest of the world was nothing to you. Nothing. But today?" She spread her hands. "If I am born in Scotland but want to live in say, Belgium, what is there to stop me? Nothing."

Connor wanted to say that that awful Brexit vote might put a spanner in the works, but he resisted. He'd learnt to control his tongue a little over the last few weeks. Rome wasn't built in a day and so he had taken some small steps. Connor had always prided himself on his dourness, his bleak outlook on life, and now it was proving a relative success on the comedy circuit. But now he realised maybe these traits weren't as fantastically attractive as he once thought. His Auntie Jojo, for example, had lovingly referred to him as a "whinger." Connor twisted the observation around in his mind and examined it from all different perspectives, but he still couldn't see how she meant it as a compliment. Life was hard for her in Ghana, but you wouldn't think it. He considered it was time to stop feeling sorry for himself and maybe start appreciating the things he did have.

He knew Ghana had a massive influence on both his mum and Jojo, on their outlook on life. He quickly realised from his trips there that his childhood perceptions were wildly distorted. Money was often sparse, but love wasn't. Time didn't seem a precious commodity. People were generous with both their time and their hospitality. Connor spent long hours at houses belonging to various relatives and they always greeted him like one of their own. He drank more in Ghana than anywhere else; he was hardly ever without a bottle of Star lager. When they said to come again, Connor knew they genuinely meant it. Sure, the church was deadly serious, but so was partying. Connor felt that over here entertainment was often organised and frequently forced. In Ghana they just went with the flow. It was never too early or too late to dance! Connor knew it must have been an incredibly difficult decision for his mum to leave her family, and in particular her sister, to start a new life in the UK.

"Just look at young Connor," Jojo said, looking at him accusingly. Connor wondered what there was to look at, what he had done wrong. He was just sat there, minding his business, staying out of trouble. "It's incredible to think what he is doing with his clowning lark. You mark my words! This boy will be the next Richard Pryor! This is a young man who is grabbing the bull by both horns," and she demonstrated with both hands exactly how forcibly he was grabbing the bull, "and then riding the bull like he is at a rodeo. And if he falls off the bull and - mark my words - he will, then he'll just get back on the bull and ride it even harder...."

Connor was beginning to feel sorry for this poor bull, but he glowed with pride that his aunt had such confidence in him. She was just like his mum. He did wonder why his auntie was so passionately convinced that he would fall off the bull, but he managed to drown that out of his mind by dwelling on the encouraging words.

"I won't let you down."

At Least the Pink Elephants are Laughing at Us

"You better not!" she threatened. "Now if I'm perfectly honest with you, Connor, and I believe that honesty is the best policy, I can't say I personally find you particularly funny. But that isn't important is it? What *is* important is that you have a gift – a gift from God – for making people laugh – people other than me - and it would be ungracious if you didn't use that gift, don't you think?"

Connor's mum nodded and smiled. She leaned forward and held his hand. "A gift from God," she said, squeezing the hand. Connor nodded self-consciously. His ears reddened. He felt immense pressure to make as many people as he possibly could laugh.

The tired voice announced that the flight to Accra was ready for boarding.

Connor's dad sprung to his feet with such urgency that Connor wondered whether he had been popping pills on one of his many trips to the airport shops.

"Accra," Alun said, nodding purposefully at the departures monitor. "That's where Ghana is."

When he saw no movement from Jojo or Nanya, he continued, "Acccra is your flight, Jojo."

"No rush, Alun," Jojo replied.

"I think you'll find there is, Jojo," Alun replied. "The plane won't wait for you, you know."

"Nonsense, Alun," Jojo said, waving her hand dismissively. Connor couldn't help but giggle.

"He's right," Nanya said. "The plane won't wait for you, Jojo. The last thing in the world I want right now is to say goodbye to you but we had better start making a move."

Alun held out his hand and helped a reluctant Jojo slowly to her feet. Once she was standing, Jojo gave him a farewell hug.

"I love you, Alun Thomas," she whispered. "You are the best thing that ever happened to my sister, you hear?"

Alun didn't say anything, he just nodded his head politely, but Connor could see he was touched.

Jojo turned to Connor next. She looked him straight in the eye. "Don't let me down now, you hear?" she said, before hugging him.

And then she moved to Nanya. They hugged, long and

emotionally. "You are the best sister in the whole world, Jojo," Nanya said.

"No, Nanya," Jojo replied. "You are the best sister in the whole world. You come visit soon, you hear?"

"I will visit soon."

And then Jojo walked away, the bright colours of her beautiful long dress fading until she disappeared out of sight.

Nanya took Connor in her arms. Her face was wet from tears. When Connor looked up, his dad's eyes were bloodshot, too. They all knew that they wouldn't visit Jojo. This was the last time they would see her.

Connor wondered what his mum was thinking, but then he realised that, for the first time ever, he knew *exactly* what she was thinking.

30 – Is the Ice Cream Man Following Me Around?

James loved playing in the sloping woodlands when he was a kid. He rode there on his beloved BMX and then hid it against the trunk of one of the bulkiest trees. He liked the way his trainers sunk into the soft ground and the subtle, delicate sound of twigs snapping under his feet. James loved the seclusion. The trees not only blocked out the sunlight but the noise and intrusion of the rest of the world. It was a sanctuary, a place of peace and contemplation.

"Dinosaur!" Rory exclaimed, pointing his stubby middle finger at a tree. "I saw a dinosaur, Daddy. A big dinosaur. Roar!"

James smiled. "I very much doubt you saw a dinosaur, Rory."

Rory sucked in his upper-lip, pushed out his lower-lip and furrowed his brow. His eyes had a manic, accusing stare. Had he been watching *Different Strokes* on replay again? James instantly recognised his son's sulking face. "Why, Daddy?"

This was potentially difficult territory, James thought. It might be a challenge explaining to a boy who wasn't four yet that dinosaurs were extinct. He could envisage how the conversation might develop. "What is extinct, Daddy?" "Dead." "What is dead, Daddy?" James remembered how awkward it was for *his* dad telling him Santa wasn't real, that grown-up people had been lying to him all these years, even though he already knew.

"Dinosaurs don't live here, Rory. They don't live in Wales."

Rory nodded his head in agreement. "They live in London, Daddy," he said.

"Come on," James said, holding out his hand and moving things away from possible "danger" discussions. "I've got something to show you."

They both leaned forward, bending at the waist, as they climbed the gentle slope. James stopped at one of the tallest trees in the wood, with an impressively wide girth for a trunk. The dry bark was flaking away. The tree was still there. It had stood the test of time; the storms, the wood choppers. James was transported back to the seventies, when life seemed so much simpler, so much more fun. He examined the trunk. There it was. He felt a sense of thrill. The names JAMES and TERRY were meticulously carved into the wood. It was significant at the time, something major. Both boys were twelve or so. They used James's trusty penknife. Over forty years later and James's son stared at the artwork, apparently bemused and unimpressed. Was this the exciting thing his dad had to show him?

"It says my name," James explained.

Rory seemed to understand this. He perked up. He smiled. His milk teeth were good, James thought, despite the many sweets his daddy gave him. James enjoyed treating his lad, especially when he was a good boy. The only problem was that Rory wanted to be treated even when he wasn't a good boy. His interpretation of a good boy was often different from his own. "It says "Daddy?"" Rory asked.

James thought it was possibly an unnecessary and fruitless conversation telling his boy it said his real name, the one Nanny Miriam gave him when he was just a baby, so instead he just nodded his head and said "It sure does, son. Come on," he continued, turning and beginning the gentle descent down the hill, "your mummy will be wondering where you are."

They appeared from the seclusion of the wood and back into the outside world, and Rory immediately held his finger up and announced, "Ice cream man, Daddy."

Goddamn, James thought, irritably rattling the few coins in his pocket. Did these people follow him around? What were they trying to do to him? The ice cream man never parked there. Why would they park there? Did they not know how much the supermarket paid him? He was going to have to be a big, strong daddy and tell Rory he could not have an ice cream.

Rory finished the ice cream on the journey home, before it had the chance to melt and turn the cone soggy. James dabbed Rory's chin with a tissue. He hoped the boy wouldn't tell his mum about the ice cream.

"Mummy, Daddy bought me an ice cream!" Rory excitedly

announced when the front door was opened, before charging into the house.

James cursed under his breath, but it was only momentary. Wow, he thought, eyeing his wife. Mummy sure is looking good. Shirley was wearing a denim skirt cut to her knees, and her legs were naked and sun-kissed. Flip flips exposed blue painted toenails. James was like a thirsty dog. He had to pop his tongue back in. How on earth had he managed to marry such a divine, beautiful lady...? How on earth had he let such a divine, beautiful lady slip out of his grasp...?

Rory appeared besides his mother's leg. James allowed his eyes to wander to the smooth, slender flesh, but he only ogled for a mini-second to ensure he didn't get caught. He turned his focus to his son. God, how he had missed his little rascal! Rory wore a mischievous grin, the one which suggested he was going to ask for something. James wanted to reach over and tickle him on the ribs, make him wriggle and kick his legs up in an adorable cycling motion. "Daddy," Rory began, right on cue. "Can I have a bike for Christmas, pl-ease?"

Shirley grinned and gently ruffled the boy's mop of hair. "It's only August," she protested. "And besides, I'm not sure Santa can afford a bike. He has to deliver a present for every boy and girl in Bridgend who has been good, remember?"

James laughed. "It's a shame *David Morgan* has gone," he said. "You got the best bikes in *David Morgan*." He turned to his boy and continued. "Don't worry, Rory. I'll have a word with Santa and make sure he brings you a bike for Christmas."

He so wanted to stay and talk to Shirley, but he didn't want to overstep the mark. Until recently he had plenty of time: time to spare and time to kill, but tonight he had things to do before it was too late. James looked up at the sky, at the fading light. "I have to go, Shirley," he said. "But I will see you tonight at the gig, yeah?"

Shirley nodded her head and smiled. "Maybe," she said.

*****

It was important she dressed appropriately. She wanted to be dignified and classy, but she didn't want to be too straight-laced and prissy, either. She saw the way he ogled her legs in the little denim skirt. Of course, he pretended he wasn't, but then if he had wanted to be convincing he should have put his tongue away, shouldn't he? Shirley smiled self-satisfyingly. It felt incredible to have somebody – no, not *somebody* – to have James, her husband, looking at her in that way again, to feel like a woman: attractive, wanted and desired. Yes, it was important to dress appropriately, but in this instance appropriate meant displaying a little flesh, just enough to tease her husband.

The wooden gate creaked open. Her heels clicked on the narrow concrete path and then pressed hard against the dry, discoloured grass. He heard her, or he felt her presence, for he turned around.

"How did you know to find me here?" James gently asked. He looked off-guard, a little awkward, but he looked pleased to see her.

"It is Saturday, and you have been with Rory all day, so I'm guessing you wouldn't have had chance to come earlier. And I know you wouldn't leave it too late. We both know this place terrifies you in the dark, darling."

James smiled. Shirley knew he was thinking she knew him too well. They'd been married for so many years; what did he expect? Shirley glanced at the beautiful fresh flowers protruding from inside the metal pot. Even when they were short of money, which was nearly all the time, James always managed to bring beautiful flowers to the grave. He didn't always manage to find money for the electricity meter, but he found money for flowers. James would have considered it an unforgivable insult to bring cheap, lacklustre flowers. Shirley did not begrudge the gesture. She thought it was sweet.

"So, have you told Bobby?"

James's eyes flickered nervously. "Told him what?" he asked. He knew what.

"Have you told him what you did to me? Have you told him how much you hurt me?"

James paused. Took a deep breath. "Yes."

Shirley knew James had told Bobby. James told Bobby everything, even the most awful things he was ashamed of, and he told him the truth; the absolute truth. James had never

At Least the Pink Elephants are Laughing at Us

confirmed this to her, but Shirley just knew.

"Tell him again," she instructed. "I deserve to hear you tell him."

James looked up at her with a pleading face. Shirley looked straight back at him with fixed, unnerved eyes; calm but serious. James surrendered to the inevitable. He slowly knelt down on one knee and clasped his hands tightly together. James bowed his head, and then he began talking.

"Dad," James said, speaking softly but clearly. "I made a terrible, terrible mistake. I was low and I was confused and stupid. I talked to a woman who talked to me back and for some reason the woman seemed to like me. She kissed me and I let her. I did not push her away – not straight away - and I absolutely know I should have. I was wrong and I am so, so sorry both to Shirley and to Rory. When I did eventually push her away it was too late. I promise you Dad, I did push her away and I promise you nothing else would have happened..."

His words faded away. James looked up at Shirley. His face was drained of colour and his eyes were damp. Shirley looked at the grave and said, "Thank you, Bobby."

She waited for him the other side of the wooden gate, on the quiet road that was empty of cars and people. The orange sun was falling so low it looked like it would disappear. Shirley took deep breaths. She paced up and down in her heels. Eventually the gate opened and James appeared from the other side, looking morose and timid and frightened. He looked at her, waited for her to speak; to give her verdict.

"You know I love you, you silly bastard," Shirley said. She gave him a kiss on the lips. "You've always been the only duck in my pond, love. But if this happens again, regardless whether you *eventually* push her away, then I promise you that not only are we finished, but I will cut those balls away from your dick. Do you understand?"

James looked at her intently and nodded his head. "I understand," he said. "And I absolutely promise I love you with all my life."

Shirley brushed a finger under her eye, knew she had probably smeared her mascara, but just didn't care. "Right," she said. "One other thing..."

"Yes?"
"Go get them tonight, you hear?"
"I hear..."

31 – Upstaged

Mandy loved going to William's flat.

There was something cool and exciting about a single bloke's pad, even though, when you read the fine print, her older brother wasn't actually single. William was like a character from one of those seventies *"Confessions Of"* films; a lovable rogue, a player, a guy about town, or – if he were a girl – a bit of a slag. She could imagine James enjoying the films when he was a youngster. Mandy was blatantly aware how easily she was drawn into stereotypes. A single woman living on her own meant lonely nights watching black and white romantic movies in a darkened room with just tears, tissues and (naturally) a cat for company. A bachelor pad, on the other hand, had beds that unfolded from the ceiling with the click of a button and Barry White whispering deep, sensual words in the background. William's flat was modern and trendy and sparse and clinical. Everything had its place and purpose. The sixty inch plasma screen stood proud and impressive and dared the other gadgets to challenge its supremacy, like a Transformer with its chest pumped out, saying what the fuck can *you* turn into, earthling?

But mainly Mandy liked going to William's flat because it belonged to William, her big, handsome older brother.

William was in the kitchen, apparently making as much noise as he possibly could, clinking glasses and slamming cupboards and pouring drinks. He was a man and that is what men did. Oh there she went with the stereotypes again. It didn't matter. William was upbeat and full of energy tonight, resembling a zany children's TV presenter or somebody who'd been sniffing white powder or overdosing on *Berrocca*. He was fantastic company and she loved seeing him like this.

Mandy, on the other hand, was slowly returning to planet earth after the show. God that had been good! Things had been steadily improving for months now, but for the first time she actually felt they could take on and hold their own at Edinburgh! She really needed that show. Distraction was a powerful force.

And when she was performing she focussed resolutely on her act. There was just no way on earth thoughts of the meeting at the train station could intrude her mind when she was up on stage.

She idly thumbed through William's CD collection, just being curious, or nosy. *The Rise and Fall of Ziggy Stardust and the Spiders from Mars. The Queen is Dead.* +. Very good. Not like her motley collection, where inclusion was primarily dependent on the offers at the petrol station. Mandy often considered taking pride in her CD's, but she usually just concluded that life was just too damn short and cash was far too sparse.

William returned to the room with a vodka and tonic (for himself), and a pint of lager (for Mandy). No nuts or extravagant nibbles. Her tummy rumbled. Mandy couldn't help but wonder what on earth he had been doing in there.

"I can't believe how good you were," William enthused. "I'll be honest with you, sis. I had low expectations. I know I've seen you perform quite a few times now, but I seriously think my viewpoint has been damaged by the memory of you as a sheep that cross-dressed as a cat in that awful school nativity when you were a kid..."

"Well thanks for the vote of confidence!"

"But that's what I'm saying, sis! When my expectations are high, I'm usually left disappointed. Now the other two guys were funny. That black guy..."

"He isn't strictly black, bro..."

"I haven't got time for any of that tonight, sis. Compared to my pasty white sister, that guy is black. It took him a bit of time to get going, don't you think? But then they say big guns take a long time to load. They *do* say that don't they? Well, Connor must really have a big gun because when that guy got firing he was really explosive! Some of his insights on the strangeness of the world were proper out there. I mean, it was proper blow your mind stuff. And that old guy..."

"He isn't strictly old, bro..."

William just waved his hand this time and continued talking. He was proper buzzing. "The old guy is much more old-school, isn't he? But he was sharp as a razor. And his timing was just perfect. He has the sort of face you can just look at and laugh without him even saying anything..."

"I'm glad you find my peers funny, William."

"But that's what I'm saying, sis. Those guys were funny but you were even funnier! My little, boyish sister was like a peacock that finally opened its wings. I literally had a tear trickling down my cheek. And I wasn't sure whether it was because you were funny or because I was so damn proud..."

Mandy blushed. And then she blushed some more for blushing. She wasn't even the blushing type. She could do with this pick me up. She wanted to tell William about the fiasco with Dad, and she would. It was just so downright humiliating though, and she knew his thoughts on the matter were completely different from her own. He was just so happy tonight that she didn't want to burst his bubble. Maybe she deserved one night of adulation from her big brother?

William finished his drink, lagging behind as usual, and then he took Mandy's glass and danced off to the kitchen. She could hear him humming. Talking to himself. She smiled. He was mimicking some of her lines from the show. Oh this really was brotherly adulation!

Mandy wandered absent-mindedly to his cabinet. She wasn't very good at just sitting still. Her feet were hurting even though she'd taken off her shoes as soon as she entered the flat. Mandy opened the cabinet door. There was a certificate from some football course her brother attended when he was a kid. A big photo of their mum, smiling to the camera. He really was a mummy's boy. Mandy really was a nosey parker. She dug her hand inside the cabinet to see what else she could find. If she ever *did* manage to get a real boyfriend who could keep up with her then she knew she would be the type of girlfriend to flick through the text messages on his phone. Not because she was some sort of crazy control addict or bunny boiler, but just out of idle curiosity, and that was an infinitely more acceptable reason.

A long plastic tub, probably used to store toys when he was a kid, dropped to the floor. The lid came off and the contents of the box scattered over the carpet. Photos. Letters. Personal stuff she should really keep her big nose out of. Mandy knelt down on one knee to put the possessions back in the tub. The booze and the exertion made her dizzy, like she'd been out in the sun for too long without a hat. One of the photos caught her eye. She stared at it more intently, and then she blinked. The room was spinning now and, she suddenly realised, it wasn't entirely from the drink.

William was back in the room, holding up two full glasses, bouncing with energy and joy. He stopped. His smile disappeared. His face became blank.

"What's up?" he asked.

"You know where Dad is," Mandy stated.

*****

James came out of the stinking toilet.

The Regency was still full of people of all ages and hairstyles mightily eager to shake James's hand, to be his best friend now the boy had done good. James didn't mind. He knew it was his brief moment in the spotlight and so he was going to make the most of it. His world would return to normal in the morning. It felt like he was doing the rounds at a wedding reception. The soles of his shoes stuck to the carpet, as they always did in this place, where spillages were the norm. James kept alert; chairs were always likely to be pushed out and block your path and trip you up. Many a punter had been left on their back with their feet up in the air over the years, which was particularly embarrassing if you were an old dear in a dress. It was always funny so long as it wasn't you on the floor. It took James a while to reach the table.

His mum spotted him and she went to stand up. James leant over, kissed her on the cheek and held her hand to make sure she didn't move. She had really made the effort tonight, James thought. It was just like that birthday when Dad turned up as a clown and Mum bought a stunning dress from the catalogue. She'd been to the hairdressers and had a trim, just tidied her barnet up a bit. His mum really was an elegant woman on a civilised night out, he thought. She deserved better than this dive, James considered.

"You were amazing, James," his mum glowed. "I almost wet myself I laughed so much!" And then she moved closer and

At Least the Pink Elephants are Laughing at Us

whispered "To be honest with you, son, I'm not absolutely certain I didn't wet myself, just a little." She rasped now, like she had a long-term smoking habit, even though she had never lit up in her life. Mrs Jones squeezed her son's cheek with her thumb and finger. "I'm so proud of you. And your dad would have been, too."

James felt his fingers tingle. All the other plaudits and slaps on the back would have been pointless if his old ma' hadn't liked his show. He lowered himself so that he could talk in hushed tones. This close he could see light liver spots on her cheek that the foundation hadn't concealed. "So it's not too difficult being in this place for you, Mum? You know, with what happened to Dad?"

His mum paused. She'd obviously considered this question, presumably before agreeing to even come out. "Its fine, son. It's natural to think about it, of course. But time stops for nobody. You know that."

James nodded his head, relieved. He was very aware his wife was sat quietly on the chair next to his mum. His eyes had longed to flicker in her direction, to check whether she looked happy, but James had managed to resist – *just* - to focus solely on his mum. James turned to Shirley now.

Shirley smiled at him. She flicked her brown, luscious hair with her hand. She looked so ridiculously sexy, just as she had in the graveyard just hours before.

"You were amazing, James."

James went to say something, maybe something clever or funny or analytical or possibly all three things. What would Ian Hislop say in this circumstance? His thoughts, though, were tangled and unstructured. Instead he just smiled and said, "Thank you, Shirley."

He turned back to his mum. "I'd like you to meet Herbert," James said. "You know: the genius who got us together in the first place. He is writing a book on our exploits. He is here with his mum tonight, too. I expect Herbert is a proper 'Mummy's Boy.'"

James held out his hand, and his mum quickly and effortlessly rose to her feet. He was sometimes surprised how agile she was, but then he often forgot she was only sixteen years or so older than he was.

This was great, James thought. He was on such an incredible, fantastic high tonight, he wondered whether things could possibly get any better...

*****

William placed the two glasses on the mantelpiece, possibly so they couldn't be deployed as a weapon of mass destruction, before he spoke at all. His motions, which had been zany and unpredictable, were now deliberate and considered, like a robot programmed to act in a certain way. He turned to face Mandy. Looked her right in the eye and then unflinchingly held the look. His broad shoulders narrowed and his head disappeared into his neck, like he was a damn tortoise.

"Don't even try to deny it!" Mandy threatened, aggressively stabbing her finger at him. She could feel her voice straining. Mandy dangled the photograph – the evidence – right under his nose. "This is a picture of you and him. *Together.* And if I am not mistaken, you don't look like an overgrown pimply teenager kid, which is what you were when he left us. You've been meeting up with him, haven't you?"

William lowered into the revolving black leather chair positioned on the other side of the room. Probably for the best, Mandy thought. Just stay far enough away from me that I cannot hit you. Mandy remembered how much she wanted to throttle that guy Dave at the train station. Dave had nothing on Big Brother right now. William tangled his long fingers together.

"I'm not going to deny it, sis. I'm sorry. I really am."

He looked down at the floor. Didn't say anything more. Mandy paced up and down the room. "Well? Don't let me stop you while you're in full stride. Where? When? Why?"

"He wrote to me. A couple of years ago. Out of the blue. Told me what he was up to. Where he was. I went to see him."

"Where?"

"He's in France. Just outside La Rochelle..."

"Doing what...?"

"He's with *her*. The woman he cheated on Mum with, although we both know there were others, of course. He lives in this chateaux; proper quaint it is. He is tanned and healthy, and although he is a little wider around the waist because he loves his fine food and wine, I'll be honest with you, he doesn't look anywhere near his age. Doesn't look like he has a care in the world in fact..."

"Well whoopee-fucking-doo..."

"Of course," William continued, talking rapidly now," he was charm-personified. Like he always was. That's when we took that photograph. He was going on about how proud he was I'd grown up into a respectable young man. All that stuff. Proper "bigged" me up, you know? Got *her* to put on these impressive spreads; salads with salmon and potatoes melting in butter and all the rest of it. Kept refilling my glass with the local wine. The works. Made me feel like a prince, you know?"

"Well, I'm glad you had a great time on your holidays," Mandy said, her tone laced with a thick, doughy dollop of sarcasm. "Prince-Lying-Scheming-Fucking-Toe Rag more like!"

"It wasn't like that, Mandy. I promise." William glanced around the room, nervous narrow eyes fleeting in countless directions. "I was going to tell you at the time. I just wanted to test the water first before reporting back to you, Tom and Mum. I know how much he hurt you when we were kids. I thought I could make things better. But I was a mug. I was just kidding myself. I pretended he was a changed man, that he wasn't the guy who abandoned us when we were just kids. On the day I left he took me to the airport. I asked him straight. I said, "What happens now, with Mandy and Tom?""

"And...?" Mandy knew she didn't really want to know. But then she *had* to know. She wouldn't rest until she heard the words come out of her brother's mouth.

"And his whole persona changed. He went quiet and started mumbling some shit. I recognised that look from years before. It just came to me in a flashback, a lightning bolt. It was the same way he looked when he lied to mum. He started coming out with all sorts, but it was just bullshit excuses. He said it wasn't fair to put Mum through any more, that he'd hurt her enough and that besides, he didn't have enough money to come back. But it was just talk. He was still the same man that cheated on our mum. He basically just didn't want to know."

"How do you know that?" Mandy demanded. "Maybe he was telling the truth! Maybe he *had* changed?"

"I *know*, Mandy," William said, more forcibly, like it just wasn't up for discussion. He looked at Mandy now, and she could see the brilliant whites of his eyes. "I got angry then. I told him to fuck off, and in no uncertain terms. I told him he had very nearly destroyed Mum and virtually ruined our lives, that he was just a piece of shit..."

Mandy cut him off. "So why didn't you tell me? Didn't I deserve to make up my own mind about him? Decide whether I wanted him to be part of my life?"

"I was protecting you, Mandy!" William protested. "Don't you see? You're my little sister. That's what I do. I didn't want to destroy this perfect image you have of your dad. You didn't need to know that really he is just a selfish little coward..."

Mandy had heard enough. She stormed over to the mantelpiece and picked up the two glasses, then launched them both at her brother. He ducked – just in time – and they clattered against the wall, leaving shredded glass on the table, on the carpet and, hopefully, on her brother. Mandy screamed at the top of her voice, "You fucking, fucking bastard!"

She headed to the door and did not dare to look back, for she feared what she would do to him...

*****

James held his mother's hand all the way to the other end of the hall. Her fingers were bony and her hand was icy cold, but her grip was firm and surprisingly strong. His wife, Shirley, was on his other side, just where he wanted her. James liked being protective. It reminded him of when he was out and about with Rory. James fully understood why Shirley sometimes tied him up in the pushchair, but for James walking was so much more fun. His little boy didn't want to let go of his hand for anything in the world, and sometimes he squeezed so tight.

Herbert was sat with his mother in the corner of the room. James could tell their leader, their inspiration, was still on a high from the show. Herbert looked anxiously their way as the three of them approached the table. His back was very straight and

At Least the Pink Elephants are Laughing at Us

rigid, like he was glued to a wooden stick and, although James could not hear what Herbert was saying, he could tell he was talking very quickly.

James introduced Herbert to his mum. They shook hands. Herbert said it was a pleasure to meet her and he did a little bow. His mother smiled nervously. Then James turned to Herbert's mother, Brenda, and offered introductions. She was a larger lady with full, rounded cheeks. A painted smile was frozen to her face.

James's turned to his own mother. Her smiled had disappeared. Her hand remained firmly by her side. Her feet were planted to the spot. "I think you'll find that we've met before," she stated.

And then, without any further words and without any warning, Mrs Jones pulled back her hand and smacked the woman hard on the side of the face.

Part Four

1 – Mr Potato Head on the M4

This was what it was all about! This was where they reaped the rewards for enduring six months of blood, sweat and plentiful tears, for surviving painful meetings and frightful gigs. This would make it all worthwhile!

Herbert blew some warmth onto his hands. He had been sucking on Extra Strong mints, and his breath was hot. Herbert wound the window down a few inches, just enough to hopefully ease the feint smell of damp. He pulled at the gear stick and forced it, with some considerable effort, into second, then steered the vehicle through the entrance to Sarn Services. "Here we go then!" Herbert announced.

The guys were going to love the minivan he had bought, Herbert considered. It was the perfect Sunday morning antedate following a heavy Saturday the night before. He'd utilised the powers of the World Wide Web and found an unbelievably good deal on *eBay*. It was without question absolutely perfect for their *very* specific needs. Herbert turned the corner and there they were – the troops – patiently waiting for him with their bags and their suitcases. Herbert's outlook felt disproportionately positive considering how recent events had unfolded.

Herbert parked the van and then jolted the door open, trying his best to keep his smug grin under control. He knew it was in vain.

"What the *fuck* is that?" James asked, pointing to the van like it was a combine harvester.

"It's a minivan, James," Herbert said, trying – again - not to sound condescending. "I appreciate it's a bit bruised in places and possibly a little rough around the edges, but that just adds *character,* yes? On the whole it's a real beauty, don't you think?"

James put his head in his hands in apparent despair. Herbert dismissed him. James was the sort of person, Herbert considered, who'd walk around the Tate Gallery shouting obscenities at the paintings, just because it wasn't the kind of art he would personally hang on his wall at home. Herbert turned to the others, expecting – hoping for - better.

The others each in turn eyed the van with suspicion or open disdain.

"Why does the van have a red nose on the front?" James asked, clearly perplexed. "And a moustache and black glasses? Is this some sort of piss-take? I thought *we* were supposed to make the jokes around here?"

"Ah yes, you noticed! It appears the previous owner was quite a character, doesn't it? I haven't ruled out it being somebody sensationally zany with an outrageous sense of humour, like Rob Brydon, perhaps? Very apt considering we're going to The Fringe."

"This guy is obsessed with Rob Brydon," Connor commented.

James managed a weak smile. "Looks like we're going to be driving down the motorway in Mr Potato Head," James said. The others laughed.

There was no time for idle pleasantries, Herbert considered, especially when the "pleasantries" weren't particularly pleasant. Herbert opened the back door and assisted with the luggage. Connor was travelling with his parents, Alun and Nanya. They seemed an absolutely adorable couple: respectable, civilised, polite and fun. Herbert shook Alun's hand and gave Nanya a hug. Herbert observed that they seemed relaxed and up for the trip, enthusiastically embracing the adventures that lay ahead.

Mandy, in stark contrast, barely said hello. What was up with her? The show had gone tremendously and she seemed in high spirits when she left the venue with her older brother. They disappeared before the drama unravelled. Mandy begrudgingly nodded and grunted simultaneously; her mouth, though, remained a fixed straight line. Herbert already knew he had his hands full with James. He didn't need Mandy causing an additional headache. This didn't bode well. James was visibly irritable and openly grumpy. Herbert would need to find the right time to talk to him about *that* little mess. It was probably best they at least made it to Edinburgh first, just in case he decided not to come.

Herbert waited until they were all snugly in their seats with their seat belts pulled over their shoulders. He beeped the horn twice to indicate the start of their journey.

He was hoping, optimistically, for a cheer, or at least an acknowledgement. The van, though, remained completely silent as they followed the sign for the M4 heading north.

*****

Nine hours later and Herbert, Connor and James stood on the pavement outside the terraced house they had rented for the duration of the trip. They each agreed the rest of the party could and should unpack and settle down inside the house. The three alpha males bounced on the soles of their feet and twisted and jerked their heads both ways, like they were at the tennis, examining the passing traffic.

"There it is," Connor announced, the relief evident in his voice.

A distinctive minivan came into view. It was distinctive because it was the only minivan they'd seen in over an hour standing on the pavement that had a red nose, black glasses and moustache. It was also distinctive because its wheels were strapped securely to the back of a recovery truck.

"No wonder you got a good deal," James stated sourly. "The van doesn't bloody work. It's a lemon. They saw you coming."

"I'm just trying to give you some new material for your show," Herbert offered, but again, like in the van, the group remained silent.

2 – Flyers, Flyers Please Do Fly Away!

Mandy handed a leaflet to anybody who looked friendly or gullible enough to take one without too much resistance. These people proved to be a rarity.

"Come to the show!" she shouted – commanded - her voice traced with a subtle suggestion of enthusiasm and a strong sense of annoyance. She felt like an irritant, a fly people desperately wanted to swat. Mandy never prided herself on being popular, but now she wasn't enjoying being openly *unpopular*.

"Why?" the person – a boy - asked.

"Why *what*?"

"Why should I come to the show?"

Jesus, Mandy thought. She preferred the ones who just ignored her. She hadn't expected so many annoying questions!

"Because the show is like proper hilarious. And it's free."

"Most of the shows are free," the boy stated. "Unless you are famous or have a unique selling point, the show will normally be free. It's definitely not a seller's market, I'm afraid."

Mandy shrugged her shoulders with visible indifference. Mandy didn't have time for this. Well, that wasn't strictly true. She had plenty of time. She'd already stood on the same spot in The Old Town, with the monumental Edinburgh Castle staring down at her from the top of the hill, for absolute hours. She wasn't going anywhere anytime soon. More accurately, she considered, she just didn't have the *patience* for this.

She spoke slowly now. "I didn't expect the 'Spanish Inquisition.' Listen, I really don't *care* if you come or not, to be honest with you. The show will still go on with or without you. But you don't seem like the type to have much else to do now, do you?"

The boy looked perplexed. He crinkled his face like he was going to say something, but then instead he just turned around and walked off. Mandy caught the skanky litterbug throwing the leaflet on the floor a bit further down the street.

At Least the Pink Elephants are Laughing at Us

Mandy had never been a fan of Mondays, like most normal people, but this Monday was much worse than most. This promotion and marketing game, for one, wasn't going as well as she had hoped. She had envisaged engaging with enthusiastic and appreciative folk who were keen to watch their free show. Instead she had either been ignored or subtly abused. It had been long, tediously boring and monumentally unsuccessful, and to cap it all she had resorted to insulting her potential customers. Even Mandy was wise enough to know that wasn't going to work.

Mandy knew this was part of the package. There were hundreds of performers doing the same thing on the wide, exuberant Edinburgh streets. Herbert warned them again and again in his "motivational" talks that The Fringe was a tough, unforgiving gig. Connor was stood further down the street and Herbert was further along again. James was supposed to be out walking the streets too, but Mandy had no doubt whatsoever he was in the pub. The man went teetotal just a few weeks ago. Well, *that* didn't last long.

They were donkey's competing at the Grand National. Mandy had to admit, if she took a step back and looked at the big picture from an objective perspective, she just didn't possess the energy, motivation or sheer drive to compete with the other comedians promoting their shows; not in her current state of mind, not with the other things going on in her life at the moment. She looked at her fellow performers - at her competition - and they were all *talking* to people, looking like they *wanted* to talk to people. Others were in fancy dress performing snippets of their act, enticing the masses to come to their show. All they saw with Mandy was a depleted, angry face. Mandy had to admit that, given the choice, she would go to their show rather than her own.

The main reason she didn't just ditch the flyers in a bin and join James in the pub was to ensure at least somebody turned up to their show. Mandy wasn't keen on adding humiliation to her list of woes. Oh, and she didn't want to let Herbert down, either; he had worked too hard, put too much heart into the project to deserve that. Mandy couldn't work out why James didn't feel the same way, too.

Mandy's phone vibrated in her pocket. Again. At least somebody wanted to talk to her. At least somebody didn't think she was invisible. Unfortunately, she didn't want to talk to them. Mandy's phone had hardly stopped ringing (or vibrating) since the revelation at William's flat. Mandy ignored the possible passing trade and stopped to type a message into her phone.

Leave me alone!

Mandy wasn't sure how she was going to perform any shows. She was supposed to be the experienced one, the shining light leading the way for Connor and James. She felt anything but, though. She felt utterly incapable, like she just couldn't function. Her mind was on a different planet from earth. It wasn't as if she had plenty of time to pull herself together; their first show was tomorrow night.

Maybe, Mandy wondered, possibly searching for the easiest route, it was best if nobody *did* turn up for the show? Would it be less humiliating if nobody was there to witness the horror?

Mandy finally showed some enthusiasm and conviction. She stormed purposefully to the nearest bin and threw away the flyers. And then she turned and tried to work out which of the many watering houses James had parked himself inside.

*****

It hadn't been the most productive of mornings, Connor thought. He pictured a D+ or a C- scrawled across the page in a teacher's untidy red ink. But then compared to his two compatriots – James was in the pub staring at the bottom of a glass, and Mandy had been sulking for the majority of the morning and then he caught her pushing a batch of flyers into the bin – Connor was a distinctive A* student and heading for Oxbridge.

Connor's initial objective had been to try and persuade punters to come to their show. He quickly realised how naive and delusional he had been. He must have been getting carried away with all these recent positive thoughts. His objective quickly changed to just getting rid of the flyers. Connor handed out the deplorable sheets of paper like they were hand grenades. And slowly but surely the pile got thinner, like the Yellow

Pages, until there were barely any left. On this basis, Connor reasoned, he had done an honest morning's work and therefore he fully deserved to head back to the house for an afternoon kip.

It was no wonder, Connor thought, taking in his surroundings, that writers like Ian Rankin managed to make a decent living from crime novels in Edinburgh. The city was a murderer's paradise! What on earth were the town planners thinking? There were endless possibilities for unsavoury people in cloaks to hide in darkened cracks and crevices. On both sides of the wide, open and vibrant strip were countless tiny narrow openings leading to spiralling, dark cobbled alleyways.

He entered through one of these openings now. Connor was reasonably sure the lane was a shortcut to the rented house. It was a relief to escape the hustle and bustle and the commercial hysteria of the city during The Fringe. Connor arched his body backwards because the path was so steep he feared he might topple over. He pressed the soles of his shoes firmly into the floor. It was amazing how quickly the noise became muffled and subdued and was replaced by an almost eerie quiet and solitude. The peace and tranquillity reminded Connor of his favourite spot down by the river back in Ogmore, the spot where his dad had recently joined him.

There was a solitary figure on the path in front of him. The figure navigated the slope slowly and carefully, staring down at the floor like he was scared it would disappear and he would fall into a bottomless hole. Connor quickly gained ground. This was going to get awkward. Connor felt like he was lurking, ready to pounce. He considered an overtaking manoeuvre. There wasn't much room to pass on either side, though. It was like the shopping aisles at Asda on a busy Saturday afternoon. The dilemma was resolved with no deliberate intervention however, for suddenly the lone figure in front of him stumbled and fell to the hard, cobbled floor.

Connor urgently bent at the knees and held out his hand. "Are you okay?" he asked. "That was quite some fall."

The person – it was a man, Connor noted – looked more embarrassed than physically hurt. It was normally the way, Connor thought. Lying flat on your back with yours arms and legs sprawled into the shape of a star fish was not generally a great look. The man hurriedly tried to get up. He blew his cheeks out and pushed his hands down against the floor, but this only lifted his feet and legs higher into the air whilst the rest of him stayed exactly where he was. He took a deep breath, pulled a face and pushed harder. His feet went higher again. Now this really was getting embarrassing, Connor considered. The man blew air from his mouth, defeated, and reluctantly accepted Connor's hand. Connor was surprised how light the guy was. The man was up on his feet and back in action in a single fluid movement. It was like somebody had pressed the fast forward button. The guy brushed himself down with his hands.

"These damn streets!" the man muttered, jerking his arms out by his sides. "I should make a claim, I tell you!" His toothy grin suggested he wasn't completely serious.

Looking at him properly now, Connor was surprised the guy hadn't crumpled into pieces when he hit the floor, just disintegrated like dust. The man was very short and diminutive. Even bouncing up and down on tiptoes the top of his thick, fluffy, white and *perfectly* combed hair failed to reach Connor's shoulders. It wasn't surprising the unforgiving Edinburgh alleyways had left him flat on his back; a gust of wind would knock him over. The guy was *old,* too, like proper old; older than the valleys where Connor was born and bred. He should be dipping biscuits into a cup of tea in a nursing home. Connor noticed how surprisingly dapper the man looked, though (and Connor liked to think he knew a thing or two about fashion). A furry white moustache matched the colour and gloss of his hair, but his cheeks were clean-shaven and they had a pink glow like he'd just jumped straight out of the shower. The man wore grey trousers and a jacket but – stylishly, Connor thought – the top button of his white shirt was undone and he wore no tie.

The guy presumably noticed Connor checking him out and looked to bite first. He glanced at Connor's designer denim jacket, covered in holes and tears and asked "Have you been attacked by a gang of cats or something?"

The man seemed friendly enough, if a tad rude for an old guy; Connor was about to explain it was just modern fashion – or so he thought – but his train of thoughts were scattered. Connor was distracted by the man's strong Welsh accent. He was of one

At Least the Pink Elephants are Laughing at Us

of his own; a Welshman fighting for his honour and survival in a foreign land full of men wearing kilts but no underpants. Connor was about to offer his hand and introduce himself when he noticed a handful of flyers scattered on the floor. It was like the flyers were following Connor around, haunting and teasing him. He'd only just managed to dispose of them after hours of hard graft and now here they were by his feet looking up at him. Connor reached down and picked them up. He realised they didn't belong to him and so he absent-mindedly passed them to the man.

"You here for the Festival?" Connor asked.

It didn't seem feasible that this old man could be performing at the mighty and intimidating Fringe Festival. But there didn't seem to be any other viable option. The old man's face stared up at Connor from the flyer in his hand.

"I sure am," the guy replied, defensively jutting his neck out like a pigeon.

"Me too," Connor replied, and now took the opportunity to shake his hand.

The guy narrowed his eyes and looked at Connor suspiciously. The cheeky bastard, Connor thought. The little cherub was surprised that *he* was playing the festival.

Connor had previously not realised just how jovial and carefree he was feeling, for the next words that came out of his own mouth were ones he had recently only uttered under duress. "Come on," Connor said. "Let me buy you a drink."

*****

Mandy knew all too well the pubs in this mysterious city were packed full of drinkers; she'd enviously eyed punters entering in droves as she stood bored and frustrated and with a dry mouth, dishing out leaflets. When Mandy had adventurously wandered away from her designated spot, she'd dared to glance inside the windows and her suspicions had been confirmed. The tables were mainly full, and the glasses were primarily empty. How she had hated those jovial, happy, intoxicated people.

The pub Mandy knew James favoured was away from the main stretch of the hub of activity. It had become a familiar sight in the few days since they'd been in Edinburgh (no hold on, they actually only arrived last night but it felt *so* much longer) to see the back of James's head (his silver ponytail) disappear through the doors to the pub. Mandy felt like an intruder now as she pulled open the heavy, sturdy wooden door. It opened with a high-pitched squeak which, she thought, was rather unexpected.

The floors were tiled with long wooden, varnished slabs. The ceilings were low. The brick walls were thick and decorated with electric guitars and vinyl records which were framed in polished glass. A single concrete step led to a stage, which was hidden slightly by red silk curtains and occupied by an impressive drum kit and a microphone on a stand. This place could be quite something, Mandy thought, when there were actually people here. James had found the only pub in the whole of Edinburgh with no punters. This was the kind of place that slept during the day and erupted with a frenzy of activity at night. A dormant volcano. Right now it felt like the joint was nursing a sore head.

Mandy ordered two pints of lager from the bar. She knew James must be here somewhere. It wasn't much of a gamble buying two drinks. If James wasn't here then she would just drink both pints.

There was a solitary table on the other side of a pillar, hidden away in the corner.

"Hope you don't mind some company," Mandy said, plonking the glasses down on the table with a wet, elaborate splash.

*****

Connor had so far ascertained the tumbling little guy from the lane possessed a Welsh accent because he was from Wales, he drunk lager because he was from Wales, he didn't mind somebody else buying his pints for him and, most interestingly of all, this was his thirty-third year performing at the Fringe.

"It started in a small hall with barely anybody in the audience."

Connor waited for him to continue, but the guy seemed content to savour the gulps of his drink that swished around in his mouth and leave the statement hanging.

At Least the Pink Elephants are Laughing at Us

"So what is it like now then?" Connor asked.

"Oh, I still perform in a small hall with barely anybody in the audience," he replied, without even a flicker of a smile.

Connor considered this. The thought of standing up in front of a barely full hall was petrifying and, if today's marketing performance was anything to go by, it was likely to become a reality tomorrow night. Connor had an urge to ask what the point of coming back was if hardly anybody bothered to watch him. He pondered this for a few moments, for it was obviously important to show tact and decorum.

"So what is the point of coming back, then?"

The man whipped out his tongue and licked foam from his upper lip. "I love it, that's why," he stated matter-of-factly.

Connor clinked his glass. He didn't really consider himself a jovial, slap-on-the-back type of guy, but Connor felt this was worth celebrating. Connor noticed the old man glanced sadly down at his empty glass, not very subtly indicating he was in dire need of a refill. He could wait, Connor thought. He was in a good mood, but he wasn't delirious.

"So would you say coming to Edinburgh all these years has been a success?" Connor probed.

The man tugged on the lapels of his jacket. "Commercially? No. Critically? No. But it has been a success in that I *have* come back every year and done the thing that I love."

Connor considered this again and slowly nodded his head. You couldn't argue with that logic, he reasoned. You couldn't argue with the guy's tenacity, either. He hadn't been deterred from coming back year after year just because of something trivial like a lack of audience or an audience that actually appreciated his comedy. He did it for no other reason than for the sheer thrill of it all.

Connor pulled his wallet out of his pocket. The old man had not given any indication he even owned a wallet, let alone any money. Connor wondered whether this was another example of getting away with things when you're old. Connor frowned at how empty his own wallet looked. He didn't even bother asking whether he wanted another drink. Connor already knew the answer. He returned from the packed bar with a hot coating of sweat on his brow and a bubbling, fizzing drink in each hand.

"Ah, Connor, you shouldn't have," the man said without even a trace of irony.

The drink was beginning to go to Connor's head. He wasn't normally a lager drinker. He wasn't normally even much of a drinker. Connor normally left the heavy drinking to Mandy and James. Where were those two? He'd finish this one, he thought, and then finally head back for that kip. Mind you, he considered, glancing at his watch, it will be bedtime soon anyway. "So when is your first show?"

"Tonight," the man replied, throwing back his head and gulping at his drink.

Connor spat his drink over the table.

Once Connor had regained his senses, he was struck by a realisation.

"You know what," Connor said. "I've been so engrossed in learning your story that I forgot to ask your name."

The old man held out a slender, wrinkled hand.

"I'm George," he said.

*****

James flicked through his phone, using the tip of his middle finger to swipe the screen from left to right. Mandy knew she sometimes did this in company, and more often recently when she'd been waiting on news of Dad, but it was irritating her now. Here she was, in one of the most beautiful cities in the country, which was absolutely buzzing with excitement in every other pub apart from this one, and she was being ignored by a grizzly middle-aged man with a stupid ponytail. Mandy was the first to admit that she was no Nicole Kidman or Jennifer Lawrence but, she considered, she deserved a better hand in life than this pile of shit.

"Trouble at home?" Mandy asked.

James looked up at her. He smiled. That was a bit better, Mandy thought. She couldn't deny - though she was sometimes reluctant to give James credit for anything - that he had a nice smile; it was layered with a generous smothering of mischief and fun. Come to think of it, *James* was layered with a generous smothering of mischief and fun. He was probably a Lothario

At Least the Pink Elephants are Laughing at Us

with the ladies back in his day, Mandy thought. Mind you, she considered, he still had something about him even now, once you looked past all the grizzle and old age and general offensiveness.

"No, actually," James replied. His smile broadened. "It is early days but we've had some real developments on that front. I'm still living at my friend's house but I've seen more of Shirley over the last few weeks. And she is giving me time to see Rory. We had a lovely day together on Saturday you know, before our final gig on Saturday night..."

James passed his phone to Mandy. "Aww," she cooed. Mandy didn't consider herself as naturally maternal, but she did enjoy a warm feeling when she gazed at the cute picture of Rory. What was happening to her? The boy's eyes and smile wore the same mischief as his dad. At least James had been ignoring her for a good reason. Mandy felt a flicker of affection towards the guy. He could be soppy under all that loud bravado and bullshit. She could see why he was so proud, too. Rory was a handsome young man. "He is adorable," Mandy commented.

"I know," James replied. "He really is, isn't he?"

There was a lone man at the duke box now, a young guy in a crinkled and torn tee shirt, a stray dog who had wandered off the vibrant Edinburgh streets and into the quiet of the deserted, abandoned pub. Mandy wasn't a great thinker, or at least she didn't think she was; thoughts didn't actually *do* anything in the real world, did they? They were confined to your head. But she did have some thoughts. Edinburgh had over seven hundred pubs, and this guy walked into this one. What were the chances? Maybe he was placed on the earth to be the one? The guy pressed a button and returned to his wooden stool at the bar. Mandy did not know it at the time, but he was leaving the scene of the crime; suddenly the quiet, homely pub was vibrating with the sound of *Uptown Girl*. Mandy thought it strange, for it did not fit in with the atmosphere at all. She concluded that this guy was definitely not the one. Mind you, she'd been texting that guy more and more recently – even though she knew it didn't make any sense – and Mandy wondered, despite herself, whether she may have already found the one.

Mandy leaned closer so James could hear her. She didn't fancy shouting. For one thing, it felt like effort. For another, what if the music suddenly stopped? James was already leant forward. In the dark corner of the pub it reminded her of the famous *Smith and Jones* dialogues Mandy had watched on rewind where the two men put the world to rights. James raised one eyebrow (Mandy noticed that he had a few stray hairs heading in different directions, and she was distracted for a moment) and gave her a look as if to say *this sounds serious.*

"Things are looking up, you say? So why do you look so flippin' miserable then, James?"

James gave her a magnified look of mock hurt, which was so outrageously over the top that Mandy couldn't help but smile. Then James glanced around at the empty pub, the half-drunk pints, the sun which snaked through the slimmest of cracks in the curtain and failed to bring any real light to the dismal proceedings, and his eyes blinked and strained. It was as though he'd been looking through the bottom of a pint glass for so long he was suddenly becoming reacquainted with the world around him. He slowly nodded his head and gave Mandy a look of recognition.

"We're a right pair us, hey, pet?" James said. Again, his mouth cracked into a smile.

Mandy was initially offended to be tarnished with the same brush as this grumpy old sod, but then she didn't want to break the rapport she had (seemingly) built with James, and so she dutifully nodded her head. "Yes, you truly are a miserable bastard!" she added, making sure she had the upper hand.

This new bond was all very nice, but Mandy wanted to know what was wrong, why James was determined to make this already likely doomed mission into a guaranteed disaster. "So what is the matter, then? You caught the clap or something, butt? Chlamydia, is it?"

James nervously glanced around, as though making sure nobody was listening (there was nobody in the pub *to* listen, apart from that idiot *Uptown Girl* guy) and then edged even closer. Mandy concluded that James didn't have bad breath (beside the feint and natural waft of lager), for if he did she would surely have smelt it.

"I've tried to just get on with it, to join in with the frivolities like everybody else. I just can't stop thinking about it, though.

And the more I tell myself not to think about it, I just think about it even more."

"Oh, that will be the pink elephants," Mandy excitedly informed him.

James looked bemused.

"The pink elephants! You try not to think of a pink elephant and low and behold all you will be able to think of is those damn pink elephants. There will be so many of them it will feel like they are mocking you. Laughing at you..."

"I'm glad somebody is laughing at us!" James guffawed.

They clinked glasses and Mandy could tell James knew exactly what she was talking about.

"It's Herbert," he said. "He isn't telling it straight. This whole thing. He has an ulterior motive he hasn't told anyone about. It all kicked off between his mum and my mum. I'm sure this whole thing is a big fat lie, and we're the punch line."

Mandy couldn't help but loudly guffaw. She put her hand to her mouth to restrain her giggles. She eyed him to check he wasn't joking. Mandy knew it had something to do with Herbert. The tension between the two, ever since they left Sarn Services on that daft minibus, was close to breaking point. Herbert was always so annoyingly enthusiastic about life in general, but even he was showing strain. What was this whole drama between the mums? Did the two 'mummies' boys' need their mummies to fight their corners?

Mandy quickly returned to planet Earth. She knew that whatever this conflict was about, James had taken it deadly seriously. He was almost unrecognisable from the James they left in Bridgend. Mandy didn't ask any questions. She looked straight at James and said, "You need to speak to Herbert then, don't you? And soon. Before you fuck this whole trip up for all of us..."

James picked up his glass and drank from it until all that was left was foam and bubbles. "Herbert knows that I know," he said, putting the empty glass down on the table. "I'm sorry, Mandy, but he needs to speak to me..."

3 – Friday Night at The Fringe

Connor was very aware he'd had a significantly better tour than the others. Connor was very aware this was not much of an accomplishment.

It was early Friday evening. They had performed four shows and only had one left. The last show had been the matinee performance earlier that day. Tomorrow night was to be their last gig, pulling the final curtain on their brutal, turbulent week together.

Connor knew, just like the others, that after four shows and with just one left, the tour had been a commercial and critical failure. It was usually one or the other, wasn't it, not both? Not with their tour. Commercially it had been a failure because hardly anybody had come to watch the shows, and those that did barely put any coins or notes in the plastic bucket (from his shop) that was passed around. Critically it had been a failure because, for example, on the third night a drunken reveller had interrupted the show by shouting "You're all fucking shit!" It was, at best, a scathing review.

Connor, though, had continued undeterred, displaying resilience and an uncharacteristically upbeat attitude. Nobody was more surprised by this than Connor himself. The other three carried the dismal failure around with them like a badge of honour. They sulked. They moaned. They whined. It reiterated what he had learnt from his Auntie Jojo. It was, Connor observed, a most unappealing look. If he had known this before then he would have been much more upbeat years ago.

Of course, he asked himself why he felt so good. Sure, there were some great things in his life right now, but then there had been great things in his life before and he'd always been a miserable sod. It felt like he had turned an invisible corner where, despite what they said, life *was* actually greener on the other side. Of course, his mum and dad were on tour with him. Under normal circumstances that would not necessarily be a good thing. In this circumstance though, there was no denying that it absolutely was a good thing. They were both undoubtedly having a fantastic time. His mum was a delight and even his dad was good, solid company. The whole gang loved them. Connor liked the fact his parents were there with him. So that was one concrete, definitive reason why Connor was feeling so damn good.

Another reason, Connor realised now, as he sat on a small and uncomfortable chair in a small and uncomfortable room in the basement of a corner pub on a backstreet that was so narrow and secluded that most people passed by without even noticing its existence, he had unexpectedly made a new friend.

*****

Mrs Henry's first-class train ticket to Edinburgh had been stored in a sealed white envelope on top of the mantelpiece in the lounge for a number of months.

Herbert, bless him, was adamant only first-class would do for his mother. He reminded her (as if she needed reminding) that she was not getting any younger and neither was her health what it had once been. He had meticulously planned the week well in advance. They were performing on the Friday afternoon, which meant they all had the evening to relax and do their own thing. Herbert had been insistent she came to the final, monumental show. It was to be the finale to a hugely successful week and he wanted her to be there to witness and enjoy it. He had booked her accommodation in a swanky hotel that was fit for a queen too, to make sure she was fresh and in good spirits for Saturday. Mrs Henry was aware that for all his plentiful faults, Herbert really did his best to look after her. The trip was pencilled onto her *Hunks 2016* calendar that was pinned to the fridge. Mrs Henry was reminded of the trip every time she opened the fridge door to nibble on the cheese that, strictly speaking, was supposed to be rationed.

She no longer led a busy or active or especially enjoyable life. It wasn't anything like it used to be back in the day when, even though she was shy and socially awkward, before she came out of her shell, she loved to get out of the house, particularly in the evenings. Now her days were normally spent on the sofa in front of the television, with just the occasional trip to the shops and the odd night out. Mrs Henry didn't have a great deal to look forward to; most of the other dates in her calendar related to trips to the doctors and the dentist. Edinburgh, and especially the circumstances surrounding the trip, was a big deal. It terrified her as much as it excited her but, she considered, at least it stimulated some sort of emotion. The trip occupied most of her waking thoughts and even some when she was asleep. She counted down the days, just like she did with Christmas as a kid. And finally, the day had arrived.

Herbert, of course, was waiting for her like a good boy at the station. She ruefully noticed he was still wearing cheap shoes from the supermarket even though he'd accepted they never lasted and usually came away at the sole. Still, her boy did look healthy and handsome, despite his recent troubles. Herbert gave her a hug, took her suitcase and then started telling her, in that fast, excitable and rambling way of his that he was going to give her a taste of the real Edinburgh. Herbert was aware, of course, because he knew almost everything about his mother, that she'd never been to Scotland before. Why would she? Who *had*? She had hardly even been to England, let alone Scotland. Her son was something of an expert on Edinburgh, or so he said. He had been there once before on a ghost tour weekend, for some unknown reason. But then, Mrs Henry mused, Herbert considered himself an expert on most subjects, didn't he? He must get the trait from his dad; not that he ever really met him, of course. Mrs Henry was quite certain that if Herbert was as informed as he said he was then he wouldn't be a reporter in a local rag. He would be running the country or an Egghead.

Mrs Henry had to admit Herbert talked with such passion about the city – the culture, the history – that he managed to stimulate even *her* stale imagination. Herbert excitedly informed her he was taking her for something to eat. Mrs Henry was careful to avoid stereotypes but still, she pictured handsome young waiters delivering food in their kilts (and she'd heard what men did or did not wear underneath their kilts) and then entertaining them in between courses by playing the bagpipes.

It did not really surprise Mrs Henry that her son had a

At Least the Pink Elephants are Laughing at Us

completely different idea of what "giving her a taste of Edinburgh" entailed. She had no idea what went through that boy's mind, really she didn't. And so, when she found herself in a leafy park that he assured her was the epitome of the beautiful and fascinating city, sat on a wooden bench opposite a statute of a marble bear, just off a wide main street that only had shops on one side of the road, Mrs Henry barely raised a bushy eyebrow. She had to admit, it was rather nice. A pleasant change. The light was fading, for it was beginning to get late. The park began clearing of people. It was peaceful.

Herbert had always been a nervous child, but Mrs Henry could tell he was more anxious than usual tonight. Her boy wasn't afraid to be open with his emotions, but he tended to beat around the bush before doing so, and even then he was usually long-winded. He was not going to be openly forthcoming tonight with his thoughts and conflicts. Mrs Herbert was an impatient lady, even if she didn't have much to rush for. He needed to be prodded. Mrs Herbert, of course, knew all too well that he had good reason to be anxious. It was partly her doing, and that didn't fit well with her.

"So how have the shows been going?" she asked.

Herbert wiped a crumb from his top lip. "It has not been a total "success" in the conventional sense of the word," he said.

That meant it hadn't been good at all then, Mrs Henry considered. She was his mother. She gave *birth* to him. And yet still, after all these long, turbulent years, he still thought he could confuse her with his fluffy, non-committal choice of words. Plus, she'd had plenty of time to piece together how events were likely to unfold. Her son really was the cleverest dumb person she'd ever had the privilege of knowing.

"Why has it been such a massive disaster, dear?"

"It is a difficult crowd to crack, mother," Herbert defensively replied. "If it was easy then every comic would be a success. You know that. And what makes one person laugh doesn't necessarily make the next person laugh. You know that, too."

Mrs Henry bit into her pie and the meat squirted from the sides. She glanced at her boy. He hadn't noticed. No need to tell him, either. She licked the gravy from her fingers. Her strange boy didn't eat meat, of course. He was trying to fob her off with standard comedian spiel. Would he ever learn? "But when something is funny, Herbert, then it is funny," she countered. "And I've seen your boys – and your girl - perform and so I know they're funny. Which can only mean one thing." She paused for effect. The gravy dribbled down the top. It was probably best just to get on with it. "There must be trouble in camp."

She could see Herbert tried to say something, but even for somebody so annoyingly articulate, the words failed him. He merely gesticulated with his hands and pulled a pained face. Eventually he said "Well, you know, things have naturally not been straightforward since that night at The Regency on Saturday night. I don't want to apportion blame, of course, but it didn't help when Miriam slapped you in the face."

Mrs Henry nodded her head. There was no denying he was right. The silly bugger obviously hadn't spoken to James though, had he? He'd had all week. There was only one show left. Her boy really needed to grow some balls. She was more than happy to tell it as it was. She wasn't getting any younger (as Herbert regularly reminded her) and she didn't have time to mince her words. But she didn't want to push her dear boy any further than she had to. He just needed a bit of poking. She often thought he didn't realise it, but she didn't like her boy to be unhappy.

"You need to speak to him," she said, simply. "You should have spoken to him long ago, but you absolutely need to now, before all of this becomes a waste of time."

She was relieved to see her son was reluctantly nodding his head in agreement.

*****

Roy sat on the bed with his back pressed against a pillow and his arms crossed behind his head. He had the house to himself. It was getting dark outside. He stared at the four walls of his bedroom. He was alone with his thoughts and, unusually for him, he had plenty of them.

Roy knew all too well that he should relax, that he should savour the peace and tranquillity of this Friday evening whilst it lasted, that the house would rapidly deteriorate into a madhouse

At Least the Pink Elephants are Laughing at Us

again when Terry, Michelle and Cat returned from the cinema, but it was difficult. Roy had to make a decision. Roy knew that, if he was brave enough to make the decision he knew was the right one, then things would never be the same again. His mind tried to talk him out of it. Why bother when things were just fine as they were? Why ruin the equilibrium? Why fix what wasn't broken? Some things are best just being left alone.

But he knew it was all nonsense. Roy placed one foot down on the floor. He pulled open the wardrobe. He stretched into the far, dark corner until his hand reached the familiar bundle tied together by a long piece of white string.

Roy sat back down on the bed, took a deep, deliberate breath, and then untied the bow.

*****

Mandy paced up and down on the only available floor space in her tiny room. The floor creaked, and she was sure she could hear the flimsy cardboard walls shake and rattle; that and her heavy breathing. She caught her reflection in the lopsided grubby mirror on the wall and could tell by the red in her eyes and the white in her cheeks that she was stressed. She just couldn't rest.

She'd been tempted to join Connor at the show to watch his new friend, the old guy, George, from down the road in Wales. Mandy had the feeling, though, more by the way he spoke than with what he actually said, that the show was kind of personal to Connor. It was sweet to hear Connor so enthusiastic. Mandy had the same warm fuzzy feeling she experienced when she looked at the picture of James's boy, Rory. Mandy didn't really want to intrude or be a gooseberry. On the other hand, Mandy had definitely been tempted to join James in the pub – again – not that he was exactly Mr Cheerful at the moment, plus she knew she'd only be drowning her thoughts by drowning copious amounts of booze (again, though, this was definitely tempting).

Mandy was fully aware that really, the way she was feeling, it was best to just be on her own. There was only so much trouble she could get into that way. Everybody else was out. Even Alun and Nanya had gone for dinner somewhere, like a couple of young lovebirds. And so Mandy left the bubbling

Edinburgh night and headed back to the bleak, dreary solitude of their house, with the cracked ceilings, the torn brown carpets and the walls which were smeared with horrific, terrifying stains.

Now though, her worst enemy appeared to be herself; she was going round and round in circles, fighting her taunting, intrusive thoughts. It was the damn pink elephants again. Mandy liked to think she was decisive. She hated dawdlers, customers who hovered by the counter in the hospital restaurant, causing queues by deliberating whether to have a flippin' latte or a cappuccino, like it was a real life or death decision. *Hurry up! They're both lukewarm and taste like crap!* But now she truly didn't know what to do. She was the epitome of indecisive. Both her options seemed unthinkable. It was such a mess. She had to do something quick. It was getting late.

Mandy stared again at her reflection in the mirror, at her fingernails which had been bitten to shreds, and at her chin, which had reddened and looked ready to be attacked by spots, and she thought, just as she had in the pub with James yesterday, that there just had to be more to life than this. All this worry and fretting could not possibly be worth it. And so, finally, she made a decision.

She was going to make a call.

*****

You could count how many people were watching the show on the fingers of both hands. Connor knew this was true because he had counted on the fingers of both hands how many people were watching the show, and there were nine. Okay, so that included a thumb. They were a decent nine, though, Connor thought. Better than the rabble that had been coming to their show seemingly intent on trouble. Nobody in the audience appeared overly intoxicated or particularly distracted. Their heads kept looking forward and their eyes focussed on the guy on the stage. They weren't exactly hysterical with their appreciation, but they did generally laugh in the right places. It was a pleasant, if low-key event.

As for the guy up on stage, dressed in a sharp suit and a flannel shirt, well he appeared ecstatic – overjoyed - just to be

At Least the Pink Elephants are Laughing at Us

there. He appeared ecstatic and overjoyed to still be alive, let alone performing stand-up to other living people. Connor could tell by the way he told the jokes (generally the same ones he told in the pub), with such passion and conviction, that the old man was having the time of his life. If he keeled over and died up on stage then he'd die a happy man. Connor enthusiastically clapped his hands and (on one occasion) yelped for joy when the punch line was delivered. A few people had glanced over their shoulder to check who the crazy guy was. Connor didn't care.

"Anybody out there listen to Radio 4?" George asked the audience. "Don't worry; you will do! When you get to my age, nobody takes you seriously. You know things are bad when you get compared to the wizard from Lord of the Rings. I can't blame it all on the age, to be honest with you, butt. I've never been handsome in the conventional sense of the word; as in, I've always been ugly as fuck. The *world* has changed, you know. Technology? Huh. I tell you, it's not all good. If you weren't particularly good looking in the first place then you are sure as hell going to be an ugly fucker in HD. And believe me, it's difficult for us old people to keep up with modern trends," George said. "It's taken me a lifetime to speak proper English and now it's all gone to the shit. A woman told me she was "pmsl" and I said don't worry, at least it only happens once a month. And things like "wtf." I mean, what the fuck does that mean?"

The show ended and George did an elaborate bow and lapped up the moderate applause. Connor hoped his friend didn't lean too far forward at the waist, for with his old bones he'd have problems getting back up again. The appreciation bucket was passed around, and when Connor dropped his note inside he was pleased to see it wasn't the only one.

George turned the light switch on and the audience began to disperse. Connor got to his feet and turned to join his mate, but then he stopped. His heart sunk. He knew this was all too good to be true. His dad stood in the aisle, on the edge of the row of chairs, hands in his pockets, quietly and nervously shuffling his feet. He had been waiting. Connor did not need to ask what was up; he could tell by the terrible, awful, solemn look on his father's face.

Chris Westlake

Auntie Jojo had gone.

*****

James stared at the clear white wall. It kept moving. That was strange. Did they have earthquakes in Edinburgh? What sort of a crazy place was this? He knew it was a different country, absolutely miles away from Wales, further away than France even; but still, he was surprised the Scots had tremors this bad.

He squinted; stared with more focussed intensity. Such vigour hurt his eyes, made them feel like the balls might pop out of the sockets. The wall started to come into focus, refrained from doing a crazy, jiggling dance. Stayed still. The wall started dancing again. *Stop moving, damn you!* The wall stopped moving. James jutted his neck out, his head forward, his eyes closer to the wall. And then he realised it wasn't a wall after all. James eyed the metal peg. The "wall" was a flippin' door.

Bang. Bang. The door shook.

"Open the door!"

James jerked his head around in a circle. Looked around. Looked up. Looked down. What the flying...? There was hardly any room in any direction. He was sat on a toilet, wasn't he? And he still had his trousers on.

He pulled the metal lock across without even contemplating who or what was on the other side. The door pushed open and slammed hard against his delicate bony knees. James jumped to his feet. The back of his legs brushed against the toilet. A bloke peered inside the cubicle. Looked straight at him. James couldn't see the bloke properly, because he kept moving with no consideration whatsoever, but he could see enough to tell he was a wide load, and he was vexed.

"We shut the pub an hour ago!" the man said. "You've fallen asleep in the toilet, you idiot."

James blurted his sincere apologies and stumbled out of the toilet and headed back into the pub, which was mainly shapes and outlines in the dark, but still seemed vaguely, remotely familiar. James briefly wondered whether it was too late to ask for one final drink, but then the decision was made for him because the heavy guy pushed James outside and slammed the door behind him.

For a fleeting moment, James's first thought was, "I wonder whether anywhere else is still open." Then some bile filled his mouth and threatened to spill out and James dismissed the idea of searching for another drinking den. James suddenly longed for the warmth and relative comfort of his bed. He desperately wanted to be away from this freezing cold night and under the covers. James decided to take a short cut. He really didn't know where this short cut led, though. He really didn't know whether it really was even a short cut. He didn't really know where he was walking, or in what direction. It was a steep, narrow passageway, and it felt familiar. James pressed the palm of his hand against the brick wall as he gained momentum down the hill.

And then he had an uncontrollable urge. The beer and food was suddenly repeating on him. His tummy rumbled and growled. There was no time to think. He had to take action, and now. James scurried to the closest courtyard, pulled down his trousers and squatted. James was hit by an incredible sense of relief. Thank God for that, he thought.

A window opened in the building just metres away. A hairy bear of a man in a faded white vest pushed his head outside. "What the hell are you doing?" he asked.

"It's not ideal but I had to take urgent action," James explained, his face smothered in sweat.

"I don't believe this," the man growled. "You're taking a fucking shit in my garden! I tell you, when I get my hands on you..." The window slammed shut.

James tore at some grass, had a quick wipe and then was on his feet, running faster than he could ever remember, down the cobbled lane. He turned left and then right and by the time he reached the bottom he was coughing and wheezing. James looked around and there was no sign of an angry gorilla in a vest. He had lost him. James took in his surroundings. He didn't know this place at all. This goddamn city! This goddamn *life*! There was just a square forecourt with a lawn and a flowerbed in the middle, which was cordoned off by black metal rails with sinister spikes on the tips. James scoped the forecourt, sniffing out possible exits. There were none. It was a complete dead end.

James looked back at the path he had taken to get here. It was all uphill. That slope looked long and vicious. Why would he head back in the direction of danger and possible death? His body ached, his head throbbed, his mouth felt like sandpaper. He wanted sleep. Right now.

He gripped the metal rail and pulled himself over with unexpected strength and agility. He landed in a heap on the grass on the other side. James stretched his body out. The flowers were soft and cushioned his sore, old body. There was no need to move. He fell asleep.

4 – Sugar and Vinegar

James knew this was one of those moments where the night before had deteriorated into the morning after and he had woken up somewhere he should not be, not entirely convinced he was still alive. He didn't know *where* he was; his mind was frazzled, his thoughts were slow and confused and his eyelids felt like they had been glued down, but he *did* know he was not under the duvet, in his bed, in the crappy terraced house. And that could only be a bad thing.

His thoughts gradually started piecing themselves together; James remembered drinking in the pub, waking up in the toilets, then being thrown out of the pub. James began thinking about what happened after the pub but then decided he didn't have the energy, or the motivation, to actually *give* a flying fuck. James released a long sigh and wondered whether he could remain lying here – wherever *that* was – for the rest of his life. Or maybe he could hibernate for a while, just like those clever, lucky animals who didn't feel the need to look busy all the time or care whether people thought they were lazy or lacking in ambition. It was very peaceful, albeit unusually uncomfortable, and absolutely stress-free; just what he needed at this point in his life. It crossed his mind that this sleeping rough lark was beginning to become something of a bad habit. The circumstances, at least, couldn't be as desperate as the last time. James tried to work out what day it was. Saturday. It was their final day in Edinburgh and then finally he could revert back to his normal, humble existence in Bridgend. The thought that it would soon be over was quite soothing.

The peace was disturbed by fluid spraying on his face. His first thought was: is a dog pissing on me? It wouldn't be the first time. He dismissed the thought. Piss was warm, or hot even, depending what you drank. This was cold. He could see, through his closed eyelids, the outline of something or somebody. It was probably a gardener, James considered, watering the plants. It was a bit inconsiderate not to ask him to get out of the way first, though! Oh no, he thought. It was that guy in a vest who was chasing after him! James managed to prise his eyes open. It wasn't a gardener. It wasn't that guy. It was the second last person he wanted to see right now. It was this guy's fault he was even in this position.

Herbert looked down on James from what felt like a great height. He really was impressively tall, James ruefully considered. Herbert smiled at him widely, but then it was a pitying, sympathetic smile and James wanted to push it right back down his throat.

"We need to talk," Herbert stated factually. He held out his hand.

James considered grabbing the hand and pulling him over the sharp metal railing and then wrestling and grappling him on the floor, just like a naked Oliver Reed and Alan Bates in that old film, but then it felt like so much unnecessary effort and completely pointless.

James took hold of Herbert's hand and pulled his head back to nod his agreement, but it banged into something hard and unmistakably concrete.

"Oh, for fuck's sake," James moaned, as his body slowly untangled and he rose to his feet.

*****

Connor liked this kind of hotel. It was his type of place. The carpets were thick and luxurious and smothered your feet, and the floorboards creaked with his every leisurely step. His hand brushed along the curved, mahogany staircase. He briefly glanced at his reflection in the polished mirror on the wall and pulled a face. Everything about the place felt and smelt old, and to Connor old meant historic, and historic meant personality. The modern hotels, in contrast, just like the football stadiums, were all clean and crisp and void of atmosphere and scents, and just far too clinical.

He stopped and stood in the long, narrow hallway and knocked.

His father pulled open the door. Of course. Dad's

movements were slow and measured and reminded Connor of a robot that needed a squirt of oil or a battery replacement. Connor noticed, though, that his hair possessed fantastic shine. His old man really was a silver fox, Connor thought. He had probably been using the free shampoo and conditioner that came with the room.

"You'd better come in, son."

*****

Herbert had these unnecessarily long legs, James thought, that belonged perfectly on an unnecessarily tall person. The man set a walking pace that was just pointlessly fast unless you were competing in some sort of race, particularly after they had just climbed up this stupidly steep brick alleyway. Was he some sort of closet Ethiopian? James wasn't sure whether the round sweat patches nestled under his own armpits were due to heat, exertion, or excessive alcohol, but he did know it wouldn't be too long before he started smelling as ripe as a porcupine.

"Quick drink?" James suggested, reasonably he felt. "Hair of the dog is probably just what the doctor ordered. I'll be straight with you, butt; I did treat myself to a few beers last night, just to let my hair down a bit after putting my heart and soul into the show, you know? I'll let you buy me a drink, if you fancy?"

Herbert didn't seem to think he was being serious, for he just continued grinning dumbly. He pulled open a white wooden door to a building that was undoubtedly not a pub. The door opened with a friendly, over-enthusiastic chime. Herbert held out his hand to let James in first. It was a cafe. James wasn't sure how his gut would handle physical, solid food right now, but he wouldn't say no to a strong black coffee with plenty of sugar.

James quickly glanced around the place, and there she was, with puffy cheeks plumped out like she was holding her breath, wearing a little posh hat that barely covered her head. James turned to walk out of the place, but his path was steadfastly blocked by Herbert.

"Come on, James," Herbert said. "She just wants to talk, too. Come on, take a seat and I'll buy you a coffee. You won't say no to a freebie now, will you?"

James turned back to the woman, who opened her mouth wide like a hippopotamus and released the loudest burp he had ever heard in all his life.

"Sorry about that. It is these flaming marshmallows."

*****

Connor sat on a chair on the edge of the plush double bed. He leant forward, his chin in his hand and his elbow on his knee. Connor noticed his dad was in exactly the same position on the chair on the other side of the bed. They both stared intently at Nanya, who lay motionless on her back, her eyes closed, in the middle of the bed.

The curtains had been pulled tight and hardly any light entered the room. The walls of the hotel were built thick and sturdy, Connor thought, for he couldn't hear any movements from the rooms next door or the corridor outside. Connor couldn't hear *anything*, in fact, except for the gentle, subtle breathing of his mum in her pink dressing gown. He dared not utter a single word to his dad, not even a delicate whisper, in case he woke her.

Connor was terrified what his mother would be like when she woke up.

Suddenly she shot up, her back completely straight, like somebody had stabbed a needle into her thigh. Both eyes opened and Nanya rotated her head to look around the room, to take in her surroundings, to remember where she was. She stopped rotating when she saw Connor.

"Hello darling," she said, her face lit by a glorious smile. "It really is fantastic to see you. You come give your mum a hug now, you hear?"

*****

The hotel provided a generous supply of biscuits, Connor mused, as he placed a plastic wrapper in the bin with one hand and sipped a digestive into his piping hot mug of decaffeinated coffee with the other. This was his first biscuit, but he'd noticed his dad had already bitten into his third. Grief and sorrow didn't appear to have affected his old man's appetite too much, he considered. Then he pictured the fun Mandy would have in this place. Mandy would probably sneak a handful of biscuits into her suitcase, Connor thought.

Connor felt strangely comfortable and relaxed nestled on the edge of the bed. His mum reached out and held his free hand. That felt good. Of course, he had so many questions, but then he wasn't sure how to ask them, and part of him wanted to savour the quiet before the inevitable storm broke. Besides, what question could he ask that would make any sense at all? Of course Mum wasn't alright; her beloved sister had just died.

"You alright, Mum?"

Mum didn't appear to think it was a stupid question, though. She smiled warmly, like she understood exactly what he was asking and felt the pain he was going through by asking the question.

"You know what? I think I am alright, you know. I don't think I am too bad at all."

This was good, Connor thought. But there again, was it good? How could she be alright? Connor looked closely at his Mum. Her smooth, flawless skin glowed and her eyes were bright, alert and lively. She didn't look like a woman who had spent a restless night fighting pain and anguish.

His face must have looked a picture of bemusement, for his mum started laughing. She turned to Connor's dad, presumably saw him munching away and then asked, "Are there any biscuits left?" Dad lowered his eyes and said "No, love. They were in quite short supply to be honest with you." Connor thought his mum must have noticed he was on his third biscuit, for she laughed louder.

"The truth is," she said, turning back to Connor and gently stroking his arm, "I think I actually *am* alright. I'm not way with the fairies, flying above the clouds, but I do feel peaceful. You see, dear," she continued, "Jojo is no longer in pain. No, she is not. And I managed to say goodbye to my dear sister. That meant everything to me. I know she has gone to a better place. I know it was only goodbye for now, that I will be seeing Jojo again, in heaven. I will."

Connor nodded his head. He searched for cracks in what his mum was saying, for signs she was deluded, evidence her illness had returned, but he could not find any.

"Of course," Mum continued, "I know and understand that not everybody is a believer. Why should they be? Take your father over there. I've always known he was more likely to believe in the Tooth Fairy than God..."

Connor's dad spluttered a mouthful of tea and an undigested digestive biscuit all over the lovely carpet. Connor was sure a blue vein throbbed from the side of his temple.

"What do you mean, Nanya?" his dad protested. His normally deep, masculine voice sounded peculiarly high-pitched. "I've always been to church with you, Nanya, haven't I? I was headmaster of a Church of Wales school for years, wasn't I...?"

Nanya shook her head from side to side and theatrically waved her hand in the air like it was a feather duster. "Its fine, darling!" she said. "I love you all the more knowing you would do that just for me. It really is absolutely *adorable*, really it is."

Alun shrugged his shoulders and smiled. Connor thought he looked like he'd just accepted there was no point arguing, like he was even contemplating turning this to his advantage. *It is no problem, darling. I would do anything for you.*

"We all have our little secrets," Nanya added. She turned to Alun. "Do you think I didn't notice you checking me out in the church that first time we met? Tssk. Why do you think I asked Amanda to swap the table names around? I was supposed to be on that happy table? Was it Caerphilly or something? No...?"

Connor's dad appeared to find this hilarious. His whole body shuddered. His mum continued talking, though.

"When it came to God, you may as well have had a sign above your head, dear," she said. "It was that obvious."

Nanya chuckled now, and so did Connor. Then she stopped, and her face became serious. "I know you can't prove His existence. I am not blind. I am not stupid. No. But I feel there is as much evidence for Him as against Him, and I feel so much safer with Him there. I choose to believe. I made a decision. And I am sure it is the right decision for me. Yes?"

Dad held his mug up in the air. "You can't argue with that logic, love. I have never argued with your belief. I respect you for what you believe in. You know I do. I respect and love you for everything you do."

At Least the Pink Elephants are Laughing at Us

Connor had no doubt whatsoever his dad did. Whatever his faults, and Connor knew there were countless, he knew his dad was a good man. He always had, despite the nagging resentment over the years.

"We'll be going back to Ghana for the funeral, of course," Nanya now enthused, turning to Connor. "It will be a wonderful, extravagant event. Ghana always puts on the best party. Of course, all of the family will be there. It will be a celebration of her life rather than mourning her death. I would love you to be there, darling."

Connor nodded his head. "I would love that too, Mum."

Nanya adjusted her position on the bed, like she was ready to get the day started, to clear the cobwebs and shake things up. "Right then," she stated. "I need to keep busy! I've been thinking of ways you can bow out of Edinburgh with a bang...!"

*****

The mug of coffee was plonked on the table.

"Could I have some water, please?" James asked the waitress. His mouth was so dry he felt the skin coating his gums was going to peel away.

"Tap water in a glass, love?"

"Tap water in a gigantic jug, please," James replied. The waitress walked away with a shake of her head. She probably didn't like Welsh people, James reasoned.

Herbert's mother, Brenda, had insisted on buying James a plate of chips, even though James assured her he was not hungry. She looked at him with concern, like she thought he would pass out if he didn't have some proper food inside him. I must look really bad, James thought. Now that the chips had arrived though, his belly rumbled and he felt surprisingly hungry. The chips were thick cut and crispy, just how his mum cooked them. James smothered the chips with a healthy dosage of salt. Herbert was one of those picky vegetarians, probably allergic to his own reflection, of course, but he obviously didn't get it from his mum. Brenda was hungrily devouring half a farmyard on her plate.

James put a forkful of chips in his mouth and then

immediately spluttered and spat them out. "What is this nonsense?" he accused. "I am sure these Scottish people are trying to kill me!"

Heads, likely belonging to Scottish people, turned to glare at their table.

"That is the sugar shaker, James," Brenda explained. "You have just poured sugar all over your chips, my lovely."

James looked at her like he, or she, had lost the plot. "You've just watched me pour sugar over my chips and you didn't say anything? What is the *matter* with you people?"

Brenda didn't look offended. She merely smiled and chuckled. "I wasn't sure whether it was a new fad or a diet or something. You have to be so open-minded about things these days, don't you? What might seem strange to one person may be perfectly natural to another? Who am I to judge? And you know what they say, 'sugar and spice and all things nice.'"

"Who the hell *are* you?" James asked, exasperated. "You're tugging on my chain now, aren't you?" He turned to Herbert for support, but the idiot was just nodding his head in agreement, like this crazy woman of a mother was talking perfect sense. James could feel his agitation quickly escalating. They'd dragged him to this awful cafe to talk, rather than to a sensible pub that served alcohol, then they'd watched him sabotage his food, yet they still weren't saying anything in particular, they were mainly just stuffing their faces. Oh, and where was that water he asked for? James could see he was going to be foaming at the mouth if they didn't calm him down soon. They would have to strap him down to his chair like that McVitee character from the book his dad was forever telling him about.

His dad. Bobby. That was why they were here, wasn't it?

"Let's cut the crap," James said, waving his fork the air. "You said you want to talk, so let's talk. I know why you got me into this group. I've worked it all out."

"What have you worked out?" Brenda asked, apparently genuinely curious.

"I've worked out that that lanky streak of piss over there," he said, pointing at Herbert. "He is my brother..."

*****

At Least the Pink Elephants are Laughing at Us

Mandy nervously dug her fingernails into the sloping wooden bench. She sometimes wondered how girls and grown-up women with fake or manicured nails managed to perform normal everyday activities, such as washing and searching for coins down the side of the sofa, without causing drama and mayhem. It was only sometimes, though. It was admittedly not exactly something at the forefront of Mandy's mind.

There was an abundance of urgent activity all around her; people striding this way, people pacing that way, all glancing up at the same round clock. Mandy, though, had located a quiet, serene spot amongst the madness. She was joined by other commuters (and idlers and thinkers) who happily passed the time reading the latest paperback blockbusters, like *The Girl on The Train* and *Gone Girl* or filling the squares of the *Times* crossword with blunt pencils. She was privileged to sit amongst the intellectuals; civilised people who possessed worldly viewpoints and reasoned opinions.

And then the large woman sat on the bench next to her brushed away the flaky remains of sausage roll from her tee shirt and released a tremendous fart that frightened even the pigeons, and with that Mandy's illusion was destroyed; the savages were everywhere!

Mandy stood up and slowly walked to the edge of the platform. This was his train now, grinding to a stop. Passengers disembarked and hurriedly fled. The crowd thinned, the numbers lowered, until Mandy was able to identify individual features and faces. It seemed she was in this position too often recently. And then she identified the face she had been waiting for.

William walked slowly, for the large, cumbersome bag he carried over his shoulder surely weighed him down, even with his strong, impressive bulk. His chin jutted forward, and he bent at the waist. The smile was slanted, cautiously, at one side. He put down the bag and held out his arms.

Mandy walked swiftly towards him, towards her older brother, and then she slapped him on the face.

*****

The plump woman sat opposite James, on the other side of the plastic table, a relative stranger, using a tissue now to dab tears from her eyes.

"It's not funny!" James scolded.

But apparently it *was* funny. Mother and son had laughed hysterically for what felt like minutes. Even Herbert's eyes were watery and runny with the joyous hilarity of it all. Brenda gave herself a visible shake to pull herself together, then glanced at James and burst into another bout of giggles.

"How on earth did you reach that conclusion? What do you think this is? *Star Wars?* You don't even look similar. My Herbert is a handsome boy and you..."

James slammed his fist down on the table. He'd had enough of this bullshit. He was up for a good laugh – it was *supposed* to be his business these days, when he wasn't earning money by serving on the till – but not in these circumstances. How dare they laugh at him? This was supposed to be his moment of emotional trauma. James felt the table rattle, even though he was pretty sure it was nailed to the floor, and he heard a loud disapproving tut from behind the counter.

"So why did my mum slap you?" he asked. "I've never seen her hurt anybody in her life and yet as soon as she set eyes on you she turned into Joe Calzaghe. What is the story, huh?"

Brenda dabbed at her cheek with the tissue, as though the sting, or maybe the memory, from the strike that night still remained.

"You need to be straight with James, Mum," Herbert stated. "Like we discussed, remember?"

The woman nodded her head and smiled. "I'm sorry," she said. "It just tickled my funny bone, that is all. This whole thing has made me quite nervous, to be frank with you, and a little light relief was most welcome. Okay. The truth." Brenda paused, then took a deep breath, as if mustering the courage to proceed. "I did know your father, James."

"Of course you did!" James retorted. "I saw you have sex with him! I was hiding in a hedge behind The Regency!"

James was aware Herbert gave him a sharp, accusing look. James was also aware his use of words didn't sound too good. He didn't care.

At Least the Pink Elephants are Laughing at Us

"No, I never slept with Bobby. I swear on Herbert's life!"

James glanced again at Herbert, and now he just looked miffed.

"So why did my mum bitch slap you then?"

"That was a sucker punch, I tell you," Brenda clarified. She dug her fork into her sausage and opened her mouth ready, but Herbert gave her a look and she decided against it. "Listen, your dad was a fine-looking man. I'm not saying I wouldn't have got 'jiggy' with him given half a chance, okay?"

James pulled a disgusted face, and when he turned to Herbert, he pulled a disgusted face, too. Brenda continued: "But the point is that he didn't give me half a chance, did he? I was just an original comedy groupie, back in the days when there weren't many of us about. We were a rarity, and not in a good way. We were just *odd*. Comedy in those days just wasn't sexy. But me?" Brenda pointed a finger at her ample chest. "I loved comedians. I went from dingy hall to dingy hall and gloomy pub to gloomy pub to watch shows. And some of the shows were absolutely *shit!* If it was a daytime show I would bring Herbert along too. That's how he got the bug, too. It was in his blood, wasn't it darling?"

Herbert nodded his head. He twisted his finger as if to indicate to his mum to get to the point. That was ironic coming from Herbie, James thought.

"First time I watched Bobby Jones, it was lust at first sight," Brenda proclaimed. "That guy was sex on legs, I tell you. I was there at every show, with my tongue hanging out. He was funny, too. If it were a Tom Jones concert I would have been one of those throwing her knickers on the stage..."

"Mum!" Herbert protested.

"But my point is, he wasn't interested, was he? And I was a shy girl back then. I wasn't exactly one to push the issue. So unless there was some sort of miraculous conception in Bridgend, James, then I can say with absolute certainty that Herbert is not your brother." She finally pushed the sausage inside her mouth. Brenda looked to the ceiling like she had a light bulb moment. "Come to think of it, the maths don't even add up. I already had Herbert the first time I watched your dad. His Aunty Linda babysat for me."

"I was even there that final night, James," Herbert added, softly. "I was just a kid, but I remember."

James thought about this for a moment, and something clicked into place. So Herbert was that little nipper running around with his mum.

"Your dad had no feelings for me in that way, James," Brenda added. "But he did respect me as a fan, and that meant something to me. Bobby had this thing about not letting down his fans. I remember a few nights before he passed away he was drunk as a skunk in The Oak and could barely stand up. But as soon as he knew I was there he was up on his feet and firing out the jokes..."

"So why is my mum so upset with you, then?"

"I became a familiar face, James. I was always there at his shows. Your mum knew Bobby was no angel and he was up to no good and she assumed – just like you – that I was a guilty party. I went to see her the day after the gig last Saturday and I assured her I wasn't. She believes me. She is a fine woman, your mum, James..."

James was shell-shocked by this. He wasn't sure what to think. He was glad his mum was feeling better, though. "I know she is," he proudly said. "She is the best."

This was all a lot to take in, and James's head was spinning, especially since that damn woman *still* hadn't delivered that jug of water. James picked up Herbert's half-drunken mug of tea and downed it. The poor guy looked slightly put out. Sod him. There was still unfinished business. They weren't getting away that easily. James turned to Herbert now. "So you...?" he accused. "Why did you get us together, then? Why us three?"

Herbert shuffled on his seat and dabbled with his hair. "Like my mum said, I got the bug too. I genuinely love comedy, James. All of that is true. I've just never been particularly funny myself, as you may have noticed. Even in the meetings my jokes fall flat..."

James nodded his head in agreement.

"We've both been attending shows for years, my mother and I," Herbert continued. "We're interested in the performers. We do a bit of digging. Some would say it is a hobby, others would say it's a weird obsession. Who knows? The plan was genuine. I swear on my *mother's* life. I really am writing my book. I did interview Mandy for my original book, but what she said about an angle really struck a nerve. I conjured up the conception for the new book there and then. Mandy had this huge personality. I so wanted her in our group..."

"Why Connor?"

"I guess you could say Connor was plucked out of obscurity. Mum saw him in a show years back, when she used to get out all the time, and although she said he wasn't very good..."

"He was rubbish," Brenda added.

"Mum said he wasn't yet the complete package, but she did say he was very unique. Now that right there is a promising credential. I started chatting to this lady who owns a cafe I frequent. Amanda is a good friend of Connor's mum. She gave me an interesting insight into Connor's background. The story hit a nerve, it pulled on my heartstrings. I wanted to give the guy a chance, if truth be told. Both Mandy and Connor have had their struggles, James. It hasn't been easy for either. And you..."

James put his hand up to stop him. He didn't need anybody else to recite his own torrid sob story.

"Can I have that jug of water now please!" he bellowed across the cafe, partly because he was gasping (had anyone ever died from dehydration at the Edinburgh Fringe?), but mainly to change the subject.

Herbert continued regardless. "As Mum said, we were both there when Bobby passed away. So naturally we felt a connection. We really wanted to reunite in some way. But you were the talented one on that stage that day, weren't you? We both hoped and prayed that you'd carry things forward, make the most of your talent. But we both know, James, that until the day I contacted you, you hadn't performed since that day your dad died, had you...?"

*****

Mandy wanted to speak to him so urgently, to let the trapped words escape out of her system, she decided to overlook the inflated prices and find somewhere to eat and talk at the train station. All this worry and fretting had made her hungry. She hadn't eaten a thing since the fry up at breakfast, and now it was almost lunchtime, for God's sake.

William took his time smothering his chips with salt and his burger with barbecue sauce. He inspected the shape (it was round) and quality (not very good) of the burger, before biting into it. He glanced around, mumbled some insignificant comments about it being busy, that he guessed Edinburgh was lively around the time the city held an internationally recognised festival. Mandy didn't have time for his rambling drivel.

"Thank you for coming up at such short notice. I know it was a very early start for you. And it's a Saturday, too. And I'm sorry I hit you," she said. "I just wanted to get one final smack out of my system, because you deserve it."

"Did it make you feel any better?"

"Hell yeah it did."

William smiled. He was beginning to look like her big, confident older brother again. "I was kind of hoping," he said, "you know, because you called and asked me to come here, that you weren't looking to fight with me?"

"I'm not," Mandy stated. "But that doesn't mean it's all going to be strawberries and cream, does it? I'm still not happy with you, Will, but I want to talk, like adults. I've been doing a lot of thinking."

William opened and closed his mouth, like he considered a sarcastic comment but chose against it.

"You lied to me. And not one of those pink, fluffy lies like telling me I look good in a dress. This was a big, fat lie. About my dad! And that pissed me off big time. Really hurt me, you know?"

William bowed his head, averted his gaze. "I know sis, and I really am so sorry about that. You have to believe me..."

"But," Mandy interrupted. "As I said, I have been doing some thinking. And looking back, you've *always* been a bit of a dick, haven't you...?"

William looked up now and visibly grimaced. "I have...?" he asked. The poor guy actually looked distraught, Mandy thought. His whole life had been a delusional failure. She felt like giving the little cherub a squeeze on the cheek.

"Yeah. You've always been sticking your nose into my

At Least the Pink Elephants are Laughing at Us

business, haven't you? You know who I bumped into the other week?"

"Who?"

"Dennis McCarthy."

William dipped a chip into a sachet of sauce and licked the tip. Mandy could see he was biding his time. The name was familiar, had some sort of ring to it, but he couldn't quite remember who it belonged to. And then he must have remembered, for he said "Oh."

"Yes. *Oh*. He was with his wife and kid playing happy families. Seeing him again did get me thinking, though. How come that nice little kid who seemed to worship the ground I walked on suddenly started avoiding me like the plague?"

"I may have had a few quiet words about a pen knife. If I remember correctly it was outside that den of yours..."

"Of course you had a few quiet words, Will! Words like "stay away from my sister if you want to avoid pain?""

"Yes," William conceded. "Something like that. I was looking out for you."

"But you know what, Will? I didn't need Dennis McCarthy to stay away from me. And you know why? Because he was a lovely kid who was only ever nice to me. And that is part of the reason you are a dick, you know? Because you get things wrong. The world is full of dirty rats and you scare off a pussycat."

Mandy's brother looked forlorn now. "Listen, Mandy, if I stopped you getting together with the man you were meant to be with then I truly am sorry. I didn't mean that at all, promise..."

Mandy laughed now. She didn't intend to sound cruel. She just genuinely found it funny. "Dennis wasn't the love of my life! Don't fret. Don't get your Calvin Klein knickers in a twist. It just made me think, that's all. And of course, you were always interfering with Dad, and now I've found out you still are."

William looked deadly serious. "Listen, Mandy. You've always been my little sister. And what with Dad leaving and Mum - you know - but now I know you don't need looking after. You're tougher than any of us. I promise on my life I will keep out of things, okay?"

Mandy wiped her hands with a napkin. "I just want you not to lie to me. The thing is that, even though you are undoubtedly a dick, I do know you're on my side. That big stupid heart of yours is in the right place. And it can't have been easy coping with having a stupid name like William Williams all your life, can it?"

That was better, Mandy thought. William's face unravelled into a happy one. He looked proper chuffed with that compliment-of-sorts. "And there are times," Mandy continued, "when I do need looking after. I fucking hate the fact you lied to me, but when it comes to Dad – yeah – I admit I let my heart rule my head. I look at him through my silly little princess eyes, and you see him for what he actually is. And you've looked after – and I mean really looked after, not just Sunday visits where I play about on the stair lift and the odd treat in the week – the one who actually deserves it, haven't you?"

Oh dear God, Mandy thought. Maybe her niceness had gone a step too far? Her older brother was looking unbearably smug now, sitting there like the King of the Castle, like Simon Cowell. She needed to rein it back in a bit, before that big goofy head of his exploded. But William spoke first before Mandy could get in a cutting remark.

"It just pleases me, Mandy, that you've finally seen me for the fantastic guy I obviously am..."

Mandy couldn't help but chuckle. And then she dampened her brother's spirits by squirting him in the face with vinegar.

*****

Mandy left William with his feet up, flicking through channels in the living room. Once again, Mandy found herself pacing up and down in her bedroom.

She dialled the number.

"Mum," she said, her voice breaking. "It's Mandy. Yes, I know you know it's Mandy. Yes, I know I'm your only daughter." She took a deep, deliberate breath. "Anyway, Mum, I just wanted to say thank you, you know, for *everything* you've done over the years. I know it hasn't been easy. Scrap that. I know it's been incredibly tough, yeah. And I love you, okay?"

Mandy paused, waited to pluck up some courage. "And Mum, listen. I'm sorry, yeah..."

At Least the Pink Elephants are Laughing at Us

*****

It was the sort of happy family breakfast setting that was suitable for a *Kellogg's* advert. Mum dutifully poured the tea, Dad browsed through the morning papers, and the daughter gleefully dug into her cereal, noisily slurping milk from her spoon. Okay, maybe minus the daughter noisily slurping milk from her spoon.

Something gnawed at Terry, though. There was a nagging doubt that something wasn't right. He glanced at his wrist watch. Where was Dad? He was usually pottering around somewhere in the house at this time on a Saturday. Terry perked his ears up. He couldn't hear any movements from his bedroom at all, not even the clumsy opening of cupboards and the slamming of doors. It was possible, of course, that he'd gone out; maybe gone for a walk in that tracksuit of his. But then the thing really troubling Terry, that really made him wonder and worry, was the fact the bedroom light was on last night when they came home from the cinema, and he couldn't hear any noise then either.

Terry folded the newspaper and disappeared to the back of the house. He knocked on the bedroom door. Nothing. He knocked on the door again, louder and more urgently this time. Nothing. "Dad," he called. Nothing.

He pushed the door open and barged inside, dreading what he'd find inside.

His dad was sat on the bed, his back upright against the headrest, legs straightened out in front of him. He was fully-dressed; wearing yesterday's clothes. He was alive. Thank God. A bundle of letters with discarded envelopes were scattered around him on the bed. Words written in black ink were scrawled in straight lines across the faded white paper. All of this was strange – curiously odd - but then it was the open-mouthed, vacant stare on his father's face that concerned Terry.

"Dad," Terry repeated, more urgently, with increased aggression. Terry positioned himself on the side of the bed.

His dad slowly turned his head, and his glazed eyes widened, like he was surprised to see his son there, as though he was oblivious to the knock on the door, to the calls of his name, to his presence in the room. "Dad? What is going on?"

Roy looked around, surveyed the scene, and although his face remained expressionless, there appeared to be subtle acceptance – somewhere - that his son deserved some sort of explanation.

"The letters," he said, holding one between his two middle fingers. "Your dear mother left them for me when she died."

Roy looked at Terry now, but Terry could tell it was a strain, like he was pushing the boundaries of courage to breaking point just to do so. "I have secrets, son," he said. "You see," he continued, his voice breaking. "I've never been able to read. Your mum tried to teach me, God knows she really tried, and she was so patient, so understanding, but it never really worked. It wasn't her fault. It was me. I just couldn't pick it up. It's only recently, since James joined us, things have gotten any better. I'm still no good, pretty useless really, but I can actually understand some words now without just pretending. You see, James has been taking me to classes in the town, with other people, just like me..."

"I know, Dad."

Roy's face remained neutral, like it was frozen into a single expression. He expressed no surprise. "James is a good man, Terry," Roy stated. "Sure, he can be a bit of a twat. But then, can't we all?"

Terry was glad he wasn't drinking tea or chewing chicken (or any food, for that matter), for he surely would have spat it out of his mouth. His dad hardly ever swore, and now he did so easily and brazenly.

"I know he is, Dad," Terry agreed. "A good man, I mean. Not a twat. Not all the time."

He paused for a moment before continuing more urgently. "But why the letters, Dad? Why did Mum write letters when she knew you couldn't read? Isn't that like buying a Porsche when she knows you've just been banned from driving?"

Terry wasn't sure whether the two things were even remotely related, or if he made any sense at all, but nevertheless his dad nodded his head. "We discussed it," he explained. "She wrote the letters partly for her and partly for me. It was how she made sense of the world, of her thoughts. Your mum was more

At Least the Pink Elephants are Laughing at Us

complex than she made out, you know? She always gave the impression she could take on the world, but she had her issues, just like everybody else. She so wanted me to read, not for her, but for me. She knew how dreadful it made me feel, carrying this secret around with me, how utterly useless I felt not being able to do something most children can. Kimberly just knew I would be able to read eventually, whether it had anything to do with her or not."

Terry clawed at the side of the bed with his fingernails. He had mixed emotions. This was a link to his mum, though. He missed her dearly. He wanted to know more. He longed to know more. "What did Mum say? Unless it is too personal? I would understand..."

Roy shook his head. "There is some stuff that is too personal, that is true." He smirked, almost mischievously. "There are other things I would like to share. Your mum said how much she loved me, that I was the only man she truly loved. She said I was a gentleman, and a perfect husband and a wonderful dad. It really touched me to hear these things, you know? Your mum said she was so incredibly lucky. And your mother spoke about you, of course. She expressed how proud she was. How she felt blessed..."

Terry's body tingled. He felt faint. His dad was staring into space. His words had drifted into nothing. There was more. There was something he wasn't saying.

"She told you, didn't she?" Terry blurted, hoping to God now that she *had* told him, that he wasn't opening a can of worms that – truly – was best kept shut. "She told you about her and Bobby, didn't she? I saw her with Bobby one time at The Regency. I was there with James but – thank God – he only seemed to recognise his dad..."

Roy interrupted him, stopped him in his tracks. "I knew all about that, son."

Terry thought he was imagining things. He had kept this to himself all these years, hidden it from his dad, and it had eaten away at him, caused him so much pain and guilt and...and his dad *knew*?

"Your mum told me not long after Bobby died. It traumatised her. You need to believe me. She adored that man

318

but she knew it was wrong and she regretted it with every fibre in her body. I know she did. Of course, we argued and it nearly tore us apart, but in the end we got over it and in a weird way we were stronger because of it..."

Terry could think of nothing else to do but nod his head, nothing else to say but "okay." But then he was struck by something. "You idolised Bobby? You still don't seem to hate him. Why don't you hate him, Dad?"

Roy shook his head slowly. "Believe me," he said. "There have been times when I have hated that damn man. But I only found out after he was gone, anyway. What could I do? I genuinely believe that man had problems. There was a good side to him, though. He didn't mean to hurt people. He was weak, if anything. James is more like him than you can imagine..."

"But you adore James?" Terry challenged.

"I do, I really do," Roy replied. "And I respect him. He's messed up before. He has the same type of struggles as his dad did. He is stronger that his dad, though. James is still here fighting, genuinely doing the right thing..."

They sat in silence for a few moments, a few minutes, who knows, before Terry asked, "So what did Mum say about the affair then?"

His dad paused before saying, "She just wanted me to know that she truly was sorry, son. I already knew that of course. But it was nice to read the words this time. You know?"

The two men, father and son, one middle-aged and the other nearing the end of his life, sat in the dark room in the corner of the house, in complete silence. It didn't feel like anything else needed to be said.

Terry couldn't quite put his finger on it, but he felt more at ease with life than he could ever remember.

5 – Mr Motivator

They gathered in the beautiful park, by the marble bear, a quiet, secluded stretch of green just down from the bridge and a stone's throw away from one of the busiest streets in Edinburgh, with roads leading in and out of the city and the shuttle taking you to the airport, to Murrayfield stadium, to a whole multiplicity of exciting possibilities. The late Edinburgh morning had blossomed. The miserable grey had turned to blue, the clouds had cleared and the sun was smiling and had its hat on.

It was in sharp contrast, Herbert considered, to the gloomy, depressed demeanour of the troops he had gathered. Herbert was aware his previous efforts to motivate the group, particularly in the meetings, had been less than successful. His efforts in the minivan on the journey to Edinburgh had fallen on deaf, disinterested ears. He had barely been able to muster a grunt from James and Mandy all week. Herbert knew this was his final opportunity to make a difference. He was uncertain whether the effects of the high-octane meeting in the cafe earlier, where his nerves and adrenaline had rocketed to new levels, would help or hinder his cause.

"I hope you have a good reason for bringing me to the back of beyond, Connor," George grumbled. "I'm an old man, don't you realise that? Admittedly, I'm not as old as I look, and I do play up the age thing just a tad, but still, I'm a gentleman of advanced years; there is no disputing that. I don't have that many days left on this godforsaken planet to waste. I should be spending my days in a pub or a strip club or something, not a goddamn *park*. All you need to give me now is some bread and you can send me off to feed the ducks, like us old people are *supposed* to do."

George irritably scratched his bare arm, then squinted like he expected his leathery skin to peel away. Connor opened his mouth to respond, possibly to half-heartedly reassure his friend they were here for a very worthwhile cause, but luckily Herbert saw the opportunity to skip the middleman and kick-start proceedings.

"Ladies and gentlemen," Herbert began, "I've gathered you together this morning to speak to you. I've been discussing with Nanya here how we can end this tour on a triumphant high. Firstly I wish to express my gratitude for what we have achieved so far this week. Now, I'm fully aware attendance at the shows has been low and the reception has been muted..."

James put his head in his hand and laughed. "Don't big us up too much, Herbie!"

"No, no..." Herbert continued, panicked. "I genuinely think we've done fantastic. I've got some wonderful material for my book. God knows how we have managed to pull off a week of shows without at least one person getting arrested. I for one thought we would never be able to."

"You didn't?" Connor questioned.

"My point is," Herbert said, changing the subject, "tonight is different from all the other nights. I'm not Poirot, but I think we've all had things going on in our personal lives that may have distracted us from the mission. But," he continued, his hands gesticulating freely, "we've turned a corner now, haven't we? If we muster all the enthusiasm and energy we have from deep within, all the talent and hilarious stories that are simmering under the surface, then we can put on a show to end all shows..."

Herbert was distracted by a display of uncharacteristic enthusiasm from Connor. He thrust his fist in the air and excreted a high-pitched yelp. This speech must be going very well, Herbert considered.

"Use your experiences to your advantage. And not just the highs, but the lows, too," Herbert suggested. "Incorporate them in your act! Bare your soul!"

He took the opportunity to give Connor a high-five, which was enthusiastically returned. Herbert's confidence grew. "Now, Nanya, could you please give some details regarding our specific game plan to draw in a record crowd..."

Nanya was in her element. Herbert could see she enjoyed being the centre of attention. There were no visible nerves whatsoever. "You can't do anything about what has already happened," Nanya stated. "Just look after today and tomorrow and life will do the rest..."

James punched his fist into the air. "That's what I think, Nanya!" he exclaimed. "I've thought that myself before, honest to God I have."

Nanya smiled at James and gave him an encouraging wink of the eye. "The first thing we need to do is get bums on seats," she explained. "This is difficult because of the huge competition. There are younger, more enthusiastic and much funnier comedians out there all competing for seats..."

Herbert went to interrupt, to say this wasn't the exact game plan they discussed, but Nanya quickly continued before he could do so. "So we need to look at our Unique Selling Point, or USP, as Herbert here keeps talking to me about. What do you think our USP is?"

The group looked at each other blankly and nobody offered a response. "I tell you what it is," Nanya said. "Our USP is George."

George beamed with pride. "And why is that, darling?" he asked, grinning goofily.

"Because you're so old, dear."

Herbert thought George looked significantly less proud now. The air had been let out of the balloon.

"Let me explain," Nanya continued. "Connor has been telling me you have been coming here for thirty-three years. Yes? Hmm. What I see is opportunity. No? I want us to join forces with you. We need to be telling people you are the longest-attending performer at the Fringe."

"But I don't know whether that is true?" George queried.

"But you don't know that *isn't* true," Nanya replied, smiling. "Sometimes ignorance truly can be bliss." Nanya glanced at Alun, and Herbert noticed his face reddened.

"I like it," Mandy added. "George looks about one hundred and one, so I don't think anyone will question it, will they?"

"No they won't," Nanya agreed. "But there is more. We want to be telling people that this will be George's last ever year at The Fringe, that it will be his final farewell..."

"But how do you know I won't be back next year?" George questioned, panic in his voice.

"But how do we know you *will* be back next here?" Nanya

asked. "How could we know that? Huh?"

"I like it!" James said. "No offence, George," he said, turning to the old man and eyeing him up and down. "I don't think anybody in their right mind would raise an eyebrow if we said you wouldn't last another week, let alone another year..."

George smirked. "I don't know whether to be offended by any of this," he said, His protests were drowned out by giggles.

Herbert intercepted. "So that is our plan then. Thank you, Nanya. I need you to go out there and believe in yourselves as much as I believe in you. Sell your show with everything you have because you truly believe the audience will enjoy it. We are on the final stretch, so one more final push...!"

The group clapped their hands and then dispersed in different directions. Herbert was left alone with his reflections. He looked up and was surprised to see his mum still there. She had been so unusually quiet he had almost forgotten she was there at all.

"I'm not into any of this sentimental claptrap," she offered. "But if you ask for my humble opinion, that was very inspirational and motivating, Herbert."

Herbert could tell she wanted to say more, but he knew it was difficult for her and besides, she'd had a funny old day. His mum started stuttering.

"I-I-I'm proud of you, son," she said.

6 – Saturday Before the Light Goes Down

James returned to the house by himself late in the afternoon.

He had been walking the streets with the others all day, handing out leaflets and enthusiastically promoting their show. James always knew he had the natural gift of the gab. The punters were interested. They loved the fact it was to be George's final year at The Festival after performing fifty years in a row (the number kept increasing as the day wore on). The old guy had inadvertently played a blinder. It was a master stroke by Herbert and Connor's mum. James distributed his final leaflet and then informed the others he had something personal he needed to attend to. They probably assumed he had to go and take a dump, but nevertheless, they didn't seem to mind. James had put in a good shift.

He gently closed the door to his bedroom, pulled the trusty laptop out from underneath his bed and then switched it on. He closed his eyes and took a deep, steady and deliberate breath. James hoped and prayed the camera was still hidden away in the same position as he had left it the previous Saturday. Please. James opened his eyes and then blew air out of his mouth.

"Hello, Dad," James said. "Just because I am in Edinburgh you didn't think I would miss our Saturday date at the grave, did you?"

Chris Westlake

7 - And the Lights Go Down...

George was flabbergasted, totally gob-smacked. Sure, Herbert had made a lovely, motivating speech and then the guys and girls had worked like dogs all day handing out flyers, but long years of disappointment had made him a tired, cynical old goat. He had never, ever performed to a full house at The Fringe and he never thought he would do, either. But now, peering through the crack in the door from their shabby, disjointed, makeshift changing room, he could not locate a single empty seat. In fact, there were even a few awkward figures stretching their legs, standing at the back of the hall. The room was absorbed by chatter, expectation and excitement. George had never felt so alive, which was ironic, really.

They each had their own individual routine to warm up, to physically and psychologically prepare. Connor was a deep thinker, a bit out there and a little bit quirky, wasn't he? He chose to meditate. Connor planted his buttocks firmly down on the grotty, hard wooden floor with his legs crossed, then closed his eyes and began to hum. He reminded George of a helicopter preparing to take off. James was old school, and he read the tabloid paper in the toilet. Mandy busied herself by eating cakes.

George, on the other hand, had never had a set routine, or any routine for that matter. George was beyond old-school. He normally continued doing whatever he would ordinarily be doing anyway, which was invariably chatting or drinking or both chatting *and* drinking, and just waited until his name was wearily called to go up on stage. George was nervous tonight, though; which was ridiculous really, he thought, at his age and with all things considered. But then - as Nanya had so enthusiastically announced earlier in the day - the whole show revolved around him now, didn't it? No show had ever revolved around George before. George was normally a lone ranger, a Clint Eastwood. There was less pressure that way; limited expectation. He wasn't used to being part of a gang. He didn't want to let anybody down. He particularly didn't want to let Connor down. The whole scenario was exciting and flattering but, at the same time, strangely – and mystifyingly - frightening.

For the first time in as long as George could remember, he wished he had a warm-up routine to occupy his mind and calm his splintered, muddled thoughts.

Herbert dimmed the lights in the audience using the switch in the corner of the room. This was it then. It was the beginning of the end. George's comedy career was either going to end with a bang or, more likely, a weak, muted fizzle.

Mandy, as the youngest and yet the most experienced of the three, strode up on to the stage. She looked energetic and confident, and she looked vibrant and pretty. Mandy had untied her strawberry hair and it flowed seductively down to her chest. George thought she looked fantastic. The audience erupted into loud applause. Somebody from the back of the room excitably shouted. "Go on, Mandy; give it to them like you did when you were a sheep in your school play!"

The crowd laughed, and Mandy did a curtsey.

"You know I'm proud to be what is now known as a BBW," Mandy began. "I fly the flag for our BBW brigade! But even I thought I might need to lose a few curves when I took off my pants the other night and realised my arse was still in them. So I went to the doctor hoping he would use one of those machines to suck all of the fat out of my body like a vacuum. But he was one of those annoying doctors living in the dark ages who wanted to talk about diet and healthy eating and the like. *Hello?* Did he think this was 1980? I said there just had to be a pill or an iPhone app to do all this for me? He said don't eat anything fatty. I was like "What no chips and crisps and the like?" The doc said "No. Don't eat anything. Fatty.""

The audience guffawed. George had never seen Mandy perform, but he liked her. She was self-depreciating but he could tell she didn't mean any of it. Besides, she was a lovely looking girl.

"I decided to go to the gym," Mandy continued, pulling a distorted, frustrated face. She paced up and down on the stage now, gaining momentum. "It was very fucking reluctantly, I can tell you! Suddenly the house needed cleaning, the ceiling needed painting; I even found time to finally shave my legs and beard, you know? I warmed up with the personal trainer and he said, "How flexible are you?" I said "I can't do Tuesdays." I decided to join one of those weight loss clubs. I lost quite a few pounds; they charged a fiver for each meeting. The social was great. We all met up in McDonalds afterwards for milkshakes and burgers. I got on the scales and the woman said, "Try again, dear; I'm not sure the scales are working properly." I decided to take off my belt because it was probably extremely heavy. And my bulky necklace. Naturally. The woman weighed me again and said, "No. The scales are right. You can put your clothes back on now. You know it really isn't standard practice to get weighed naked, dear."

The audience was in full flow. Mandy flowed effortlessly from the perils of internet dating, to being misjudged as a lesbian, to the joys of having two older brothers looking after her. She left the stage beaming brighter than ever. George gave her a hug and Herbert excitedly bounced up and down and assured her she was amazing.

James appeared on stage in his blue jeans and denim jacket, his hair tied back in his familiar ponytail. George thought he appeared much fresher and exuberant than the grizzled guy from this morning who looked like he had spent the night sleeping rough in a flowerbed or something. James's placid, dour face burst into a broad, energetic smile. The audience laughed. James had one of those fortunate faces that were funny without the need to even say anything.

"I became a new dad a few years back," James announced. The audience clapped. A few gasped. "Don't look so fucking surprised!" James protested. "I'm not *that* old! It's been a hard life. I'm from Bridgend. And besides, it's incredible what they can do with test tubes these days, don't you know? I'm lucky because I know I'll never become one of those single dads you see trying to join in at the playgroups. My wife will never leave me, you see. Admittedly, it's not necessarily from lack of trying. She did send her photograph to a Lonely Hearts club just after we got married. They sent the photograph back, though, saying they weren't *that* fucking lonely. I'm not the easiest guy to live with, you see. No, I'm being serious. I once dated a hoarder, but even she threw me out..."

The crowd loved him. They could tell he was a genuine rascal. The guy didn't need to try very hard to be funny. George knew all the stuff about his wife was nonsense, though. James hadn't stopped going on about Shirley all day. He had proudly shown George a picture of her, too, and she was a real stunner.

"To be fair," James continued, "my wife is actually something of a sex object. No, honest. Every time I ask for sex, she objects. I will say, though, that she has a peculiar way of looking at the world. We were watching this kid's film where this talking tow truck gets knighted by the Queen, who is naturally a Rolls Royce. "This just isn't realistic!" my wife protested. "That talking tow truck is American! You can't knight an American!"

James wiped his brow, which was glistening with sweat. George knew it was because of adrenaline, though, and not the heat that penetrated strongly from the bright lights. "I tell you what, these so-called children's books are scary as fuck. I read *Three Little Pigs* to my little boy and it was me who hid under the duvet! It wasn't The Big Bad Wolf that scared me; it was Mummy Pig. That pig doesn't fuck around, honest to God. She got out of the wrong side of the sty one morning and she was like, "You three have got too fat and so I'm kicking you out today! The Big Bad Wolf will eat you for dinner, but oh well. Fuck off!" You do pick up the different approaches to parenting when you're out and about. One mother will be, "Spatial awareness, Timothy. Spatial awareness, dear." Another mum in the same situation will wake up the whole shopping centre by yelling, "Brittney, get the fuck out of the way!" You notice that mums get carried away with naming children after whoever happens to be in the limelight at the time. I did think things had gone too far, though, when I overheard one mum chasing after her daughter in Tesco's shouting, "Lady Gaga, come back...!"

James returned backstage with his arms lifted triumphantly above his head, the deafening sound of clapping behind him. George shook his hand and said, "Well done, young man." James was ecstatically embraced by Herbert.

Connor was next. This was the one George was really interested in. He adored this guy. George just hoped he didn't succumb to nerves and he produced the performance he knew he was capable of. Both his parents were in the audience, hoping and praying for the best, and George longed for Connor to do them proud.

"Just be yourself and the rest will look after itself, George said, shaking Connor's hand.

Connor wore a luminous red Hawaiian shirt and baggy red shorts. His crazy dress sense had accidentally (it seemed) become part of his act. It contrasted sharply with his persona. The crowd were again giggling before Connor had uttered a single word. George hadn't seen Connor perform either, but he had a good idea what his act would be like.

"You may or may not have noticed," Connor began, "but I'm not what most people would call "white." No Sir," he continued, leaning towards the front row, "it's not just the lighting in this joint. My mum is Ghanaian, you see. Now let me tell you, and you may be surprised to hear this, but there weren't that many of us growing up in Bridgend in the 1980's. Most folk in the village weren't exactly sure where my mum was from, but they managed to narrow it down to Africa. I remember this time I was in the Post Office with my mum when I was just a boy and we overheard two old dears with matching tea cosies on their heads trying to work it out. "I think she might be from Nigeria," one of them suggested. Now my mum sure as shit didn't like that, let me tell you! "No, no, no!" she said, waving second-class stamps at the two frightened old women. "I don't care where you think I'm from, so long as it's not Nigeria!" Those two countries aren't best friends, if you know what I mean. And this goes back way before they tried selling the rest of the world timeshares..."

The audience chuckled and so did George. He was so relieved. Connor was exactly how he expected – and hoped – he would be.

"Now I've been to Ghana a few times," Connor continued. "And it truly is a magnificent country. One thing though, I didn't see a single sports shop. And yet half the children were running around in Brazil football shirts! Do *Amazon* deliver to Ghana? And you think the people who go to church in this country are religious? Tssk. You must be crazy. They only go for an hour! I went to church in Ghana and people had a change of pyjamas with them just in case. That show goes on all day! They don't just do the expected stuff like singing and praying. No, they get up and dance, too! It did have a miraculous effect on me. When I got back to Bridgend I felt truly blessed that, when my mum dragged me to church, I'd be back in time for dinner!"

George wiped a wet tear from his eye now. His friend was doing great out there. He was proud of him, and he knew his mum and dad would be, too.

"You might be surprised to learn that when I was a kid I wasn't what you would automatically describe as a typical red-blooded boy. Don't laugh! No, please do! I enjoyed my own company and art and drama and reading. I carried around a dark secret that ate away at me for years. My dad was the headmaster of my school and as straight as they come. I was terrified of telling him my dark secret, of breaking his heart. But one day I sat him down and just blurted it out. "Dad," I said. "I don't like rugby!" But he has managed to get over it now. After all, it's been two weeks since I plucked up the courage to tell him!"

Connor returned to the dingy little room and George could just tell he was floating on the ceiling. His smile stretched the full circumference of his handsome face. George hugged him, really clung to him for dear life. "You were amazing, Connor," he said truthfully, and he patted him heartily on the back.

George was next. The nerves had vanished. It didn't seem to matter anymore. He could just go out there and enjoy it. The show had already been a success regardless of what he did. George released the hug and looked Connor in the eye. He only had moments to speak before he was called up on stage. "Your mum was right, you know? This will be my last show..."

Connor narrowed his eyes and looked at him confused. Concerned.

"It's cancer," George explained. "The type that doesn't get any better. Not at my age. That's why I'm determined to make the most of what I have left, you know?"

Connor nodded his head and then gave him another hug, really squeezed his body.

"Just go and get them," Connor instructed, and George just knew, as he walked out onto the stage for the very last time, that he absolutely would.

Part Five

1 - Man Lurking on the Train

2017

Herbert had replayed the scenario countless times in his head.

He catches a train and – oh what an absolutely remarkable surprise - the commuter sat opposite just happens to be reading his book. Herbert casually and indifferently asks whether they are enjoying the book and gives a dashing and non-committal look which suggests he might just be tempted to read it himself. The commuter smiles and says the book is absolutely fantastic, one of the best they have ever had the privilege of reading. They say that if you read one book this year then this should be the one. Herbert returns the smile, says he is glad they enjoyed reading the book, because he sure enjoyed writing it. The reader excitedly glances at the cover, does a double-take, laughs bashfully and then asks whether he would be so kind to sign the book. Herbert graciously signs the book and, of course, pens a personal message.

The scenario was bound to evolve eventually. It was a simple law of averages. Herbert had been catching trains all over the place to ensure it happened; he had even bought a season ticket, even though there was absolutely no need. He trawled the narrow aisles, moving from coach to coach, often colliding with the buffet cart, eagerly hunting for his book. And *finally*, there it was.

She sat on her own by the window occupying a table seat. From experience at book signings, she was not Herbert's typical reader. Herbert's core readership was primarily comprised of women over seventy. This lady must have been in her twenties. His audience was expanding, he considered. Herbert bided his time. This felt like a pinnacle moment. He wanted to savour it.

"So what do you think of the book then?" he croaked, trying

to sound casual, cold sweat glistening on his forehead.

The woman put down the book and looked at Herbert. "It is *alright*," she said, and shrugged her shoulders.

"Just alright?"

The woman crinkled her nose. "Yeah," she said. "No great shakes."

"Really?" Herbert challenged. His hands gripped the edges of the table. "Well I've been told it's really good," he said.

The woman looked at Herbert more closely now. This was the moment she realised who he was, he thought. She pressed her arms on the table and leant forward. "Listen," she said, "you asked for my opinion and I gave it. I'm not sure whether this is how you normally come on to women, but let me tell you now, it isn't going to work with me. Okay...?"

Herbert nervously nodded, frantically wiped the dripping sweat from his forehead with his sleeve. The two commuters sat in painful silence for the next ten minutes until the woman eventually – *finally* - disembarked. Herbert released a deep sigh of relief.

That hadn't really gone to plan, he considered.

His phone vibrated, gladly interrupting his morbid thoughts. He did not recognise the number. "Hello?" he cautiously said.

A male with a distinctive Welsh accent enthusiastically spoke on the other end of the line.

"Rob," Herbert exclaimed, his voice breaking into near-hysteria. "Of *course* I am still available for that interview!"

2 – Big Brother

"So how did you say you two met?" her mum asked.

Mandy squeezed her boyfriend's hand under the table and smiled. She was not prepared to give the whole truth and nothing but the truth, but a rough depiction was fine. "We started emailing each other after I met one of his very best friends, and then it sort of progressed from there. Didn't it Dave?"

She hadn't really intended it to be an invitation for him to fill in the gaps and add some meat to the bones – an interested nod of the head would have been sufficient – but really that was naive of her. She knew by now that her new boyfriend was an excitable and rapid talker and besides, it was the first time Dave had met her mum and he was naturally nervous and keen to make an impression.

"I think that pretty much says it all, Mandy," Dave agreed. Thank God for that. There really was no need to give any details. "But to give you some details," he continued, "we met at a train station and then we had an almighty row which I take full responsibility for, then we made up, kept in contact and now here we are today; deeply in love and waiting for our starters to arrive..."

Mandy glanced at Dave and gasped. "Love?" she asked. She shuffled around and glanced at her coat, which clung to the back of her chair.

Dave wiped his lenses with his forefinger. "Yes," he quickly replied. "I thought we talked about this, Mandy. You know, after we had breakfast in bed and then – you know – and I said I loved you, and you said..."

Mandy cackled loudly. "I'm messing with you, Dave..."

"Oh," Dave nervously laughed. "Well that is an almighty relief, I can tell you. Phew! And after I spent all that money on a ring..."

"Ring?" Mandy choked.

Dave patted her shoulder. "You're not the only one who can make a joke, Mandy," he said.

Mandy's mum was chortling now. She looked happy. There was colour back in her face. She wore lipstick and mascara and her hair was freshly cut with stylish streaks of blonde.

"And what about you two...?" Mandy asked.

"We met at one of our awful work functions years and years ago when I was still with your father. I thought Spencer was adorable, of course, but obviously there was no attraction at the time..."

"There wasn't?" Spencer asked, face twisted into mock disappointment. Mandy observed that he had an unusually pointed head and never tired of looking down her mother's top.

"Well I was a respectable married lady, dear. I wasn't so open to you being a bad influence on me at the time..."

"But how did you get together now?" Mandy asked. "All these years later?"

"Well it's all down to your brother really."

Mandy turned to William, who was busily devouring the white bread and apparently not really listening. Of course. Golden Balls. He seemed so much more naturally adept at making Mum happy than she was, but Mandy loved him for it. William raised an eyebrow as if to ask – *what – you talking about me?*

"It was that computer he bought me, wasn't it? One day Spencer popped up on my screen and he asked if I would be his friend and I said yes and we have been friends ever since. And recently, we have become more than just friends, haven't we?"

"That's so sweet," Mandy cooed. Dave gave an eager guffaw of approval. Mandy realised it really was sweet, that she was glad her mum was happy. It felt odd they met through her dad, but who cared? She met Dave through her dad too, and really those circumstances were much, much weirder.

Mandy offered to go to the bar to get some drinks. Dave said that he would go, but William suddenly woke up from his daydreams and said no, that it was his round.

"Just to let you know," William said when they were both at the bar, "that when your new feller goes to the toilet I'm looking to follow him and give him a few quiet words about making sure he looks after my little sister..."

Mandy giggled. "Of course. I would be disappointed if you

did anything less, big brother," she said. "I like the fact you're a bit "chopsy" with my new feller. You're supposed to be looking out for me, after all."

She knew William wanted to say something, but was trying to work out how. It must be difficult, because he could be a real charmer when it came to words. Mandy knew *exactly* what he was thinking. "You look really pretty tonight, sis. I guess you must really like this Dave character if you have worn a dress for him, huh?"

Mandy turned to her brother and smiled. "William, I'm not wearing a dress for Dave, silly," she said. "I'm wearing a dress for Mum."

William looked a little bewildered, but then his handsome face broke into a smile and he nodded his head.

3 – Brown Bread

It had been a beautiful service, absolutely perfect, a wonderful tribute to a seemingly much-loved man.

Connor sat on the second row of pews, just behind George's family. He was tightly nestled between his mum and dad. Connor was so glad his parents had the opportunity to meet George, too. They all had such fond memories of the trip to Edinburgh. The rest of the gang sat a few rows back, a little more inconspicuous: Herbert, Mandy and James. None were as close to George as Connor, of course, but they too had happy memories of George from the tour and they were there to pay their respects.

The whole congregation respectfully stood to sing hymns and knelt to pray at the appropriate moments. Connor couldn't help but glance at his dad and observed he dutifully joined in where required. The church was filled with shiny faces that swelled with bubbling emotions. Tissues wiped away tears and mascara from moist eyes. There was a commotion behind him as somebody blew their noise so forcefully it nearly blew the roof from the church. Connor just knew, without turning around, that it was James.

He knew this would happen. Everybody all around him freely displayed their emotions, and yet however hard Connor tried, he just couldn't. It felt a part of him was missing since George left the world. He was incredibly empty and sad. And yet that just didn't equate to a physical display of affection and mourning. It made him feel self-conscious, made him feel guilty. What was wrong with him? Why was he such a cold, heartless fish? He felt he'd be judged, but then he felt guilty for thinking that, too. Who did he think he was? Why was he so unbearably egotistical? Today wasn't about him. Who cared how he felt?

They filed out of the church in laboured, considerate lines and Connor shook hands with the family and with George's friends. It was a lovely blue spring day outside, and the brightness of the daffodils and freshly cut green grass were a

At Least the Pink Elephants are Laughing at Us

pleasant, welcome contrast to the dimly lit confines of the church. Connor stood in line at the buffet, waiting for Mandy to find enough space on her plate to add some more cheese and pickle sandwiches, when he was gently tapped on the shoulder. Connor turned around to acknowledge George's eldest daughter, Angela.

"Would it be possible to have a quiet word, Connor?" she asked.

She took his hand without waiting for a reply and led him outside. They sat on one of the wooden benches in the beer garden out the front. Angela kept hold of Connor's hand whilst she continued talking.

"Dad was incredibly fond of you, Connor," she said. "He said so many times. He thought you were a true friend. He just wished he could have met you earlier, to have enjoyed more time with you."

Connor nodded his head and smiled. "I really valued our friendship, too," he said. "It will probably surprise you to know that I don't make true, meaningful friendships easily."

Angela's neutral expression suggested that – no – she wasn't particularly surprised. Connor continued, "I've always thought the same thing. I really wish I could have met George earlier. I guess we should be grateful our paths crossed at all."

Angela placed a dark wooden box down onto the bench. She did not open the lid. "Connor," she began, "on the very day Dad died – and you know he died peacefully at home – he made me promise to give you this. I have no idea what is inside, but I'm sure it is personal to you."

Connor vacantly stared at the box for a few moments. Angela slowly rose from her feet and affectionately kissed Connor on the temple. "I'll leave you alone," she said. "Promise you'll keep in touch with us, you hear?"

He assured her he would, and it was far from an empty gesture. Connor was left alone now, in the beer garden, in complete silence. He tentatively removed the lid from the box. There was a letter inside, with words scrawled in blue ink in shaky handwriting.

Dear Connor
How you doing, butt? If you're reading this then I'm brown bread. I'm happy enough with that. It was a good ride whilst it lasted. I just wanted to say a few things. It may have been better to have said this when I was still alive, you know, but I just run out of time. I thought the world of you, Connor. I valued our friendship more than I valued the taste of Guinness, and that really is saying something.

I never really made it as a performer, but I was happy enough with that. I lived the life I always wanted to live as a kid, you know. You though are a clever sod and you have more talent in one of your skinny fingers than I had in my whole body. I'd like you to really have a go at things. When you are famous you can tell people that you knew me once, you hear?

Anyway, I've enclosed some of my happiest memories from my time as a performer.

I hope to see you soon, but not some time too soon,
George.

Connor eagerly flicked through the photographs. Right at the top was the picture taken in Edinburgh on the final day of the trip, the whole group together, before they took on the world and held their own. The pictures went back in time, over a fast array of decades, until finally Connor reached a faded black and white Polaroid. George was just a youngster, barely out of school. His smile was broad and distinctively goofy. George was stood next to a portly middle-aged man with a round face and an impressively thick head of hair, in front of a wooden Punch and Judy hut. The photograph was signed. Connor was not sure exactly what it said, but it looked like *The West Virginia Wisecracker*. Connor wondered what sort of god-awful name that was.

Connor bowed his head and put his face in his hands. He hoped the beer garden was still empty of people, for he sat on the bench and cried uncontrollably.

4 - Love

It was a hot Sunday afternoon.

The Sunday roast had been happily devoured, and James and Shirley resisted the temptation to fall asleep in front of the television (bellies full and heads sleepy) and instead they knotted the laces on their trainers and ventured outside. The curtains in the living room had been pulled together, to keep the house cool and the deadly sunlight at bay, and so James was alarmed by the heat and brightness when he opened the front door.

"Flippin' hell, Shirley," he exclaimed, putting a hand to his eyes. "Have we been living in a cave? It's roasting hot out here! Should we go back inside? You know I have delicate skin. I'm a sensitive guy. I'm a 21st century guy. I'm a 'metrosexual', you know?"

Shirley turned to her husband, smiled, and said, "The best thing for you right now would be a spoonful of "Man Up." Give me a 20th century guy any day of the week. We live in Bridgend, darling, not Kenya."

James tugged at his faded tee shirt and sniffed at his armpit. He lifted Rory by the waist, up and over a concrete sty, wary to avoid the overhanging, overflowing nettles. "There you go, Tiger," James said. Rory planted both feet on the bumpy grass and eagerly sped off, enjoying the freedom of the large and open field. The field was smothered with dried cowpat; cowpat that quickly turned wet and soggy when stepped on, but Rory didn't mind. His back was straight and his head swung from side to side.

"He runs funny," James commented, like he'd never seen his son running before.

"He runs like his dad," Shirley stated.

"Have you got something to tell me? Who's his dad, then?" James asked. "Kriss Akabusi?"

The boy seemed happy. James dangled his hand invitingly by his side and Shirley took hold of it. James inhaled and was hit by the fresh, country air. He looked around and noted the sky was clear and beautifully blue. It sure was hot, and James was not used to the heat, not round these parts, but there was a gentle breeze that made it refreshing and satisfying.

James was suddenly hit by a thought, a thought from long ago.

"You know what, Shirley?" he said, squeezing his wife's hand. "All we need now is a dog – maybe a little Jack Russell - don't you think?"

At Least the Pink Elephants are Laughing at Us

Did you Enjoy this Book?

If you enjoyed this book, then it would be much appreciated if you left a review on Amazon.

If you would like to hear more about future publications by this author, then please www.chriswestlakewriter.com and sign up to his mailing list.

About the Author

Chris was born and bred in Bridgend, South Wales, but now resides in Birmingham with his wife and two young children. *At Least the Pink Elephants are Laughing at Us* is Chris's second novel. He is currently planning his third with a notepad and pen. You can find out more about Chris on his website www.chriswestlakewriter.com

Acknowledgments

Thank you to my wonderful wife, Elizabeth, for giving me the time and encouragement to write this novel, especially with two young rascals running around the house, causing mayhem. Thank you to my beta readers, Nathan Ali, Christoph Fischer and of course my dad, Steve Westlake. The Bridge Boys (Dave Wright, Gareth Baker, Gary Mason, Arian Fisk and Matthew James) were a great help filling in gaps in my memory and knowledge. And a special mention to my Tenby expert, Steph Sambidge.

Thank you all.